THIEF OF SOULS

BEC MCMASTER

Want to know when my next book is released? Want behind-the-scenes exclusives? All the McMasterverse news?

Sign up to my mailing list!

Too many emails in your inbox?
Try my New Releases Only newsletter.

Here are some other ways to stay updated:

* Follow me on Bookbub
* Like me on Facebook
* Or visit my website at becmcmaster.com

I drown a thousand times.

Every day, for months. Sometimes twice a day. Sometimes three times. In the cold, dark silence of the Abyss it's difficult to keep track, so it's only when the winch starts clanking that I get my first warning that we're going to play this game again.

My stomach tenses, and I jerk out of the half-comatose reverie I've been existing in. *No. No, not again.* Pain screams through my shoulders. I've been hanging in these chains for so long that the only time I can feel my arms is when they threaten to dunk me into the pit of water below.

My throat is raw from screaming, and there's no point.

There's no one here to hear me anyway.

This is the cost of failure.

As the chains lower me back into the watery pit, I can't stop myself from shaking. I don't want to do this. Not again.

But when I returned from the Court of Dreams without

the Dragon's Heart I was sent to steal, my father sentenced me to three months in the Abyss.

Three months hanging in chains over a watery pit, just waiting to drown again.

It won't kill me.

I might, however, begin to wish I could drown and be done with all of this.

That's the problem with being a half-breed. The fae are long-lived, and wraiths are difficult to kill. I can heal from almost anything, if given the chance.

It's both a gift and a curse.

Because the ability to heal from most things means the ability to *survive* most things.

The first shock of frigid water hits my bare toes.

"Stop!" I grab for something to save me—anything— and then I suck in an enormous breath.

The chains rattle faster as I'm plunged into a watery grave. The cold iron that burns around my wrists shoots straight for the bottom, taking me with it.

No matter how many times this happens, I still fight. Far above me, high in the tower, is a single lantern, and I can see that firefly glow slowly fading as the chains haul me lower.

A bubble escapes me—an unconscious cry of fear— and then several more as panic starts to set in. Kicking hard, I yearn for the surface, but the weight, the wretched weight, is dragging me down, down, forever down—

Pressure crushes my chest.

Please. Please, no. I'm sorry. I didn't mean to fail. I won't fail you again, Father. I won't. I promise I won't—

It's so hard to keep holding on. My lungs kick like a

mule, heaving at my ribs. Nothing. There's nothing there. Only my ears threatening to pop, and bubbles slipping from my mouth as I try to capture them with my hands and hold such precious oxygen in….

The first mouthful is the worst.

I scream, but there's no air. Only thick, wet weight that sinks through my lungs and the anchor that hauls me to my doom. Maybe this time will be the last time. Maybe this time my father will keep me down long enough that even *my* body can't heal itself.

Darkness roars over me, but it's not the warm cocoon of nighttime. It's a greedy fist locking around my throat and choking me.

Please! Please help me!

A little spark of light burns to life in my chest like a hot coal.

Magic. Pure magic.

I reach for that spark with desperate hands.

"Merisel?" whispers a startled voice in my head.

A male voice.

Merisel? That's not my name.

Why would he call me…?

My eyes blink open in horror, but it's too late.

Because the spark of magic is consuming me, right at the moment where consciousness meets that dawning darkness.

Heat and flames snap around me, and I'm pulled through time and space until I finally slam into the world again.

I suddenly blink and find myself standing within an enormous bedroom. The first gasp of air sends me to my knees, slapping wet palms on the tiles. I can breathe again. Hot, blistering air that burns my ravaged throat and lungs. *Warm.* The tiles are warm. I want to kiss the floor and bathe in that heat. Or maybe just collapse. Water pours from my body, my shirt clinging to every inch of me. I can't move. I want to, but I simply don't have the strength within me.

This is some sort of gift, but fate never deals me a hand like this. Miracles are for pretty blonde fae princesses who have never known a day of toil in their life, until the moment they're horribly cursed or prick their finger on an enchanted spinning wheel. There's always a kiss stamped into their destiny, a twist of fate, hope.

But even though my silvery hair might charitably be called blond in a certain light, and my father technically *is* a king, I'm not that princess. I'm the villain of the story. I'm the thief, the liar, the girl of storms with her mercenary heart.

I am the Wraith King's daughter, and if this is fate, then it's about to punch me in the teeth.

Get on your feet then, I hiss to myself.

Because the first thing I ever learned is not to crawl. Not for anyone.

So I push my head upright and realize fate is a tricksy bitch after all.

Merisel, he called me, and there's only one male who

knows me by that name. Even though it is—like the rest of me—a lie.

A warm breeze billows through sheer curtains, and I sense someone prowling along the balcony. My breath catches, and I squeeze my fists tight in order to control the response.

I know who it is.

But the part of me that descends from a long line of fae that lived their lives in dark forests, feels the glint of the wolf's eyes lock on me. I'm not alone, and I'm not trapped in the dark, but something is still hunting me and my body knows it.

The curtains shift and then he's there, pausing just inside the room as if he's a little surprised to see me standing there.

Keir.

Prince of Chaos and Dreams.

Our gazes collide and even though it's been several months since I escaped his court, the impact of his presence hasn't abated one bit. Dark hair brushes against his collarbone, and his thick brows highlight the intensity of those green-gold eyes. He owns me with a single look. It's the kind of look you can't practice. Hundreds of years of overweening arrogance combined with centuries of knowing you're at the top of the food chain and anything and everything around you is your prey. You are either born with it, or you surrender to it.

"Merisel." He breathes the word.

The truth hits me like a wall of solid stone: He isn't looking at *me* like that. *No.* He still thinks me Merisel of Greenslieves.

I wince. Two months ago, Prince Keir sent out a summons in search of a bride, and over twenty prospective princesses and ladies attended in the hopes of capturing his heart.

When Father ordered me to steal the Dragon's Heart from the Court of Dreams, I'd kidnapped the Lady of Greenslieves and used her alias in order to get inside.

It should have been the perfect cover.

I had the invitation. I had a new identity. I just had to avoid the prince, find the relic, and steal it.

Instead, somehow, I'd captured his eye. And for a second—just a second—I'd known what it felt like to want something for myself, something I knew I couldn't have because I'm tainted and ruinous, but that didn't negate the strength of the feeling.

I wanted a handsome prince to whisk me away and save me, but the truth is: I'm a wraith-born bastard who is owned by her father. There is no handsome prince coming to save me. All I have is myself.

But he looks at me, and it's as if we're both drawn back into the past.

We both feel it—we both wanted something else too.

A pretty little lie.

"No." The truth dies in his eyes. "Not Merisel. I never did catch your real name…?"

"I never gave it."

Keir glances down, his silky lashes hiding his eyes for one small moment before he looks up again. There's no green in his eyes anymore. Only the dragon staring back at me—because that's his little secret.

He looks like a fae prince. He acts like a fae prince.

But long ago, when the fae went to war against the dragon kings, rumor says they turned from this world, turned to stone, stepped into the long Unwaking....

Sometimes I wonder if the dragon kings set those rumors themselves, because one of them is right in front of me. Locked into mortal flesh, his eyes blazing as though his fae prison can barely contain him anymore.

"Where have you been?" he demands as his gaze slides down me. "I've summoned you a half dozen times."

Drowning. Repeatedly.

But he doesn't need to know that.

I shrug, but the shiver that runs through me ruins the effect. "I told you that you weren't the only one to whom I owed a debt. Sometimes, I'm not at liberty to attend."

His eyes narrow. "You're dripping wet. And freezing, by the look of you. Where are you?"

"What? You've never taken a bracing swim in a glacial fjord?"

"Not clothed." Keir bares his teeth. It's not a smile. "I see how easily you do it now."

"Do what?"

"Lie," he growls before he holds his hand up and makes a gesture.

Water sluices down my body. It feels like a warm tingle running over every inch of my skin, and I do mean every inch. A gasp steals from me as puddles of frigid water hit the floor, and then I'm warm and dry and blessed gods, I almost forgot this feeling....

It's enough to make my eyes water as I stagger.

Warmth. Actual warmth.

I can survive almost anything my father wants to do to

me—I *will* survive—but the sudden shock of such a comfort almost breaks me.

It's not real.

Somewhere out there, my body is coughing and spluttering as the inevitable finally happens and I'm forced to choke down a lungful of freezing water. But just for a moment I'm safe and warm, and I don't have to be strong anymore—

I hit my knees, palms slapping against the tiles.

It's as if my body simply gives out.

Bare feet whisper over the tiles in front of me and then his shadow looms. It's enough to make me flinch back, but there is no weapon to grab and belatedly I realize Keir's not attacking me. His hands are still an inch from my arms, the expression on his face arresting.

"I'm not going to hurt you," he says softly. Gently.

"You…." I clear my throat. "You caught me by surprise."

I look up the length of his body.

There's no longer a golden claw hanging around his throat—my sister, Soraya, stole it and presented it to Father, thinking it was the mythical Dragon's Heart relic that was going to break our wraithbound curse.

Keir turns his hand over, offering me his fingertips.

And a sardonically arched brow.

My brain finally starts working again. "Why did you summon me?"

"I need you," he says.

Every girl's wet dream.

I know better. There are invisible glyphs painted into the skin of my forearms, counting out the days. I owe him a year and a day of service, and now he's calling in his favor, and it has nothing to do with me seeing any more of that glorious skin and everything to do with me being crushed between two opposing forces.

"I am at your disposal, it seems," I manage to drawl as he draws me to my feet.

Keir cuts me a hard look, then sweeps past me, the hem of his robe brushing against my calf. "Follow me."

Just a small touch, but it feels as though he's lashed me.

I don't know if it's the bond between us or something else, but the sense of awareness between us seems to be growing.

"Please," I mutter, curling my fingers into my palms as if I can somehow trap the sensation of his hands on mine.

"What?" he calls over his shoulder as he vanishes between the gauzy curtains.

It's a simple courtesy, one I lost many years ago when my father trapped my soul in the small vial he wears around his neck. Since that moment, I've lost the right to demand courtesy, and Keir condemned me to a similar fate several months ago when he demanded a year and a day of service from me.

A sigh escapes me. I have no choice.

I've never had a choice.

And so I follow.

The balcony overlooks an azure sea.

The Court of Dreams is anchored to the real world, but it exists in a plane outside of time. The only way to reach it is through a portal Keir controls—or through your dreams. Indeed, he commands every aspect of the entire island, because he created it with his power.

It was the first sign he wasn't quite as fae as he seemed.

Platters of food rest on a table in front of me. Dates and stuffed figs, along with the finest cheeses, and biscuits cut so thin they'd melt in your mouth…. My mouth waters, even as my mood plunges. Keir can't know how long it's been since I was fed, but this feels like a new sense of torture.

If my father ever discovered it's the key to breaking me, then he'd have more than my soul. I would give him everything.

"See something you like?" Keir's voice is rough velvet

as he gestures and one of the chairs sweeps back on an invisible gust.

My stomach twists. It wants food so desperately that I have to dig my fingernails into my palms to control the urge to stuff my face. "Are you referring to the cheeses, my prince?" I glance at him from beneath my lashes. "Or a certain dragon?"

He smiles a little dangerously. "You don't need to pretend to flirt with me anymore, Merisel."

That's not my name.

And he knows it bothers me. This is only a means to force me to tell him the truth.

"Fine," I tell him. "The food looks delicious."

I pluck a grape from a platter and stuff it in my mouth before he can even reply. Sweetness bursts across my tongue. I swear I almost have an orgasm. I need more.

"Is this even real?" It feels real beneath my fingers, the date sticky as I squeeze it. "This dream?"

"What makes you think it a dream?"

I laugh. *Because my life is a nightmare, and this is a mirage.* "You're the Prince of Dreams. This is not the first time I've woken to find myself walking these halls."

He pauses. "You never came. I've summoned you a half dozen times."

Maybe they were fever dreams.

Keir leans back in his chair, one arm slung over the chair beside him as he watches me. "And it can be."

"Be what?"

"Real."

I pop the date into my mouth, and flavor bursts over

my tongue. Gods, I barely chew it before I swallow it down. Maybe it's not enough to fill my stomach, but I don't care. With a flash of the knife, I slice a thin, crumbly wedge of cheese. "So you seduce you me with such pleasures first," I murmur, "and then, I presume, comes the torture."

His gaze drops to my fingers as I lift the cheese to my lips. "This is not seduction, Merisel. You will know if I ever decide to seduce you."

"Then what is this?" The cheese melts on my tongue. I'm a little too quick to reach for another piece.

"Why would you think I intend to torture you?" There's curiosity in his tone.

I pause, swallowing my mouthful and then licking the remnants from my thumb. That was a slip. He's questioning it. "Why would you not? You own me."

"Ah, yes." There's a quirk around his mouth. "Our bargain. I was a little angry with you when I made it. I thought I'd found a bride and here you were, using false pretenses to try and steal from me."

This time, it's my turn to arch a brow. "I never tried to capture your interest. If anything, quite the opposite."

I can't help hearing the words he spoke to me when he realized my deception: *I've never been more intrigued by you.*

I set the fork down. "What do you want? It isn't to watch me eat. It isn't to remind me of the past."

"You dined with me once. Perhaps I wished to repeat the experience."

"Now I see how *you* dance around the truth."

Keir laces his fingers together. A dangerous intensity springs to life in his eyes. "Rumor abounds that an ancient magic is reawakening. The world trembles with its presence, and every power-hungry lordling and prince in all the lands will be desperate to find it. I want to get my hands on it first."

I pause, nibbling on the stuffed fig. This feels familiar and it's a relief to finally get to the crux of the matter. "An ancient magic…?"

"The cauldron," he replies. "The Goddess's Cauldron."

I drop the fig, and my fork ricochets off my plate. He cannot be serious. The cauldron was gifted to the fae by the goddess herself. When the dragon kings used the power of the cauldron in order to defeat a half-bred monstrosity, they were forced to surrender their magic to it and retreat from the world.

It left behind an enormously powerful magical relic created by a goddess, and filled with the power of ancient dragons.

And every fae in the land wanted it.

A wise old king at the time stole the cauldron and sailed out to a small island off the coast of the Court of Storms. He begged the Goddess of the Sea to take the cauldron and hide it, for fear that one would rise with the power to wield what should never be wielded.

The other courts hunted him but they were too late.

The sea rose in anger, driving their boats back to shore. By the time the storm died down, the island had vanished. The king and the cauldron with it.

No one has seen it since.

"Well, fuck." I stare down at my bodice. Clots of soft goat cheese are spattered across my breasts, and leaves of thyme cling to my skirts. The fig is nowhere to be seen. I haven't been that clumsy since I was a girl.

"That's all you have to say?" Keir looks amused. "I've just offered you the greatest quest of all time and this is your response? You could be famous."

"Or dead," I point out. "The answer is no. No, I will not steal your cauldron—"

"I don't need you to steal my cauldron," he purrs. "I just need you to find it for me, and to do that, I need you to get your hands on the Horn of Shadows."

More myths. "The horn that leads the Wild Hunt?"

He leans toward me, every inch of him fixed in predatory intent. "The hounds of the Wild Hunt were born of the cauldron. They can find it. But to control them, I need the horn."

There's a moment where I consider pushing my chair back, climbing onto the railing, and diving into the water far below.

And right now, I hate water with a passion.

Maybe I can appeal to the Goddess of the Sea? Maybe she'll make me disappear too?

But this is his realm.

He'll probably simply pluck me out of the sea. There's no escape there.

"The hounds of the Wild Hunt make Wyrdhounds look like a child's bedtime story," I grind out. And one of *them* nearly killed me three months ago. "To blow the horn means binding your soul to it forever."

"'Til death," he corrects. "Only one fae can blow the

horn at a time. Once bound, the horn becomes useless to anyone else. Unless the blower is killed."

"There's an easy solution to that problem, Your Highness. If you get your hands on that horn, every prince in the land will make it their personal prerogative to slit your throat."

"Worried about me?" There's a slight quirk to his lips, and his eyes flare gold as he lets his glamor slip, just for a moment.

I don't know how I never saw it before.

The dragon peers back at me, smoldering in golden flames.

My heart skips a beat. "You can still die. The fae managed to kill the rest of the dragon kings. Even you can't survive the removal of your heart."

"Did they?" Another faint smile.

I stare at him.

Keir sips his wine. "Some of my brethren chose to fight. Some of them chose to sleep. And some of them… chose another way to live."

He's not the only dragon out there?

"How many? Who?" Because surely they wouldn't be masquerading as lowly peasants. No, they'd be kings. Princes.

"If I tell you that, my love, then I will either have to kill you or capture you."

"Capture me?"

His smile holds all manner of sin. "Bind you to me forever. Lock you away in a tower where you can't ever escape me."

On second thought…. "Keep your secrets then."

"Aren't you curious?"

"Not *that* curious."

"About the horn," he whispers, a dangerous hint of smile tugging at his wicked mouth. "About the cauldron. An ancient prophecy states it will be reborn, Merisel. Someone's going to find it. Don't you want to be the one who does?"

My thief's soul quivers at the thought.

But I wipe at the goat's cheese staining my lovely gown. "There's always an ancient prophecy. There's always an angry goddess—or god. And there's always some idiot thief who finds themselves talked into a job like this." I toss the crumpled napkin aside. "Do you know what happens to that thief? They die. I know how this story ends, and my answer is no. Find yourself another thief. I don't want fame. I don't want glory. I don't want anything to do with power-hungry fae princes and a mythical cauldron everyone wants to get their hands on."

"You haven't heard all the details."

"I don't want to hear all the details!" I drag my finger across my throat. "Because this is what happens to curious thieves."

"What do you want then?"

Freedom.

"Something I can't have."

He gives me a considering look, but wisely, he doesn't pursue that line of thinking. "You owe me a debt."

I set both hands on the table and glare over it at him. "Then take it out of my hide."

He leans forward. "You tried to steal from me, and I'm

just as dangerous as any of the fae princes in the lands. Don't tempt me, Merisel, because if I demand payment, then you won't like my terms."

Every inch of me stills.

"Perhaps this will help you change your mind." He tosses something on the table between us, though I swear his hands were empty just now.

It's a sheet of paper, curled up on itself. I unroll it and a line drawing of my sister's face appears, along with the word "Wanted." The reward is ten thousand groats, which makes my shoulders deflate.

For ten thousand groats, every hob and selkie and brownie in the lands will be looking for her.

Soraya and I have a complicated history.

Once upon a time, she was the other half of my soul. When our father plucked us from the world and threw us into the training camps, she was the only one I could turn to. We would sleep in each other's arms at night when the nightmares threatened. If I was flogged for failing in my training, she'd be the one who cut me down from the posts and tended my back. If she was starved, I was the one who stole food and water from the cook tents for her, despite the risk to my own life.

You never forget that.

I needed her with a desperation that went soul-deep, and I'd thought she needed me too. And then our final trials began and she left me behind because I was injured —and if neither of us crossed the finish line in time, then we would both die.

She chose herself over me.

And there's a part of me—the part that was raised in the wraithen court, where mercy only ever cost you—that understands that.

There's also a part that bleeds, because we were supposed to be more than that. We were supposed to be better than the rest of them. Instead, she only proved my father's point.

I have no family.

The only one I can rely upon is myself.

But still....

"What do you mean?" My voice roughens as I smooth the paper out. "Where is Soraya? What did you do?"

"Me? Nothing."

It's difficult to believe. "She *did* try to kill you."

"She's not the first," Keir replies with a shrug. "And she won't be the last. No. I had nothing to do with her disappearance."

"Disappearance?" This time my gaze snaps to his.

"Curiously enough," he continues, "it was how I discovered the existence of the horn. Your sister wasn't in the forefront of my mind until one of my spies happened to chance across her. Or her description, rather. I plucked his memories from his dreams and imagine my shock when I saw her face."

"The horn? What does the horn have to do with—"

"Your sister was in a position to find it and considering your interest in certain relics—" His fingers brush against the bare skin around his throat. "—I found it interesting that she just happened to be using a false name in a place that is abuzz with news of the horn. When my spy moved to apprehend her, she was gone. And in unusual circumstances. She simply disappeared. Her room was in disarray, and there were spatters of blood on her pillow."

The warmth drains out of my face. *Blood*. I suck in a sharp breath, but then my mind starts racing. Soraya doesn't lose. She's one of the most dangerous assassins in the Blessed kingdoms. If there's blood in her rooms and she's vanished, then there's a reason for it and it's not because someone has buried her in the forest somewhere.

What would my father want with the horn? Because if Soraya is using a false name, then she has to be there on his orders.

The cauldron.

Power.

It was reputed to hold the might of the dragon kings. It could break the curse that shackles all of the Forbidden into their wraithbound shapes, and what my father desires most of all is to break the curse on his people.

"Where?" I breathe.

"I thought you weren't interested." The lazy gleam in his eyes holds a dangerous smile.

The prick.

I bite down on my frustration. "Maybe I can be convinced."

"I thought you might be," he purrs. "She was at the Court of Blood."

"The Court of *Blood*?"

It's one of the most dangerous of the Blessed courts. The only other court that might come close is the Court of Frost and Fangs.

What was Soraya doing at the Court of Blood?

How does it factor into the location of the horn?

Keir must see my confusion. "Three years ago, the crown prince of the Blood Court funded a private group of treasure hunters who began digging into a dragon king's private hoard in the Frostfangs. Malechus thinks nobody knows about it. He is wrong. According to one of my sources, the group found something but apparently all died of a blood-hungry curse. The last survivor was found rambling in a tavern about how the dragon's cave was haunted."

Haunted treasure trove. Blood-hungry curse. Crown Prince of the Blood Court.

I watch as Keir bites into a fig, his sharp teeth cutting cleanly through the goat's cheese. It's far too distracting. "Strange. I thought curses like that were almost the sole province of the Court of Blood's royal family. Not ghosts."

Keir flashes me a smile.

"They found something in the dragon king's hoard." My mind starts chasing down thoughts. It's always been my curse. "Malechus wanted to keep it quiet."

"Oh, it's far more interesting than that," Keir says, licking at his fingers. "Malechus wanted to get his hands on it. It seems the lead treasure hunter realized exactly what he'd found and wanted to make more money than what Malechus was offering. He ran with the treasure."

"More fool him." There are certain fae princes I might consider stealing from—Malechus is not one of them. Not even for all the souls around my father's neck. "You can't spend coin in the Shadow Lands. So Malechus has the horn."

"Uncertain. The last treasure hunter was traveling through the lands of Mistmark when he died. He thrust an object into a serving girl's hands and begged her to bury it. He choked to death on his own blood that night, and the girl vanished."

That changes everything.

Three years ago…. I can't help thinking that my sister was sent to assassinate the Lord of Mistmark roughly about the same time. My father never did say why.

And it's one of Soraya's only failures. She never breathed a word about it, but…. A mystical relic crosses the Lord of Mistmark's lands, where it's passed into a servant girl's hands.... And my father—hungrily searching for the power to break an ancient curse—sends his finest assassin to kill the Lord of Mistmark.

"Mistmark has the horn," I breathe.

"Interestingly enough, the Lord of Mistmark is now betrothed to a princess of the Blood Court. Malechus is hosting the wedding of his dearest cousin within ten days. Every prince and princess in the Blessed lands will be in attendance."

"Mistmark is marrying Malechus's cousin? They must have made a deal."

"I keep thinking the same thing, but why would the Lord of Mistmark give up the horn in exchange for a princess? There are dozens of them if he wants one." Keir arches a dubious brow. "There's an entire court between his lands and the Court of Blood. To wage war, Malechus would need to convince Prince Angmar of the Court of Storms to allow him to cross his kingdom with an army. There's no love lost between the Court of Blood and the

Court of Storms. And the Lord of Mistmark has enough power to ward off a blood curse."

"Who knows? Maybe Mistmark is a coward?"

"Alaric is many things, but he's not a coward."

Alaric. "You know him?"

"I know all of them," Keir replies. "Alaric plays the game and deeply. If he's marrying sweet Belladonna, then there's a reason for it. And that's where my trail vanishes." His gaze holds mine hostage. "I need someone to enter the Blood Court and discover if the Lord of Mistmark truly has the horn and if he's promised it to Malechus as a bridal tithe."

Oh no.

No Blood Courts for me.

Soraya disappeared from there.

I close my eyes, trying to harden my heart against the little piece of me I haven't managed to kill.

Soraya can handle herself. She left you to the Prince of Dreams' mercy, after all. She wouldn't come looking for you.

The problem is, I'm not entirely convinced of that.

You can spend an entire lifetime threatening to murder your sister, but if anyone else dares try and touch them….

Still… how do I even escape the Abyss? I can't. I've *tried.* And Father will never let me go.

If he even suspected the Prince of Dreams owned some part of my loyalty….

"I'm sure if you attended, they'd let you in," I point out. "You are the Prince of Dreams, after all. Powerful, mysterious, handsome, and… a bachelor who's recently made it clear he's searching for a bride. They'll roll out a red carpet of welcome and fling a dozen nubile virgins in your direction."

His smile holds teeth, as if to say *I am a very good dragon, and I'm not trying to put your back against the wall at all.* "Oh, I can get in. But I'd be watched. I haven't left my court in three centuries. If I attend that wedding then all eyes will be on me."

"Take a spy. I'm sure you have dozens."

"This is the Horn of Shadows, Merisel. I want the best. I want you." He holds up his arm, his sleeves falling around his elbow. Little golden marks flare to life on his skin, and I gasp as I feel mine answer his magic. "You very nearly stole my most powerful asset—my heart—and I didn't even suspect you until it was too late. You're good."

I am good.

But I'm not going to fall for that little bit of flattery.

"It's a pretty story," I point out, "but unless you force me, I'm not going anywhere near the Court of Blood and this mythical horn. Sorry, but I'd rather let you torture me than dare fall into Malechus's hands."

Something tells me Keir's punishment would be eminently less painful than having every ounce of blood wrung out of me by the Prince of Knives.

Keir stares at me, drumming his fingers on the table. It's a test. He could do it if he wishes. He's marked me and until the end of the year and a day, I *must* obey him.

But to do so means he must force me to his will.

Hot flame licks at his irises and then it's swiftly smothered. Reaching inside his shirt, he tosses something on the table in front of me.

It's a locket.

Ancient silver, heavily pockmarked with use. A crescent moon linked by a trio of stars. Barely worth a handful of groats, but valuable all the same—because the last time I saw that locket, it was hanging around my sister's neck.

The breath slams out of me. "Where did you get this?"

"I told you I have my sources."

I snatch the locket into my palm. Soraya would never lose this or leave it behind. It belonged to her mother and was all she had of her when she was stolen from her people and brought to the training camps. Sometimes I'd find her sitting on the top of the tallest tower of the wraith court, staring at the moon and rubbing the locket between thumb and forefinger.

I don't have a locket.

I don't have anything of my mother's except for her pale blue eyes and silvery hair, my father once snarled.

And if I did, then I would kill anyone who dared touch it.

"*How* did you get this?"

"It was sent to me by the man I hired to track her down." Keir continues, pouring himself a goblet of wine and then filling my glass. "You think she's up to something, don't you? You think her disappearing act is merely a ploy of hers… but I'm not so sure, Merisel. I think your sister is in trouble. And as much as you don't care about the horn, you do care about your sister, don't you?"

You son of a—

Stars suddenly ricochet through my vision.

It's enough to make me blink.

What was that?

"Merisel?" Keir growls. "I asked you a question."

"Cauldron's piss," a voice hisses. *"Turn her over. Quick! The king has sent for her and we can't deliver a corpse to him! He'll have our lungs torn out through our nostrils."*

"My name is not… Merisel."

I stagger out of the chair, trying to grab hold of the balcony. The whole world begins to reel around me.

"Then what is it?" Keir demands. "What's wrong?"

"Zemira," I whisper, staring down at my hands. "My name is Zemira."

My fingers vanish.

It's as if I'm evaporating into thin air.

"Zemira!" Keir shoves to his feet, reaching for my hand, but some strange force sucks me backward, until he's merely a pinpoint of hot, flaming gold—

The world around me grows dark around the edges.

I'm wrenched into a world of shadows.

Hard floor beneath me. The burning ache of iron shackles around my wrists.

Pain screams through my shoulders and I choke and kick, my lungs spewing water as someone slaps me between the shoulder blades again.

I retch and retch, until my eyes are bugging out of my head. Just when I think my brain is going to explode from the pressure, it's finally gone. *Air.* I can breathe again. And the first lungful tastes as sweet as Night's Bloom—the most delicious poison I've ever tasted, and the most painful.

It was a dream.

It was all a dream.

Keir. The island. The cauldron.

Soraya.

Because the next words reveal the nightmare: "Get up, dog." A boot drives into my middle, and I cry out and curl around it, as someone grabs a fistful of my hair and wrenches me close to his face. "The king wants to see you."

The guards haul me to the throne room.

There's another supplicant on his knees before the throne and I'm relieved I'm not the center of attention as I'm dragged through a ring of guards.

"Please, my king. *Please.*" A wraith begs for mercy, clasping his hands together as he scrambles forward to try and touch the king's boots. "I have been a loyal servant for nearly a century—"

"Show me," the king says, his voice echoing through the throne room.

Guards pin the wraith and tear his shirt open, hauling his head back by the hair so the king can see his chest. All three of them wear gloves and they move with grim, ruthless efficiency, as if they dare not get too close.

The entire court draws back with a gasp. Horror fills the guards' faces—hardened wraiths who've killed time and time again for their king and yet, they tremble at this.

I know what they're looking at, even with his back toward me.

I've seen it too many times.

A dark, mottling across the skin that sometimes resembles a bruise over the heart at first. Except it keeps spreading, creeping across the ribs and shoulders, little snaking tendrils that wind down arms and abdomens. It never reaches the legs. By the time it's gone that far, you can see it in a wraith's eyes—dark veins bleeding through the whites of their eyes as if in warning.

The blight.

One last mocking twist of the curse the fae gifted us with long ago,

"It's not contagious!" the wraith screams. "The lore masters say it's not contagious!"

But my father's face is implacable. He pushes to his feet, fury hardening his jaw. "How dare you bring this among our people? How dare you hide it?"

"You promised us a cure!" The wraith cries, and for the first time his anger overtakes his good sense. "You said you would break the curse. You said you would fix this blight upon us!"

"And fix it I shall. Guards." My father waves at his men. "Remove him from this court before his carelessness afflicts us all."

"*No!*"

My heart kicks into my throat, but it's all over in a matter of seconds. Steel flashing in the torchlight. The meaty thud as a head hits the ground and bounces.

I turn my face away, eyes clenched shut as I swallow the pool of saliva in my mouth. *Curse it.* I was hoping to find him in a generous mood. A little tremor shivers down my spine as I lift my eyes to my king.

I'm next.

And my eyes can't help finding the body of the wraith as the guards drag it from the throne room by its heels. A scarlet trail paints the floors behind it, and someone has its head by the hair.

The Forbidden Court is not a kind place to live.

Once we were as glorious as the fae, albeit the darker of the courts. Unblessed by the goddess, they named us, saying that she had turned her face from our kind.

We weren't always wraiths.

Once we were a court within the Seelie hegemony, until the other courts turned on us during the Dragon Wars. A mighty battle against the dragons was fought—a battle we should have won—but treachery ruled the day.

I don't know whether our long-ago king stabbed the king of the Dawn Court's son in the back, or whether the Crown Prince of Dawn—fueled by an age-old resentment —forced a duel upon the field in which he was not prepared to win. Accounts vary, depending upon whom you listen to.

Either way, the Prince of Dawn died and his father swore vengeance. He named us tainted and proclaimed our unruly blood was costing the Blessed courts the war. He called us Unblessed—a blight on the Goddess's glory.

With the blessing of the other courts, King Anselm forged a weapon that stripped the fae magic from our bodies. He said that if we were no longer of the light, then the sun would shun us. It burned our skin, burned our eyes, and forced us into the night. Our immortality bled from us, leaving us sickly and dying. My grandfather, Prince

Rakulh, was forced to curse us into a new form in order to survive.

Now we are the Forbidden.

No longer fae. Wraiths, instead. The shadow remnants of our fair brethren, with our pale skin, darkened claws and twisted magics.

Thankfully, I resemble my fae mother more than my father—enough to make it possible to walk among the Blessed courts with a little glamor to hide my glowing skin. It looks as luminescent as moonlight if I don't tamp my magic down inside me behind chains of glamor. After years of doing it, it's almost as natural as breathing.

I can walk beneath the sun.

And my ability to heal and regenerate is almost fae-like.

But in recent years it's become clear the curse Prince Rakulh used to save us is slowly destroying us.

Rumors of the blight whisper through court. Everyone's heard of someone who has an uncle, a brother, a grandmother who's suffered from it by now. The king has spent years crushing such rumors, but no matter how many of the afflicted he kills, more arise.

And no one knows what's causing it

At first it was one or two suffering from this sickness. We knew nothing of it, except for its aftermath. It happened in the south the first time, during a blizzard along our southern walls. A shattered guard tower broken apart as if by beasts. Bodies torn apart and drained of their blood. Not a single survivor left to tell the tale.

I saw the report sent back to the king. One of the guards was missing, and to all appearances the guard tower was locked and warded against outside forces. They had to assume the guard had gone on a killing spree, but no one knew how. The puncture marks left on the bodies spoke of sharpened canines and elongated claws, and while wraithenkind are considered abominations by the Blessed fae, we're not animals.

My father set the report aside. There were wars to plan and fae princes to manipulate. It wasn't until the second attack came at a town much closer to the court, that he sent someone to investigate.

Six months passed. There were more attacks, vicious and bloody. The guards dragged one of the afflicted back to court, revealing a creature with maddened eyes and fangs and claws. It was as though everything the fairer courts spoke of us had sprung to life, as if some strange magic heard tell of their tales and conjured a monster right out of their nightmares.

A Nightstalker.

It was not an illness. Nor a poison. There was no rhyme nor reason to the blight's occurrences. It simply happened. And kept happening.

I'm one of my father's favorites. I've knelt by his feet as he's heard the reports, and seen the fury and fear mingling in his eyes when his seneschals retreat.

"The curse," he'd whispered once. "It must be that the curse is… evolving."

And ever since that moment he's been obsessed with breaking it.

"Well?" Father barks, shattering my thoughts. "What now?"

"Your daughter, Your Highness," one of the guards says stiffly. "You sent for her."

"She looks half dead." There's a hint of menace in those words.

"Half dead is still half alive," I manage to rasp. My throat feels like someone reached down it and ripped my lungs out, but the warm tingly feeling means my fae heritage is healing me. I barely have the strength to push myself to my hands and knees, every inch of me shaking.

But I swore myself an oath when I was a little girl.

No matter what happens to me, I will not crawl before this creature.

I will never beg.

I will never abase myself.

Slowly, my chin lifts until our eyes meet.

"Father," I say.

"Stand up," the Wraith King snaps.

Stand up, they yelled in the training camps when I was forced to endure trial after trial in order to prove my worth to this creature in front of me.

And if you didn't stand then you earned a slit throat.

I force my muscles to move as I slowly push to my feet.

And then I behold the true horror of the Unblessed king.

Raesh Ghul had any sense of mercy whipped from him as a boy and it shows in his face. An enormous troll's skull is carved into a crown atop his head, and his long, raven-black hair is bound into a myriad of plaits. If not for his ghostly white skin—maggot pale—he'd almost be handsome.

And maybe that's the true horror, for a monster lurks within that fair façade. One who stole my fae mother from her bed one night and bred a child on her to forge as a weapon against her kin. A child with the gifts of both sides of her heritage—and one who can pass as fae if I'm focusing on my glamor.

A half dozen soul-traps hang from his throat. He likes to leave his fur cloak open, so they're visible. One of them calls to me, the wisp of pale blue mist caressing the glass it's trapped within as if it can sense me.

My soul.

It was cut from me the night I was born in order to ensure my loyalty. With it, he owns me. Without it I can never truly escape, for he can snuff my life simply by closing his fist around that small crystal cylinder and crushing it.

I've heard stories of my birth. There's something about the meld of wraith and fae that often makes delivering a half-born child difficult. Some say it's the curse cast upon us, fighting to twist the fae mother's magic. In defense, my mother's power sought to protect her, which nearly killed me. My father cut me from her womb in order to save my life, and she was left to bleed to death in her bed as he beheld all his hopes and dreams... and found them utterly lacking.

I was small, sickly, and gleaming like mother-of-pearl. In the eyes of my father, who had hoped for a strong child born of two powerful bloodlines, I was an abject failure. He cast me at a wet nurse and told her that if I lived, then I was to be brought before him at the age of five in order to see if anything could be redeemed of my worth.

The first I knew of the world was the small hovel where I was raised. The potential of my bloodlines was too important for the wet nurse, Thia, to dare let me starve, but there was no kindness to be found among the several bastards she raised in exchange for my father's coin. With three older "brothers" and a "sister" who liked to cuff me when nobody was looking, there were only scraps of food to eat, and a small nest of hay under the bed to sleep in.

The first time I ever Sifted—slipping from shadow to shadow—was when I was four, and a pair of my "brothers" tried to drown me in a well. All I can remember is that I was terrified and desperate enough that I somehow managed to reach my magic, and when I came to, I found myself drenched and shivering in a nearby forest.

It became my escape from a lifetime of misery.

I became adept at stealing from the markets near our house. One sidestep into the shadows, and suddenly, I could take everything and anything I wanted from the market stalls. I stole to eat. I stole to survive. I stole because sometimes it was the only way to revenge myself upon those older brothers who liked to hit, and kick, and ambush me in dangerous places. I'd leave those treasures in their boots and other hidey holes, where they'd be found. It earned them several thrashings and nobody ever knew it was me.

When my fifth birthing day came around, I was hauled before the king. I knew who he was and that I had to please him or the money would stop being sent.

I feel the same weight of condemnation now.

Somewhere, deep in my heart, I will always be that sickly child who knows she needs to prove herself.

"Daughter." The king's cold black eyes lock upon me, and then they slide down my length. "You look unwell."

"Torture does that to a body," I rasp, and can't stop my right fist from curling in upon itself.

He notices. He notices everything.

I'd love to say I have the wherewithal to mutter "Fuck you," but I'm pretty sure I do nothing more than tremble as the chancellor sweeps his torch closer to me.

"Is she even in any sort of condition to do this?" The chancellor asks.

My father's eyes harden. There is no choice. Whatever he wants of me, I *must* do.

"The other one failed, after all," says a new voice, coming from my right.

A chill trembles through me. I cut a sharp look toward the newcomer as he strolls out of the shadows, toying with something in his hands. Black hair tumbles over a pale forehead, but where my father is wildness and aggression, Ruhle is cultured malice. Every inch of him is sleekly poised, from the gleaming leather of his body armor to the silver skull ring on his finger. His boots gleam, and there's a joke among the court that you don't want to get on Ruhle's bad side, or your tongue will be the one that polishes them.

My father has sired many children.

But few survive the training camps, and those that do are the killers. I didn't have the killing instinct—I still don't—but Soraya did, and those were the days when she had my back.

Ruhle is the eldest of the wraith king's children and heir apparent. He was the only wraith-born bastard who survived the training camps during his year, and some whisper there's a reason for that. The first five to get across the finish line of the year-end challenge are allowed to live—but he was the only one who returned from the mountains.

That doesn't mean he works alone.

No, he has his own little circle of wraiths to do his bidding. Seven of them, to be exact. And they're all as cruel and malicious as he is.

"How was the Abyss?" he asks of me.

"Somewhat chilly. How was exile?" I return, squaring my shoulders. Drawing his attention is never wise, but cowering before him is a certain means to earn his full attention. He preys on the weak and after years of small aggressions, if I give him one good reason to believe me unable to fend him off, I'll find him in my bedchambers one night with a knife in hand.

Ruhle's lip curls. "It was never exile—"

"No?" I turn my full attention toward him as he prowls toward me. "Three of our brothers die, and you are sent to the watchtowers along our southern flank during winter? Perhaps it was a gift instead, a boon for our precious crown prince to learn to control his temper."

Father hates that title.

He rules. Absolutely. And with his longevity, the concept of an heir makes his lip curl.

"The Blessed courts were starting to look north," Ruhle grates. "Someone had to ensure they didn't cross the Shadowfangs."

"How brave of you, to take a captain's job—"

"You little slut." Ruhle starts toward me, his fist clenching. "Your bitch sister isn't here to save you now—"

"*Enough.*" The word cuts through us and we both kneel toward Father as he watches us with simmering fury in his eyes.

The word echoes through the throne room with all the finality of the chancellor bringing his staff down on the slate floors with a ringing thump.

"Yes, Father." Both Ruhle and I parrot, as we bow our heads.

But I can sense my brother's cold glare.

I'll pay for that little moment, but he won't dare try to kill me. I'm still valuable to my father, and while Ruhle might have murdered three of our weaker brothers, he doesn't dare touch the king's Shadow Walker.

He'd also have to catch me first.

"I have a task for you, Zemira," Father continues as we both straighten.

Twice in one night. A girl can only be so lucky.

"And here I thought you were prepared to welcome me back into your loving embrace," I reply. "Imagine that. What would you have of me?"

"You failed me this summer. I sent you to steal the Dragon's Heart from the Court of Dreams, and not only did you fail to find it, but you mistook it for this worthless scrap of gold."

He flings something at my feet.

A golden amulet shaped like a dragon's claw. It fetches up by my bare feet. The last time I saw it, it hung around Prince Keir's muscled throat, but my sister stole it and presented it to my father as the Heart.

Stillness runs through me. This moment is dangerous.

Because I mistook nothing.

The Dragon's Heart was never a relic. No, it was a story twisted to hide the truth of the matter: Many, many years ago, Keir was one of the powerful dragon kings who ruled this world. Rumors abound that when the fae went to war with the dragon kings, the dragons turned to stone and withdrew from the world.

But Keir merely focused his magic upon himself.

He forged a new body, one that looks fae enough to pass, and he tore his court from the mortal planes, anchoring it in an Other World that sits alongside ours. Now he's nothing more than a powerful prince in the eyes of the Blessed courts.

If anyone knew the truth of his heritage, there would be war again.

It was never a relic I was searching for. But his heart is another matter. If my father could cut it from Keir's chest, he wouldn't merely have the power to break the curse that afflicts wraithenkind and binds us to the icy north, he could tear apart the entire Seelie hegemony.

And I can stop him.

All I need do is keep this one secret from him. I can finally thwart him, even if it costs me.

So I lower my eyes. "My mistake, Father. I'm sorry."

Ruhle's smile is the kiss of a knife against my throat. "We're only ever allowed one," he whispers. "You seem to be at your quota."

I swallow down the temptation to retort. "What would you have of me, my king?"

"Your sister is missing," Raesh tells me.

Not a dream. It wasn't a dream at all. Which means that Keir truly demanded I find the Horn of Shadows for him.

"What do you mean?" I ask slowly, because I need to sound surprised.

"I sent her to carry out a task for me, and she hasn't responded to the last three of my communications." The king clamps a hand around one of the vials around his throat. "She's not even responding to this."

"What happened to her?" I can't stop my gaze from dropping to the tiny vial. The wisp of her soul lies still and dormant at the bottom of the soul-trap. They're never quiet like that.

For the first time, I feel true worry.

When Keir mentioned her disappearance, I shrugged it off. Soraya is a survivor. No matter what she must face, she puts herself first. Even the sight of her amulet wasn't enough to know true fear.

But this....

She's not dead. The little wisp of soul in that glass vial would have evaporated if she was, but something is wrong with her.

The king waves off my concern. "She will either return or she will not. What matters now is that her task remains incomplete. And you will finish it." His eyes become hard. "The Lord of Mistmark is marrying the Prince of Blood's cousin. I want you to steal something from Malechus—"

I almost laugh, barely hearing the words. What are the odds? If he dares say it....

"I've heard rumor the Lord of Mistmark has managed to get his hands on a certain horn..., one that controls the hounds of the Great Hunt. And those hounds can lead me to the Cauldron of Creation."

Fuck you, Fate. Fuck you, you capricious bitch.

"The cauldron?"

The Wraith King leans toward me, both pallid hands curling around the ends of his throne. "I warned you once that I would have an end to the curse that binds us to these misbegotten lands and tethers us to this warped flesh." He holds up his claws. "You failed to bring me the Dragon's Heart. The only other relic with the power to shatter our chains is the goddess's cauldron."

"There has to be another way." The words blurt out of me. I can't let him do this. I can't let him say the words. "If we—"

"*Enough.* Bring me the horn," my father declares. "And I will break our curse."

What am I going to do?

If that was truly not a dream, then Keir just demanded I fulfill my debt to him. I can feel the magic of his glyphs under my skin. The agony as they branded themselves into my skin was indescribable. I can only imagine what would happen if I dared defy him.

But my father….

My lungs still ache. Every inch of me is cold and clammy and echoing with the caress of death.

If I betray my father, then he won't just kill me.

He will make me suffer endlessly.

And with my lifespan, it might be centuries before I ever see the mercy of light again.

"Yes, my king," I breathe, bending knee once more

before I turn toward the doors in a flurry of sweat-fueled nerves.

"Zemira?"

I pause, glancing back over my shoulder.

"No more failures," the Wraith King says in a menacing whisper.

Ruhle smirks at me from his side. "Fail again and maybe I'll ask for a boon. Maybe it will be my hand that ends your wretched life."

It's not an idle threat.

I have no choice.

The only one who can save me is me.

My shoulders straighten. "I will find the Horn of Shadows. I will not fail you again, Father."

I do not dare.

Even if I have to betray Keir in order to do so.

4

Torn between a vicious king and a powerful prince.

I sigh as I stare at the ceiling of my bedchambers at the inn I'm staying at. All I really need right now is to throw my treacherous sister into the mix, but she's missing.

And the Lord of Mistmark's name keeps being mentioned in relation to Soraya. My sister was sent to kill him and for the first and only time, she failed.

I know how she played the ruse.

From what little I know of the Lord of Mistmark, he's powerful, dangerous, and rules his own lands, separate from any court. She tried to seduce him and something went wrong, for she either couldn't kill him, or she didn't have the *heart* to kill him.

Until this moment I wouldn't have thought her to *have* a heart, but I taunted her about him once and she nearly put a knife in me. I saw the look that crossed her face. Just one fleeting, unguarded second of pain. It was a look of lost hopes. And dare I say it, broken dreams….

And now he's marrying another and my sister, who was sent to steal the horn he has in his possession, has vanished into the winds.

The Court of Blood is one of the most dangerous of the Blessed courts. It's ruled by King Aswan, but his son is hungry and ambitious, and his nieces no less so. They're gifted in the art of poison, and it's said that some of them mix torture with sex. Narcissa, one of Aswan's nieces, was one of the potential brides summoned to the Court of Dreams three months ago, and although she died, I wouldn't have liked to have crossed her.

Why would the Lord of Mistmark want to marry Belladonna?

Why would he want to marry *any* of the Court of Blood?

They've been passed over for centuries—one of the reasons Narcissa was so desperate to capture the Prince of Dreams' attention—and if sweet little Belladonna is as poisonous as her sister, then it would be like bedding down with a viper.

If Mistmark caught a glimpse of my sister's face, then he might be responsible for her disappearance. He's definitely at the top of my suspect list, though certainly not the only one on there.

I need to get into the court to find answers.

But I don't have an invitation to the wedding.

The Court of Blood will be locked down tighter than my sister's heart. With so many of the Blessed courts in attendance, the guards will be thick and alert. Servants will be known and vetted. I could kidnap one and glamor myself to look like them for short periods of time, but that's a dangerous route to take. One must have time to study one's prey and their mannerisms.

But several princesses saw my face three months ago. They knew me as Merisel of Greenslieves, and while my skills of glamor are good, they're not good enough to completely change my appearance. It's a twist of the cheekbones here, a slip of the nose there…. You're constantly working to hold the glamor in place, because different angles change perspective. Too many people would look at me and wonder why I seem familiar.

Who knows what kind of traps and glamors the Prince of Blood has laid over his court? He didn't earn that moniker because he's a kindly soul.

The answer to my dilemma is clear: I can't get into the Court of Blood in disguise.

The only way to get in is if I'm invited.

Or more to the point, if *Merisel* is invited. And there's one fae who *isn't* invited, but will be welcomed all the same.

Pushing upright, I scowl.

Sometimes I hate the twists my mind takes.

Fate trails her icy fingertips down my spine.

I cross to the fireplace, pour myself a goblet of wine, and stare into the flames. I've never tried to contact Keir but I can feel the link between us, etched into my skin with his magic. Four hundred and thirteen days I owed him—a year and a day—and now roughly three hundred and fifty marks remain. They're invisible to anyone other than myself and Keir. Each day a little tingle shivers through me as one of the runes vanishes.

"Hello?" I whisper, stroking the mark on the inside of my wrist. "Can you hear me?"

There's a moment of silence and then a foreign awareness turns toward me. I don't know how to describe it. One second the room is empty, and the next I can almost feel an enormous body brushing against mine, his breath whispering over the back of my neck.

The prince.

Keir's not here, of course, but it *feels* like it.

"Zemira?" His whisper is intimate. "What happened? Where did you go?"

I swallow hard. "You want me to steal the horn? Fine. But I'll need a little help to do so."

There's a long, drawn-out pause. "What do you need?"

"You."

THIS IS THE SECOND TIME I'VE PLANNED TO BETRAY THE Prince of Dreams.

I wait by an old castle's ruins, right on the border of the Court of Blood. Trees sprawl over tumbled rock walls, vines snarling around broken towers. It's as though the forest is trying to reclaim the castle, eating it inch by inch, year by year.

One day, there will be nothing here but trees and future fae will stub their toes on mossy stones and wonder why they're rectangular.

The eastern road passes by here. It's one of the least known entry points to the Court of Blood and lightly guarded. There's no trade into the mountains, and the threat of the Forbidden are far to the north.

Or so the fae think.

Thousands of years ago, when the dragons lived they ruled the world. When the war forced them to treat with the fae, they returned their magic to the cauldron so that their kind could live, and yet a spark remained within their breasts.

The loss of their magic stripped them of their immortality too.

And when they died, it took years for the fae to understand that that spark of magic slowly bled into the world beneath a dragon's bleached bones.

We call them barrows.

When their bones melded with the soil, they forced the earth around them to become *different*. Magic leached into stone, and roots, and trees. Old forests grew—the kind of forests that whisper of an ancient time. It slowly seeps outward, infecting the earth around it. Year by year, the barrows grow. They're an Other World, a place cleaved from the real world in time and space, even though they look the same as the world around them. You can always tell when you enter a dragon's barrow. It feels like walking through an invisible shock of lightning. It's just enough to make your breath catch, and then the world around you is a little brighter, and there's a faint hum like the far-off buzz of cicadas.

Nothing lives in a barrow beyond the trees and the grass. It's an eerie, silent place. No wind blows. Nothing moves. And yet, there are eyes on you somehow. Invisible eyes watching and judging you. They even say the dragon's spirit lives on, lost in dreams, and that if you're not careful, you can be drawn into such dreams yourself.

Few would ever venture inside willingly, but if you find the heart of the barrow, then you can sidestep into another Other World, another barrow.

And walk out of it a thousand miles from where you entered.

The fae don't use them, considering them haunted. It's forbidden to enter one, and without a ward against the barrow's magic, you can be lost to the Other Worlds.

But my father's been slowly mapping their paths, sending his wraithen scouts to test the pathways. Many don't return—the issue with exploring such newfound paths is that nobody knows the dangers of a dragon's dreams until it's too late. But the risk is work the reward in my father's eyes.

He yearns to deliver an army right into the heart of any court in the land if he so wishes.

The Blessed fae would be practically defenseless.

But first we have to shatter our curse so his wraithen armies can walk beneath the sunlight without being struck down.

I saunter through an ancient arch of a broken castle, a shiver running over my skin as I exit the barrow. Sound intrudes again. A chatter of squirrels nearby. None of the fae know just how vulnerable they are. They barely even guard these places.

The jingle of tack echoes through the air.

There. Sunlight sparking off something bright. A carriage, by the look of it. One drawn by a brace of matching fae horses, their coats rippling silver beneath the light. I hide in the shadows, my heart skipping a beat.

Keir.

He's here.

In the flesh.

Suddenly, I can taste betrayal in my mouth and my heart skips a beat. Keir and I spoke once of trust and I remember the look in his eyes when he realized who and what I truly was.

There's no coming back from that.

For either of us.

But he doesn't *need* the horn. He merely wants it in order to control its power.

And I *need* it.

I watch the carriage spill into the clearing below us, where it draws to a halt and someone steps down from it. I can barely see him. A tall figure, garbed in a cloak. Tugging his gloves from his fingers, he circles the ruins. Looking for me, I think.

Keir.

I Sift through the shadows, watching him stalk through the broken stone towers. His shoulders are broader than I remember.

To see him in my dreams was dangerous enough, but there's a potency about him in the flesh that can't be denied. He towers a good five inches over me, and every inch of him is lean, hard-cut muscle. To see him is to be reminded of what he is all over again. A predator in the body of a handsome fae prince. Hard. Dangerous. Lethal. There's something sinuous about the way he moves, as if, even after centuries of pretending to be fae, the dragon still exists.

"Zemira?" he calls, the wind caressing his shirt against his body.

I Sift through shadows, following him.

"I know you're here," he whispers, and somehow the breeze carries his words right to my ear.

I peer from around the stone arch I'm hiding within.

Gone. He's gone.

I press my back to the stone wall and swallow. I'm still half in the shadows. He can't see me. But he'll have sensed me.

Wind stirs through the ruins.

I can almost hear a roughened laugh.

He's hunting me, and we both know it.

Sound whispers to the left of me—perhaps a boot on stone.

I turn right and slam directly into a hard chest. It's almost an exact reenactment of the night I first met him.

Gloved hands capture my forearms and the prince's shadow falls over me. He tears me back out of the shadows, and the shock of sudden light is near blinding. My fae half protects me from the burn of sunlight, but it still hurts my eyes.

"Here you are," he breathes, his voice rough-edged with delight.

He's real. Real and solid, and I can smell his cologne— something spicy that never fails to twist my insides. Hot, golden eyes lock upon me. He's not even bothering to hide the dragon within him—or maybe now I know it's there, I can see it.

The first time I laid eyes upon him, he'd been a target, a means to an end. I'd been focusing so hard on my mission—get into the Court of Dreams, ensure nobody broke my cover as the Lady Merisel, and find the Dragon's Heart—that I'd relegated the actual prince of the court to merely a male I needed to avoid.

Instead, he was everything I could have dreamed of.

I was wraithenborn. A monster in a fae world.

And if I looked back on the events of this summer, it's easy to see where I went wrong.

The first time a boy kissed me, I was sixteen and preparing for my final trials. The kiss took me by surprise —he was the son of one of my trainers, brought in to spar with me over the autumn—and until that final night, neither of us had thought the best of the other. He was handsome, cocky, frustratingly arrogant. I didn't even really care for him.

Five of the trainees make it through the final trials, and our particular year was incredibly competitive. I'd spent half the night polishing my blades and trying to calm my racing heart, when Rian gave me a piece of information about the forthcoming trials that might save my life. Maybe he felt sorry for me. Maybe those hours of earnest sparring had earned me some slight reprieve. After years of barely daring to let another into my life, his kindness made me falter where nothing else could have.

It was the first time I let down my walls.

And when I survived, I fell into his bed with a desperation neither of us could quench. I needed some sort of connection to another living being after Soraya's betrayal. I wanted to be something else, someone else. I wanted to bury myself in Rian's arms and pretend I was merely a fae princess somewhere in the Blessed lands, holding onto her beloved.

Except, it was very clear I wasn't.

A month later, I was brought to court, where I was raised among my father's personal guard, and Rian vanished back into the army. I never saw him again.

Stolen kisses whilst I was sent into the world were all I had. Sex became a secret pleasure I stole for myself whenever I was on a mission and a stranger caught my eye. It was a moment of pretend. Just for a night I could snuggle into another's arms and dream that I would wake in the morning in a new life, with a new destiny. I could be a princess in a land where food was never in short supply, I didn't have to lock my door every night, and nobody would ever beat me again. I wanted that dream so badly that every night when I slipped beneath my sheets, I would conjure a nameless, faceless prince who would steal me away from my wretched life and make me happy.

And then I was sent to steal Keir's heart.

I knew the moment my father's spymaster set his file into my hands that he was different to my usual marks. The small miniature of his face barely did him justice, but at the time his green-gold eyes had made my breath catch. A ruling fae prince of a mysterious land, handsome and dangerous and wickedly sinful. Every mention of the Court of Dreams promised everything I could ever want. The night before I set out to break into the Court of Dreams was the first night my dream-like lover had a face.

It was safe.

Nothing could come of it.

I would slip into his court, get a better glimpse of the dream, and then steal his relic and never have to see him ever again. There were nineteen other princesses vying for his attention. He would never choose me.

And to ensure this fact, I made myself absent from the group gatherings where he would be present. I gave him a polite smile, and disengaged from any of his attempts to draw me into a conversation.

I made a fatal mistake.

Of course a dangerous fae prince is going to chase the one woman who doesn't seem to like him. He had nineteen princesses kissing his polished boots. Of course he was going to set his sights on the one who barely gave him a hint of attention. No matter what I did, he found ways to tempt me out of the role. We flirted. We dined. There was a breathless moment where I even began to forget why I was there.

And the worst thing was… I liked him.

Truly liked him.

When I asked him what he wanted, he whispered that he dreamed of a queen to rule at his side. Someone to love. Someone he could trust with his whole heart. It was like he conjured my own dreams to life and then instantly set a sword to them.

Because the woman he dreamed of wasn't me.

I was bound to betray him.

Nothing has changed.

But those wretched old feelings resurface just long enough to make my throat thicken, and then Keir's lashes flutter low over his eyes, and he brushes his thumb against my cheek. "I almost didn't think you were going to come."

My heart skips a beat. "I was the one who asked you to be here."

"We both know you tell lies."

For a second, I think he's going to kiss me, and panic flares. He's only ever kissed me once, and that was to bind me to him.

I don't even know why I'm thinking of kissing.

"Your Highness," I blurt.

"So formal." He hasn't let go of me. "Considering I once overheard you call me His Royal Studliness."

"*I* didn't say that. That was Calliope."

He arches a brow, and I'm reminded of all the ways I shouldn't mention that name—mostly because she tried to kill both of us.

"Where did you go? You were in my dreams, and then you were gone."

"I woke."

Something dangerous lurks in his eyes. "You're lying."

"I'm not." I push past him, desperate for some space. "Isn't that how one escapes a dream?"

"Not mine." Keir's voice is a shiver over my skin as he prowls after me. "Once you're in my dreams, Zemira, you can't escape me. So I would like to know how you achieved it."

I drowned.

I still the shiver fighting to break free. I'm not going back there to that time and place, not even in my own memories. I'm alive, in the here and now, basking in the warmth playing over my skin. If life has taught me anything, it's to never look back. "Perhaps your power isn't as absolute as you would like to think it is."

His eyes narrow, and I'm fairly certain I haven't convinced him. Those dangerous eyes rove over me. "I like the vest." His gaze turns hot. "I like the breeches too. Much better than the silk and lace you once pretended to thrive in. This suits you."

"It's easier to move in than the pretty gowns I once wore." I shoot him a challenging look. "Did you bring what I need?"

Keir gestures me toward the carriage, his eyes glinting with challenge. "As my lady commands."

Don't call me that. But it's the plan, after all. And it's my plan.

Two servants haul a trunk down from the carriage even as I studiously ignore him.

A simple flip of the latch, and there it is.

The perfect weapon.

I wince as I pick up the corset on top of the pile of gowns. "I'd almost forgotten how uncomfortable all of this is."

"If you want to be invited in," Keir murmurs, "then you have to look the part, my lady Merisel."

I hate that name so much.

"It bothers you, doesn't it?"

"What?"

"Her name." Keir leans his back against the carriage, turning just his head to look at me.

I shake out the dress on the top of the pile. The silk feels surreal beneath my callused fingers. Little chips of diamond glitter from where they're sewn into the skirts. "It's just a name. Just an alias. I've spent my entire life slipping them on and off like old clothes." I can't help arching a brow. "This is cut to my size perfectly. Is it real?"

"No. It's crafted entirely from my dreams," he purrs. "Careful, or I might simply make it all vanish, right in the middle of the wedding."

I nearly drop the gown. "*What?*"

"You wanted a distraction, did you not?" He actually rolls his eyes as my jaw drops open. "It's real, Zemira. It's all been made just for you."

"You have an entire trunk of clothes cut to my size?" Not even a brownie with the best homespun magic can simply magic up an entire wardrobe of clothes like this.

"I like to be prepared," he says. "I have a year and a day of your service, and if I need you to do something for me, then I don't want to have to wait until you have a wardrobe." His gold eyes lock on me mockingly. "You have an entire suite of rooms awaiting you at my palace. You have a wardrobe of gorgeous gowns. You have books. You have a set of goblin-forged knives, spelled to cut through any ward and keyed to your hand only. Everything you might need and desire."

"Goblin-forged knives?"

The goblin court was named Forbidden during the same wars that branded my people with that title. The goblin king vanished his court from fae eyes and swore that his court would not deal with the fae while the sun was still in the sky. A goblin-forged blade is worth a small earldom. They're rare. Impossibly rare. And to get his hands on an entire set of them....

For *me*.

I can't breathe. A horrible, giddy feeling sweeps

through me. Soraya has one goblin-forged blade she stole from the collection of a centuries-old fae who captured pretty mortal girls and chained them to his dais. She killed him with his own knife, set the girls free, and then burned his palace.

It's her most treasured item.

"When you say 'set,'" I manage to sound almost calm, "precisely how many knives are you talking about?"

Keir laughs under his breath. "I should have known that would be the gift that would get your attention."

Gift. Every inch of me stills.

Soraya used to give me gifts for my birthing day every year. Small things like honeyed cakes she'd stolen from the kitchens, a flask of mead when we came of age—which is probably the reason I can never taste it again without gagging in remembrance—and a string of dandelion seeds with which to make wish after wish.

She stopped leaving them on my pillow after she betrayed me in the trials.

And nobody else has ever given me a gift since.

I stare at him, reminded once again that he's a fae prince with all the luxuries that title can buy him. It probably means nothing. As he said, he has plans for me and needs me to be able to infiltrate a court at his beck and whim.

But still....

I blow out a breath. *Mind on track.* I have the wardrobe required to infiltrate the Court of Blood. I have the prince. There's just one little problem....

"Speaking of Merisel, is she going to become an

issue?" I ask. "I can't imagine that having two of us appear together would be wise."

"My sources tell me she rarely leaves her manor. Something about a digestive disagreement she had the last time she traveled, which caused her to lose her chance at attending a prince's summons. You wouldn't know anything about that, would you?"

"If I'd ingested that much Monksflower, I probably wouldn't leave the manor for a while either. Or I'd travel with a personal chamber pot."

"That doesn't sound very kindly of you."

I cut him a scathing look. "My sister wanted to feed her a heavy dose of hensbane. I thought Monksflower to be the kinder alternative. I didn't want her dead. Just indisposed." The look on his face…. "What?"

His eyelids hood. "Nothing."

I start tugging on the buttons of my shirt. "I'm a thief, Keir. A pragmatic thief. Dead bodies bring questions. They also inspire lofty notions such as vengeance or justice in ones enemies. The best thieves are the ones no one ever knows about. I don't need to be known as the Scarlet Hand or the Black Hood. Or—"

"The White Wraith."

"What?"

"The White Wraith," he murmurs, a faint smile toying about his lips. "That's what King Angmar named you when you stole his trident."

That fucking trident. It's going to be the bane of my existence.

"He did *not*."

Oh, he's enjoying this moment. "There's a reward

poster and all. It seems you're not as unknown as you might wish for." He cocks his head. "Though the painting on the poster doesn't quite do you justice. You're much lovelier in the flesh."

I drag my hand down my face. "All my sources say Angmar won't be attending."

It was the first thing I asked my father's spymaster.

"He's not. He made some excuse about mermaids attacking one of his watch towers along the shore. I daresay he feels a little naked without his source of strength, especially when Prince Malechus would love to see him humbled."

"The trident wasn't *that* powerful." My father tried to use it to break the curse on one of his guards, and the gold in the trident simply warped as the magic lashed back. "If he can't face another ruling prince without it, then perhaps he should pass his throne on to one of his siblings."

"Oh, I think it won't be long before one of them takes it."

Perfect. Angmar won't be in attendance. I'm sure he'll send an emissary, but nobody else saw me the night I stole the trident, and my glamor is strong enough to make my face just different enough to his reward poster.

"There's just one more little problem as far as I can see," Keir says.

I've been through all of my plans. Nothing has been left to chance. Nothing. "What?"

"You said you had another master." A certain intensity comes over his face. "I can't imagine he'd be pleased to let you off his leash. Does he know where you are?"

This is the dangerous part. I know he wants to know who rules over me.

"It won't be an issue."

"It won't?" There's a dangerous look in his eyes.

"My sister is missing," I point out. "If I can find her… then my king won't question it. He'll think I merely went to save her."

Keir examines my face and then gives a curt nod.

He believes me.

I turn away with the dress in hand.

I have little more than a week before the wedding takes place.

A week in which to locate the horn, find my sister, betray Keir, and escape an entire court who will most likely want my head for what's about to take place.

A week to figure out a solution to the oath that binds me to Keir.

At least this time, he knows who and what I am. If I steal the horn out from under him, that's his own cursed fault for trusting me a second time. I don't have to worry about the entanglement of feelings or whether I'm going to break his heart.

He'll hate you for this.

But it will be done, I argue with myself. *He'll never trust you again. And he doesn't truly* need *the horn. He won't suffer for any of this.*

"Are you alright, my lady?" the maid asks.

"Just preparing myself for this torture contraption," I reply, picking up the corset. I throw Keir one last glance over my shoulder. "Do you mind giving me some privacy?"

The heat in his eyes smolders. "You have five minutes."

And then he and the footman vanish around the corner of the carriage.

Dressing swiftly, I accept some help from the lady's maid he's provided for the corset and other undergarments. Soon, I'm drowning in silk. It's as blue as a field of cornflowers, and I can't help fingering the little cap sleeve that sits on my shoulders. Dozens of silver mesh flowers are embroidered on the bodice, spilling into the skirts with such abundance it looks as though I rolled in starlight.

If I was to conjure a dress out of my dreams, it would be this dress.

You can't afford this dress.

Still, it's so *pretty*.

Keir falters as I walk out from behind the carriage, trying to haul my silken skirts out of the dirt. I can barely move my legs or breathe, and I don't care one whit. There's a look on his face that momentarily makes me pause. For a second I can't identify it.

Hunger.

The realization makes my breath catch.

For all my faults, for all that's come between us, he still wants me.

"It's the same color as your eyes," he whispers. "I wondered whether I'd imagined it the second I saw the silk...."

For the first time in my life, I can't get the words out. They're trapped in my throat, right along with the need to breathe. "*You* chose the silk?"

His face shuts down, all of his emotions locked away.

"Someone had to. Shall we?" he murmurs, offering me a hand to assist me into the carriage.

I take his hand.

The horn awaits.

But I can't help feeling as though I've just made a dangerous misstep in the game somewhere.

5

The Court of Blood is housed within the heart of a mountain. Long-ago fae chiseled halls and rooms from within the slate, and each gaping "window" looks like the mournful eye of a monster. Stars glitter like a shimmering cloak draped over the mountain's shoulders, but it's the blood moon in the sky that captures my attention.

Many years ago, the king of the Court of Blood was married to a daughter of the Court of Frost and Fangs. He despised his new bride and ridiculed her by parading a never-ending cast of hundreds through his bed. In retaliation, she fled to her father's court and cast a curse on the Court of Blood by the power of the blood moon.

The waters of the court would run with blood. The stone of his mountain court would crack. And the king's… ahem… would never flourish again.

He could look. He could admire. But he could never, ever rouse, even to a lover's touch.

The only way to break the curse was for one of his lovers to sacrifice herself—willingly—to the bonfire.

It's a little inauspicious to begin a wedding beneath such a powerful astral sign that did so much damage, but the Court of Blood have always been a little strange.

A maze leads toward the entrance to the court.

It's formed of hedges of bloodstar, with their dark red leaves and silver branches. There are whispers they water the trees with blood, which gives the leaves their stunning color, and the entire effect is eerie.

The Court of Blood isn't pretending to be anything it's not.

It's a malevolent trap. A warning. An imposing fort with an elaborate welcome mat and a trap door that's prepared to slam shut behind you.

Getting in without an invite is impossible.

Luckily, I have the most delicious-looking invite a girl can find. The Prince of Dreams is the coup of any social event—a reclusive prince with enormous power, a gorgeous face, and, whilst my way in is on his arm as his betrothed, technically, until the ceremony happens, he's still unmarried.

The hardest part of the entire affair is convincing the powers-that-be that *I* belong here.

Me. A wraith-born bastard forced upon my fae mother. A monster cut from her womb.

My fingers dig into my palms. I feel sick and shaky all of a sudden, though I could have sworn I banished these moments long ago.

She loved me. She had to have loved me, because she named me true, and named me thrice before they stole me from her arms. Every fae child receives the gift of three names from its mother. Without them you are truly Unblessed.

Zemira Ashburn. Gravekissed, the Black Hawk, Winterborn.

No one knows those names except for me and my father. They're imprinted on my soul and bind me to my oaths. A fae's true name is what forces them to uphold their word, once given.

Armed with my true name and my soul, he can control every inch of me.

"Merisel," Keir murmurs, his golden eyes watching me in a way that makes me feel as though he can see right through me. "Are you all right?"

I breathe through the moment, swallowing it all down like poison I've consumed far too many times to fall prey to it. "I'm fine."

His face remains chiseled from stone. Impassive. He sits across from me, clad in sophisticated black velvet with golden dragons embroidered down the lapels. Rubies glint on his fingers, so dark a red that they seem almost black.

I have no idea what he's thinking.

Can he see it on my face? That I mean to betray him?

Surely not.

He wouldn't be lazing back against the carriage seat across from me if he was.

I have to believe that, and yet, for some strange reason, that knot of tension is back within my chest. I toy with the sapphire rings on my fingers, forcing my shoulders to square.

"We're nearly there," he says, glancing through the windows.

"You've been here before?"

"Once." His lashes shield his eyes for a second. "Though these lands did not belong to the fae then." Something makes him hesitate. "This court was the summer residence of Igrainne, my king's daughter."

Igrainne.

The daughter Queen Mab begot on the dragon king she married—before she betrayed him. I cannot even remember a time when it wasn't ruled by the Court of Blood. It makes me realize how truly ancient Keir is.

"It's beautiful," I tell him in a quiet voice.

"It is as nothing to what it was then," he replies as if he sees something else. "These lands were wild and free. We called them the Lands of the Golden Lakes, for the summers here seemed endless. And the mountain halls were wide enough for even a dragon king's wings."

"Do you miss it?"

He looks at me quickly.

"Your people," I point out.

"I miss… aspects of it." Keir sighs under his breath. "I am much changed from what I was then. At first I thought this a welcome disguise, but sometimes I wonder if the body's alchemy changes the very patterns of one's mind. I am more fae now than I ever was dragon, in some ways." His focus turns upon me. "And what of you?"

"Me?"

"You are half fae, half wraith. Which side of your nature calls more strongly to you?"

I look away. "I have never been fae. My father's court

would burn me alive if they suspected I yielded to my fairer nature."

"That wasn't what I asked."

His voice is so soft it almost seems as though it's gilded with sympathy. I close my eyes against it. "When I was born, my father took one look at me and sneered at my weakness. I was small and sickly and I gleamed like mother of pearl—"

"Mother of pearl?"

"Some twist of my bloodlines, no doubt."

"Hmm."

"It's true." Some wraithenkind glow in the night like fireflies, unless they tamp down their magic, but I've never seen another wraith with skin like mine. "My fae nature was more ascendant when I was a little girl, I'm told."

"What happened?"

Restlessness itches within me. This is not something that is spoken of—I don't think I've ever spoken of it, and it feels somewhat akin to revealing a weakness. "To remain weak meant to die. I quashed any and all of my mother's magics. The first thing I ever learned to do was to hide the glimmer of my skin." A shrug. "It's second nature now. I don't even have to think about it and sometimes I wonder if I could ever go back."

We stare at each other.

There's a sad little smile on his lips. "Yes. Something like that." He glances out the window. "Here we are."

Our carriage makes its way up the enormous driveway that parts the maze. And then it's all happening. Keir's footmen open the carriage door. A step is brought forth. Court of Blood servants turn to glance at our carriage, their eyes turning into saucers when they note the colors and sigil. The Court of Dreams is marked by a swooping dragon, which is probably Keir's idea of a joke. One of them goes running—presumably to find Malechus and inform him of his newest arrival.

I hate this.

I'm made for the shadows, not the glittering lights that flicker over the Court of Blood entrance. My glamor is firmly locked in place—no one will catch a hint of the faint luminescence of my skin—and yet I feel utterly naked.

"Breathe," Keir tells me, stepping down from the carriage and offering me his hand.

I'm scanning the entrance, tracking the guards, noting their weapons, potential escape routes, everything…, and his words jolt me out of the abstraction.

I look down, and there's a handsome prince offering me his bare hand. Our fingers meet, and despite my misgivings I can't help sucking in a short, sharp breath at the sheer heat of his skin. His mere touch promises I will burn if I were to ever give in to the look in his eyes.

It's a game.

Punishment for my betrayal.

He knows I desire him, and he's going to torment me at every turn with that desire.

"Come, my lady Merisel," Keir says, his eyes burning through me as he lifts my hand to his lips and brushes the chastest of kisses across the back of it. "Let us go and introduce the world to my bride."

෴

His words chase themselves through my head as we mount the stairs.

I'm not supposed to be his bride—well, I am, but that's just the cover we intend to use. He's supposed to be bound by his choice during the Summons, but he is to ask for two rooms and will spend his time hunting with the other lords and dancing with the ladies. The servants will gossip of course, of how there stands a door between our beds.

It's supposed to encourage the ladies of the courts to compete for his fractured attentions.

Maybe he made a mistake, they will whisper.

Merisel of Greenslieves is some backwater lady who just happens to have a distant queen in her family lines. She's not particularly pretty—not like the glamorous fae princesses bound to be in attendance—and her tongue is boring and her wits slow.

I will fade into the background, some mere plaything the Prince of Dreams is growing tired of and he will attract all the attention.

Precisely as planned.

We're led toward the ballroom, with flustered servants appearing from nowhere. If we've timed it perfectly, all the gallant fae will be dancing in celebration of the Blood Moon. It's the first night of the wedding celebrations, an omniscient start to a weeklong orgy of merriment.

Tonight, they'll crown the Willow Queen—she who was once offered to the bonfires to ward off the curse of the blood moon.

It might sound like a sacrifice, but the first Willow Queen was a clever little thing. A lowborn nixie, she drank as much water as she could from the pond and filled her veins with it before offering herself as sacrifice. She went to the bonfires and broke the curse, but she did not die. The fires couldn't touch her.

When they dragged her from the ashes, the Blood Court's curse was broken, and the king of the court was so enamored with her that he took her as his second wife.

Her family was blessed with skin that would ward off even the sharpest knife, and her weight in rubies.

I don't know what happened to the first wife. Her name was lost to memory, and the very fact they honor the Willow Queen each and every blood moon tells you something about the first queen's ending.

The doors before us open, and a self-important kelpie in a pomaded wig draws a deep breath and bellows, "His Royal Highness, Prince Keir of the Court of Dreams, and his betrothed, Lady Merisel of Greenslieves."

Heads turn.

Gasps echo through the chambers.

The entire dance comes to a stop, as even the members of the string quartet in the corner tilts their heads to look at us, with one last discordant shriek from the cello.

I have never wanted to fade into the shadows so much in my life.

"Come, my love," Keir says, taking my hand and drawing me forward into the light, as if he can sense my horror.

They're all looking at me.

Hundreds of whispering fae. I think I'm going to vomit.

Focus on the job. I swallow it all down, and even

though I'm no longer feeling sick, I know my skin has paled.

"Prince Keir," a brunette breathes, her eyes wide with joy as she welcomes him. "An honor."

"Your Highness." Another woman swims out of nowhere, dropping into a deep curtsy. "We never dreamed we would have such an illustrious guest."

On and on and on it goes as the females of the court swarm toward us.

But it's the impossibly handsome fae prince on the throne who draws my attention. Malechus is the Crown Prince of the Court of Blood, the last in a long line of vicious, dangerous males. His father, King Aswan, may rule the court, but it's said he keeps Malechus here at Castle Blackrock in virtual exile, far away from the throne and any ambitions his son might foster.

A crushed velvet doublet the color of a black-red rose spans his broad chest, with black edging clinging to his shoulders. Rings glitter on his fingers, winking in the light, and I catch a glimpse of midnight leather shifting over his thighs as he finally sights us through the crush.

Instantly, he stills, like a panther sighting its enemy.

His brown hair hangs in a wavy curtain to his shoulders, and eyes the color of a crystalline lake lock on me, even as he plucks a golden goblet from his attendant's tray and nurses it negligently. He slowly lifts the wine to his sulky mouth, but he barely sips it. Instead, he watches us over the rim, his blackened claws scraping on the gold.

Or no, not us.

Me.

That look shivers all the way through me. It's intimate,

as if he's picturing stripping the gown from my body or drawing me into the embrace of a knife.

"You've met before?" Keir murmurs in my ear, clasping his hand over mine as he leads me toward the dais.

"No." Though there's something about the way the prince looks at me that makes me question the truth of that myself. "Maybe he's met my sister. Soraya resembles me in some ways. Her hair and eyes are black, but otherwise we could be twins." My voice roughens. "A little bit of glamor and she fooled even you, after all."

"Mmm." Keir strokes my knuckles. "Then I don't like the way he's looking at you."

Me either, but— "If you kill the prince, then we won't get what we both want." Though the Prince of Blood is going straight to the top of my suspect list for those involved in Soraya's disappearance.

"Prince Keir." Malechus strides down from the dais, a dangerous smile on his mouth as he clasps hands with the prince and draws him into a swift embrace. "If I'd known you thought to attend, I would have sent an invitation."

"If I'd known you would invite me, I would have made my intentions clear." Keir's smile is a knife.

The two of them part.

And though Keir has an inch on him, Malechus feels in no way less dangerous.

"Please allow me to present my lovely bride-to-be, the lady Merisel," Keir purrs, a hand coming to rest in the small of my back as he gestures me forward. "She wishes to lure me back into the world."

"Ah yes." Malechus reaches for my hand and brings it

to his lips, his eyes settling once more on me. "I've heard many things about the lovely lady. Twenty potential brides accepted your Summons, and yet it was this one pretty little dove that caught your eye."

"A dove?" Keir laughs under his breath. "I consider my love a peregrine instead."

"And she's captured fair prey," Malechus says, breathing the words over my bare knuckles. He straightens abruptly. "You are very brave, my lady, to have survived such a dangerous ordeal, for others were not so lucky. You may recall my dear cousin, Narcissa?"

The last I saw of Narcissa, she was entombed in a wall and only her hands—forever clutching for help—remained free of the marble.

"A terrible tragedy, Your Highness." I never liked her, but nobody deserves to die that way. "And it was not bravery that saw me win the day, but luck."

Malechus glances at Keir beneath his lashes. "Tell me… did you bring me her killer's head?"

Keir stares him down. "No. I burned Calliope's body and gave the ashes to the forest."

"A pity." Malechus's lips thinned. "I should have liked to have set it on my castle walls."

There's a hard truth in Keir's eyes. "I should have liked to have had a chance to… discuss many things with her before I was forced to kill her."

A shiver runs through me.

Calliope claimed she was born from the bloodlines of Queen Mab—the fae queen who married the most powerful of the dragon kings. Mab birthed a daughter,

Igrainne, who bore half of her mother's magic and her father's power, and all of the hunger for more.

Calliope was a direct descendant of Igrainne.

She tried to kill me.

She very nearly pushed me into a wall, leaving me to suffer the same fate as Narcissa. If I'm a little swift to snatch a glass of elderberry wine from a passing servant, it's only because drowning isn't the only death that makes my heart race.

But it's the first time Keir has mentioned Calliope's name.

She was part dragon herself, determined to eat his heart in order to fully transmute herself into "what she was meant to become."

As I sip the wine, I can't help stealing a glance at him. Does he wonder if he could have reached her and swayed her from her mad plan? Or does he wish he had time to personally question her, in a chains-and-rack kind of way?

"Come," Malechus says, gesturing us into the hallway. "I shall have servants sent to make chambers for you. In the meantime, you must greet our guests."

A gasp comes from behind.

Glass shatters.

I have the hilt of a thin dirk in my hand as I turn, but the danger doesn't come in the form of a weapon.

No. It comes in the form of a voluptuous redhead wearing a gown of seafoam draped with gold netting, her jaw gaping open as she stands in the wreckage of what was once an elegant wineglass.

Princess Ismena.

The sister of the King of Storms, and the woman I

saved from Calliope's murderous wrath the night she was killed.

"Merisel," she says in faint horror, and relief floods through me as I realize she still believes me to be Merisel of Greenslieves.

If her brother has my face plastered on reward posters, then I need to ensure my glamor doesn't slip, even once.

Is that why she's looking at me as if *I* was the one who tried to kill her?

What does she know?

Keir pushes past me, using his body to force my hand down. I shoot him a glare and vanish the knife.

"Your Highness," I greet.

Ismena recovers well, pasting a smile on her lips as she glances toward Keir at my side. "Such an honor, my prince. I did not expect to see you here—either of you."

And then she makes a swift apology and virtually flees.

I exchange a look with Keir.

This might be a problem.

"I forgot how much I hate these shoes," I groan as I climb the stairs toward our rooms. They're endless monstrosities of polished alabaster and my heels are a good four inches high. I'm fairly certain my calves are about to commit mutiny, and my toes want to scream. "Do you think anyone would notice if I Sift to the top?"

"I forgot how much I hate balls," Keir mutters as he eyes me. "Here."

He sweeps me into his arms before I can react and resumes our quest.

"What are you doing?" I blurt.

"Carrying my beloved," he mocks. "As any heroic prince would do."

My tongue stills. No one has ever carried me and it's a strange thing to be in his arms like this. It takes me back to the Court of Dreams. To the first time he kissed me. I found his strength and presence overwhelming then, and if anything time has only worsened that impression.

But I also forgot how warm he is.

A shiver runs through me. I can't stop myself from thinking about what it would be like to have all this weight pressing me into a mattress. I'm trying not to touch him, but up close and personal, all this muscle is distracting.

He sets me down outside the door to our rooms, my skirts slithering down around my calves.

"There," he whispers. "Better?"

I'm not entirely certain the answer to that is yes. "Thank you, but if anyone was to see us, they're going to think you've fallen for me."

Keir's smile remains dangerous as he reaches past me to unlock the door to our rooms. "Anyone who saw us this summer would know I had already been a fool for you." His smile fades. "If we're going to continue the lie, then we have to sell it. Anyone who knew me would know that my feelings for you would not fade so swiftly."

I examine the stern lines of his jaw as he opens the door. If a sculptor was ever to create that face out of stone, they'd be lauded through the ages.

"You're a prince," I point out as we sweep into the

antechamber that lingers between our bedchambers. Despite my distraction, my breath catches when I see them.

Malechus has certainly spared no expense in outfitting his court—or perhaps he set his servants to scrambling the second he realized Keir was here. Or did he simply cast another couple out of these rooms?

They're gorgeous.

Sumptuous red silk cushions. Low divans and rugs. The room itself is carved out of the mountain, and enormous columns of polished quartz circle the room.

"What does that matter?" he asks, kicking the door shut behind us.

"You have princesses throwing themselves at your feet at every turn, as evidenced by what happened below. I think it highly likely your feelings for me would have waned in such a short amount of time."

"Oh, that you think me so inconstant." He tugs his coat off revealing the fresh lawn of his shirt.

"I *don't* think you inconstant," I snap, "but you know the truth now. You have no reason not to let your eye linger on others." Tugging at the bracelets around my wrist, I toss them on a low table. "You're my decoy. I want Malechus—and the rest of the court—focused on you."

"Fine. How far do I take it?"

"How far… what?"

"These flirtations?" Keir tosses the coat aside as if it's a challenge, and his shirt clings to his chest with static. "How far do I go, Zemira? Do I focus on one princess? Or maybe I dangle two of them on my knee…. Or would three suit?"

"That's your decision. I don't need to know how many."

"No?"

"*No.*" Goddess-have-mercy, but suddenly I'm right back there in his arms, trying not to feel the flex and pull of muscle as he holds me. Pouring myself a wine, I try to take my attention off him, but all I succeed in doing is nearly drowning on my first gulp.

Keir watches me with those hypnotic eyes as he stalks toward me. "All these princesses that fling themselves at my feet.... I'm almost starting to wonder if you're jealous?"

"*What?*" I choke on my next mouthful.

"That is the plan, is it not? When they wilt at my feet, I'm supposed to be entranced."

"*Yes.*" The way he looks, serving him up as a distraction is the best idea I've ever had. Nobody will be looking at me. *Nobody.* The males will see a challenge, the females will want to conquer him.... There is nothing about this situation that could be bad.

Except....

I drain the goblet. More wine. I definitely need more wine.

"The very idea I would be jealous is ridiculous," I tell him as I go in search of another flagon. "Besides, that's not our biggest problem."

"No?"

"Ismena looked horrified to see me," I point out. "Not merely shocked, but horrified. She *knows* something about me."

"The last time she saw you," he points out dryly, "Calliope was trying to kill her. Even Ismena suffers from nightmares of that time."

I arch a brow at him. "Does she? Has someone been peeking into his potential bride's heads?"

He crosses both arms over his chest. "I owe those women a debt. Calliope came to my halls to murder me. She killed several of those women out of frustration and left the others with the sort of nightmares that will haunt them forever. I chased the nightmares away, nothing more. I can give them that, at least."

My eyes narrow. It sounds entirely too altruistic.

I don't like any of this.

An emissary from the Court of Storms would have been bad enough, but my former nemesis?

"What did you learn tonight?" he asks.

"Malechus knew Soraya to look at. He took one look at my face and I would swear he recognized me."

My glamor's good, but the more changes you make, the more magic you need to wield. It's easier to make subtle shifts here and there and to restrict them to elements that don't move very often. My mouth remains untouched along with my brows. My cheeks are a little softer, my eyes not quite as blue, and my hairline lacks its distinctive peak.

All in all, you wouldn't pick my face out of a crowd of beautiful women. I've designed this face to be pretty but unmemorable.

And Soraya taught me the art of glamor.

"You're sure he's never seen you before?"

"Never." And Angmar's reward poster won't be circulated this widely.

Has Ismena seen it? Has she put two and two together?

I feel like I need to get a good look at this reward poster. When I stole the trident from her brother, I lured him back to his bedroom with a smile and a wink, drugged him the second we got to his rooms, and then left him snoring on the floor, naked. It's not my fault he was so quick to shed his clothes that half the royal guard saw his flaccid cock.

Since I was playing at the seduction game, I would have emphasized my features with glamor. Soft mouth. Long lashes. Curves that would have made a man trip over his tongue. I'm fairly certain I'd been wearing a long, blonde wig, with golden curls the color of wheat, and a pink gown that was cut to reveal slashes of skin in strategic places.

I doubt anyone looking at the poster would see the resemblance to me, but the concern has to be noted. And Ismena is the one fae who might be able to knock a candle into all of my plans and set them on fire.

"Tell me about your sister," Keir says.

I curl my fingers around the wine and kick off my shoes with a small groan. *Bliss*. Scrunching and flexing my toes, I fist handfuls of the skirt that has suddenly tumbled around my feet, and venture to the fireplace. "Why?"

"Why not?" He sinks into his chair, one boot hooked up on his opposite knee. For some reason, he's looking at my toes. "She did try to kill me, after all."

"Was this before or after she kissed you?"

Keir's eyes narrow. "You know I thought she was you." He pauses, those dragon eyes turning to full smolder. "And I'm fairly certain your interest in me was a ruse."

Fairly certain? As in, he's not entirely certain?

"Why was she sent here? To this court?" he demands.

There's something in his voice that stirs the magic within me. I want to answer him. It's an urge that bubbles up my throat, where I trap it behind my teeth. He may own my services for a year and a day, but he has no claim on my secrets.

"I don't know. The wraith king said Malechus had something that belonged to him," I say instead.

Technically… true. My father does believe the horn is his for the taking.

And Soraya's been here for nearly three weeks, ingratiating herself within the court as per protocol. The wedding was announced far and wide, and two days later she was working her way inside the court.

"If you want to steal something, you send a thief." Keir stretches his arm along the back of the chair, but he doesn't force the magic. "Your sister is not a thief. You are. So why did he send her and not you?"

The thought occurred to me too.

"Maybe because he was too busy drowning me for my failure in cutting your heart from your chest" dies on the tip of my tongue.

I don't share such secrets.

But it also doesn't feel like the truth.

"Cauldron's piss," I whisper. He lied to me. My father looked me in the eye and lied. "Soraya wasn't sent here to retrieve something. She was sent here to kill someone."

"But who? You must be able to guess," he says. "From all my information, it seems she infiltrated the lady Anissa's household as her maid. Was the Lady Anissa her target? Was she trying to fool her the way you fooled me?"

"It won't be Anissa. And," I point out, "I tried to avoid you. I tried to give you every reason to pursue some other princess." Even though avoiding him earned me nothing more than his interest. "I was there for a job. I didn't want to mislead you—if you'd just accepted my rebuff, we wouldn't be in this situation."

It's not the whole truth.

My heart is not mine to give. Without my soul, I'm my father's puppet. I don't even have the autonomy to allow myself to care.

And yet, I couldn't stop myself from wanting him.

I couldn't avoid the guilt that came with each lie I told him.

For the first time in my life, I yearned to be free to make my own choices. I've never been so envious of a fae princess in my life. The other potential brides might have been fools, but there was nothing standing in their way should Keir have looked at any of them.

Except, he was looking at me.

And I didn't dare return the favor.

Something in Keir's expression hardens. "You play an excellent part. Tell me..., does lying come so easily to you?"

"Yes. It does." Learning to lie is the only thing that kept my head on my shoulders during my trials. And I can't stop my eyebrows from rising. "You had twenty princesses kissing your boots. You were hardly lacking for female worshippers. Don't tell me you bear a grudge because I didn't wilt at your feet."

"No grudge." His voice roughens. "I just don't like being lied to. Particularly when it comes to matters of the heart."

"Oh, please. The only reason you decided I was the one you wanted to pursue is *because* I wasn't kissing your boots. You had no personal interest in me."

Keir's finger circles the rim of his glass, and if he had a tail it would be lashing behind him. "Do you know the worst part of this entire debacle?"

"What?"

Our eyes meet.

"I would have married you," he says coldly. "I would have taken you as my wife and I could have loved you. Forever. So thank you for revealing your true intentions before it was too late. Because it would have been the biggest mistake of my life."

He drains his wine and pushes to his feet, turning to stir the hot coals in the fireplace with the poker.

"Take the room on the left, Zemira." He strides toward the door. "I'm going to return to the ball."

"The ball—?"

"You want me to be a distraction? Then I will be a distraction." His smile as he reaches for the door handle is vicious. "After all, we're both fae, are we not? Marriage is merely an alliance. Nothing more. Nobody will care whose bed I'm in. Yours… or someone else's. I will be the best distraction you could have asked for."

The door slams behind him, leaving me staring after him helplessly.

Someone else's….

"Right," I mutter under my breath, sitting on the edge

of the mattress and then letting myself crash onto my back. "This is just a job. Find Soraya. Find the horn. Fuck them all."

It's so much easier now he knows the truth.

Now I don't have to pretend.

It hurts the same though.

6

K*eir would have married me.*

I don't know what to make of those words.

They torment my dreams, and when I wake in the morning, I find myself no better rested. I've spent hours being chased through the Court of Dreams by a rabid wolf, and every time I think I've escaped pursuit, I burst into a room and there it is again.

Waiting to devour me.

The sooner I find my sister and the horn, the better.

The first candidate on my list of suspects to question is Lady Anissa. Soraya pretended to be her lady's maid. I don't know what sort of deal she struck with the fae lady, but I do know Soraya prefers blackmail.

"Trust is a knife waiting for your back. I'd rather have a noose around their throats," she once purred.

And yet Lady Anissa is clearly not Soraya's target.

For one thing, she's still alive.

For another, you don't ingratiate yourself in the household when you're planning to kill someone. You'd be the first suspect. No, you plant yourself in a household that will give you access to your target's household.

So someone Anissa knows.

Soraya's rooms are locked. I try the handle early the next morning before continuing on as though I've merely lost my way to the breakfast room. Also unusual, for she's been replaced with a brownie that Lady Anissa spends half her days harassing, and it would be expected that the brownie would be given the rooms Soraya used.

But she hasn't.

Which means I need to get inside to see what they're hiding.

Maybe Anissa wasn't Soraya's target, but that doesn't mean that the constantly vexed brunette didn't ensure Soraya went missing.

I eye my target over teacakes and scones.

Anissa is a minor scion of the Court of Dawn; a random cousin of the king there. Her gown bares her shoulders—which appears to be the latest of fashions—but it's made from silk that looks like last year's pattern. Cut down perhaps, in order to appear new, which tells me she doesn't have as much wealth as she pretends, and yet, she's desperate to mingle with the elite and pretend to be one of them. Gossip tells me she's ventured to the Court of Blood several times this year, ostensibly on trade business. There's some suspicion she's got her eye on Malechus and may even be in his bed already, but when the prince himself appears, she doesn't even glance toward him.

Considering she was seated at the far end of the hall last night, I have to imagine Belladonna—who would have laid out the dining arrangements—has little liking for her.

Few have surfaced after last night, and so I spend the afternoon adding names and faces to my repertoire.

There's no sign of the Lord of Mistmark, who is someone else I want to acquaint myself with most desperately. Nor is the blushing bride here.

And Keir is currently making several women laugh. Maybe he said something outrageously funny, but I doubt it. The ruse is working. He's barely looked at me. I am out of favor, left on the sidelines to my own devices. One of the women cuts me a sidelong glance as she daringly strokes his sleeve.

He didn't return last night.

I know, because I spent half the night tossing and turning, before I finally slammed the pillow over my head and fell asleep.

I make my excuses and leave the tea party.

Before I punch her pretty white teeth through the back of her head.

FIND WHAT HAPPENED TO SORAYA, AND YOU FIND THE HORN.

I haul my mask over my face as I climb through the window in my room, and then look toward the bridal suite in the eastern tower that the Lord of Mistmark has been given. The mask is glamored to make me invisible in the night, even when I'm not Sifting.

I barely saw the Lord of Mistmark today. Just a distant figure dressed in strict black as he swung a pretty blonde in a red gown around the dance floor tonight. There were too many nobles between us—every fae in the kingdom trying to gain his favor, for he's the toast of the court this week.

Perhaps it's a good thing.

I'm a little too curious about him.

What sort of man conjures mercy in my merciless sister's heart? What kind of lord could even capture her attention, let alone any tender feelings?

I need to find out.

Night is the time I come alive. There is nothing more than shadows here, and they're my home. I Sift toward the Lady Anissa's rooms, flickering into being on one rooftop and then the next, until I'm sitting on her window ledge. There's no one inside her rooms. I can tell when a room is empty, and so I dart along the ledge, leaping from window to window with effortless grace until I fetch up alongside the window that leads to the rooms Soraya was using.

I pick the lock and ease the window open. A second later, I'm inside.

Maybe it's being in the Court of Blood, but I feel uneasy as I enter. A shiver runs over my skin, lifting all the tiny hairs on my body. Over the years, I've learned to listen to my instincts and they're all telling me to run, but a swift visual inspection reveals no sign of a trap.

And I have the shadows if I need them.

Servants' chambers are small and tidy, in general, but the sheets on the bed are rumpled. A trunk rests at the foot of the bed, clothes hastily strewn inside it and the lid slammed shut, with half a gown sticking out.

My sister is organized. Tidy. Not like me. Every morning she folds her clothes and makes her bed, until you'd barely know she's even been in the room.

Something happened to prevent that.

I examine the trunk again.

Did someone search it?

I squat down to examine the lock, and that's when I see a splash of something dark on the floor.

Blood.

It's long dried, and as I lean down, I can see where someone's mopped up more of it. The patch of floor in this corner is suspiciously clean, whereas hints of grime beckon along the rail that dissects the floor from the wall. They missed this one fleck.

Maybe it's a whisper of sound or a glint of light beneath the door, but my senses suddenly scream at me.

I punch into shadows, hovering on the edge of form just as the door explodes open. There's a knife in each hand.

Two shadowy figures sweep inside, garbed in cloaks. Women, I think.

One of them gestures with a hand—definitely a woman from those elegant fingers—and bloodied orbs of glowing light follow her around the room.

It's the pretty blonde from the ballroom. The one who floated in the Lord of Mistmark's arms.

Belladonna of the Blood Court.

The Blood Lily, they call her.

She lowers her scarlet hood, and I finally get a good look at her face. It's like seeing her sister, Narcissa, in the flesh again. There's an insolent curl to her painted red lips, and her blonde hair tumbles in elegant curls around her face.

"What is it?" whispers the ethereal brunette who follows on her heels. Lady Anissa.

Ah, so they're friends or allies, or… working together either way.

"Come out, come out, wherever you are," Belladonna whispers. "Don't you know who I am? I can burn the blood in your veins, little thief. And I know you're here."

I press my spine to the bed and stay still, barely feeling my heart beat.

Belladonna sweeps closer, her angry red orb floating over her shoulder hungrily. "That tugging feeling you can sense on your skin? It's a ward layered over the window. You tripped it the second you entered."

Curse it. I *knew* something was wrong.

And I let my desperation to find my sister distract me.

"Do you think it's the kidnapper?" Anissa whispers.

Belladonna cuts a sharp hand in her direction, which is interesting.

Kidnapper?

Damn it, Soraya. Where are you? What happened to you?

"I think," Belladonna whispers, her gaze cutting right through me before it searches on, "that someone has returned to finish the job." She steps closer to me. "What are you searching for, little thief? Didn't you find it the other night?"

I glance toward the open window. It's a temptation and a lie, because she'll be expecting me to go for it. And Anissa stands between me and the door.

Anissa starts tugging the sheets out from under the

mattress, lifting the corners of the bed. "The letters have to be here somewhere."

I just need her to move a fraction to the left—

There it is.

I Sift toward the door. The only problem with my magic is that it's restricted to line of sight, and so, if I wish to escape the room, I need to be able to open the door to see past it.

"There!" Belladonna cries, and something—a slash of magic—cuts into my back. "There's blood! Near the door!"

I jerk the door open, solidifying just enough to be able to use the handle and then—

The door is torn from my fingers, slamming closed.

Another Sift, and I'm behind them.

Belladonna turns as if she can see me—or maybe she can scent my blood—and then she has a knife in her hand.

This is what I know. My body reacts as that blade lashes out and I catch her hand, rolling beneath the blow and tossing her over my shoulder. A startled squeak escapes her. I'm punching in and out of shadow, forming for the barest fraction of a second—just enough to throw her—before I vanish again.

It must feel like wrestling with a shadow.

Belladonna lands on the bed and her knife drives into the wall beside Anissa, point first. Anissa screams, hands jerking up far, far too late. The knife missed her by an inch.

Belladonna's focus locks on her friend and then knife, and then an expression of pure rage twists her features.

Past time to be going.

Belladonna rolls free of the tangle of sheets, and then whips her hand toward me as if she's throwing something.

A sharp slash of heat whips across my abdomen.

There's four feet between us but she might as well have a knife in hand.

Blood magic.

And here I am, with only my shadows to save me.

I know when the odds are against me. I punch into shadows, reforming on the window ledge with one hand clapped over my wound. One last look back, where I catch her startled glance, and then I throw myself out the window.

The wind catches me, and then I Sift again.

Gone.

Unseen.

But not unnoticed.

7

"What happened?" Keir grabs two handfuls of my shirt and tears it apart, revealing the blood that weeps down my side.

He was pouring himself a drink when I staggered over the windowsill, and the second he saw me, his eyes turned gold with rage.

Though perhaps it wasn't aimed at me, for all he did was haul me into the wash chambers and hiss under his breath.

"I told you what happened," I growl, sitting on the edge of my vanity, where he's cornered me. "There was a ward set over Soraya's room. I triggered it when I entered, and then Anissa and Belladonna appeared. I didn't know Belladonna had the ability to bloody me from such a distance."

"She's a princess of the Blood Court."

And clearly, I am an idiot.

"It's rare that the royal bloodlines breed down so strongly," I mutter. "I know Malechus and his brothers have the blood magic, but I didn't expect Belladonna to wield it. Narcissa didn't."

Every royal court is ruled by the strongest family in the lands—marriages are kept firmly along certain lines so as not to dilute the magic in the royal line.

But dilution happens.

It's rare for any but the direct heirs to wield the kind of magic the court is renowned for.

Some fae marry for love, even though they know their children will suffer the consequences. Some are passed over again and again and must settle for a lower-born marriage. And some reject court life and the pressure of upholding their family's honor.

For a minor cousin to wield the family's magic so strongly, it means the Blood Court is not just dangerous— but have spent centuries on carefully selective breeding.

It also means Malechus had best watch his back.

"Narcissa didn't," Keir confirms. "She was also desperate to try and lift her status within her family." A muscle hitches in Keir's jaw as he surveys the wadded-up shirt I stuffed against my side. I wouldn't let him touch it until now, and clearly my attempts to contain the bleeding have fallen short. "Who taught you to medic yourself? A pig farmer who's never seen a needle and thread in his life?"

A wraith warrior who cared less about what a wound looked like after he was done, and more about salvaging what he could from the training camp ranks.

"I'll heal."

"Not from this, you won't." He gently touches my flushed skin and I wince. "That's what makes them so dangerous. Many members of this court can cut you from a distance, but if a royal cuts you, then you don't stop bleeding."

No wonder I'm ruining a second shirt.

I bite my lip. It's such a little wound but hasn't stopped bleeding. The one on my back is shallower, but it's weeping blood too.

"Here." Keir tugs a knife from the sheath at his hip and I flinch. He pauses, noting my sudden discomfort. Dark eyes search my face. "I'm not going to hurt you, Merisel."

Cauldron's scurvy surface. "Zemira," I grate out. "The rooms are warded, so nobody will hear you call me by my name in here. And it's a professional hazard of the job. Knives make me nervous."

He flips it, capturing it by the handle before he offers it to me. "Then you do the honor."

The honor? I stare at the knife.

Curling my fingers around the hilt, he sets the tip of the blade to his wrist and slashes a thin line across his bronzed skin.

"Goddess's mercy! What are you doing?" I rip the knife well away from him.

Cupping a hand at the base of my skull, he brings his wrist up. "Drink."

I slam my palm against his chest. "I don't know what sort of proclivities you might have, but where I'm from, we don't drink blood. That's just a stupid story the fae conjured."

Keir glares at me. "My blood will heal you. Don't tell me you're squeamish?"

"I'll... heal."

"No, you won't. And not in time. I need you whole and hearty, not fainting on the floor in the middle of the fucking wedding from blood loss. Drink, Zemira."

Help. He used my name.

"Where's my pragmatic wench now?" he croons.

Currently feeling a little overwhelmed.

But he does speak the truth.

I have a horn to steal, a betrayal to plan, and a prince to escape.

I give into the pressure of his hand and allow him to draw my head forward. The first brush of his wrist against my lips sends a shock of lightning through me, but it's the wetness of his blood spreading over them that makes me shiver.

It tastes like copper and iron. It's not unpleasant, but the second his blood hits my stomach, heat spears through me. Weariness sloughs off me and my wound tingles as if the magic in his blood has found a weakness and targets it.

It feels like starshine in my blood. Like heat and warmth, and a tingling sensation that lights through me *everywhere*.

I fall back against the wall, gasping. I think I just had an orgasm. If the fae knew his blood had the ability to do this to them, they'd be bottling it.

"Better?" The knowing look in his eyes makes me slap his shoulder with the heel of my palm.

I stare at him.

There's a promise in his eyes. One that says he can take me away from here—from all of this. One that will protect me at all costs. One that says there's a court of dreams out there, with a gorgeous sun-kissed palace filled with servants to tend my every need, and beds draped in silken sheets. I can almost hear the sound of waves dashing against the sandy beaches below that palace. The taste of dates explodes in my mouth as if I just bit into one, and the caress of fingertips skates up my hips.

If I close my eyes, I'm right there.

Feeling those dangerous lips chase their way up the slope of my neck, the graze of teeth threatening to dig deep into the muscle at the base of my shoulder—

This is his most dangerous aspect.

He gets inside your head.

He gets inside *my* head and conjures a dream of a new life, where I never need worry about my father again.

If only I could promise him my heart, my body, and my soul.

For one breathless moment, we stare at each other, and I'm surprised at how much I want that lie.

Because it is a lie for someone like me.

My heart is a fist of stone within my chest. My body a weapon I use at will. And my soul? If I owned it myself, I would never, ever let another dare take it from me.

"Better," I rasp, swinging my legs off the vanity and letting my boots hit the floor.

He doesn't back away.

I'm left pressed flush against his body, curling my fingers into fists before I can touch him. It's like his blood now calls to me. A little shiver of that post-orgasmic bliss steals through me. I want his hands on my skin. I want that connection.

Damn it.

"I need to wash," I growl out, because I desperately need him out of this room.

Keir finally gives me space, sidestepping toward the oils sitting on the vanity. "So what next? Since Belladonna and Anissa are clearly not responsible for your sister's disappearance."

"They're involved in something," I correct.

Belladonna's a royal princess, and the lady of the Dawn Court may—or may not—be involved with Belladonna's cousin, according to gossip. And what had she meant about those letters?

Why would she be searching Soraya's room for them?

"But not your sister's disappearance," he points out.

"Mistmark, then," I tell him, trying to ignore the shiver of desire in my blood as I turn the faucet on. "He and Soraya had a certain history together. He'd recognize her on sight and would move to strike her down if he saw her. Besides, if anyone is going to know where the horn is, it's going to be him."

Keir scowls into the distance. "How are you going to get to him?"

That is the problem.

"You're not going to enter his rooms the way you did tonight." There's a hint of anger in Keir's voice. "You nearly died."

I blow a breath of frustration through my lips. "A slight exaggeration, my prince. And no, I'm not going anywhere near Mistmark's rooms."

Not until I know how he thwarted my sister's assassination attempt all those years ago.

"No," I repeat. "I need more information. I'm working

blind here. Normally I know what I'm looking for. It's simply a matter of finding it. Now… I need more information. Time to go play simpering lady of the Greenslieves."

THE MEN SPEND THE MORNING HUNTING THE WOODS, including Keir. I plead a headache and leave the ladies to their own devices on the front lawns. From a stolen glimpse through the window, it looks like they've set up a field of archery. Several servants appear to have been roped into the game, and they're wearing targets over their clothes. I don't know what the ladies are shooting with— their arrows appear to have blunted ends, and every time they strike a servant, a colorful cloud of powder erupts, until the servants look like they've been dusted with powdered sugar.

It gives me time to ghost through the castle, avoiding both servants and nobles alike as I work out the layout of the palace.

I try the door to Mistmark's room, but it's locked. Usually not a problem, but a servant's footsteps echo through the hallway, and I'm forced to retreat. I don't want to enter after last night's fiasco, but it doesn't hurt to check.

Malechus's rooms are guarded by heavily armored guards. Belladonna's chambers sit at the opposite end of the hallway to his, and there's a redcap squatting outside her door. Definitely not someone I want to meet on a dark night.

I retreat to the garden so nobody starts to wonder about my actions.

"Lady Merisel!" calls one of the archers with a malicious glee. "Come and try your hand at the targets."

The targets look like they're drunk. One serving girl with a fox tail falls into another's arms, giggling and nuzzling at his neck. From the tails on his coat, he looks like the butler, but no butler alive would grab a housemaid's bottom like that.

My eye locks on those colorful splats of powder staining their clothes. Now I know what it is. It's rapture, a fae aphrodisiac that the nobles of certain courts sniff. It's also a little dangerous, because it strips you of your control and makes you desire nothing more than hedonistic pursuits.

Tomorrow that serving girl is going to wake with a giant's hammer of a headache and possibly the butler in her bed.

"I'm afraid I prefer my targets to be a little less lovedrunk and a little more in control of their faculties," I reply. I hate such mindless cruelty. The servants have little recompense here. They owe their lives to Malechus—and his guests'—favor.

They can't refuse to play.

And the appearance of the drug strips them of any remaining choices in regards to their bodies.

"Oh, pish," says the woman. I'm starting to put a name to her face. Rhea, perhaps? She belongs to the Court of Whispers, though I can't remember whether she's part of the ruling family there. "Where's the fun in that? If she wanted to avoid her current situation, then she should have run faster."

I should give a shrug and laugh before slipping amongst the women. I have a reason to be here. I want to find out exactly what the relationship between Belladonna and Anissa is. Because if Anissa is Malechus's lover, then I doubt she'd be friends with Belladonna. To all appearances, Belladonna is displeased with her cousin's efforts to push her into marriage.

But it's that callous disregard for a servant's choice that rubs me the wrong way.

I've disguised myself as a servant before.

I've had lords' corner me in darkened rooms, their faces twisted with malice and dark desires before I showed them the error of their ways—and the pointy end of a knife.

I've had fae ladies play similar games with me, as if I'm a mere amusement and not a woman with my own hopes and dreams.

I've been able to avoid such vicious endeavors purely because my role in their worlds has been a ruse and I've been able to escape.

The serving girl with the fox tail has no choice. She has no escape from this.

I turn toward Rhea. She wants to play games? Okay. We'll play. Right now, I have a position of power, even if these women would tear me down if they knew the truth.

"Your bow?" I ask Rhea, who was the same female I saw sliding her hand over Keir's sleeve.

I can't help myself.

I take the bow and arrow from her hands.

And then I smile at her. "Indeed, let's make this a little more challenging. Let's see if *you* are faster than the serving girl."

Every head in the vicinity tracks toward me. The other ladies look delighted. Some whisper behind their hands, and I can see they think me jealous of Keir's attentions toward Rhea.

"You wouldn't dare," she snaps, backing away from me.

"What's wrong?" I set the arrow to the bow. "Do you prefer to pick and choose your own partners? Would you perhaps desire a prince? Would you try to *steal* him?"

Jealousy is a lovely little motive to hide behind.

And maybe there's a little bit of truth in it.

"Run," I suggest. "Run fast."

Rhea takes off with a squeal, shoving her way through the horde of silk.

"Doesn't she make a fine rabbit?" I ask the woman beside me as I draw the bow back. If I hit her, then I'm virtually declaring war on the Court of Whispers. "Let's make her think I have her measure. Where shall I aim? That tree in front of her?"

"Right in the back," the woman replies with a malicious smile.

I loose the arrow, and it hits the tree right in front of Rhea. She squeals as she darts to avoid the puff of pretty pink powder that explodes into the air.

I lower the bow. "While I would love to send that smirking little wretch to her knees, I think a warning sufficient for the moment. But perhaps you would care to do the honors?"

With a wink, I pass the bow to my crestfallen partner.

It breaks up the gaggle of predatory women. They're no longer focusing on the servants, and the servants—with some relief—are slipping away while they're no longer visible to the gathering.

I laugh with several of the ladies who think my ruse was amusing to watch. They'll turn on me in an instant. But for now I've won entrance into their little group, which was an unexpected advantage.

And as I watch the serving maid, I see the moment where she staggers against the hedge, feeling overcome with rapture.

Slipping out of the group of fae women as refreshments are brought, I pass behind a tree and vanish, reappearing at the girl's side where I capture her in my arms.

She looks at me in a mixture of glazed shock and hunger. Even the simple act of my hands on her skin have set off the rapture coursing through her veins.

"Let's get you back to your rooms," I murmur.

"No, please, my lady. I don't…."

I understand. She thinks I intend to overwhelm her. "You're safe," I whisper. "You need to sleep it off. I'll get you out of here."

I hate the fright in her eyes, but this one time, I have been able to use my power for good.

Even if it makes me a powerful enemy.

By the time I've set the little maid in her bed and returned to the gathering on the lawn, the bows and arrows have vanished and the men have returned. There's no sign of Keir. Perhaps he's cleaning up after the hunt.

A blur of darkness captures my attention.

The Lord of Mistmark slips away from the party as if he's heading toward the castle to refresh himself—but halfway there, he takes a sidestep and vanishes into the maze.

"Excuse me," I say to a princess who's trying to insult me. I think she's one of Rhea's friends. "I have to… fix my hair."

And then I walk away from her, ignoring her shocked gasp and her pointed "how rude."

I slip into the shadows as I enter the maze. The world is abruptly muted. It's like looking at everything through a diaphanous gray veil. Fine details are lost, and everything becomes soft and blurred. It strips the hard edges from a fae prince's face and eases the harsh lines and avarice in a princess's expression.

I steal from shadow to shadow, tiptoeing along in the wake of the Lord of Mistmark.

He's the one mystery I haven't been able to solve.

He reaches one of the final turns of the maze and glances over his shoulder. A lock of raven-dark hair tumbles over his brow, and I catch my first glimpse of alpine-blue eyes. They're amazing eyes. Even with a veil of shadow between us, they make my breath catch.

Okay, maybe it was the eyes that caught Soraya's attention.

She's always had a thing for pretty fae lords with sulky mouths and dangerous intensity. Or lords who are clearly up to no good, because Mistmark is obviously meeting someone here. Someone he shouldn't be.

Maybe someone female?

I wonder what your dearest Belladonna will think of this….

We slip through the maze, and Mistmark clearly knows where he's going, because within minutes he paces into a clearing where a hundred oak trees stand apace, clipped into uniform precision. It's not the heart of the maze, but one of the "rooms" inside. We passed dozens of them: a fountain carved of alabaster—shockingly white against the reddened leaves of the maze—stood alone on a field of lawn carefully mown into checkered squares akin to a chessboard; a water garden edged by hedging caught my eye; a dozen cascading pools babbled like a brook in another; a folly; a grotto; even a spun-glass butterfly house, with dozens of tiny winged fey trapped inside.

"Where are you?" he calls softly.

A figure appears from around the trunk of one of the mighty oaks. I start, because although I'd scanned the garden the second I approached, I didn't see him there.

It's a fae male I don't know.

Someone fairly prominent, judging by the dark green velvet coat and the diamond earring stabbed through his ear. It glitters like a star. Despite the clean lines and cut of his clothes, the way he wears them tells me he likes to look good. His cheeks are so smooth I want to run my hands over them just to check if he even grows stubble, and the way his hair is raked back looks like he's spent a decent allotment of time soothing it into place.

Mistmark, on the other hand, is simple good taste.

Black velvet. Black leather gloves. Slightly scuffed boots. Careless hair.

It's all expensive—and I'm fairly certain I recognize a glint of demorari silk embroidered into elegant roses in the weft of his coat, which is the latest of fashions in the southern courts—but Mistmark looks as though he paid good money to a tailor or three, and simply let them loose on his wardrobe.

Something simple. Something fashionable. Make me look like a groom who's comfortable in his own power, and not someone forced to bend knee before another court…. Nothing too fussy….

Whereas the blond looks as though he made half a dozen tailors and their assistants sweat as he pored over every scrap of fabric, and then fingered the seams before sniffing and insisting they did them again.

My eye lingers on the newcomer. Even from the shadows, his hair gleams like spun moonbeams. There's an uneasy sensation within my breast—a feeling I know this stranger, when I could swear we've never met in our lives.

I study his face, but no recognition dawns.

I've never seen him before. I'm sure of it.

"Well?" Mistmark tugs his leather gloves from his hands, finger by finger.

"It is done," the stranger says. He tosses Mistmark a scroll of paper. "You're playing dangerous games. Malechus won't appreciate it."

"Malechus started the game," Mistmark says coldly. "If he doesn't like my rules, then he shouldn't have challenged me."

Ooh, interesting.

The stranger laughs under his breath. "I admire your brashness, Alaric. Very few seek to take on the Prince of Knives, and few do it out in the open like this."

Mistmark unfurls the scroll, a faint smile edging his lips as he examines it. "You found the questing beast."

"It found *me*." The stranger flicks a speck of dust from his sleeve. "It could scent me, even if it couldn't see me."

"You look none the worse for wear, Falion."

"Tell that to my hunting leathers," Falion drawls. "The bitch can breathe fire. It took me all morning to lure it into the maze and then I had to make a hasty retreat into one of the ponds, where I managed to finally lose her."

A questing beast? In the maze? A little shiver runs through me. They're usually monsters formed of several different animals and viciously dangerous. Some say they were fae who were cursed or betrayed by former lovers, and now they seek to take their vengeance on all fae.

Or maybe they lose the part of themselves that retains any sense of identity and become merely rage-driven beasts hungry for fae flesh, consumed with an unwitting fury for all of my mother's kind.

Rule number twenty-six in the unwritten Codex of Thieves: Do not try to steal from a questing beast, unless there's a knife to your throat.

"What's it going to eat?" Mistmark murmurs.

"Hopefully the bride."

They exchange a long, steady look.

"Unkind," Mistmark says, his lips quirking in a smile. "I don't want her dead."

"Who? The questing beast? Or Belladonna?"

Mistmark laughs. "You're in a rare foul mood, my friend."

Falion pushes past him, running a hand through his hair. "My boots are ruined, I've lost my best knife, and I'm not allowed to kill Malechus. You promised this would be fun. So far, your description of the word doesn't seem to match mine."

"What's not to enjoy?" Mistmark spreads his hands wide. "There are beautiful women everywhere you look, and weddings are prone to make them sentimental. You might get lucky and have someone take pity upon you."

"Ha, ha." Falion crosses his arms, flicking lint off his sleeve. "I'd laugh if I wasn't so certain you were going to end up with your heart cut out of your chest."

"Belladonna's no more allowed to renege upon this bargain than I am—"

"I wasn't talking about your intended," Falion drawls.

That cuts through Mistmark's smile. "Yes, well. Allow me to worry about that. First we have to find her. And my bridal tithe?"

"Safely guarded by that fire-breathing bitch."

"Excellent."

"I was talking about the beast, not the woman who's going to cut your throat. Nobody's getting near it until this ceremony is over, and I can retrieve it but—"

"Play nicely." Mistmark taps the scroll against his lips. "We're one step closer to getting this noose from around my throat and rescuing her. You can afford to smile for once in your life."

"I wouldn't want to steal all those ladies from their lords."

Mistmark contains a laugh in his fist.

What noose?

A little quiver runs through me. This marriage has never made sense, but if Malechus is blackmailing Mistmark into joining his house....

But how?

Or rather, what?

And this bridal tithe.... I was right. It has to be the horn.

It's always expected—when marriages are conducted between courts of unequal power—that the lesser of the courts is the one to provide a bridal tithe to the more powerful court.

But why would Mistmark give it to the questing beast to protect?

Is he planning to double cross Malechus?

I Sift closer, slipping from shadow to shadow. It's easy here, where the hedges cast large banks of shade.

I can see their faces better now.

Mistmark is still gorgeous, his features cut from the mold of the Blessed courts. But I can't stop my attention from shifting to Falion's face. There's something... ethereal about his features. Finer, sharper, more dangerous than any other fae I've ever met. His cheekbones are cliffs, and his mouth is as soft and full as mine. Light gleams off the angles of his face as if it suffuses him.

The thought sets off a slow-burning twist of anxiety deep within me.

He looks a little like me.

I turn and press my back to the oak I'm hiding behind

as my heart erupts into a stampede. I can't stop myself
from grabbing a twist of my moonbeam-pale hair.

I have my mother's eyes and hair.

It's a rare combination among the fae courts. They're
comprised of all the colors of the rainbow, and I've always
considered my pale skin to be a curse my father's bloodline afflicted me with.

But what if it's not from my father?

My fingers tremble. There's a pearlescent glow
beneath my skin if I let my glamor slip. I haven't let it
show through in years, indeed, keeping it locked away
within me is more natural to me than breathing these days.

I steal another glance at this Falion, at the ripples of
light playing over his features. If I didn't know any better,
I'd say his glamor was relaxed in the presence of his friend,
and he wasn't bothering to hide the gleam within him.

"Captured starlight," my wet nurse once told me. Then
her face had twisted in a rare moment of warning. *"You
shouldn't let your father see it."*

I've never known who my mother was or where she
came from.

"You could simply refuse to marry Belladonna," Falion
says. "Or I could cut her throat and end this before it's
begun."

Mistmark turns toward his friend sharply. "You know
what happens if I refuse the marriage. I will *not* let it
happen. *No.* We bide our time. We make the exchange.
And then we turn this all on its head and—"

The stranger suddenly looks up, and his head turns, as
if he's scenting the air.

"Falion?" Mistmark tenses in response. "What is it?"

"There's someone here," the stranger whispers, and his gaze locks right on me, as if he can penetrate my veil of shadows. "Someone watching us."

"Who?" Mistmark draws steel, turning toward me.

I've seen enough.

I clench my fingers shut, obliterating that faint gleam, and vanish in a whirl of darkness. It takes a half dozen leaps before I feel there's enough distance between me and the pair in the heart of the maze, but my heart keeps skittering like a rabbit's.

He knew I was there.

He turned and looked *right at me*.

Falion.

I don't know who he is. I don't know his face. But I know him, deep in my heart.

I finally clear the maze, the landscape rushing by, and then I stumble out of the shadows just in time to snatch a glass of wine from a servant's platter. I steal a little acorn cake from a different servant, and press close enough to a group of fae women that I might be considered part of the group if anyone was to look.

Just in time.

Two seconds later, Falion appears at the entrance to the maze, his hands in his pockets as he surveys the gathering on the lawns.

He cleared the maze impossibly fast.

I throw my head back and titter as one of the ladies makes a ridiculous joke, and then sip my wine, stealing glances of him out of the corner of my eye.

Pasting a smile on his face, he prowls into the gathering, but he's clearly looking for someone.

Now I know who is he is.

He's the Lord of Mistmark's assassin. He has to be.

Every court has one, and while they're usually less… visible, Mistmark would want to keep his well in hand in an enemy court.

And he somehow saw right through my shadows.

8

Two hours later, there's no sign of Keir.

What is he doing?

I pace the party, trying to hold my own with people I don't care about and trying to avoid both Falion and Mistmark. Someone laughs about how "Malechus is keeping such a close eye on dear Anissa," and the group I'm passing all exchange secret smiles. I slip among them, hoping for more information, but the only other thing I glean is that with Belladonna marrying, Malechus's stakes as a bachelor just increased.

And that's when I finally see Keir, surrounded by a flock of pretty fae woman.

Our eyes meet across the garden.

This was my idea. But I hate the way it feels to see him with a pair of handsome blondes practically perched on his knees.

Stop it, I tell myself. *They're hardly perched upon him. And they're gigglers. He hates gigglers….*

It doesn't matter if he hates gigglers or not, because he's doing exactly what you asked of him.

"Stop staring at him. Stop staring at him. Stop staring at him," I whisper under my breath, and turn to intercept another servant with a tray of iced lemons.

I've eaten three already.

But I should have been watching my back, instead of Keir.

"The Lady Merisel of Greenslieves," Belladonna purrs, linking her forearm through mine as she slips out of nowhere. "Walk with me."

Clearly, there's little choice. "An honor, Your Highness, though are you not busy with your forthcoming wedding?"

"For you, I'll make time." She cuts me a smile and leads me toward the maze.

What is with this maze?

If I were Malechus, I'd send a dozen dryads into it to hide, and I'd have every secret that's available at this bloody court.

The thought makes me look closely at every tree in the row. Not a single face is revealed in any of the trunks, but a shiver runs down my spine regardless.

And then my mind helpfully conjures a recap of Mistmark and Falion's conversation.

Not helpful.

It's a big maze. It's not as though the beast will be lurking near the party....

You can always throw Belladonna at it....

"The wedding celebrations have been lovely thus far," I say, though I'm terrible at small talk.

And who needs to make it right now?

Clearly, she's not dragging me in here because she thinks I'm a stimulating conversationalist.

I can get away, I remind myself. She can't chase me through the shadows.

"Then thank Malechus." Is there an edge to her voice? "He's the one who's hosting this entire mockery."

Mockery? I cut her a look. "You care not for the Lord of Mistmark?"

"I care not for marriage." Belladonna turns directly toward the wall of trees on our right and whispers something to them. The trees shift apart—they actually uproot themselves and walk—and then we're facing a low stone wall, a little secret garden in the middle of the maze.

There's even a door with a brass knob.

Belladonna pricks her finger on a needle she has tucked in her belt, and then presses the welling bead of blood to the handle. The door swings open, and she shoves me through into a walled garden filled with dozens of nocturnal flowers.

A circular pool dominates the little garden. The moon's reflection shimmers there, and though gorgeous night-blooming blood lilies decorate its surface, I catch a glimpse of little foxfire lights dancing among their red petals.

I don't dare go closer, just in case the flowers ensorcel me.

This is the Court of Blood, after all, and *something* has to feed them. Beneath the surface are bound to be yards of tangled vines. Hungry, strangling vines. It's what gives the plants their name.

I face the princess. "What is going on? What do you want?"

"Poor, sweet Merisel," she says, watching me with her back pressed against the door. "I've had my eye on you from the moment you arrived, did you know?"

I arch a brow. "Me?"

"I wondered what sort of woman had stolen his heart," she says coldly. "I wondered what sort of woman had survived the plot that saw my sister killed."

Ah. She wants to know how Narcissa died. "It was a terrible thing—"

"A terrible thing indeed," Belladonna cuts me off. "I saw the horror in her eyes when Prince Keir had her body returned to us. And I know my sister. Narcissa feared nothing. And yet some sort of dream-forged monster stains her corpse with terror? I think not."

I can see the wall again and those hands clutching for safety.

Narcissa was entombed alive and by the time Keir had her chiseled free of the marble, she was long dead.

I very nearly suffered the same fate.

The horror of that moment lingers still, like a phantom fright within my heart that needs only receive a single thought of remembrance in order to rear itself again.

"Your sister was brave," I say softly. "But Calliope was… a monster."

I don't even know if that was the truth. I liked her. Until she decided to kill me, I thought we were friends. But from what she'd said, her mother had poisoned her mind. She spent years telling Calliope she was special, and that if she ate Keir's heart she would be able to transform into "what she was meant to become."

"You're a liar." Pushing closer, Belladonna suddenly digs her fingers into the barely-healed wound across my hip.

Despite years of conditioning, I hiss and grab her wrist.

Her green eyes light up. "Ah. Then I *was* right. What were you doing in Anissa's maid's room last night? Come to finish the job?"

"The job?" I push her hand away from me. "I don't know what you're talking about. And Anissa? The Lady of Withenwold? I barely even know her. Why would I be in her rooms?"

Belladonna's lip curls. "I know you're up to something, you poisonous little toadstool. I don't deem it coincidence that you were there when my sister died, and last night I just happened to cut an intruder in Lady Anissa's rooms with my magic. Show me your right side and prove it wasn't you."

Protest dies on my lips. If I refuse her, she'll know for certain it was me. "Would I not still be bleeding if it was me that you'd cut?" The dress I'm wearing is a confection of black silk, with ample amounts of flesh showing. The fabric drapes around my throat, crosses in the front over my breasts, and then flows into my skirts. My lower back and navel are bare and there's a gold collar around my throat that holds it all together. It took me two maids and a lot of guesswork to get into it.

And some inventive cursing toward Keir.

I tug one of the pieces of material aside, revealing the curve of my right flank. The skin there is pink and tender.

"See? No cut. I bumped into the corner of the vanity this morning though, so I daresay I'll expect a bruise."

Belladonna traces a clawed fingernail down the phantom remnants of the wound, and I grit my teeth.

If I was free to be myself, I'd punch her in the face, but I'm not.

Sweet, innocent Merisel would never confront a princess of the Blood Court.

She shoves me back, toward the pond. "Your innocent smile doesn't fool me, you little wretch. I've questioned every princess who was at the Court of Dreams that night. Ismena said you were the only one unaccounted for the night my sister died and that you were friends with this Calliope. My sister could kill a fae from a hundred feet away. So how did a single madwoman manage to take her down?"

Another shove, and I feel my heeled slippers take in the edge of the pool.

I shoot the pond a wary look.

The foxfire lights in the blood lilies flicker with frenetic energy. A vine slithers through the water toward me as if it senses my shadow.

If I land in that water, I won't be coming out again.

"Tell me the truth," Belladonna snarls. "Look me in the eye and tell me you had nothing to do with my sister's death. Tell me you didn't see a chance to thin the competition and whisper Narcissa's name in your friend's ear."

I grab a fistful of her gown. If I'm going in, she's coming too. "I had nothing to do with her death! Calliope fooled me just as much as she fooled the others! I'll bet our dearest Ismena forgot to mention what happened the night Calliope tried to kill *her*? I was the one who saved her. And when Ismena bolted for safety, Calliope tried to shove me in the damned wall too. Does that sound like I was involved?"

"Oh, she mentioned what happened." Belladonna's hands capture my wrists. "You came out of nowhere, she said. You appeared as if you'd leapt out of thin air and drove them both to the ground."

I still.

I'd Sifted and attacked Calliope from behind. Ismena had been so panicked, I'd hoped she'd been confused enough in the rush for her to think I'd run at them.

"I know you were there last night," Belladonna whispers, pushing me backward until I'm arching over the pond. A hungry tendril reaches for me. "And I know what you can do. It was you last night in Anissa's rooms, wound or no wound. Admit it."

I panic as my heel slips on the edge.

The only way out of this is to Sift—which will prove her point.

"If you truly thought me involved," I try to bluff, "then you wouldn't be questioning me. You'd have simply pushed me in the pond by now. So what do you truly want from me?"

There's a moment where we stare at each other.

And I see it in her eyes. I guessed right.

She sets her sharp fingernails to my chest, right over my heart. A sudden pain spears through me, leaving my head spinning.

Suddenly, the pond is the least of the possible dangers here.

"I don't know how you turned yourself invisible last night." She leans closer, her lips whispering against my ear. "And I don't care. Kill my future husband, Merisel, and all is forgiven. Kill him and bring me his heart, and I won't snap shut the curse I just twined around your heart. But do it soon. Before this fiasco of a wedding ceremony is completed."

I MAKE IT BACK TO MY ROOMS AFTER BELLADONNA SETS me free, the hem of my gown sodden and my heart racing.

An idiot.

I was an idiot.

Slamming the doors to my rooms shut, I cross to the mirror and jerk my gown apart. There's a bruise mottling my skin, right over my heart. It's in the shape of a knot of thorns. A blood *curse*. *Fuck*. What am I going to do?

I was complacent. I truly didn't think she could hurt me, not after everyone had seen us very visibly enter the maze together. I allowed the protection of Keir's claim on me to dull my senses. I'm in the middle of the cursed Blood Court, and I blithely followed its princess somewhere private, assuming she didn't dare hurt me.

Why would she demand I kill the Lord of Mistmark? I'd tried to protest that I was no killer, but she simply tossed me on the grass and told me to find a way since I was so resourceful.

What in the Wild Hunt is going on here?

If Mistmark dies before the wedding, then there will be no tithe. He's not a fool—judging from his conversation today he hasn't handed the horn over to Malechus already, and probably won't until the wedding is done. No, it will be a deal of some sorts—*if you kill me, then you'll never get your hands on it....*

Does Belladonna even know what she might cost her cousin?

Or does she simply not care?

A sharp rap comes at the door.

I jerk my hands from my gown just as Keir abruptly enters, shutting the door behind him.

"Come in," I call, eyeing him challengingly. "It's not as though I'm naked."

"I knocked."

"It's usually polite to wait for an answer."

At that, his gaze slides down me somewhat posses-sively. The last I saw of him, he was draped in naiads. It's the role he's meant to play—to draw attention and leave me in the shadows—but I'm irritable enough with the entire situation that it only sharpens my fury.

Maybe he sees it on my face, for his eyebrow arches as he slips his cloak off and tosses it over a chair. "I tried to find you at the party, but you didn't come back from the maze."

"You didn't notice," I correct sharply. "You had a blonde on each knee."

His eyelids lower lazily, thick lashes concealing his thoughts. "I would have noticed if you'd returned. Blondes or no blondes. What happened? Belladonna was practically smirking at me."

"A few playful threats. Some name-calling. An attempt

to drown me in a pond full of blood lilies. You know how these princesses are."

He takes a sharp step toward me before he pauses, clenching one fist. "You're all right? I hated watching you enter that maze with her."

"She knew I was in Anissa's rooms last night. She's been questioning Ismena about her sister's death and seems to think I can glamor myself invisible."

"How did you get away?"

"I didn't. She cursed me," I grind out. "She wants me to kill the Lord of Mistmark, or she'll unravel the curse and let it eat my heart."

Keir strides toward me, fury etching hard lines in his face. "She did *what*?"

I repeat myself, but if anything, he only grows angrier. "Show me."

This time it's my turn to arch a brow. "Is that what you say to all the girls?"

Keir rests both hands on the vanity on either side of my hips, and for the first time I realize I must have backed against it. "Show me."

The words are soft with menace, and yet they still somehow steal my breath. Because his anger isn't directed at me.

And maybe I do need his assistance, though the asking of it is impossible.

"I need help."

I turn and lift my hair out of the way. The catch of my dress is at the back, and it's complicated enough that I don't bother with it myself.

There's a moment of hesitation, and then Keir's fingertips brush another lock of my hair out of the way. He works at the clasp of the collar, and the silence is suddenly warm and intimate. It feels as though the room is closing in on us.

He's barely touching me.

Just the dress.

But I can feel his breath stirring over the back of my neck, and my nipples go hard. Heat emanates from his body. I can feel the wall of it against my back.

I want it.

I want to drown myself in that heat. I want to lick it from his skin and taste it on his mouth. I want it inside me. I would *kill* to get those hands on my skin.

A soft gasp escapes me.

His hands still.

He knows.

It's like all my shame pools within my abdomen, leaving me slick and molten.

"I shouldn't have let you enter the maze with her." His fingers fumble with my gown.

"You're not 'letting' me do anything," I point out. "This is what I do, Keir. This is how I'm going to find your horn for you."

I catch a glimpse of his jaw as I turn. The look on his face says, "fuck the horn." But I can't be reading that right, because the only reason we're here is to get our hands on it.

Goddess, he's getting to me even now, because I want him to care more about me than the horn, and now I'm conjuring it in every interaction.

Taking a piece of fabric in each hand, I part the gown

until I'm barely shielding my breasts. The curse is written large against my skin. It looks almost black now. A tangled knot twined around my heart.

Keir doesn't look down. Instead, he peers straight into my eyes, almost as if he can see right through me.

"The curse," I growl.

I can't read the expression on his face as he glances down. He splays featherlight fingertips against my skin, as if he's trying to untangle the knot of it. Heat shivers through me. It's a honey-slide of sensation, and it warms me from within.

His magic is a dangerous drug.

Then his gaze shutters. "I can't undo it. She's set it to activate the second anyone tries."

Instantly, the heat is gone. A sick feeling pervades me. "I didn't expect you to." *Cauldron's piss*. I am bound to the princess's will.

Killing Mistmark is no answer—even if I had the instincts for it, which I never did. If I harm a single hair on his head, I'm dealing with Malechus—the Prince of Knives himself—who is infinitely more dangerous than both Belladonna and Mistmark combined.

How do I get myself into these messes?

"Well," I manage to drawl as I retie the dress behind my neck. "At least you're going to be free of your betrothal if this all goes wrong."

It's the wrong thing to say.

Keir is a dragon. A protective dragon. I'm still thinking of him as a fae prince, callous and toying with the whims of others, but I know the deaths of Narcissa and Lady Altrea affected him. They were under his demesne when they were murdered. And now he thinks I'm part of his party.

Snapping his fingers causes his cloak to fly across the room and alight on his shoulders. "Let me deal with the so-called Princess of the Blood."

Alarm floods through me. I Sift into shadows and reappear in front of the door just as he reaches for the handle. Our bodies collide, but I manage to get a fistful of his cloak. "Don't you *dare*. If you go down there and drag the bride out of her rooms for daring to curse me, you'll ruin our little ruse! They'll know we're working together!"

Hard hands clamp around my waist, and Keir shoves me back against the door. "Let them," he breathes, but some part of his power must catch on the words, because I shiver as they etch themselves in my ears. "I can tear this fucking court apart stone by stone if I will it."

"Because she threatened me? Believe it or not, my prince, it's not the first time I've had my back against the wall. It won't be the last."

"Because she dared curse you," he spits. "You. My bride. Under *my* protection. It's a threat against you, it's a mockery of me, and it *will not* be tolerated."

Ah, now I understand.

A male's oath of protection is like his cock. You do not mock the size of it, you do not suggest it can't handle itself, and you certainly don't laugh in the face of it.

Belladonna just did all three, metaphorically. By cursing me, she's suggesting she doesn't find Keir's power and status threatening.

Which is possibly a huge mistake, I note, as the muscles in his forearms flex.

"If you kill her, then we lose our chance at the horn," I warn.

"Fuck. The. Horn," he enunciates very clearly, a strange light in his eyes.

Heat bleeds out of me. I can't lose this chance. I can't. If Keir ruins this entire situation because of some sort of overweening fae arrogance, then I'm dead.

"Don't you dare." I grab another fistful of his cloak and realize I've got it all bunched around his throat. "Stop thinking with your pride. Whoever gets the horn has the power to find the cauldron. I know she insulted you, but—"

"*Insulted* me?"

It's like trying to wrestle a runaway carriage that outweighs me by a thousand pounds. "Yes," I hiss. "I'm the one with the curse looming over their head. So you can take your territorial foot stomping and put a fucking leash on it."

He freezes.

It's not, as immediately suspected, an improvement in the situation.

Keir captures my chin in one hand. "Let me be perfectly clear since you seem to be leaping to the wrong conclusions. I don't give a fuck about the insult, or my pride, or any of this so-called territorial foot stomping. If she snaps that curse shut then you are dead. And I will *not* have that."

I suffer a moment where I have no fucking idea what that means.

And then it comes crashing down on me.

He's... angry because he thinks I'm going to get hurt.

"Because you won't be able to find the horn," I whisper, trying to reel in all my conflicting feelings.

His thumb strokes the curve of my neck. "Oh, Zemira. The lies you tell yourself.... *Yes*," he hisses, pressing closer. "Because I need you to find the horn. Because if she steals you from my side, she's insulting me. Because this is a game, and all I care about are the whims of foolish little fae princes. Do any of them feel like the truth?"

I can't look away from him. His eyes blaze and I realize I have a furious dragon by the collar, and I don't know how to defuse the situation, because I truly don't know why he's so angry.

He must see it in my eyes. "I will kill her because this is not the first time she's dared attack you. Last night can be forgiven—she didn't know who you were. But now she has no excuse. I will kill her because you are *mine* and she hurt you. I will kill her because I promised myself I would protect you. No matter what the cost."

Kill her? My eyes widen. *Mine? What is this?*

"Stay here," he says, trying to push me aside. "I will be back."

He's going to ruin everything and in so doing, cast me to the wolves. Or, to be more precise, my father's lack of mercy.

There's only one thing to do—

I kiss him.

There's a moment of stillness as if I caught him by surprise. Hands lock around my forearms as if he seeks something to steady him.

And then, it's as though he surrenders utterly to the sensation. Keir kisses me hard, shoving me back against the door, his soft mouth claiming me. His tongue lashes against mine, the stone wall of his chest pressed firmly against me.

I knew his body was carved of pure marble by some long-ago artisan who conjured him into flesh, but the sensation of it.... All that muscular flesh pressing me into the door, grinding me there until we're practically struggling for breath and surrender, steals my wits.

Maybe we aren't the ones fighting—maybe we were fighting our own desires—because it feels as though desperation twines itself through my body.

I need to kiss him.

I need his hands on my skin.

His tongue in my mouth.

I need this like I need air. Or water.

He kissed me once, his oath biting into my lips and drawing blood. At the time I was frightened and reeling, and though the memory of that kiss has replayed itself a thousand times over in my head, it wasn't entirely something enjoyable.

But now I'm not thinking about pain, or oaths, or stopping him.

Now all I can taste is his mouth.

That hard, relentless mouth that tastes like all manner of sin. I can taste apples on his tongue, tart and sweet, and his hands slide down my hips, capturing my ass in both hands as he hauls me up, driving into the welcoming embrace of my hips.

A gasp tears loose from my ragged throat. I should stop this right now. This is dangerous, like throwing oil on a fire, but I can't. Just a second more. Another second.

I'm stealing seconds and drowning in the passion of his claim.

Keir doesn't just kiss me.

He steals my breath, my thoughts, my tremulous heart… and if I'd had my soul, I think he'd be engraving his name permanently on that too. His magic runs through my veins like molten honey—or slow-acting poison. It slides through every inch of me, igniting something within me that I've never felt before.

A hand cups the back of my neck, fisting in my hair.

"Zemira." My name is a gasp on his lips, and then he's no longer being kind and gentle. Instead, he claims me with some sort of desperate growl, stirring a beating hunger within me. It feels like we're eating at each other, as if I'm inhaling some sort of primal essence from him and breathing it into my lungs.

It's too much.

I break away, shuddering for breath as I rest my forehead against his. The slam of my heart against my ribs feels like a mule kicking its stall walls. I don't know what just happened. Except whatever did occur, I can still feel it, like lightning dancing through my veins.

Our eyes meet. I see the storm within him, dark clouds bubbling on a distant horizon. This is the primordial darkness within him. The conqueror. The prince. And he wants to claim every inch of me until he owns me.

Oh no.

I think I've roused the dragon.

"Put me down," I whisper, heart racing like a carriage out of control.

He turns and strides toward the bed, carrying me in his arms. "Good idea."

"Not like this—"

My back hits the mattress and Keir kneels between my thighs. Reaching down, he tries to capture my mouth again, but if he does all is lost.

Because I won't let him out of this bed again.

I shove his shoulder, and we roll, me ending up astride him.

I don't know who's more shocked. Him, to find himself flat on his back, with my thighs straddling his lean waist, or me, to discover that the position, whilst the dominant one, seats me right where I shouldn't want to be.

I freeze, fingers curling in his shirt.

Someone's happy with the situation. And if what I can feel grinding into my ass is any indication, I do not want to unleash that battering ram for fear it will conquer me as surely as any castle.

"What the fuck were you planning to do with that thing?" I squeak, looking down as I heave my weight forward onto my knees. "Broach the castle walls?"

Keir captures my thighs in his hands, his eyes lazy-lidded. "Maybe I'll fuck you into oblivion instead. Maybe we can dispense with these stupid games and simply skip to the enjoyable part."

Another squeak of shock escapes me. "Games?"

"What's wrong, Zemira?" His thumbs ride up the inner slope of my thighs. "You can take it. You know you can take it all." A dangerous look enters his eyes. "I'll even let you be on top."

Oh no. This is a bad idea.

My body begs otherwise.

"We're enemies," I blurt. "You locked me into a year and a day of service. You're a dragon. You're *supposed* to be concentrating on the horn!"

"Keep lying, my love." His thumb digs into my inner thighs as he runs the other hand up my leg. "Maybe we'll both believe it."

What is happening here?

He rolls me onto my back again, and then he's kissing his way down my throat and I *let* him.

"They're all truths," I blurt as his lips reach the edge of my neckline. I can't believe the dress is still in place.

He lifts his head, his eyes shining like lighthouses in the night. "You're only my enemy if you believe it, Mira."

Mira.

I can't breathe. *No.* No, this isn't happening.

"And yes, I will hold you to me for a year and a day." His roughened palm skates up the silk of my dress, right where I want it. I gasp and can't help undulating as it curves over my breast. "I will hold you to me forever, if you let me."

"I. *Can't.*"

Frustration firms that sensual mouth, and his hand stills. "Why not?"

Why not, indeed?

"Because you're a prince!" I yell. "You *own* me." And my father will kill me if he catches wind of this, or worse —he'll see a means to bend the Prince of Dreams to his whims. I don't know which is worse. I have to stop this. "And you are meant to be flirting with other women! What happened to our plan?"

"Change of plans." His eyes are like molten pools of fire as he stares down at me. "There will be no more of this distance between us. You belong to me. You're my promised bride." He leans closer, his breath stirring against my scalded lips. "And I don't care what anyone thinks. You will be by my side until this plays out. You'll sit on my fucking knee if I have to make you. You don't leave the room without me, you don't vanish into thin air—"

A growl of frustration escapes me. Trust a fae prince to start making power plays when I definitely do not need them. "Why not just tattoo 'property of the Prince of Dreams' on my ass?"

There's a look in his eyes, one I don't like at all. "Don't tempt me."

"You're *supposed* to be the distraction. Not painting glowing foxfire all over me that says 'this bitch needs to be watched.'"

He captures my chin. "You're already being watched. You have a fucking blood curse wrapped around your heart, Zemira." His voice comes out half-growl, all menace. "You want a choice? Then here's your choice… you obey my new rules, or I'll go after Belladonna and remove the threat of that blood curse."

He's going to set the entire court on fire.

Or maybe rip her heart right out of her chest.

I can see it in his expression.

I shove against his chest and escape the close confines of his body. "Fine. No more solitary sojourns. Drape me over your knee, pretend I'm the woman who stole your heart, stomp the ground and beat your chest like some pagan beast making his claim, but do *not* ruin this for me.

If you kill the princess, I lose any chance we have at getting our hands on that horn."

And that, I can't allow.

Keir's lips curl in a satisfied smile. "I won't kill her, Zemira. But an affront to my claim on you like this must be satisfied."

I thump his chest with my fist. "Don't—"

He captures my hand and presses a heated kiss into the palm of it. "I'll do nothing that will risk the horn. I swear to you, by the Goddess who Blessed me, I won't harm a single hair on her head."

It will have to do.

I finally nod.

And then I escape to the antechambers so I can breathe again, knowing I just left a territorial dragon in my bed unsated.

"Did you sleep well?" Keir purrs the next morning, leaning down to brush a kiss against my throat as I stab a plump berry on my plate.

The brush of his lips lingers like a particularly irritable ghost long after he's taken his seat across from me at the breakfast table. But his words conjure an entire night of tossing and turning as a shadowy figure crouches over me, his golden eyes gleaming as he kisses his way down my abdomen.

"Barely even moved," I lie.

"Liar." He plucks a raspberry from the bowl and places it in his mouth with such innuendo I can barely contain myself from shifting in my seat.

"Stop it," I snarl. "Stop with the kissing. Stop with the touching. Stop this… foolishness. And stop sending me such dreams! I get it. I embarrassed you and now you can make me dance to your tune, but I want you out of my head! If you want your horn, then I need sleep!"

Keir's hands pause on the lid of the honey jar as he

glances up at me. I have a horrible moment where I see the confusion on his face turn smug and knowing.

Oh no.

"Dreams?" His voice has always been his most dangerous weapon, and there's a roughened edge to it that scrapes over my skin. "If you're suffering from dreams, then you should know… I did not send them. I have been most meticulous in staying out of your head, as any good ally should." He licks the honey from his spoon, slowly and enticingly. "Tell me, *my love*, do *I* feature in these dreams of yours?"

He… didn't send them?

Cauldron's piss. I want to cringe under the table. Heat floods my face. "No, you do not."

"Liar." He points the spoon at me. "Am I naked in these dreams of yours?" He sees the red in my cheeks, and his smile widens into a predatory curve. "Or are *you* naked? And my love, if I wanted to punish you I wouldn't be sleeping in a separate bed. I would have you bound to mine with silken ropes, and you would be begging me for—"

"Stop!" I clap my hands over my ears, because my own mind is quite sufficient at torturing me itself. I don't need him to provide inspiration—though clearly my own perceptions have been a little limited.

Bound? By silken ropes?

Oh, no you don't. I hastily haul my eager imagination back into line.

Horn. Cauldron. Betrayal.

In that order.

There will be no naked princes involved.

He laughs under his breath as he leans back in his chair. "You're so ridiculously easy to rile."

"I'm not the one threatening to murder a princess."

"Who said anything about murder?" His eyes gleam. "I said she'd regret it."

"Not today, she won't."

He smiles.

"You promised."

"I promised," he tells me. "But you need help, Zemira. This isn't your world."

"This isn't yours either," I point out.

"No, it isn't. But power games? Posturing and preening? Having a knife at one's throat? Those are things I know." Setting both hands on the table, he leans forward. "I grew up in a world where every breath I took and word I spoke was liable to be held against me." His eyelashes shadow his eyes. "These puny fae lords think they know power. I will show them power. I will make them dance to my tune before I am done. I'm not afraid of them, Zemira. And I will help you with this mystery. That's not an option."

"Those puny fae lords broke your precious dragons," I remind him, "and chased you into oblivion. Don't underestimate them."

A spark of anger smolders in his gaze. "It was never the fae who broke us. We did that to ourselves."

"And you shouldn't be speaking so openly," I hiss, glancing at the walls of the breakfast salon in our rooms. "If they find out what you are, they'll cut your heart out of your chest for the sheer power contained within it."

"The rooms are warded," he points out. "Nothing can

overhear us. And they can try." There's something about the smile he gives me that tells me he wants them to. "I would *like* to see them try."

He's going to get me killed.

Worse, he's going to get us both killed.

"I don't work with amateurs."

"Tell me again… how *did* Belladonna lure you into a trap?"

"Because I'm trying to play by the fucking rules," I growl. As Merisel, I gain entrée to the highest circles in the land, but it also comes with its own shackles.

"Wrong." Keir leans back in his chair. "You're trying to work alone. You had your sister to watch your back when you stole into my realm. This time, you will have me."

It's like arguing with a brick wall. I throw my hands up. "Fine. On one condition: I'm in charge. And you will obey me. If I tell you to do something, then I want to see you do it. Immediately."

"Agreed." Just like that, he eases back in his chair.

Oh, no. I'm not that foolish.

He wants something from me and thinks he just managed a way to get it.

But what?

"Talk to me about your plans," he says.

"Something's going on with this wedding." I suckle the yoghurt off the spoon. "Neither the bride nor the groom seems to be satisfied with the arrangement."

"Did Belladonna give you a timeframe in which to kill Alaric?"

"Before the wedding." I frown at the wallpaper. "I'm

not sure what to do there. I have four days to kill the Lord of Mistmark—or die myself."

"You're not going to die." There's a faint hint of the growl back in his voice.

Fine. We won't return to that argument—because I'm fairly certain it's only going to end with me pinned to the breakfast table.

"So next move?" he asks.

"There was something Anissa said about letters. 'The letters have to be here somewhere….'" In my experience, it's the little details that deliver the dragon's horde. "Since Soraya was posing as her maid, I have to presume she somehow got her hands on compromising letters."

"Blackmail?"

"Maybe." I tap the spoon against my lips. "It's not the way I'd play it. The point is to remain unseen."

"The question is: Does Anissa think *Soraya* was the one blackmailing her or did someone else take the letters and use her to cover their tracks?"

I have no answer to that. "More questions, no answers."

"Then what's next?"

"Mistmark's assassin, Falion, said he gave the bridal tithe to a questing beast."

Keir looks up sharply. "Assassin?"

Right. I haven't quite had a chance to fill His Highness in on the entirety of the previous day. I swiftly tell him about the meeting between Mistmark and Falion in the maze.

"And he saw you in the shadows?" he muses.

I recall the way Falion searched the party. "I don't

think he saw me. I think he sensed someone watching him. He knew someone was there—don't ask me how—but he didn't know who."

Keir brushes his thumb against his mouth thoughtfully. "Hmm. I don't think I've seen anyone in Mistmark's party matching that description."

"Do you.... Do you think there's another Shadow Walker out there?" The urge to clear my throat is incredibly strong. I've never met anyone like me before. I've never met anyone who even knows what I *am* apart from Keir and my father.

His gaze cuts to me. "It's possible. It was an ancient gift that was bred through the bloodlines of only two courts; the Court of Shadows and the Court of the Moon and Stars. Both royal houses could walk the shadows, thanks to a common ancestor, though until you appeared, I was under the impression the gift had been long-lost to the Court of Shadows."

"It is. Or it was." A frown etches itself between my brows. The Court of Shadows is my father's court, though the Seelie refer to it now as the Court of the Forbidden. And my father was thrilled when I began to Sift. It's the one thing that's stayed his hand all these years—my rare talent, and the way he can use it. "Court of the Moon and Stars?"

I've heard the name, but know little about it.

"It was destroyed nearly twenty or thirty years ago," he says. "It bordered the Court of Dawn, but their king was beginning to grow ambitious, and the power of the Court of the Moon and Stars was growing. A new queen was rising to power within that court, and some say King

Ryddhaen of Dawn couldn't bear to see her come to power. The old queen died, and the night before Princess Zyra's coronation, her household was attacked. The court was burned, Zyra's sisters were slaughtered, and her body was never found."

"Twenty or thirty years ago? That's a large span of time, Keir. Your specifics are terrible."

"What is time to a dragon?"

I tap my spoon against my lips. "If this Falion has the gift, then he had to belong to the Court of the Moon and Stars." And was most likely of their royal bloodlines. "What in the Shadow Lands is he doing with Mistmark?"

"The territories of Mistmark abut the lands that belong to the Court of Moon and Stars." Keir shrugs. "If someone survived the massacre then he may have sought refuge with an ally."

Interesting. I know why I want to continue this train of thought—it's personal—but it's not the most pressing matter in play. "I'll keep an eye on him then. Falion may be dangerous. And speaking of dangerous, I've heard of questing beasts before, though I've never heard of one obeying a fae master. What am I dealing with here?"

"We," he counters. "And we are dealing with a creature that is both deadly and vicious. They have the neck and head of a dragon-like creature, the body of a leopard, and the legs of a hart. I believe they spit acid, and they're impervious to mortal weapons. I don't know a lot about them. They were conjured in the third age while I was hibernating within my court."

"Whatever it is, it can breathe fire." *And thank you for reminding me precisely how old you are.*

He shrugs. "So can I."

"I've never… asked you about your other form." But I've seen the enormous spines of dragons buried in the forests. I've walked within the hollow sockets where their eyes lay.

He stills, his attention focusing entirely upon me. "Would you like to see my big, scaly tail, Zemira?"

There's something about the smile that touches his lips that makes me swallow. "No, I think I'm fine with not seeing it."

His laughter sounds like a rough-edged purr. "I never took you for a coward."

"Not a coward," I point out. "Just careful."

He laughs again.

I clear my throat. "Now, if that is done, I'm going to go see if I can discover why Belladonna wants Mistmark dead. Unless you have an objection?"

Keir drums his fingers on the table.

I can tell he wants to say something.

"Well?" I demand.

"You own me," he says softly as our eyes meet. "Last night you said 'you own me.' You think I would force you into my bed as payment for your debt?"

His words steal the winds from my sails. "No. I don't think you would do that."

I've faced a dozen lecherous fae lords in my time, but there's nothing about Keir's mannerisms that make me nervous. If anything, the desire he inspires within me is the thing that makes me uncomfortable.

The wanting what I can't have.

The temptation to start dreaming….

It's all there. A future I can never live taunting me at night like a beckoning Will o' the wisp leading me to my doom.

His eyes narrow to thin slits. "I would never do that. I want you in my bed, Zemira, but I want you there of your own accord."

"I *know* that."

"But you hesitate." He leans forward in his chair, his hands clasped between his knees as if he's trying to solve a particularly complex equation. "You kissed *me*. You kissed me and then you pushed me away. Why?"

"Because...."

"You're attracted to me." He says it as though it's a fact. "You want me."

"I want a lot of things that aren't good for me. It doesn't mean I choose to pursue them."

"Hmm...."

"You want to know what the problem is?" I snap. "You're a *prince*. You're a fucking dragon. When you walk through a forest, everything flees because *you're* the predator. You can take what you want without consequence. For you, a kiss is just a kiss." I hold my arms up so he can see the glyphs inked into them with magic. We're the only ones who can see them. "For me, a kiss can never be just a kiss. The balance of power between us is skewed in your direction. You. *Own*. Me. Maybe you won't insist I share your bed as payment, but even if I was to fall for your charms, the truth remains: We're on uneven footing within this... partnership. And thankfully, I came to my senses last night before it was too late."

His mouth opens, but....

For the first time since we've met, he appears to have nothing to say.

I roll my sleeves down and grab my knife off the table before sheathing it at my hip. "Now, I'm done playing by the rules. It's only going to get me killed. Anissa and Belladonna are hiding something. Belladonna wants her betrothed dead. Malechus is holding something over Mistmark's head in order to force him into marriage. Basically, we have two fae who do *not* wish to be married, and I want to find out why."

Malechus is the key, I feel.

And in order to find the horn and Soraya, I think I need to know more about what's going on with Malechus.

But I can't tell Keir that, or else his hackles will rise again.

"You want to help?" I throw over my shoulder as I head toward the door. "Then keep Belladonna distracted for the afternoon. Just don't kill her."

"How in the cauldron's name am I supposed to keep her occupied?" he growls behind me.

"I don't know," I call back. "Maybe you can show *her* your big scaly tail and see if *she's* impressed."

10

B oldness is the order of the day.

I spend the morning searching for certain herbs in the kitchens, blaming it on my moon courses—but what I ask for is foxglove and a four-leaf clover, and a flower spike from the lords-and-ladies plant. The clover is the giveaway. It tells the servants I want a charm, and they direct me to one of the towers that curls out of the mountain slopes.

Inside is the Ragwort Man. He's a tiny brownie with brown-stained teeth and by all accounts serves as the apothecary here in the court. "Foxglove, you say? And lords-and-ladies?" he asks, as I press him for the clover. "That sounds like a nasty bit of charmwork to me."

"It's not real," I tell him with a smile, as I examine the glass bottles and small tinctures on his shelves. For a brownie with good intentions, he certainly has a decent assortment of poisons, including a single ruby-red drop of miroire oil carefully sealed in a glass bottle. He's sealed the bottle with lead too, which tells me he knows just how dangerous it is. Someone knows his trade. "It's just a game we ladies play.... I want to deliver a message to one of my rivals."

Arching a tufted brown brow, he produces the ingredients I ask for. "If anyone ingests that foxglove—"

"It's not meant to be ingested," I tell him. "I plan to tie it all up in a little satchel of black velvet, and leave it in the bed hangings of my rival. They say it brings misfortune and bad dreams."

"Aye, that it does."

"And if she finds it, then she'll know to keep her hands off my prince."

He doesn't look convinced. "I've had three young ladies in here this week, looking for medicinals."

"*Three?*"

"Best check under *your* bed," he says through a nasty little smile.

"Oh, I always do." I toy with a ring on my finger. The door is closed, but I make a great mimicry of checking it is latched. "Perhaps you can help me with something else.... Do you know if any of the servants have any abilities with natural remedies? One of the kitchen hands said there was a woman here...."

"Remedies to what?"

"The usual sort of feminine problems." Which could be anything from avoiding an unwanted child, to removing a rival. Permanently.

The brownie pauses to polish his spectacles. "There was a young woman working here for a few weeks who had some interest in such remedies, but it appears she's moved on."

"Moved on?"

"Her name was Violet." He puts his spectacles back on and peers over the top of them at me. "Took up with a fancy lord, I was told. Seems she preferred silk sheets to scrubbing her mistress's floors."

Violet. There you are, dear sister. Cultivating the same habits as usual. Soraya prefers not to carry her own poisons with her—it's too easy to be searched. But most courts have an apothecary and I've never met one she hasn't charmed.

It was an educated guess.

And it tells me more than he knows.

Violet is the persona Soraya uses when she wants to play the slightly mysterious maid. The fact she was offering hints that she might be able to assist in certain feminine complications means she was trying to get close to one of the ladies of the court.

She ingratiated herself as Anissa's maid.

But was her target female?

Or was it this lord who she's allegedly run off with?

I slide the ring off my finger. "Which lord? I might have use of her...."

The Ragwort Man eyes the ring. "Can't say I remember."

Placing my palm flat on the table I slide it toward him. "I would very much like to talk to her."

His mouth works, as if he's fighting against his instincts. And then he scowls. "Keep your baubles, my lady. Violet's gone. As I said, she caught the eye of a fancy lord. I ain't seen her since."

"And there's no one else?"

"None," he says curtly.

"Maybe I'll just leave this here," I tell him, lifting my hand off the ring. "And if you think of someone, you come find me."

He grunts inconclusively, but makes short work of wrapping up my herbs and then practically pushes me out through his door.

Interesting.

I let the glamor I'm wearing dissolve, sidestep into the shadows, and then settle down to wait. The ill-fitting gown I stole does me few favors—it's too tight through the hip and bodice, meant for a frame smaller than mine—and I can't wait to return it.

The ring, however, is lost forever.

Good thing the lady of the Dawn Court doesn't need it. It makes me feel all warm and fuzzy inside to know I've managed another strike against Rhea.

But first, let's see where this little tidbit takes me....

It takes him barely five minutes.

Peering out, the Ragwort Man sees the tower steps are clear and then bustles out, locking his door behind him.

I follow him down the stairs, lingering in every pool of shadow and listening to him mutter under his breath.

The sun's still high in the sky as he crosses the court-yard, which gives me plenty of shadows to hide in, but avoiding the stream of servants scurrying about their daily business requires all my concentration.

Every step we take leads us further into the court and tightens the tension in my chest.

We're heading directly into the private wing of the royal family.

There's a small study just past the first ring of guards, and the Ragwort Man knocks brusquely.

"What is it?" calls the fox-faced fae sitting at the desk. He doesn't bother to lift his head from his correspondence, but his dark red doublet has the Court of Blood's insignia upon its breast, and there's an enormous set of keys resting beside his inkwell.

"Might be nothing," the Ragwort Man tells the seneschal, "but one of the ladies here for the wedding's been asking about Violet. Maybe you ought to mention it to Himself?"

The seneschal's disdain clears sharply as he looks up. "Which one?"

The Ragwort Man shrugs. "Said her name was Rhea." He flicks the ring at the seneschal. "And she gave me this as payment to find her."

MY HEART LEAPS ALL OVER THE PLACE AS I HURRY DOWN the back stairs onto the enormous lawns that stretch before the court. Brushing out my pink skirts, I pluck the pins from my hair and rearrange my tightly coiled curls down my back in loose waves. I ditched the other dress in one of the kitchen ovens, and dropped Rhea's rings down a well. My own gown was neatly wrapped and stowed away in a linen closet. And now I'm late for lunch by ten minutes. I promised Keir I'd meet him here at twelve O'clock, and yet I didn't dare rush away after the Ragwort Man disappeared, leaving the seneschal staring after him.

The Ragwort Man went straight to the head of the servants. He *knew* "Violet" hadn't disappeared, which means he knows who took her.

And what does "Himself" mean? Even I heard the importance of the way he said the word.

I have this horrible suspicion I know exactly who took Soraya.

But why?

Lunch is being served on the lawns as I search for Keir, and several ladies appear to be trying their hands at croquet.

Just my luck, the lady of the Dawn Court spots me as I circle the green.

"Tell me," Rhea taunts as she aims the ball in my direction and steadies her mallet, "where have you been scurrying about, little mouse? You ought to be careful that someone doesn't steal your prince while your back is turned."

She hammers the ball toward me.

Instinct takes over. I slap it away with a sharp chop of the hand, and then belatedly squeal and throw my arms up like some lily-livered maid.

Glass smashes.

"Hey!" someone shouts.

By the time I peer over my arms, the Duke of White-haven is lowering a shattered wine glass and gaping at it.

All eyes turn upon me.

I turn my stare upon Rhea, but she's somehow been absorbed back into the crowd of ladies with mallets.

One of them is Ismena, and as our eyes meet across the green, I almost take a step back at the look of malevolence she shoots my way.

Seeing her unnerves me, as always. She can't suspect I'm the one who stole her brother's trident. She'd have said something by now. Wouldn't she?

But why is she keeping company with *Rhea?*

"Merisel. There you are." Keir appears out of nowhere, capturing my upper arm. His lips compress tightly over his teeth. "My apologies, Your Grace. She's a little clumsy at times."

The duke's ire softens when he sees who's with me. "Apology granted, Your Highness. Though I'll expect to ride with you this afternoon. You can make it up to me."

"Of course," Keir says and extracts us with polite nods. "This way. We're dining over here."

A smile here. A nod there. It's easier to maintain my composure in the smaller gatherings. Right now, it feels like the eyes of the entire court are upon us.

And it makes me nervous.

"A little clumsy?" I hiss, the second we have some distance between us and the duke.

"Where have you been?" Keir practically drags me across the lawn. Tension vibrates through his hard frame. "You're late."

"Doing a little fishing."

"And?"

"It appears I caught a shark." I can't keep the grimace off my face.

He drags me beneath one of the gardens stone follies. Everybody can see us and from this distance it probably looks like we're arguing. Perfect.

"Who? What?"

"I think I know who took Soraya," I blurt, and then tell him everything. "If the seneschal is covering it up, then he has to be obeying Malechus's instructions. But why would the Prince of the Blood Court kidnap my sister? How does the seneschal know?"

"You don't think Malechus found her out?"

"Unless she made her move on her target and was caught...." I think about the rumpled sheets, the blood.... "No. She hadn't made her move yet. She wouldn't have returned to the room. She wouldn't have left her locket in the room.... When she strikes, she's always packed those belongings she wants to keep and spirited them away. She grabs them, runs, and she's never seen again."

Keir brushes a long pale curl behind my shoulder. He tugs at the chain around my throat, and the locket that's hidden beneath my bodice spills free.

A crescent moon and three stars.

Soraya's locket.

I hastily stuff it back inside my dress. I found it in my trunk along with all the other jewelry he's had commissioned for me, but something made me put it on today. "I'm just keeping it safe for her."

The amber heat in his eyes flares a myriad of colors. "Sometimes I don't understand the relationship between the two of you."

"That makes two of us," I grumble, but he lets me tuck it away.

I hate the way he looks at me as if he sees right through me.

Grabbing a fistful of pretty pink skirts, I pace to the edge of the folly. "Malechus has to be our chief suspect. But what would he have done with her?"

"Dungeons?"

"I checked," I admit. "It's why I was late."

"His rooms?"

"All feature glass windows," I reply. "I wafted past them the second night and saw His Highness in bed with a blonde. He doesn't have Soraya stashed beneath his bed."

"She's not dead," he points out.

"Then why did he take her? What purpose does she serve?"

"Maybe she was discovered," Keir points out, "and Malechus seeks to learn who sent her?"

Plausible. But again, there's been no sign of her in any of the cellars I've found. All the usual places are devoid of stubborn wraiths.

"We know who took her," Keir says with more gentleness than I'd expect. "We know the horn is in the maze. We just have to find the both of them."

"What happens if the horn's the easiest object to find?" And there it is. The question I've been trying not to think about.

Our eyes meet.

"I'm fairly certain if you find the horn first," he drawls, "I'm not going to know about it until after you've rescued your sister."

I can't stop myself from wrapping my arms around me.

Guilty. I shrug. "I'm the only one she has to watch her back."

His voice roughens. "Would she do the same?"

I hate the fact I don't have an answer to that question.

Keir sighs. "I'm trying to decide if I care. She *did* try to kill me."

"If Soraya truly wanted to kill you, then you would *be* dead," I point out.

"Not unless she knew what I was." Keir captures a handful of my skirt, glancing down as he fingers the fine silk, rubbing it between his thumb and forefinger. "I'm not so easy to kill Mira. And if someone didn't know what I was and caught me by surprise well… they'd only do it once." He takes another step, his thighs pressing against my skirts. Slowly, his gaze lifts to mine. His voice is a dangerous thing. It whispers inside me, like the velvet stroke of a glove *beneath* my skin. "The *only* way someone gets a shot at me is if you told them the truth."

Little lightning sparks shiver down my spine. The wall of the folly is against my back. Nearly seven foot of repressed dragon is staring down at me, his eyes gleaming like a shark's. There's nowhere to go. Nowhere that won't out me as surely as if I suddenly flashed into being right in the middle of the lawn. Even from here, I can tell there are eyes upon us. Somehow, we've become the talk of the court, which was precisely what I'd hoped to avoid, and no doubt half the party is dying to know what he's saying to me.

The dress clasps around my ribs. It was one of the few I could wriggle into without assistance, but it's so tight that every breath betrays me. He notices too, his attention drawn down to the deep dip of the bodice in an utterly male fashion.

Stalemate.

"I haven't told anyone you're a dragon." I hate the way he looks at me like that. "I wouldn't."

Instantly, the sounds from the garden vanish as if he's warded us within an impenetrable bubble. All the better to keep our secrets. "I have to admit that I wondered whether you would or not."

That earns him a glare. But to do so means I have to look up into his eyes. He's so close I could touch him. So close I could kiss him. But fury itches through me. Is this truly what he thinks of me? That I would betray him like this?

"Is that why you didn't insist I keep my mouth shut about our pact? You were testing me?" It never made sense.

Heat flares to life in his eyes. "Maybe."

If he's thrown down the gauntlet, then I don't hesitate to pick it up. I poke a sharp nail into his chest. "I *may* have a sliding scale of morals in regards to the ownership of certain items, but I wouldn't tell someone such an important secret. If the fae of these lands knew the truth, you would have no rest. Regardless of your intentions, all they would see would be war."

The dragon kings were too powerful. Ancient spirits who were blessed into being by the goddess. In this world, where every fae prince measures his importance by the size of his dick, knowing there was a dragon out there would be so humbling they wouldn't be able to abide by his sheer existence.

"You were protecting me," he says.

"War is bad for business...."

"Horseshit. It's the perfect time for a thief to reign. And your king would like nothing better than to cast the Blessed courts into chaos." There's a dangerous light in his eyes as he leans down. "You were protecting me. All you had to do was reveal the truth, and this year and a day of loyalty that so chafes at you would be gone. You know it. I know it." He bares his teeth in a reckless smile. "So tell me, Mira, why didn't you?"

"Is it so impossible to understand I don't want to see you dead?"

"You could have cut my heart from my chest and used it to—"

That's enough. I dart beneath his arm, spinning in a flourish of skirts. Keir whirls, every inch of him poised like a cat prepared to pounce.

"The fae are watching," I point out.

"Let them watch." He graces them with half a glance. Not to be distracted, not by something so inconsequential as a half dozen fae lords and their princes. "If I threw you over my shoulder and hauled you away to our rooms, nobody would think anything of it."

"But if I drove my knee into your balls," I reply sweetly, "then maybe they'd have something to talk about."

Impossibly, he laughs. "You're so fucking stubborn. Why can't you just admit you care about me?"

The words catch behind my teeth. I liked him, of course. There was a part of me that could even imagine falling for him. Dreaming of him. Wishing there could be something between us….

But I never realized until this moment that I'd taken it quite that far just yet.

The heat steals from my cheeks.

It leaves me breathless, and a little off-balance.

No. Absolutely… no.

The smile slips from his face, his eyes widening just a fraction. "You didn't know."

"I didn't…. I don't…."

"Stop lying to yourself." It's like my words steal all his hard-won control. Hunger stares back at me, naked and demanding. He wants me. The dragon wants me. "It took me a long time to realize what you came to my court for. You knew the truth of what I was, the power in my heart…. All you had to do was breathe a word of it to your king, and I would be looking over my shoulder for wraith assassins. I was angry, Mira." He prowls toward me. "So angry, when I realized your deception. Until the day I wondered *why* I hadn't seen you again. What were you waiting for? What was holding you back from betraying me?" He stares down at me, an indecipherable look on his face. "And there is only one truth that can explain it: You couldn't bring yourself to do it."

It takes everything I have to tilt my chin defiantly. "I'm not an entirely wretched creature. *Yes*, I care. Sometimes I care too much. It's always been my downfall. But the truth, Keir, is that it doesn't change a cursed thing."

"It changes everything."

I snatch my hand back into a fist as he reaches for me, and if there's a quiver in my voice, then so be it. "It changes nothing." I shake my head. "You're a dragon prince. You rule your own court. And I'm a wraith born bastard with a murderous… king who will never let me go. It wouldn't—"

"What do you mean he won't let you go?"

Shit. I knew I shouldn't have said it. I wave the words away. "My oath of fealty is as heavy as a chain around my throat." I give him a cruel smile. "You know what I can do, Keir. He's never going to let me go free. He's never going to give me up. I'm too important a tool for him to wield." Pushing my hand against his chest, I head for the exit of the folly, desperately needing to fill my lungs with oxygen. I can't breathe here, with him demanding more of me than I dare give. "Not even you can gainsay the whims of my king. So thank you. I'm flattered that you still find me intriguing enough to pursue, but we are done here." I pause at the edge of the folly, hand resting against one of the stone columns as I glance back. One more time. "Business partners make bad bedfellows they say, and we both have our parts to play. I want to get my sister back. And you need the horn. So let me do my job and forget this foolishness."

11

It's almost as if he didn't hear a word I said.

Keir fills my plate with all manner of bite-sized delicacies as we take our place at the banquet. He granted me a moment's grace before he followed me from the folly, but there's no escaping the heated look in his eyes.

This conversation is clearly not done.

Not even by half.

But I'll play that game when it comes at me.

The enormous truncheon tables cover the lawn and groan beneath the weight of the food. Keir's thigh presses against mine as he leans forward to slice more venison, and from the quirk of his lips he's aware of it. A little shiver runs through me.

"You're not tempting me," I whisper in his ear as I sip my wine.

"Not even a little?"

"Not even an inch."

"Liar," he breathes, spearing some of the meat for me with his fork.

I stab his hand with my fork as he moves to put it on my plate, shooting him a sharp look. If he keeps this up, then everyone is going to wonder at his solicitousness. This is the kind of bullshit male fae get up to when they're intending to claim a female.

A slow, dangerous smile curves over his lips and he simply dumps the meat on my plate, despite the white pressure marks my tines left behind.

I dare you, that smile says.

I tear my gaze away, taking out my anger upon my plate. I should never have admitted there's a spark of something there for me. He's going to be insufferable now.

"Keir," calls a voice, startling me out of my misery. "Is this the lovely young woman you were telling me about the other night?"

The Lord of Mistmark appears, crisp in a dark blue coat with gleaming gold epaulets on his shoulders. A red cloak falls from one shoulder, the golden chain crossing his chest. His ever-present gloves are in place.

I nearly choke on a scallop.

Curse Keir. The last thing I need right now is distraction, and yet, clearly, I lost track of the mark.

"Merisel, my love," Keir says, leaning back in his chair, his expression as genuinely warm as I've ever seen it, "allow me to introduce my friend, Alaric of Mistmark."

Mistmark drags out a chair opposite us, and it's only then that I realize Falion is on his heels like a well-trained dog. Clad in a silvery-green tunic with patterns that shift in the light, he's somehow ridiculously hard to notice. Catching my eye, he arches a well-chiseled brow as if to demand to know what I'm looking at.

I am sitting at a table with my sister's *maybe-true-love, maybe-merely-a-conquest*.

And his assassin.

Who is an unknown entity, considering I'm fairly certain he can Sift.

Somehow I manage to spit the half-chewed scallop into my napkin before I gag on it again.

"And this is my friend, Falion," Mistmark says, noticing the edged looks we're both sharing.

Sweeping his cloak back, Falion kicks out a chair and slides into it with effortless grace. I blink the second the cloak retreats. There's some sort of magic in the fabric, I think. One that makes it difficult to look at him when he's wearing it.

"Well-met," Keir says. "Merisel and I were just discussing the hunt this afternoon."

We were?

I need to get my head in the game for wordplay, before I give the entire game away.

Mistmark grimaces. "I heard there's a white hart. I wonder if Malechus has had the creature imported in from the northern fens just for the occasion."

"It's exorbitant," Keir replies, "so presumably, the answer is yes."

It's an auspicious sighting for the wedding. The White Hart is a messenger from the goddess; often a good omen. If you capture it and steal a lock of hair from its hide, it may grant you the answer to a question.

But it's said that if a hunter manages to bring it down and eats its heart, then he—or she—will be able to see directly through the goddess's mists, which will grant them the ability to divine the future itself.

"I heard rumor the ladies are actually invited to ride today," I murmur. "I wasn't sure if he was going to set us free from our embroidery for the afternoon."

Mistmark shoots me a conspiratorial smile. "Don't take it personally. Malechus is a little old-fashioned. Maybe he's worried you'll beat him to the mark."

Falion makes a snorting noise under his breath, though his attention is riveted upon the platter of sweetmeats, dried figs and cheeses in front of him.

Did he just… snort? As if he found the idea inconceivable?

My stare grows a little more piercing.

"Careful," Mistmark says in a stage whisper. "I think you just roused the ire of Keir's bride."

"I have a name." It's not entirely Mistmark's fault my voice comes out cutting, but it does draw the attention of all three of them. Lunging forward with my knife, I steal the fig Falion's reaching for from the platter, and pop it in my mouth. "'Bride' is such an antiquated term I have to confess I'm starting to wonder if there's any difference between the three of you and Malechus."

Mistmark winces. "My apologies, my lady. That was ill-spoken of me. I meant no offense."

Falion's arched brow holds entire shades of condescension. Clearly, he doesn't share his friend's smooth tongue —or intentions.

I stare back. And chew a little obnoxiously.

Delicious fig.

Falion smirks, and then slowly reaches out and chooses another.

"Is this some kind of territorial marking of assassins?" Keir muses in my mind. *"Are the two of you going to start throwing knives in a moment? Or urinating on the ground? I'm not sure how this works."*

"Knives could be arranged," say my eyes as I glance sideways.

But he merely laughs under his breath.

Keir's arm stretches along the back of my chair. "It seems your appearance is a fortuitous one, indeed. You've spared me my lady's ire for a few minutes."

"This mood looks good on you," Mistmark admits, his eyes darting between us. "I did wonder what sort of woman would catch your eye."

"Only a challenging one."

"The best," Mistmark demurs.

I wonder if he's thinking of Soraya? There's no hint of emotional disturbance on his face. Mistmark wields a smile like a mask, I think.

"Forgive me." I pour myself another goblet of wine. "But how do the two of you know each other so well? I was under the impression Keir locked his court away from the world for several thousand years so he could twiddle his thumbs and write melancholy poetry. And yet, you seem to share a certain familial ease…."

They share a look.

"Keir is a collector of rare books," Mistmark finally says. "And *I* am the custodian of the Library of Arrenhahl. He might have been in self-imposed exile, my lady, but that didn't mean he didn't simply come and go from the world as he pleased. He merely didn't bother to announce his presence. Every now and then I turn around in my library, and there he is with his feet kicked up on the sofa, and a glass of my good brandy in his hand."

"Bottle," Keir corrects. "You have excellent taste in reading material and fine liquors."

"Yes," Mistmark says in some exasperation, "but most of my acquaintances *ask* first."

He'd said he was friends with Mistmark—Alaric, he'd called him—but it's the first time I think I've seen him treating another male as if they stood on even footing.

"It drives Falion mad," Mistmark says to me. "My castle is meant to be impenetrable, and yet Keir keeps getting in. Falion's tried every spell, every ward and alert system, and somehow he bypasses them all."

I could tell them how he's doing it, but I don't think that would be wise.

I do, however, smirk at Falion.

And then I lace my fingers together. "Library of Arren-hahl? Is that not the repository of the Living Oracle? They say there are copies of every book ever written within its walls."

"I *could* tell you," Mistmark says in an apologetic tone, "but then I would have to kill you. I am its Guardian, after all."

It's tempting to point out how he is clearly failing if he can't keep Keir out—and that gives me some insight as to why my prince…. I mean, why *Keir*, keeps stealing inside it.

Because he can.

"Interesting. Have you read every book within its walls?"

Mistmark smiles. "I'm not *that* old. Not like Keir."

"But I'd imagine you've learned so many intriguing things. And you're clearly an intelligent male." I rest my arms on the table and lean forward. "Perhaps you can settle a bet between me and Keir?"

Keir's hand comes to rest upon the back of my neck. *"What are you doing?"*

I don't know how he's in my head—*please tell me he can only send private thoughts and not pluck them from my mind*—but I ignore him.

"I'll try, my lady."

"Excellent." My smile holds teeth. "You see, we were having a silly little argument about something and Keir thinks I'm wrong. Perhaps you can clear it up for me?"

"Zemira. You can't ask him about the horn." There's tension in his touch. *"We're friends, but I'm not entirely certain I trust him."*

"I can only try," Mistmark muses, noticing Keir's strain and clearly mistaking it.

"When a fae male sends out a Summons for a truemate —a bride—he knows she's out there," I say, "because he's been granted a vision by the goddess. Keir claims he could foretell my arrival by the constellations in the sky."

Mistmark stiffens as though he realizes I've just pushed him out onto a frozen river and I'm about to throw him an anvil.

And Keir's stare *incinerates* the side of my face as his head whips toward me.

Oh, you didn't expect that question at all.

"Sometimes the goddess is so merciful, yes," Mistmark says carefully.

Falion finally looks interested in something other than the figs.

"What if they get it wrong?" I ask, because I'm not above pushing Keir out onto that ice with an anvil too. "How can they tell if she's truly the one?"

Both males wear an expression as if they heard cracks lancing through the ice beneath them.

Keir cuts in sharply. "I told you—"

"A male can tell by a single kiss." I arch a brow at him. "Yes, I know what you told me while you were wooing me at the Court of Dreams."

"Ah...." Mistmark looks toward Falion in search of a lifeline.

Strangely enough, it's the assassin who answers me. "It's the combination of a female's scent, her taste, her pheromones.... It ignites a recognition within the male. It speaks to the territorial nature of the beast he once was, when we first conquered these lands, these forests. So when he says he knows by a single kiss, then he *knows*. Every instinct within him is clamoring to take her to bed and never let her out of there. The urge to breed his child upon her is almost impossible to deny." Falion shrugs. "It's a little uncouth, but I've seen men I previously thought to be sensible fall prey to such utter nonsense. It happens."

"It's not nonsense," Mistmark warns him, as if this is an old argument they've had a million times over. "One day, my friend, you are going to be minding your own business when a female drops into your lap and you're going to lose all good sense, and I am going to *laugh* myself silly over it."

"Highly. Unlikely." Falion's tone drips with frost.

"Hmm." This is unexpected good fortune in the turn of the conversation. I thought it would take me longer to steer it in this direction. "You've felt such a calling before, my lord?"

Mistmark tears his focus from his friend, a faint scowl etched between his brows. "We all know I'm getting married, do we not?"

"Strangely enough, I think I've heard the odd mention of it. There's some low-level betting going on about whether you're going to get the bride to the altar or not. Some expect *you* to cry off, and some expect the bride."

He sighs. "What can I say? I was granted a boon by the goddess. There are certain stars aligning in my very near future that seem to be playing out precisely as predicted. The Blood Moon is in the skies. I am several days away from being brought to heel. Each and every element is falling into place. Though I have not yet kissed my intended, I daresay even I may be overcome...." His vision grows distant for a second. "Although.... I already thought I'd found her, a long time ago. But I was clearly wrong. So perhaps there is something to be said for some confusion. Is there more than one mate offered for each male? Perhaps. And now I don't know if I've helped your cause, or Keir's?

I already thought I'd found her....

A little flight of butterflies take wing within me and it's all I can do to not blurt out, *"Three years ago, perhaps?"*

Somehow, I keep my mouth shut through sheer force of will.

"Merisel prefers solid facts she can see and feel," Keir replies, closing his hand over mine. "My lady doubts my intentions."

"It's not your intentions I doubt."

I love the challenge I see written across his face. It feels like Keir's been in control of this arrangement at every step of the way. A year and a day of service. I owe him some unruly behavior.

"There you are, *my love*," says a clipped voice behind me. "My brother's been looking for you."

Belladonna. With Anissa standing right behind her like an ever-present shadow.

And here we were, just getting to the interesting part.

"Ah," Falion mutters under his breath, "I didn't realize harpy was on the docket for the hunt."

I'm fairly certain I wasn't meant to hear that.

I'm also fairly certain I need to do something. Fast. Before Keir makes good on his threat to remove the danger Belladonna presents.

I curl my fingers through his, leaning into his shoulder so he can't make any sudden moves without dislodging me.

"Beloved," Mistmark stares at his bride-to-be like a man eyeing a blank chessboard, and plotting his opening move. He offers her a hand. "Would you care to join us?"

"Alas," Belladonna replies, though her tone belies the smile pasted on her lips. "It appears we're not going to be having that afternoon to ourselves that we hoped for."

Dogs bay in the direction of the stables.

"A true shame." Mistmark finally lowers his hand as if realizing she doesn't intend to take it. "What's going on?"

"The huntsman just sent word. The white hart has been seen in the forests near the lake," Anissa tells him. "Malechus wants to start the hunt early."

She, at least, sounds excited.

"Early?" Falion looks at her sharply, as if she just tossed an explosive spell into the middle of all his carefully laid plans. "What do you mean by early?"

"Now." Belladonna doesn't bother to hide her dislike of him.

This presents a conundrum.

Am I Team: Belladonna? Or Team: Falion?

I could also be convinced by a fairly weak argument to join Team: Sword Match To The Death between the pair of them, and if I'm not mistaken, there's some serious silent challenges as to that affect being thrown between them.

"I need to change into my riding leathers," I say, pushing to my feet. I shoot Keir a warning glance. "Saddle my horse for me?"

That ought to keep him busy.

He looks amused.

Until Belladonna links arms with me. "I'll escort you back to the court. I need to get rid of these shoes."

"Of course." Just what I want. Another moment alone with Her Iciness.

"Just make sure you return her," Keir tells the Blood Lily, and if I thought she and Falion were preparing to throw down their gauntlets, I'm fairly certain he just took it to another level because Belladonna squares her shoulders like she's facing an entire cavalry by herself.

"Wouldn't dream of doing anything else," she purrs.

And then she hauls me toward the house, with Anissa scurrying along on our heels.

"Enjoying yourself?" Belladonna whispers as we cross the lawn.

"The best part was when you showed up," I admit. "I get the feeling you're not overly fond of Falion."

Interestingly enough, her cheeks turn red.

"If you think your precious prince will save you," she hisses, "then you should think again."

I grab her wrist. "I don't think Keir will save me."

"*No?*" There are dark shadows beneath her eyes. "You think I'm fool enough to imagine last night was happenstance?"

"Last *night*?"

Belladonna leans closer. "Tell him to keep his filthy claws out of my dreams, and I won't have to strike back. Now do what I asked. Kill Mistmark and we won't have a problem."

She stalks away.

Anissa gives me a pained smile. "It's the wedding. She's on edge."

I rub at the knotted curse suddenly writhing in the center of my chest. "You have terrible taste in friends."

Anissa gives a sad little shrug. "I know. But someone has to be there for the Evil Queen. She's not all bad."

Horns suddenly echo through the air.

Dogs go wild in the distance.

I shake my head. "A rousing endorsement." I see Belladonna shoot one last vicious glance over her shoulder. "I think you're being summoned."

Anissa flees after her mistress as though she doesn't want to be punished by lingering.

I decide to test the theory that Keir can hear me. "What. Did. You. *Do?*" I growl in his direction.

There's a long moment with no response, and then I can sense him inside my head. Hot possession. The scent of burning amber. A very smug sensation, somewhat akin to a cat purring. *"I told you. I will take care of it."*

"Stay out of my head." I turn for my chambers. "You're going to get me killed."

"Never," he says.

And then he's gone again, and I hate the fact that I feel a little alone.

1 2

The hunt went overlong, and somehow, the white hart managed to escape into the swampy fens to the north of the court.

The huntsman was confounded. Its tracks simply disappeared into the swamp. The dogs ran around in circles. And nobody got to kill the beast.

"It just… vanished," the huntsman finally admitted.

I caught a glimpse of the look in Keir's eyes as he watched Malechus rant and track mud through the edge of the swamp, until he was forced to finally concede and send us all home.

I didn't dare ask him if he had done something.

As if in retaliation, Malechus is in a rare good humor tonight. He calls for more wine. More mead. More music. He will have his glory, no matter whether he must wring it from us in blood.

I dance and dance until my feet ache.

There's a wildness to the music that brings a rush of blood through my body. Or maybe it's the company. Keir spins me in his arms, again and again, until I'm dizzy with it. For once we have this one night in which there is nothing to do beyond enjoy the pleasures to be found. There are too many curious eyes upon us, and one must make certain appearances if one is to be beyond suspicion.

"I need something to drink," I plead as the music lulls.

"I'll be back." Keir bows with a vicious smile. "Don't fall in love with any strangers until I return."

I watch him go, slightly bemused by his good mood tonight.

Maybe it's you. Maybe he's enjoying himself because he's with you.

The thought sours my mood a little.

I turn and almost walk right into Rhea.

The second I see her, her kohl-rimmed eyes bright and malicious, my heart skips a beat. "What are you—?"

"A little gift for you, toadstool."

She blows a handful of powder in my face.

I jerk away, trying not to suck it in, but the merriment has left me breathless. It's too late. The powder hits my lungs.

Grabbing her by the dress, I shove her against the wall of the ballroom cavern, a knife pressed low to her abdomen. "What did you poison me with?"

"Not poison," she says with a laugh, her arms wrapping around me with an intimate embrace. Our bodies twine, and then she's undulating against me, careless of the knife. "I wouldn't dare." She breathes the words against my neck. "Your prince can take no umbrage with this, can he? Tell him it's my little gift to him."

My heart skips a beat, but it's the stealthy slide of lust

through my veins like raw honey that makes my eyes widen with horror.

It's not poison.

Fingertips trail between my breasts, setting me alight. The tips of my nipples harden, and I shove away from her. It's too late. I'm on fire. Burning within.

I've never inhaled rapture, but the fae of the Blessed courts use it to enhance their celebrations.

Snorting a pinch of it is enough to transform lovemaking. A male will be hard for days, driven only by the urge to fuck his way inside a female. A female, on the other hand, will want to rut with anything that's hard enough....

I've heard talk that some of Malechus's wildest debaucheries are filled with little bowls of the stuff, and small straws through which to imbibe.

No. No, no, no, no....

I have to get out of here.

I shove my way through the gathering.

Slamming into the hard planes of someone's chest, I fight to trap the gasp that echoes in my throat. "Sorry—"

Malechus.

Hard, lean, staring down at me with predatory intent.

"I'd like a word with you," he says with a chilling smile. "Dance with me."

"I'm afraid I have to—" There are hands on my wrists. Hands that shackle and bind. Hands that make me wilt into his touch.

"This way," Malechus says, leading me toward the balcony.

Every instinct inside me starts screaming, but my feet, treacherous beasts that they are, carry me after him.

~

"WOULD YOU CARE FOR A DRINK?" MALECHUS ASKS, snapping his fingers to one of the servants as he pushes me —none-too-gently—onto the balcony.

The ballroom beckons through the gauzy curtains. The music seems discordantly jarring, until I want to scratch my nails down my forearms. There's sweat down my spine. Under my nose. If I grind my teeth together hard enough, maybe the feeling won't overwhelm me?

"No." I need to get out of here, before the rapture has me at its mercy.

Malechus takes a bottle of elderberry wine and pours us both a goblet, regardless of what I said. "Relax," he purrs. "I have a good friend taking care of your handsome prince. We won't be caught."

"Caught?" *Caught doing what?*

He offers me the goblet. My choice is either to take it, or dare risk having him touch me.

Instantly, my mind throws half a dozen sensations into view. Malechus's hands gripping my wrists. His teeth on my throat. His tongue on my skin....

I'm heating up.

How long does it take for this drug to fully take hold?

"Thank you." I grab the goblet and retreat to the far end of the balcony.

"It's my pleasure," he murmurs, his blue eyes alight with heat as he stalks after me. "Or it could be...."

"Could be?" It's too hard to focus on my words. All I can do is repeat his.

"Merisel, was it?" His eyes seem amused, and I cannot, for the life of me, work out why.

"Yes." I half-snort a mouthful of wine in my eagerness to distract myself.

He rests one hand on the railing beside my hip, and every inch of me tenses. "I always wonder what sort of secrets a woman hides." He breathes the words, trailing his fingertips barely a quarter inch from my body as he follows the contours of my gown. "Let's find out, shall we?"

And then his finger comes to rest between my breasts.

Heat ripples out from his touch in concentric circles. I bite back on a moan as the prince leans closer.

"Ah, there you are. Such pale, pale skin you have…." His smile turns vicious. "I wonder whether Keir has any idea what a delightful gift he has to unwrap…."

Heart pounding. Breath catching. I bite into my knuckle. It can't be mere coincidence that Rhea accosted me half a minute before Malechus sought me out. "Did you do this?"

"Do what?" His voice is little more than a roughened purr.

Before I know what I'm doing, I shove him back against the wall, putting my knife to his throat. I can't remember drawing it. It's like I'm making jagged leaps forward in time. "Did you send Rhea?"

"Rhea?" Malechus tilts his head back, but he appears completely unconcerned by the threat of the knife. "Oh, I can see why you've caught Keir's attention." He suddenly fists a handful of my skirts. "Be careful, my lady. If you start such a dangerous game, I will finish it."

"I'm not playing a fucking game." That hand. In my skirts. I'm sweating again. Need to get out of here.

But he seems to sense it, because his thumb strokes against my thigh.

"I like games," he whispers. "That's the one thing my father taught me—set the board, cast your pieces in play, and see what reckless mayhem ensues. Every fae prince will show his true face when you twist their arms. This entire elaborate scheme is bringing all the secrets to the surface."

What is he talking about?

"Stop it. Get your hands off me."

"Is that truly what you want?" He steps forward.

Somehow, my back is the one against the wall. I can't remember moving. Malechus captures my hand, squeezing it tight around the blade. He turns it, forcing the point against my throat.

Everything within me goes still with liquid anticipation. I want to scream with frustration that my body's barely obeying me at all.

I need to twist this back on him somehow.

"Your father. The king of the Court of Blood? I thought... you'd be a little careful... about playing games with him."

Malechus's smile deepens as he leans closer. "Want to know a little secret, Merisel?"

I shake my head. Desperately.

But his lips graze my jaw, and it's all I can do not to melt into him.

"In two days' time, my father will no longer matter." The knife trails down my throat, pressing against the curve of my breast. "I will finally have the power to destroy him."

The horn. He has to be speaking of the horn.

"You're going to overthrow him?" Maybe that's what this is all about—he wants the power of the horn to wield against his father.

Malechus withdraws, just enough to search my expression. "Why the fascination with my father?"

"He's the king. He's the one who rules. You can play these pretty games, but none of them truly matter. He's more powerful than you will ever be." I bite my lip, trying to force my brain to think. "Is that why he's not here? He wasn't invited? You didn't want to risk a confrontation with him?"

If I just keep talking, then maybe I can ignore the influence of the drug.

Instead, Malechus slides the tip of the knife down my throat, letting it slice through the thin lace decorating my breast.

Every inch of me goes still.

And he knows it.

"My father is *un*important. Do you know what power is, Merisel?" he whispers.

"What?"

"*Truth.*" He angles the blade until its point draws a single bead of blood. "So many of the fae lie. They lie with a dozen little truths, all half-twisted. But they don't know that I can see right through their lies." The blade presses deeper and I gasp. "Tell me: Why did you—?"

"*Merisel?*"

Keir.

I break away from Malechus with a soft cry as Keir appears, stark and imposing in black.

"Ah," he says, his eyes raking over us. "You found her. My thanks, Malechus."

The Prince of Knives runs his tongue over his top teeth, but the blade in his hand has disappeared. "So I did. All yours, Keir."

He captures my hand in his before he goes, pressing a kiss to the back of it. "Enjoy the night, my prince. She's ripe for the plucking."

And then he's gone, leaving me shaking from head to toe. I've never been so relieved to see Keir.

"Merisel?" His frown turns stern.

"Get me *out of here.*"

I can barely breathe by the time Keir drags me into the maze. The itch riding beneath my skin makes my vision waver. All I am is want. Need.

I need to fuck him. I need his hands on my skin. His mouth.

We pause somewhere, and he growls under his breath as I grind against him and slide my hands beneath his coat.

"*Zemira.*" Capturing my wrists, he lashes them within one fist as he fumbles with some sort of latch. "Damn it, stop it."

"Why?" I kiss his throat, licking at the throbbing pulse of his vein.

"Because I know you don't want this," he growls, shoving open some sort of door. We stumble through, and I manage to get my arms around his neck. "Not really."

"I do." He does too. I can feel the thick fist of his cock driving into the silk that covers my abdomen. "Kiss me."

"No." He unwraps my arms from around his neck. "No," he repeats, pushing me away.

Every vein in my temples throb. I want to scream. I want him. I don't want him. My heart's pounding so fucking fast, I can barely breathe.

"What happened?" he demands. "Who did this to you?"

"Rhea."

Somehow, we're in the hidden garden where Belladonna first tried to kill me.

I turn and wade into the pool of blood lilies, trying to choke down the scream that wants to escape me. Underwater vines lash around my skin, and it hurts, but the feeling *isn't* pain. It's denial. It's lust, driving through my system like a carriage tumbling over the edge of a treacherous mountain path. If I don't let myself crash, then the pain of sheer, unresolved lust will drive me to tear my own skin.

"Zemira!" Keir crashes into the water after me.

Hard arms lock around me.

No. No. I fight to free myself, but it's like dragging my own fingernails down my skin. I want him. I want him so much I want to scream.

"Don't touch me," I gasp, Sifting away from his arms until I'm trapped against the wall of the garden. Even the rasp of the stone against my skin sets me on fire.

"I'm going to kill her. Slowly," he promises, stripping his coat from his arms as he stalks out of the water, tearing at the lashing vines that wrap around his thighs. "Here."

I don't want his coat.

No. My eyes drop to the sleek press of his shirt against his body. I want to run my teeth over his skin.

Then I'm in his arms, punching out of the shadows and sliding my hands under his shirt. The sensation of his skin takes away some of the edge. *This.* This is what I want. What I need.

"Zemira, no." He captures a fistful of my hair, forcing my hungry mouth away from his. "Let me knock you out," he whispers, hands cupping my face. "At least until the drug is out of your system."

"It hurts."

"I know." He lowers his forehead to mine. "I *know.*"

I don't even care anymore whether this is real or not. "Make it stop hurting." My hand slides down his abdomen. "I want this. I want you to fuck me—"

"No, you don't." He captures my hand. "Trust me." His pupils are ringed with solid gold. I've never seen the dragon so close to the surface. "Let me make you sleep until this is over. I'll watch over you, Zemira. I promise nothing will hurt you."

I can barely breathe.

Instead I nuzzle into his throat, desperate for the touch of his skin upon mine. The ache between my thighs burns like acid. I need him. *There.* Inside me. I need this.

I need help.

"Please," I gasp before my treacherous mouth can say anything else.

"As you wish," he breathes, and then the world grows hazy around the edges and I collapse into his arms as darkness overwhelms me.

13

I dream of a dragon trailing his claws through my hair, and kissing his way down my throat.

"*Mine*," he hisses, and then he thrusts inside me, sinking his teeth into my throat hard enough to bruise.

Then a gentle hand soothes my hair. "Sleep," someone says. "Sleep and it will all be over. You're safe."

Safe. "I don't think I even know what that word means," I mumble.

The hand stills. Someone growls under their breath. "But you will, Zemira. You will. I will always protect you."

I snuggle into warmth. I can't fight it anymore. I don't want to keep fighting.

"I don't want to be alone...." I whisper.

Maybe I'm imagining it, but there's a soft sigh and warm hands lock around me. "Never," he promises.

WAKING UP FEELS LIKE BEING HIT SQUARE BETWEEN THE eyes by a hammer.

Light gleams through the curtains, my mouth tastes like something shit in it, and I feel like I wrestled a bear last night. Maybe I did. I vaguely recall Keir having to pin me to the bed, and not in an amorous manner. The sheer indignity makes me furious. It's not enough that rapture steals all your wits and leaves you with nothing more than furious desire, but now I get the post-rapture headache.

And humiliation.

"Thirsty?" There's a Keir-shaped blur sitting on the edge of the bed—well out of touching distance by the look of it.

A vague memory of me begging him for his cock chooses that moment to replay itself. I groan and roll onto my face, dragging the pillow over my head. "Go away."

He laughs under his breath. "Ah. Safe to come closer then. Here. I have water. It will make you feel better."

As much as I want to crawl under the blankets and hide, my tongue is cleaving to the roof of my mouth. I could drink the Burning River dry right now.

Coming out from under my pillow, I reach for the glass and gulp it down without looking at him.

"None of what happened last night is your fault." Keir's voice roughens. "I want you to know that."

And there it is….

"I should never have confronted Rhea the first time." I grind my thumbs up under the hollow sockets of my eyes. "I knew she'd return the favor. I just didn't know how." *Stupid. Stupid. Stupid.* "I failed the Third Rule of Thieves Code: Don't ever get involved."

There's a long moment of silence.

"You rescued a servant from a fate over which she had no control," he says quietly. "I don't consider that a failure, Mira. I consider it an act of courage."

I drag my hands lower. *He knows about that?* "How did you—?"

Keir's lashes shield his eyes. "I heard talk of it. The ladies of the court think you jealous. But in the serving halls, they whisper of your bravery." He looks up. "I like the fact you fought for someone who didn't have the means to fight her own battles. You can call yourself an honorless thief, Mira, but I see your heart."

Grabbing the pillow, I try and smother my face with it. "That's *not* a compliment. Someone like me cannot afford to have a heart."

Keir tugs the pillow down. "If you don't care about others, then what's the point of living?"

It makes me grit my teeth. He has no idea what it's like to be powerless and forced to obey the whims of others. "How kind of you to say so…. You, who stands at the top of the rule of order. You, who could crush this entire court into pieces if you will it…."

"You think it's any easier to wield such power and keep yourself in check?" A hot flush of anger brightens his cheekbones. "You're right. I could destroy this court and every fae in it. I could obliterate this entire *kingdom* with a mere thought. Don't think it hasn't crossed my mind at times. But I'm the one who has to look myself in the mirror every morning. I'm the one who looks at Malechus and sees what I could become if I were to lose the very core of what makes me honorable. The choice to care—to have a heart—is the only thing that restrains me."

I'm too tired to argue with him.

And maybe the arguments I'm voicing are only echoes of my father's voice.

There is no kindness in the Court of the Forbidden.

But nobody's managed to quite beat it out of me yet.

"Fine. You win." I toss the blankets back. "I need to… wash my face."

He lets me stagger toward the wash chambers. "I had to take your dress off. It was soaked. But that's all, Mira. I promise."

Cheeks burning, I duck inside the wash chamber. I'm still wearing my undergarments from last night. It's a little bit of a relief, despite the fact it's all seen better days.

Until I see my reflection in the mirror.

"Well, if that's not going to chase him away…."

I take care of the necessities, then wash my entire body of its cold sweat. The last to go is the remnants of last night's powder from my face, including the thick kohl that seems to have migrated down to my cheeks. I can't get it all off. My face looks like some sort of weird frog that has eyes painted in the middle of its back to warn off predators. It will have to do.

Slipping into my dressing gown, I tie it around my waist and venture back out.

"Here." Keir moves away from the bed on cat-silent feet, crossing toward a small cart I hadn't noticed. "Breakfast. Or lunch. I assume you're ravenous."

Oddly enough, I'm not. *Me*. Who's spent every gathering so far at this court perusing the banquet table. I know he's noticed my love affair with honeyed breads and lemon cakes—every time I've licked the icing from my fingers, I've looked up to see him watching.

But food is a privilege.

You never know when you're going to get another mouthful. And if there's one thing I enjoy about these missions my father sends me on, it's that I get to eat and drink whatever I can steal.

Zemira Ashburn. The White Wraith. The Greatest Thief in the Blessed lands.

And the best heist I've ever pulled off was one that saw me forced to hide in a chocolatier's shop.

I can still taste the caramels.

He sets a tray on the bed as I climb back into it, lifting the silver cloche as he sinks onto the mattress.

I try not to think about the muscles shifting in those powerful thighs. He's wearing his riding leathers again— evidently there's another hunt on the cards for today—and while I'm sure they're exquisitely useful in avoiding saddle chafe, they stir remnants of the rapture within me.

Too large. Too close. Too… male.

I try to breathe through it.

"I'm…. Is that pie?" I inhale the scent, and my mouth waters. Distraction. *Please.* "Venison pie?"

Keir's smile is wicked as he wafts the steam toward me with the lid. "Venison and onion with a red wine gravy."

"Are you trying to seduce me with your pie?" I challenge.

"My very delicious pie."

I swear I'm drooling. "Sir, I shall have you know I am a lady of very refined tastes." I reach for the fork. "I shall eat your pie—your uncouth pie—but never let it be said that I was tempted."

"You can eat as much of my pie as you want."

I arch a brow at him. *Are we still talking about the pie?*

He tries to steal my plate at the last second, and I threaten to stab him with the fork.

Keir laughs, and then pushes the plate back toward me with one finger. "All yours."

"I swear I'm not going to fit in any of your lovely dresses if you keep feeding me." I tear off a piece of pastry and stuff it in my mouth. *Oh my… gods.* I think this sauce is the best thing I've ever eaten. I was wrong. I'm ravenous.

"You'll have to go naked then, and that would be such a shame."

I peel off another piece of pastry. "Excellent response."

"The only response."

My eyes narrow. I suppose, when you've lived three thousand or so years, you become adept at avoiding certain traps. Holding out the pastry, I offer it to him as a reward.

Keir's eyes heat as he leans forward to take it. He calls my bluff, and what began as an incongruous move ends in a lengthy stalemate as he carefully closes his teeth over the golden pastry without touching me.

Curse it.

"Is it my imagination, or are you always trying to feed me?" I murmur, withdrawing my fingers before his lips can graze them.

Keir licks the crumbs from his mouth, and I force myself to focus on the pie again, but the sound of his low voice is doing dangerous things to me. "Shadow Walkers tend to burn a lot of energy when they use their magic."

I pause, a scalding piece of meat in my mouth. "They roo?"

He pours me a glass of water and offers it to me. "All the transfiguration magics do. Shapeshifting is a demanding process. You're shifting levels of your body on a minute level. In your case, you're not just shifting your body, you're changing states of matter. A state of being."

I have never, ever realized that what I can do has anything to do with shapeshifting.

"There were also some that said that Shadow Walkers could manipulate light too," he says. "And not just the absence of it."

I swallow down my lump of meat and take a sip of water. Long ago, one of my father's ancestors could walk the shadows. I've always thought my gifts a throwback to him, but there's only been two other wraiths in the last two hundred years who could Sift—and neither of them survived long enough to master the gift.

I know virtually nothing about my talents.

"Manipulate light?" I ask, popping another pie of pie in my mouth. Light burns when I'm Sifting. Stay to the shadows and you'll be safe, but if there's one weakness I own....

"It's not advisable," Keir points out. "Light is a Shadow Walker's weakness, except for the very rare few who learned to bend it, and they were true masters. Kings and queens of their courts. They transcended their gifts."

"How do you know all of this?"

He smiles. "I may have known a Shadow Walker or two in my time."

"Hmm." I eye him. "Just how long does a dragon live?"

"Why do you want to know?" There's a challenging note to his voice. "A great deal of the lore of dragonkind has been lost to the ages and maybe that's the way I like it."

"You're already trusting me with your secret." I've never truly thought about what a rare gift that is—to be the only person in possession of information that might be able to destroy him.

I look at him anew.

He's never once threatened me to hold my tongue. He may have locked me into a year and a day of service, but it's almost as if he gave me the key to his demise and then dared me to do something about it.

A chill runs through me.

He's testing me. He has to be testing me.

Does he want to know if I can be trusted?

Or is it... something else?

"A dragon lives for many thousands of years," he replies, his fingers stirring over the blankets as if he sees and feels something else. "We were the goddess's favored children, torn from the stars themselves and forged into beasts who ruled the skies. But it is one thing to own the possibility of living for eons, and quite another to live it. The toll of time comes to a dragon, not so much in the weight of his bones, but in the weight of all he has lived and lost. Mated pairs follow each other swiftly into the grave. But others who lose children and grandchildren and great-grandchildren sometimes make the choice to slowly turn to stone. And others still, return to the stars, using their power in one last defiant surge to shoot through the night skies like a comet. We call it 'chasing the stars.'"

"And how long have you lived for?" I whisper.

Our eyes meet.

"Long enough for me to begin to feel the burden of my loneliness." He looks away suddenly, scrubbing a hand through his hair. "Long enough to feel my heart start to slow, and my blood to thicken in my veins. Long enough to drift in dreams for centuries, barely caring of what events transpired around me."

I have to ask it. "What changed?"

He closes his eyes and tilts his face to the ceiling. "When I dream, I dream of the skies. Of chasing those very stars. I was very close, perhaps, to igniting. But one night a new star appeared. One that sparkled and winked on the edge of my consciousness. One that called to me." He releases a harsh breath and looks at me. "Twenty-four years ago, I think. I've been searching for that star ever since."

I don't know what to say.

He sent out a Summons because he said the right constellations were in the sky, but I thought that was only a fae thing.

And when his astrologers consulted their lists, they narrowed down a list of princesses and ladies who fit their timeframe.

Twenty-four years ago.

I am twenty-four.

It's impossible. My name wasn't on that list. It was

pure chance that saw me take a tilt at the Dragon's Heart during that precise moment. I don't even know the time of my birth. Sometime in the winter. Sometime when the snows kissed the ground.

It can't be—

Keir reaches out with a sudden smile and bops me on the nose. "Stop thinking so hard. You don't believe in fate, remember?"

"I know." But I can't help thinking that *he does.*

He'll never let you go. Not if he thinks you're truly his.

My heart is suddenly racing.

"What do you believe in?" he asks.

"Myself," I blurt.

He laughs.

Keir crashes onto the mattress beside me, lacing his hands behind his head. It's an innocuous move—his attention is on the ceiling—but the second I see his shirt cling to the thick muscle in his biceps, a pulse of heat goes through my lower abdomen.

Want. Need.

Maybe the rapture's not entirely out of my system. Or maybe I'm still panicking.

"I like this," he says.

"What?" I force myself to lick the gravy from my thumb, even though I can barely taste it anymore. I'm too busy trying to control myself.

Keir tilts his head to look at me. Hot, amber eyes flare like a dragon's. I can't breathe. I can't look away. And I imagine that it felt a little like this to blunder into a dragon's den all those years ago and come face to face with the great beast itself—knowing that you were prey.

"This," he repeats, his voice like rough gravel. "I like it when you relax, when you talk to me. It's what I liked about you from the beginning. You never looked at me as if I was an object to be hunted down. You looked at me as if you saw me. *Me.*" He looks away abruptly, staring at the ceiling. "Sometimes I hate that the most…. That it was all pretense for you."

The breath bursts out of me. Panic sets in. It's exactly what I needed—an icy bucket of emotions thrown all over my lust.

I can't tear my gaze away from him as he stubbornly refuses to look at me.

Instead, all I can see is the Court of Dreams.

And his smile.

The way he teased me.

The way I smiled back and *felt* it, deep in my heart.

But I can't say it. I can't say any of it.

Keir pushes upright, slinging his legs over the edge of the bed. "Malechus wants to take another tilt at the white hart. You should stay here. Rest."

I drag the blankets around my shoulder as he heads for the door.

Say something….

Common sense tells me to let it lie.

This is a *good* thing. I can't afford to encourage him. I don't want to hurt him when it's all over.

But….

"It wasn't… all pretend," I blurt out as his hand hits the doorknob.

Keir pauses with the door half open, throwing a hot-lashed look over his shoulder.

Our eyes meet, and there's something in that silent duel that makes my heart skip a beat.

I can't stop my mouth. "It doesn't change anything. This.... Between us.... It will never last. There is no future. And I know it. I know it every time I look at you. Being with you is like a guilty pleasure I can never give myself over to wholly.... But I wanted you to know that. It wasn't all pretend." Drawing my knees up to my chest I rest my chin on them and close my eyes for a brief second before summoning the courage to look at him. "And I wish it was. I wish it hadn't felt real."

Keir's shoulders still.

Tension fights within him.

My fists curl into the sheets.

I want to take those words back.

Even as some part of me rages to set them free.

Turn around. Turn around. Turn around.

Look at me....

Maybe I'm not the only one who can hear his voice in my head. Because the door clicks shut. He slowly turns around. And looks at me.

"Say something." Once again, my tongue takes control of my scattered wits.

Heat blazes to life in his eyes. "One chance, Mira. One chance. Say no. Tell me to go on the hunt and I will. I will walk out of here. I will go. I will leave you alone. But if you say yes, Mira.... I won't stop. Not today. This is your choice. This is *always* your choice." His voice roughens. "But if you give me even one hint...."

The seconds tick out.

I can barely say it.

"Kiss me," I whisper.

It's a *yes*.

It's always been a *yes,* hurtling toward me with the slow inevitability of a carriage wreck. From the moment I met him, I've wanted him.

A growl echoes in his throat. "Good."

THREE STRIDES AND THEN HE'S UPON ME.

The kiss takes me by surprise.

One moment I'm sitting there in bed, daring a dragon to kiss me, and the next second his mouth is upon mine, his hand sliding through my hair to cup my nape. The warmth of his touch explodes through me. It's like there's some kind of furnace burning within that enormous chest and the lash of his tongue goes right through me.

Hunger.

Fierce need.

I'm drowning in it. In his kiss. In his touch.

"Mira." His hands tremble as he goes to his knees on the mattress and captures my face in both hands. "*Mira.*"

We stare at each other for a single, shocked second, both too breathless to speak. And then his mouth claims mine.

Tumbling onto my back I drag him down, gasping as the heat of his body slams over me. Every inch of him grinds between my thighs, and my legs part like wantons, capturing his narrow hips between them.

All of that delicious weight, driving me into the mattress…. The firm claim of his mouth…. Whatever restraint he'd been using to shackle himself into a semblance of control, it's gone now, breaking apart with a single spoken command.

Kiss me.

Kiss me forever. Make me forget. Make me feel. Make me dream.

I moan into his mouth, fingers twining in the thick luxuriousness of his hair. A hand slides down my side in response, fingers digging into the soft flesh of my ass. Hauling my thigh up higher, he thrusts against me, licking into my mouth.

"*Mine,*" he growls, and then he's biting at my lower lip, his golden eyes flashing.

I get a hand under his shirt, searching urgently for bare skin. Lust ignites within me. Last night was nothing as compared to this. That was all chemical, all haze, all mindless desperation to rut.

This is fire in my veins. A hollow ache between my thighs, slick and restless. The urgent need to have his mouth on mine, until we're eating at each other, desperate to merge.

Keir must sense my need.

He rears up on his knees, reaching over his shoulder to haul his shirt over his head. A scowl emerges, but I'm too astonished by the cut of his body to truly notice it. I throw my arms around him and kiss him. The assault is too much for his balance. He goes down on his back, and then I'm splayed over 280 pounds—give or take—of furious muscle.

"Oh, gods," I breathe, licking my way up his throat. "Tell me again why I was resisting this for so long?"

"Some apparent need to torture me," he breathes, his teeth flashing and a wild look in his eyes. "I think you exist to torture me."

"Don't tempt me," I purr, kissing along the line of his jaw and finding his ear. I rock against the steel fist behind his trousers. "Because I might take that as a challenge."

An enormous hand splays over my ass, grinding me against him. Sensation shoots through me, stealing a gasp from my lips. "Careful, my love. Or maybe I'll throw down my own challenge."

"Mmm." I kiss the words against his lips. "And what… might that… look like?"

Suddenly there's a hand in my hair, and he rolls me onto my back. "Something like this." His teeth sink into my breast, his hands slipping under my silken nightgown. "First to cry mercy."

"Mercy?" I throw my head back and give a smoky laugh. "Have you met me?"

There's a growl in answer, and then a heated laugh against my skin. "Oh, Zemira. You're so brash right now. But you just took the leash off the dragon. Think you can tame him?"

He kisses his way down the center of my chest, hands parting the silk of my robe.

"I know I can," I whisper, looking down the length of his spine and shivering.

Muscle ripples in his back. Keir looks up, amber eyes locking upon me as his hot mouth closes over my nipple. The lash of his tongue burns, the hot suction of his mouth lined up directly with something between my thighs. I arch into him recklessly. *More*. I want more. I want teeth and pain and pleasure and sin. I want him to ruin me.

The ache within is too intense to contain. Gripping fistfuls of his hair, I ride his thigh, desperately trying to demand more. Teeth rake over my nipple and then he simply fists the thin fabric of my chemise and tears it apart with a wet-seeming sound.

The second my other breast is free, his mouth closes over it.

"Keir," I gasp, but he's not finished yet.

He tears apart the entire chemise in slow jerks until it lies in two halves. I'm losing control of my glamor. The faintest of lights starts to glow beneath my skin.

"Pure starshine," he whispers, kissing his way down my abdomen. Our eyes meet again. "No mercy. Just remember that, Mira."

Slipping his thumbs under the edge of my drawers, he lures them down, seeking out the throbbing mess between my thighs. Lifting my hips, he draws my undergarments down my legs, and then he's tossing them aside and returning with a vengeance. Splaying me wide, he dives between my legs like a man determined to devour an entire banquet.

No mercy.

Not even a single word of warning.

He goes after me as if he's spent weeks, months, *years* dreaming of this moment and he's not about to waste a single moment more.

The hot lathe of his tongue swipes up my entire slit, even as he pins my thighs down. *Fuck.* My eyes go wide as pleasure shocks through me. The gravelly rasp of his stubble on my inner thighs provides the bite of pain, but it's the way his tongue delves inside me in some defiant parody of the way he kissed me that sets me alight.

Keir groans, and then he's kissing his way into my wet, swollen flesh. Thrusting his tongue inside me, then dragging it up, flickering it over the bud of my clit. Pushing me toward that edge as if he intends to throw me off it without giving me a single chance to breathe.

I scream as he shoves a hand flat against my abdomen, forcing my spine to flatten. I want to grind myself against his mouth, but I'm not in control here. He is.

"Beg me, Mira." It's a hot breath against wet flesh. "Beg me for release."

Never. The defiance lights through me, but then, hot on its heels is the thought: What the fuck am I fighting him for?

"Please." I moan, grabbing shameless fistfuls of his hair and arching against him.

His tongue stabs into me again, teasing, torturing. He knows where I want it. "More."

"Please. Oh, fuck. *Please!*"

He finds my clit and suckles it into his mouth, even as he drives two fingers into me.

There is no warning.

I simply shatter like a thousand radiant stars. Heat and ecstasy. Burning so hot I'm going supernova. White light fills the room. *Me.* I'm glowing, until I can see the shadow of Keir between my outthrust legs. The force of climax arches my spine obscenely, until I'm screaming his name, even as he thrusts and kisses and bites and licks at me.

There is no mercy.

Collapsing against the mattress, I beg now for relief. "Stop. Stop! Oh, gods! *Keir.*"

Drawing his fingers from my body, he licks them clean, and then kisses his way up my abdomen. Little flinches of aftershock jerk through me with each touch, and I can't stop my gaze from dropping to the hard, tented jut of his erection.

I kiss him.

Simply slide my hand behind his neck and drag his mouth down to mine, tasting myself on his lips. Those wicked hands make short work of the strip of chemise that's still draped over my elbows. Searching between us, I find the buttons on his trousers. Snap them loose. Tug them open, until the heated steel of his cock tumbles into my hands. He licks at my mouth, a groan tearing through him as I curl my eager fingers around him.

"Inside me. Now."

Keir breaks free, a reckless light in his eyes. "But, my love, you're not in control."

A rough laugh echoes in my ear and then he flips me onto my stomach. It's a chance to escape, but no sooner do I think it than a hard, mountainous body comes over me, grinding me into the bed.

Oh, fuck.

A treacherous gasp steals from my lips. Arching my spine, I shamelessly thrust my ass back into him.

"*This,*" he hisses, sliding his cupped palm between my legs from behind, "belongs to me now."

Gods. Every inch of me bucks at his touch. But I can't just let him claim me like this. "What are you going to do?" I throw over my shoulder. "Leave your mark on my ass?"

Hard teeth sink into my shoulder. It startles a scream from me.

But worse than that is the breathy gasp that follows.

"Maybe I'll just ruin you for all others," he growls in my ear, his fingers forming themselves to my slit. He finds me, fingers gliding through my wet folds. "You want to choose? Then choose, Mira. Tell me yes. Beg me to fill you. Beg me to ruin you." His teeth sink into the flesh of my ear lobe. "*Beg.*"

It feels like his teeth have a direct connection with my clit. A cry escapes me and my hips thrust backward, pushing into his touch.

"Oh no," he warns. "You have to do better than that. You want this, Mira? Then tell me you want it."

I don't even know what I'm asking for. "I don't beg anyone."

His hand stills. I want it back. I want those fingers driving into me.

"All those dreams…. With you in my head…." He growls. "I am done with this wanting. I am done with you taunting me—"

Shoving my knees apart, he drives two fingers into me from behind.

I cry out again, but it's got nothing to do with pain.

Fuck. I curl my fingers into the sheets as he fills me up to the second knuckle. Slow, fierce thrusts that work my body until I swear I might even be able to handle him.

"Do it!" I yell. "Do it! Ruin me for all others! I don't care. Just don't stop. *Please* don't stop—"

"Fine," he growls, his fingers leaving me bereft.

"No, wait!" I grab his wrist, but he's not abandoning me in the bed.

Instead, he tears his leathers down his legs and flings them aside. "Fuck," he hisses, as leather tears.

"I'll buy you a new pair," I taunt. And then I can't stop myself from laughing.

Rough hands capture my hips and haul me back toward him. He stuffs a pillow under my hips and drives me into it, so my ass is in the air.

Fingertips trail down my spine. I shiver, tensing as his touch slides between my cheeks, dipping inside the lush wetness of my body. Our eyes meet in the mirror that hangs on the opposite side of the room. Whatever I've thought of Keir—whatever I've suspected—vanishes as I see the dangerously carnal look in his eyes. It's not merely a predator playing with his prey. It's a hint of what I've always sensed.

What I've always known.

"Mine," he whispers, lowering his face and pressing a scalding kiss to the small of my back. "All mine, Zemira."

"Never," I breathe into the pillow, but the word turns into a gasp as his tongue follows the same trail as his fingers.

Shoving my thighs wide he drives his face into me from behind and I scream as his tongue thrusts inside me. Again.

It's savage. Hard. Brutal.

Unrelenting.

I scream and scream my pleasure as he fucks me with

his mouth and fingers, until I'm spent and writhing on my knees before him. Begging. Desperately.

A hand knots in my hair as he winds the silvery length around and around his fist until I'm practically mobile.

"Beg me for my cock," he breathes in my ear, forcing my spine to arch.

I bump back against him, feeling the brutish weapon slick between my thighs. "Please. Fuck me. Make me yours. Just *do it*."

His fingers slide down my abdomen and delve between my swollen lips. "Mine," he whispers in my ear. "Say it. Say it's *mine*."

"Never."

His eyes blaze and the edge of his fingertips quirk up, teasing through the swollen mess of my cunt. "You always have to fight me, Zemira."

A hard slap shocks a cry from me.

Did he just…?

I clench around him, shuddering as I lower my head. "I *can't*."

"You can."

"It's yours." The words burst from me. "It's always been yours. From the second I saw you."

He reaches between us to guide his cock to my entrance. The first inch makes me sweat. The second inch is torture. It's the sweetest of aches, leaving my thighs trembling. My eyes go wide, nails digging into the sheets as he feeds it into me so slowly that my muscles melt around him. He's so *thick*.

Panting from desperation, I gasp, "I don't know if I can—"

"You can." Curling a hand around my throat, he draws me back against his chest, until I'm sinking down upon him, taking him all. Somehow my moan combines with the sharp hiss that exhales between his teeth, and then he's driving into me that last, final inch.

The dance begins.

Slow. Bone-melting in its intensity. A dangerous grind filled with soft gasps, and the slap of flesh on flesh. This is not merely fucking. He's working my body until we're one. Driving us both closer to a single peak, until my thighs shake with the tension of holding myself in place.

"More," I gasp.

A hand curls around the back of my neck and then he's pushing me down onto my hands and knees. Long, slow, driving thrusts. Getting faster and faster, until his thighs slam against mine. The wet suck and pull of flesh does things to me. Fingers find me, flickering over that restless ache. I want to scream again. I want to bite into the pillow, beg him for more, simply take it....

Keir pounds into me, and then his fingers find my clit and he pinches.

It sets me off again, until I'm crying his name, shattering upon distant shores.

Tension shivers through him. Clenching around him, I try and force him to come with me.

"*Mira.*" It's a breath. A curse. A plea on his lips.

Shuddering with release, he spills inside me with a growl, fingers digging into my hips so fiercely I know they'll leave bruises that I'll relish.

Collapsing against me, he gasps and pant, until we're a

mess of arms and legs. Slick seed spills from my body as he withdraws with a gush.

"Oh, gods." I don't think my heart is ever going to stop racing. "I can't move. I think you're ruined me."

"Mmm." Another hot, sloppy kiss captures my mouth as he spills me onto his back. My pulse kicks against his lips. "Did you think we were done?"

And then he laughs as I simply lie there and shake in the aftermath, his tongue tracing the slope of my neck.

14

I wake with a gasp, a scream trapped in my throat.

For a second, I was trapped in the dark, with not even a single candle to light the way, and the roof closing in upon me. It felt so real I could almost taste the stale air of whatever cell I was contained within, and the old scar across my palm—where Soraya and I once bound ourselves together—is throbbing.

"Mira?"

I turn into Keir's body, my heart racing. Every inch of me is deliciously bruised and sated, but it's the way his arms curl around me that does so much damage.

"Bad dreams," I whisper.

He strokes a hand through my hair. "You shouldn't be having any bad dreams. Not while I'm near."

I shudder. "I thought…. I thought it was Soraya, reaching for me."

He rolls onto his side, so we're face to face. "We'll find her."

"I know."

"She'll be fine."

"I know."

Long seconds tick out as he strokes small circles over my arm. "You love her," he whispers. "Even after everything she did to you."

I can't possibly explain.

But I want to.

For the first time, I want to.

"I don't know who my mother was." The words come from my mouth, but I don't recall beckoning them. Still, it's far too late for regret. "I thought perhaps she was from the Court of Whispers, thanks to something my wet nurse once said, but... I've been there many a time. She wasn't of the Whispers."

He says nothing.

I want to say nothing further.

And yet, the words are rising up within me, choking me with all the pain and sorrow I've never been able to hide. "My father forced himself upon her. It's what he did to all of them. He sent his wraiths to find him fae brides, and when they were brought to him, he forced them to bear his children. He wanted a child that could pass as fae. One that could walk these lands and bring him what he wished. He wanted a child who could break the curse that afflicts us."

All the horror spills out of me. "There were dozens of us. Hundreds over the years. Whatever curse afflicts our kind, it breeds true. Barely one in twenty resembled their fae kin. And of those few, only a rare handful have the ability to wield their fae magics." I hold my hands up and let the glamor slip. It washes from my skin like a warm blanket being withdrawn. A chill settles over me. I'm wraithenkind enough for my flesh to feel like marble. A faint glow settles over my skin, as if the moon itself shines within me.

Not all wraithenkind bear such innate power.

Most of them are maggot-pale and coldblooded. But in this my breeding ran true on both sides. I have the power of my wraith father and the magic of my fae mother.

"Soraya is the only one who stood at my back throughout my childhood. And I watched over her. It doesn't matter how many times she betrays me, Keir, because she is all I have." A single tear leaks down the side of my cheek.

The faint light cuts shadows across Keir's cheekbones. He lifts a hand and rests it, gently, against my hip.

His skin burns feverishly, and my chilled flesh drinks in that warmth as if it longs for it. His thumb brushed against my abdomen, and our eyes meet. My skin explodes like starlight, painting shadows across the wall.

Suddenly, I can't breathe.

"Who is your father?" he breathes.

A week ago I wouldn't have given him a name. But there's a weakness within me that I can't hide. I yearn for the heat of his touch, for the look he gives me.

And maybe there's a part of me that is all swept up in this game of pretend.

If I close my eyes, maybe I could still *be* Merisel, his beloved future bride.

"You know who it is," I whisper. "There is only one wraith that could steal hundreds of fae maidens from their beds."

"Raesh. The King of the Wraiths." His fingers skim the slope of my side from hip to ribs. His thumb works its devastating magic, for it brushes, just faintly, against the undercurve of my breast. "I knew, Zemira, but I wanted the truth from your own lips."

I shudder.

"Leave him," he says simply.

An incredulous laugh bursts from me. "And go *where*?" I hold up my glowing arms. "One hint of this and my head is removed. There is nowhere I can go."

Nowhere that is far enough to escape my father's wrath, and nowhere that would welcome my kind. Not to mention my soul....

Heat burns to life in his golden eyes. "There is one court that would have you."

What? My throat grows tight.

Keir rolls onto his hands and knees, his knuckles resting on the bed on either side of my hips as he leans forward. "I told you I was searching for a bride, Zemira. I told you I had waited hundreds of years for this moment. The stars aligned when I sent out that Summons. She was always going to arrive at that moment of time. My bride was going to walk into my court, and I was going to claim her. And the second you appeared, I knew you were the one fate had gifted to me."

"No." My protest is weak.

"Leave him. Come to me. You want the truth? You have rooms awaiting you at my court. You have an entire wardrobe of clothes. You will be safe. Protected—"

"I can't *leave* my father!" I wrap my arms around me. And I would. I would if I could, but with that soul-trap around his neck, my father owns me. "He'd kill me if I even think about it."

"He has to get to you first," Keir points out.

I rake my fingers through my hair. This is a nightmare. Because he tempts me so. "You don't understand. He doesn't have to find me. He doesn't have to get to me. He can kill me with a single snap of his fingers at any time he chooses."

Keir goes still. The dragon's a dangerous presence lurking behind amber eyes. "How?"

I shake my head. This isn't happening. This is surreal. I can't believe he *still* thinks I'm the bride who was meant for him, even after everything I've said and done.

Dreams *don't* exist.

Fate isn't meant for girls like me.

"Please don't." I wrap my arms around myself. "I know what I am, Keir. I've made my peace with it. And while it's incredibly tempting, I'm a wraith. You're accepted within the Blessed courts now, but if you take me as your bride, you won't be."

"I don't give a fuck about their acceptance."

I meet his eyes. "I can't be what you want me to be."

Keir stares at me for long seconds before he sighs in surrender. "You're not merely a wraith, Zemira. You're fae too. And if you want the truth, I think your mother was of the Court of the Moon and Stars."

"*What?*"

The Court of the Moon and Stars is mere myth to most of the fae these days—though I *have* wondered whether my gifts came from there. Once upon a time it sat high in the Forbidden Mountains, a palace carved of alabaster that gleamed like the moon itself.

It was destroyed several decades ago by an avaricious king.

"Why would you say that?" I can't bear to sit still any longer and push off the bed. There's some escape in movement, in pacing—some escape from the emotion clawing its way up my throat. For as long as I can remember, my mother has been a mere shadow to me.

I don't know her name.

I don't know where she came from.

I don't know if she had sisters or brothers, or parents. Or if she liked cheese or blackberries or riding or painting. I don't know anything about her.

All I know is that she had eyes as clear as an alpine lake, just like mine.

And that she gave me three names.

She loved me. She loved me enough to name me true, according to the old ways. I have to believe that. I *have* to. But it's a knot that twines its way around my heart like strangler vines, because no one and nothing has ever loved me, and if I cling to that… then it makes the stone weight in my chest feel a little like a heart.

"Because the Queen of the Court of Moon and Stars was a Shadow Walker, just like you," he finally says. "It ran in her blood, and some say it's the reason her court was shattered. She had three daughters, each as fair and lovely as the others, and each one powerful and dangerous. Myrinda, Amithiele, and Zyra Starsworn."

My breath catches as he conjures a ball of light into his hands. Movement swirls within it as it spins, letting shadows dapple over the walls. It's like a snow globe. A child's snow globe. But it's not glass. No. It's a dream. A fragment in time, captured within a tiny pocket realm and fused into the shape of a globe.

Three fae women appear.

One is blonde and lovely, clad in a gown that shimmers like the moon off the waters of a lake. The second has her ashen hair bound into a braid, and her earrings are little daggers. There's no mercy in her face, and the sword at her hip has a moonstone set into the pommel. But it's the last one that captures my attention.

The one with hair like spun starlight, clad strictly in black leather with a hunting bow at her side.

The one with the emblem of a slashing hawk carved into her belt.

"The Starsworn," he whispers, and the other two women vanish like smoke as he forces the third princess to lengthen until I might as well be looking in a mirror.

All I can see is her face, lovely and dangerous.

Something hot slides down my cheek as I reach for her. The second my fingertips touch her cheek, she's gone, ghosting into mist. The globe dissipates.

But for a second, I felt her.

And I saw her eyes widen as if somewhere—long ago —she felt a phantom caress on her face.

"Why did you show me that?" Rage and sadness threaten to overwhelm me.

"Because Raesh is but one half of you, Zemira. It's the only half you know. But you are fae too. You were born under an ancient moon, and you have the stars in your blood. You were made of the shadows, and you have the power of an ancient fae queen thrumming through you."

He reaches toward me. "Do you know why King Ryddhaen broke the Court of Moon and Stars? It's because the queens that ruled there were powerful beyond belief. Thousands of years ago, a long-ago fae queen found a fallen star high on the mountains, where she eventually made her court. The stories say she swallowed it, and nine months later she gave birth to a daughter who glowed like the stars and had the power to shift the tides themselves. You are a child of that bloodline, made of starshine and shadows. You are unmatched by any among the Blessed courts."

"I am also a child of darkness and despair," I breathe.

His face is merciless. "Yes. You are."

My heart sinks like a stone.

"You are darkness and you are light, and if you could ever bring yourself to accept the entirety of your nature, then even your father would fear you. You could kiss the stars themselves, Zemira, if only you would let yourself."

"And you?" I whisper.

"Me?"

"Would you fear me too?"

A dangerous glint comes into his eyes. "I fear nothing, my lady of starlight. I never have, and I never will." Flames suddenly flicker in his eyes. "Because I am Fire and Fury, and if I were to ever unleash myself from these mortal trappings, then the very world would burn." He captures my chin. "I do not fear you, Zemira. Even though you could be my undoing."

No matter how much I try, I can't stop the violence

trembling within me. "If you continue to offer me such terms then I *will* be your undoing." My throat goes dry. "He'll kill you, Keir. My father will kill you. No." I turn for the wash chambers, desperately needing a moment alone. "This is all we can ever be."

15

I know what I have to do now.

I Sift along the hallways of the court, searching for my target. I checked on Keir before I left and found him sleeping, which means this is the perfect opportunity to take. My heart might be in turmoil, but my head is clear.

I can feel her, deep in my heart, stirring, reach for me—

It feels like days of mulling over the court, the gossip, the rumors and lies, has finally cleared the mess in my head.

Malechus has spent the days hunting and drinking, and the night's debauching himself in his private grotto. I can't get into his bedchambers, and there's no sign of Soraya in the rest of the court, but there's one place I haven't looked for her.

The grotto.

It's an old sunken limestone cave that's been turned into a garden of sorts. Thousands of candles are tucked in nooks and crannies around the walls, and thick vines tumble from the roof. The floor is a carpet of moss and night-blooming flowers, and a little brook babbles somewhere in the distance. Ancient stone sarcophagi line the room. The stone is so old the symbols on them are rubbed bare, but they don't seem like anything I've seen before. Someone whispered that they were the tombs of ancient dragon kings, long since turned to stone, and I haven't dared asked Keir about it. There was rumor that they opened one of the tombs last night, just to check, and the enormous vault was empty, except for an eerie puff of dust that was unleashed when they levered the lid off it.

Malechus's debaucheries aren't for the faint of heart.

I've seen the masked recipients coming and going— always from a distance—and there are rumors that Malechus simply pours the rapture on the nearest table and lets his guests fight for it.

A young brunette casts her mask free as she tumbles into the arms of a naked faun, the pair of them vanishing into one of those hidden chambers that line the grotto. Snatching her mask before it hits the ground, I Sift into the shadows and then step out of them. Binding her mask around my face, I check the position of my knives, before I steal a wineglass from a passing tray with no intention of touching it.

I swirl the wine, breathing it in as though I know the difference between whether the berries that brewed it came from the mountainous slopes of the Shadowfangs, or whether it's low country swill.

Really though, I'm testing for poison.

It's one of Soraya's favorite weapons and we spent our

youths tasting poisons and antidotes. Even over the scent of a cloying wine I can pick out the faintest hint of hensbane or wolf fever, but this is innocent enough. Adding a little saunter to my stride, I step into the light and join the party. Instantly the music assails me.

Clear head. Clear heart. Clear eyes.

I'm going to need it.

I know she's here.

I've sensed it ever since I woke to that dream.

Malechus stalks into the grotto, his chest bare and a long black silk robe falling from his shoulders. A pair of loose silk trousers hangs low on his hips. It should look ridiculous, but there's something about the way he moves that makes me suspect he could wear a jester's bells and still pull it off. Dozens of hands reach for him, and the fae cry out in welcome.

Gorgeous golden sigils are tattooed across his chest. I recognize a crescent moon, a sun, a spear, dozens of others....

"Every single one of those marks represents a fae house that he's destroyed," whispers a woman beside me, clearly following my gaze.

"Someone's ambitious." There are dozens of them.

"Hungry," she says, watching Malechus with the same blaze of need in her eyes. But I half suspect she doesn't desire his body—only his throat. "He was born hungry, that one." Her mouth twists. "Though some say his father drove him to it."

It's not the first time I've heard of tensions between the king and his son. "Oh?"

The woman smirks and drinks a mouthful of her wine.

"His older brother was stronger than he was, and the king spent years pitting them against each other for his love."

"That doesn't sound like love to me."

The woman takes her first full look at me, as if surprised to find someone so naïve here. "Well, the brother's dead now. Hunting accident, they say. Though Malechus *is* fond of his hunting…. Now they say he's starting to see a crown in his future."

"Is that why the king's not here?"

"The king wants no part of this mockery. He cast Belladonna out of his court long ago."

Again, I'm missing threads. But I don't say it this time. "Have you placed a bet on whether the wedding will take place yet?"

"My money's on Belladonna," the woman replies. "I hope she takes them all out. She's earned a little peace and quiet."

I stare at Malechus. "Oh, I think she's making plans to that end. I just hope he's not going to present too large an obstacle."

The woman laughs as if I'd said something incredibly droll, before she walks away.

A golden statue moves next to me, and I nearly leap out of my skin.

No. Not a statue. A fae youth.

Naked. Painted gold from head-to-toe. Even his lashes and hair clump together, as if he's been gilded. The shock of the whites of his eyes and his blue irises is a little eerie, but he presents a tray of goblets to me.

I shake my head and circle the room. One thing is

becoming clear. Malechus likes his displays. Everything screams of excessive wealth and power. Who imports a white hart all the way from the fens? Who unwraps an ancient dragon king, just to see if he's turned to stone?

I'm finally starting to put all of the pieces of the puzzle together.

Mistmark claimed the horn when it crossed his lands.

Malechus wanted it.

And so, what? He threatens war? *No.* The Court of Storms is dangerous enough that even Malechus wouldn't dare cross its king. And then there's his father, who considers his ambitions dangerous enough that he'd quash even the merest notion of war.

The king would not dare let his son come into possession of an army.

I rub my temples as I rest my back against the grotto wall. I think this is all a power play. Malechus doesn't have the strength to stand against his father, but if he gets his hands on the horn, he will wield the Wild Hunt. He can challenge his father. Kill him. Take his crown.

But the question always came back to: How did he force Mistmark into marriage?

What did he use against the lord in order to blackmail him?

It had to be something Mistmark would kill to get his hands on.

I already thought I'd found her, a long time ago....

My breath eases out slowly. It all comes down to Soraya.

My sister is missing—the same sister who lost more

than her killer's touch when she was sent to kill Mistmark, the same sister who won't even breathe so much as a hint of his name.

Malechus has her, I'll bet every coin in the treasury on it.

And he's using her to blackmail Mistmark.

There are still so many unanswered questions—how did Malechus even know my sister would blunder into his court?—and yet my head is spinning as it all locks into place.

"Every time I see you, you look so melancholy," says a cool voice.

As if summoned, Malechus swims into view, watching me with those shark's eyes.

"Have you tired of your prince?" he asks. "Are you come to try something new?"

I can't stop my knife from slipping from my sleeve and finding welcome in the warmth of my hand. He sees it too, and his lips quirk. "Perhaps I was curious," I tell him. "But you will keep your distance."

"I'm not here to harm you," he murmurs.

"No? You certainly had no compunctions about sending your little handmaid to do your bidding the other night."

"Handmaid?" His eyebrow arches. And then comprehension dawns. "Ah, you think her mine. Alas, my dearest Rhea has found another master who suits her purposes. Or should I say, 'mistress.'"

He smirks at me as if he knows something I don't know.

I think of every time I've seen Rhea.

Ismena is always nearby, and Ismena hates me.

Maybe he's telling the truth. Maybe he merely came along and took advantage of my rapture-addled state. Maybe he didn't plan it.

"I was wondering if you'd ever win free of Keir." He prowls closer. "He's so protective of you, my sweet. It must be chafing. But then, what is it they say? Keep your enemies close?"

I run my tongue over my teeth. I need to play this right. "Sometimes. But sometimes I like knowing he gets jealous."

"Such a cruel game you play," he whispers.

"Aren't they all?"

A smile.

"A gift for you," he murmurs, conjuring four long thin hair needles out of nowhere. He certainly wasn't hiding them behind his robe.

"For *me*?"

A denial dies on the tip of my tongue as I catch a glimpse of the little jeweled ornaments on the end of them. A crescent moon adorns the largest. The other three are glittering stars, encrusted with tiny crushed diamonds.

"For you," he murmurs. "For you shine the brightest of any here."

Now I know he's full of shit. As amazing as I am, the women here are beautiful. "That's so sweet of you."

Circling around behind me, he slides the first pin into the hair twisted on top of my head. "Sweet. Now I know you're mocking me." Another pin. "Does it amuse you to have two powerful princes chasing after you?"

"Are there two of them?" Even though my voice

sounds flirtatious, I can't quite manage to soothe the tension from my shoulders. He's right behind me with a weapon in hand.

"There could be." Another pin. And then the final one, sliding into place within my hair a little painfully. He strokes a strand of hair over my shoulders. "Where *has* he been hiding you?"

"Keir?" I take a nervous sip of my elderberry wine, then force myself to spit it back into my glass before he notices. It's not every day a girl finds herself the center of a prince's attention and I'm not fool enough to think this has anything to do with me.

No. Malechus is playing games.

I'm just the pawn he's using to take a tilt at Keir.

Something about Keir unnerves him.

"He's kept you from every court in the land," Malechus muses. "Just think of all you've missed out on because of him."

Murderous fae. Blood curses. Overly ambitious predators. Oh, yes, such a shame. "Maybe His Highness makes up for it in other ways."

His smile is dangerous and knowing. "You remind me of someone."

"Was she beautiful?"

He leans closer, forcing me to put my back against the wall in order to maintain some semblance of distance. Over his shoulder I catch a glimpse of the room. He's managed to herd me away from others quite nicely. "She was beautiful." There's hunger roughening his voice as he slips the sleeve from my shoulder. "But better yet, she belonged to another and I wanted her. I like taking what I want."

Pressing a finger to his chest I arch a brow. "Then your father should have taught you to share better. Being the bone caught between two dogs is hardly flattering, Your Highness."

His hand curls around my wrist. "Only when you think you're the one with the leash in hand, is it?"

There it is.

The glimpse of something ugly in his face that I saw the other night.

This seductive tease is nothing more than a mask for his true intentions.

"Tsk, tsk, Malechus." A voice calls out. "Chasing sloppy seconds again?"

The Lord of Mistmark appears, winding his way between sarcophagi. Falion lurks at his heels like a watchful hound.

A muscle in Malechus's jaw ticks, and then he pushes away from me, his brow clearing of any irritation. "Ah, my reluctant groom. I didn't expect to see you here. I thought you disdained such attractions."

"I find them tedious." The look Mistmark gives me, however, is anything but bored. He's clearly curious as to why I'm here, and perhaps asking if I want to *be* here. "I find the entire affair tedious."

"Ah, yes." Malechus slinks toward him. "But the game is nearly done."

"Mmm, perhaps." Mistmark tugs his sleeve into place. "I do like your ambitions, however. It wasn't enough to merely cross me, but now you're going to take a tilt at Keir? My, my, someone has grown bold." He looks at me directly. "You ought to leave, my lady. This isn't a place for you."

"Oh, I don't know." I smile at him. "All the dangly bits painted gold are kind of interesting to look at."

Falion stares at me as if he can't quite work out what type of woman I am.

"Falion will escort you," Mistmark says, and Falion's head tracks toward him as if to say *when-the-sun-shines-in-the-Shadow-Lands*.

"That's very kind of—" There's a hissing sound across the grotto.

A trio of rambunctious fae have levered open one of the sarcophagi and are peering inside it. One of them screams as if he sees something staring back at him, and then he tumbles inside the enormous casket.

"Those fucking *morons*." Malechus's face goes white with rage. "Do they have any idea what they're doing? There are dragon spirits leashed into that stone—"

The sarcophagi simply explodes outward.

Falion's eyes widen and then he slams into Mistmark, wrapping his arms around him before they both vanish. I stagger to my knees behind one of the remaining sarcophagi, with Malechus—of all fae—shoving my head down.

Screams echo through the grotto. And then laughter. Malechus, however, is not laughing.

"Stay here," he growls, pushing to his feet and stalking in the direction of the explosion.

They're... gone.

Not merely across the cavern. But gone. Completely. Out of line of sight.

Falion Sifted him somewhere beyond this room, which was, until this point, something I considered impossible.

I gape at the room, slowly lowering my arms.

One of the wreaths is on fire. The grotto is mayhem. Half naked males and females spill from small nooks, clutching arms across breasts and buttocks. Malechus strides through it all, seemingly intent upon murder.

I couldn't get a better distraction if I'd tried.

I CIRCLE ONE OF THE ENORMOUS COFFINS, THE ONE THAT calls to me the most.

It occurred to me that there's one place to hide someone right out in the open, when you don't want them found. Somewhere that you can keep a close eye on your prisoner. Somewhere that nobody would ever be able to escape from.

A stone tomb, built to house a dragon's spirit.

I press my hand against the stone and lean my forehead there.

"*Forever*," Soraya whispers in my memories as she slices her dagger across the palm of her hand, forcing blood to well. "*You and I against the world forever.*"

We bound ourselves to each other that long-ago night.

The link between us is still there, buried deep in my heart and chained down by treachery.

I reach for it and metaphysically dust it off, and on the

inside of the sarcophagus I swear I feel her suck in a sharp breath as if she feels it too.

That son of a bitch.

Keep your enemies close indeed.

Now how the fuck am I going to get this cursed thing open?

"Soraya?" I whisper through the stone.

I've tried everything I could to shift the lid. The sheer weight of it is impossible to move, and the distraction across the grotto will only last so long. Which means the only way I'm getting through it is by using my magic.

I pace around the sarcophagus.

Falion Sifted beyond sight.

But how? How did he do it?

Pressing my hand against the sarcophagus, I try to reach through it the way I reach through shadows. Nothing. Nothing but cold stone against my touch.

I can't help thinking about the first time I ever Sifted.

My two foster brothers hurled me over the lip of a well, and I woke up in a nearby forest.

Nearly a mile away.

I did it once.

But how?

I was four. I can't even remember what I was thinking that day. It's my first formative memory, but it's as shadowy around the edges as the gloom that fills this room.

The well. Strong hands levering me over the edge.

"We're done feeding you, you little bitch," my eldest brother said.

I can't even remember his name.

But Riori? I remember him. I remember that you never dared allow yourself to be alone in a room with him, and as he held me over the edge of the well, he leaned close enough to whisper, *"I hear you sniveling at night. You're scared of the dark, aren't you? Well, this ends in darkness, you little bastard. And the only people who will hear you scream are the two of us. The well monster's going to feed well tonight."*

And then he lets me go as he laughed.

That day filled my nightmares for years. Sometimes I wonder if my recollections of it are even real, or whether they've become some twisted amalgamation of my dreams.

I fell for what seemed forever.

And then the icy shock of cold water swallowed me whole.

I couldn't swim.

It was so dark down there I could barely breathe.

I thrashed, and I screamed, and I looked for them, but all I could make out was a thin circle of light above me, with two dark heads peering over the lip of it before I went under again.

And then something touched my foot.

Something cold and slimy curled around my ankle, like a bony hand that was half-rotted.

"You're not the first brat we've fed to the well," Riori said as he dragged me out of the hut. *"You're finally going to go meet the rest of our brothers and sisters."*

I screamed and screamed and screamed.

Please. Please!

A glowing hand reached out to me, plunging through the dark waters like a full moon rising.

"My little girl," whispered a voice in my head, *"if you ever need me, reach for me. I'll be there for you. I promise. I love you… I love you…."*

I took that hand, and it felt like a doorway opened within my mind. I finally fell through it.

And then I was sobbing in the forest and that door was still open somehow, an invisible hand stroking through my hair before the sensation faded and a pair of dry leaves skittering over my skin as the wind stirred them.

My eyes blink open, and I'm standing in front of the sarcophagus.

I'd forgotten about that hand, that voice….

I Sifted beyond sight that first time.

Yanking my hands off the stone, I strip the glamor from my skin and stare as a faint luminescence bleeds through. I've spent my entire life hiding that light. It's a dangerous kind of weakness to show before my wraithen brothers and sisters.

Before my king….

Swallowing hard, I curl my fingers around the glow. Spears of light stab through my clenched fingers. I don't know what it means. I don't know what any of it means.

But there's one thing that's starting to embed itself in

my mind: Shadow is the absence of light. Light is the death of shadow.

What if I was able to manipulate more than mere shadow?

You are not merely wraithenkind, Zemira....

I let the light escape along with the exhale of my breath. Even if I am half fae, there's nothing for me in this world. My ghostly pale skin sees to that. I can hide it behind glamor, but I'll always be hiding it. I would be forever living a lie, no matter how much I yearn for that lie.

There is no place of acceptance here, even if I wish I could escape my father's court....

The only one who has ever accepted me—betrayals or no betrayals—is entombed alive within this sarcophagus.

Soraya is all that matters. I'll need her if I'm going to be able to pull off this heist.

Or maybe I just need her.

It's a bitter antidote to swallow.

I place my hands on the stone again.

And this time I push through them.

Soraya. Soraya. Soraya. I try and channel that focus, that desperation I had the first time I Sifted beyond my limits. Darkness flickers in and out of my mind—there's something....

There.

I plunge through the sarcophagus, and then I'm tumbling onto a warm body.

"What the fuck?" Soraya bursts out, grabbing me by the wrists.

I'm groggy and disorientated, but I have precisely

two seconds to remember she's an assassin and will probably take to my sudden appearance in a similar way to a sleeping cat that's suddenly had a dog thrown upon it.

"It's me!" I hiss as she wrestles with me. "Soraya! It's me!"

Harsh gasps burst through the small space as she freezes. "Z?"

I wilt against her. "Hold tight." There are chains around her wrist. "I need to pick these locks."

She clutches my hands as I pick the manacles, her breath coming loudly in the dark.

The dark.

She hates that I know this, but she always sleeps with a faint light because she's afraid of the dark.

"Did Malechus talk you into these shackles, or did he actually fool you? Because I'm going to be very disappointed if you fell prey to the crown prince of the Blood Court," I tell her in a conversational tone.

"How did you find me?" she snaps. "What are you doing here? You were in the—"

"Abyss?" I finally get the second lock open. "Apparently Father was getting a little concerned that you weren't checking in. He sent me in to finish what you started."

"What I started?" I can't see her in the dark, but I know her head just whipped toward me. The movement throws me forward until I have a knee in her thigh. "But you're not...."

"Not what?"

"Goddess's breath, are you done?" she grinds out. "There's not enough air in here for two."

I was hoping she'd spill her secret mission, but it appears she's starting to think again.

"I'm done." I slip the lockpick back into my belt and curl up against her side. "Just how much do you want to get out of here?"

"What do you mean?" And then she stills. "How did you intend to get me out?"

"That's the problem. I can't lift the lid—"

"*Zemira.*"

"Just hold still. Really still." I let my body relax, melting into shadows. But this time, I hold myself right on the edge between corporeal and incorporeal.

Falion did it.

He took Mistmark into the Sift—an act I'd previously believed was impossible. And while Mistmark didn't look too happy about it, I have to presume he was still in one piece when he arrived.

"Don't you dare." Soraya stiffens. "Zemira. Zemira! Have you ever done this before?"

"Sshh."

The bond between us flickers to light. *There.* There she is. I feel her flesh, feel her breath in her lungs, her heart racing. I sense her eyes going wide, and then I plunge us both into the Between.

A single second that stretches to an eternity.

I don't think I could do this if we weren't bound by blood.

We burst onto the flagstones of the grotto floor, and Soraya scrambles out of my arms, whipping a knife into her hand and staring at me with wild eyes. It's one of her little tricks: It doesn't matter whether she's been unarmed, she can always Summon a weapon when she needs to.

"What the fuck did you just do?"

Her words are a slap in the face. So much for the warm welcome, the gratitude. "I'm fairly certain I just rescued you."

"*Rescued* me?"

Soraya's stern façade lasts all of a half second, before she's paling. "I think I'm going to be sick."

And then the staggers for the nearest statue and vomits behind it.

"So MALECHUS GOT THE JUMP ON YOU, HUH?" I RUB HER back after she spends fifteen minutes retching into an urn. I hauled her into the hallway and well away from the grotto before Malechus could deal with his fire. Now we're sitting in some underground room somewhere, that might have once been a cellar. "You got sloppy."

Soraya sits back on her heels, scrubbing at her mouth. "If I didn't still feel like I'd been turned inside-out and then put back together again, I would punch you."

"Please. You'd have to catch me first. And you can't even do that when you're at your best. Also, you're welcome. I saved your ass. I'll accept any favors and gratitude you can throw my way."

Soraya shoots me a murderous look.

The last time we confronted each other, she was glamored to look like me as she tried to drive her knife into Keir's chest and steal the amulet around his throat. We both thought it was the relic our father was looking for, and she double-crossed me at the last second.

It's not the first time.

It won't be the last.

And yet, despite everything, it's good to see her again. She's the one constant in my life, and even if we're often at odds, if some outside force wants to harm one of us, he'll have the other to deal with.

"You look better than I would have expected, considering you were in the Abyss for three months," she says gruffly.

"You look like shit."

Soraya shudders. "Some asshole just pulled me straight through a stone sarcophagus. All I can taste is bile and granite. What did you expect?"

"My abject apologies. The only person I know who might be able to lift the lid probably has you high on his kill-on-sight list. I went with the only option I thought might be able to work."

At that, her gaze sharpens. "What are you doing here? Who are you with? What does Father want?"

"What he always wants. A means to break the curse. He wants the Horn of Shadows. And I'm here with Prince Keir—"

"Keir?" She actually pales a little.

I can't resist a smile. "Nearly seven feet of furious, slightly-territorial fae prince? You might remember him from that time you tried to cut his heart out of his chest. *He* certainly remembers it."

"And you're working *with* him?"

"He wants the horn too. It seemed an easy way to get into the Court of Blood."

"Yes, because that's exactly what I'd call him—easy. Cauldron's piss," she growls, "were you even *thinking*? What were you going to do? Use him to get in, bat your lashes at him a few times and then double cross him the second you caught a glimpse of the horn? Because I'm fairly certain that's how you played it last time, and as far as I recall, it left you hanging in chains in the Abyss. He's not going to fall for the same ruse. I don't even think he fell for it the first time."

My conscience chooses that moment to replay the look Keir gave me the second he realized I wasn't there to become his bride—but to betray him.

I've taken a knife to the chest a few times and that look felt exactly the same.

I can't let her see it though, so my voice is all mock bravado. "If he's foolish enough to trust me twice, then he'll get what he deserves—"

"Or he's playing his own game."

There's nothing I can do except shrug, because I know she's speaking the truth. I haven't figured out what stakes he's playing for, but Keir definitely has some kind of game in play. "Most likely. But until we find the horn, the point is neither here nor there. We're using each other, we're both aware of it, and now that I've dragged your sorry ass out of your stone prison, I'm about to put the winning piece on the board. I just need one or two pieces of information."

She rolls her eyes. "What?"

"Who did Father send you to kill?"

A hint of steel settles over her expression. "Mistmark."

"That makes no sense. You've tried before." I watch her expression closely, because this is Soraya's weak spot. I don't know how. I don't know what happened exactly. But I do know she squirms like a worm on the hook whenever his name is mentioned. "You failed. And why would Father send you to the Court of Blood? How did he know Mistmark would even be here?"

She throws her hands in the air. "Ruhle said Mistmark was arriving for a tense negotiation with Malechus. I wasn't in a position to argue."

And there it is....

"Ruhle," I whisper. "He's the one who brought the information to Father. He's the one who set this game in play."

Soraya flexes her knuckles as though she's thinking about conjuring a weapon. "You think Ruhle set this up? But why? We're the ones in the field. If one of *us* brings the horn to Father...."

We'll be the heroes. Not him.

I can't stop my feet from pacing.

A thousand thoughts misfire through my brain. "Maybe he thinks he'll earn his way into Father's good graces for the sake of the information." No, that makes no sense. Father doesn't give credit to those who sit back and wait. He urges for us to strike and strike hard. He admires bravery, fierceness, courage and determination.

But he also admires manipulation.

Play the game right, and you earn a pat on the back. Play it wrong, and you're right back there in the Abyss.

I think of everything I know about Ruhle and his seven

wraith lackeys.

"If Ruhle set this into play then he's waiting for us to retrieve the horn," I say. "He'll hit us hard the second we get our hands on it. Then *he* delivers it to Father." I frown. "But why… why didn't he send you straight for Mistmark? Why make the play here? At the Court of Blood? If Mistmark had the horn, then why this elaborate ruse to draw him out of his castle?"

Once again, there's a flicker of some unknown emotion in her eyes. "It's not that easy getting into Mistmark's castle. Or getting out."

"Well, yes, I have met Falion."

She scowls. "So have I. Indeed, I promised him a reckoning should we meet again. But Falion's not… he's not the only weapon Mistmark has up his sleeve. The castle… it exists within an Other World, outside of time. He makes the rules there. He controls the entire castle. It's shrouded in mist, and it's hard to gauge sound and sight within those mists. There's also something that hunts the forest around the castle. To make it past both…."

"How'd you get in?"

Soraya snorts. "Damsel in distress. How else? I appealed to his sense of mercy. When I 'woke' I was tucked carefully in his bed with a healer hovering over me."

In his bed? *Interesting.* But there's no point dwelling on that. I feel like there's a knot within this chain of thought that needs to be untethered. "Mistmark's impossible to breach. Ruhle knows Father wants the horn. But how did he know that Mistmark would leave the castle?

What did Malechus have on Mistmark in order to draw him out?"

This time, I'm not mistaking the heat in Soraya's cheeks. She glances to the side angrily.

"*You*." It's all starting to make sense. "You were the prize Malechus used in order to get his hands on Mistmark. He blackmailed him—marriage to Belladonna and the bridal tithe paid in exchange for you." *But how did he...?* A thought occurs. A terrible thought. "Ruhle's working *with* Malechus."

It's the only way Malechus would have known that Mistmark swore bloody vengeance upon my sister.

Maybe the Blood Prince doesn't know who our brother is. Maybe they struck a deal. Maybe they think they're going to double-cross each other. But there's no other way that Malechus would have known what Soraya meant to Mistmark unless that information came from within the wraithen court.

"Falion's the only other one who had that knowledge," Soraya counters.

"Falion's tongue is so far up Mistmark's ass, I don't think he would ever betray him."

Soraya cuts me a dangerous look. "I haven't seen a single glimpse of Ruhle or one of his little lickspittles."

It doesn't mean he's not pulling strings behind the scenes. "If he's here, then this game has more moving parts than either of us can handle."

I don't like the odds stacked against me. Father. Keir. Mistmark and Falion. Malechus. Ruhle.

Not to mention a certain vicious Blood Court princess whose curse is currently weaving its talons into my heart.

"The horn's somewhere here at court." Regardless of whether Malechus or Ruhle are the ones behind this ploy, they've managed the set up the play quite neatly. A little thrill runs through me. A means to steal the fucking thing right out from under their noses. "Malechus is watching both Keir and Mistmark. Falion's out there somewhere, and he doesn't like Malechus either. I don't know what Belladonna wants, but I think she'll take the chance to stab her cousin in the back if she gets one. And none of them will work with Ruhle. If he truly *is* behind all of this, then he's going to have to keep his head low."

"What are you thinking?"

"Father wants the horn. Ruhle wants us both dead. Malechus and Belladonna have both attempted to kill us. And I don't know what Mistmark wants with you, but he ventured out of his locked vault of a castle in order to get his hands on you. It's all leverage." I meet her eyes. "I can't negotiate this mess by myself." It's a breathless realization. Once more, my back is against the wall. "And you're wanted by at least three men."

Soraya looks speculative. "What do you have in mind?"

I can feel the hungry edge to my smile. "Easy. Like I said, the horn's right here. Falion hinted that it's in the maze somewhere. He gave Mistmark a piece of paper—it might be a map. I'll slip into his rooms and search for the paper. Then you and I are going to steal the horn. And we're going to play the others off against each other in order to do so."

The hardest part about managing this entire scenario is a certain handsome dragon.

I keep my thoughts close to my chest all day, dressing for the final ball, my skirts whispering around my ankles. Tomorrow is the wedding. It will all be over then.

Keir catches sight of me as I walk into our shared antechamber. The sight of those hungry, hungry eyes makes my stomach drop. I pleaded a headache this morning, but I know he can sense something is wrong.

"How are you feeling?" he murmurs, his gaze sliding slowly over me.

It's not real.

It can't be real.

I don't know what I'm going to do.

Steal the horn. Break the curse. Betray.... My thoughts eddy away into pathetic little undercurrents. It was so much easier when I hadn't come to know him.

I like him. Too much.

I could love him, if I let myself.

"Nervous," I admit, my voice barely more than a whisper. "Tomorrow is the last day we have up our sleeves in order to kill Mistmark, or else—"

"We'll break the curse," he growls, taking my hands between his and warming them. "I've been thinking about Belladonna. You're right. I can't kill her. And we can't kill Mistmark—"

"Somewhat of a conundrum," I point out.

"But we don't have to," he says slowly. "We just have to make it *look* like he dies."

My heart goes still.

There's a ringing silence in my ears.

"What do you mean?" I breathe the words out.

"I'm the Prince of Dreams. I can craft illusions so beautifully they almost seem real. Tomorrow, I'll simply make it look like Mistmark dies, right in front of everyone. The second Belladonna breaks the curse she's woven around you, the truth can be revealed."

I tug my hands free. "Are you going to let Mistmark in on this secret? Or Falion?"

His jaw tightens and he gives an imperceptible shake of his head. "I cannot. They cannot know what sort of powers I have."

And for him to wield them in front of the entire court is a huge risk.

"What if someone sees?" I hiss. "What if someone guesses what you are?"

"I'll deal with that if the matter arises."

"Keir, *no*. It's too great a risk."

"We don't have another choice," he says bluntly.

My mouth drops open, but… he's right. The only other

option is to kill Mistmark and—

Kill Mistmark. That's it.

My stomach falls to my feet. Keir's right. We just need it to look like Mistmark dies. And I need…. "Fine," I force the word past my lips. "We'll play it your way. An illusion to make it look like Mistmark is dead. Break the curse. And then we steal the horn."

Keir gives a clipped nod and then offers me his arm. "One last ball. Are you ready?"

"For this to all be over." I rest my hand on the muscled flex of his arm. "Yes."

And no.

Because once this is over, I don't know if I'll ever see him again.

~

The skies open up as we make our way toward the enormous orangery that stands in the heart of the maze. There are guards along our path, all of them carrying torches. One or two servants have disappeared during the maze this week, and I think Malechus is taking all precautions.

Of course, he's probably not aware there's a questing beast lurking within it.

The glasshouse is where the final ball will be taking place, though Malechus hasn't counted on the weather obeying his commands.

"Under here," Keir says, tugging me beneath an enormous oak as the winds whip at my skirts.

In the distance, lights gleam within the orangery.

Malechus will be there. Mistmark. Belladonna. All of them playing one last game....

Keir peers out to check the skies, as if to see if they're going to let up long enough for us to make a run across the last stretch of grass. My silvery skirts are already spattered dark gray in patches, and though he shielded me with his coat as we ran, my hair is a mess.

I press a hand to his chest. His heart is beating steadily, but the look he gives me is anything but steady.

And I can't stop myself from asking, "Why do you want the cauldron so badly?" It can't be power. He was born a dragon king. According to the stories, he gave most of his power up, gifting it to the cauldron in order to bring peace between the fae and dragonkind.

Keir gives the clearing a savage look, his answer clear. *Not here*. Not where there are so many listening ears.

"The folly," I say, tilting my head.

Away from the glasshouse.

Away from the ball.

Away from the politicking and backstabbing, and the tremulous threads of betrayal sweeping me toward a final, treacherous conclusion.

Keir tugs me out from under cover. We run through the rain, my heels sinking into the lawn and rain slicking my gown to my skin. I can't stop myself from laughing breathlessly.

"This way," Keir yells, hauling me to the left.

There's a folly there.

One crafted of scrolled iron and glass. Several fae lanterns hang in the rafters, and wisteria curls its way around the iron. The firefly flicker of light hovers around several bunches of its flowers; Will O' the Wisps humming like fat bumblebees in the night as they steal nectar from the flowers.

The night is still and humid around us. All the other guests seem to have fled in the direction of the orangery.

We're alone. In the dark.

Alone and somehow, I've never felt more vulnerable.

Rain glides down the glass ceiling above us. A Will O' the Wisp drifts past Keir's shoulder, highlighting the stark planes of his cheekbones and those hungry eyes. His black lashes are clumped together with the wet, and the effect only makes those amber pupils more hypnotic.

Hunger darkens his eyes.

He traces the glyphs marked into my arm with his magic, and as his finger strokes down my clammy skin I shiver. Each rune is the promise of a single day that I owe him. A year and a day of service. Every morning I wake there's one less rune.

And maybe I'm a fool, because there's a little part of me that mourns their loss.

Once they're gone, he'll be out of my life.

A complication I never wanted.

A dream I don't dare dream.

As though it has a mind of its own, my hand lifts to his cheek, palm scraping over the roughened stubble of his jaw. His hyphen mouth rarely shows softness, but as his lips part I'm caught in the yearning that fills his gaze.

Neither of us dares exhale.

"Tell me what you're hiding from." His voice roughens. "Tell me why you won't give yourself to me fully. I know you want me. I can feel it in every breath you take, in every look you give me.... But something holds you back. Who? What?"

The words shatter the spell he wove.

Here I was, thinking about how that mouth would taste and his entire focus is upon unearthing my secret.

You're such a fucking fool for him....

I turn away, scraping the wet hair from my temples. "I told you...."

"Nothing," he grates out, stalking after me. "You've told me nothing. All I know is that you were working for the Wraith King, and you're *still* working for him." His face darkens. "You have no intention of leaving his court, do you?"

It's not as simple as that. My soul.... "I'm not fae, Keir." I hold up my hands, letting the faint illumination spill through me. Suddenly I'm a firefly in the night, a pearlescent glow. It's getting easier and easier to let my inner light shine through. "I don't belong here. I'll never belong here and you—"

"You belong with me." There's a dangerous edge to his expression as he steps closer. Every inch of his shirt clings to his skin, lovingly caressing the hard muscles of his chest. "You are mine, Mira. You said you were mine."

Those words.... They do their own sort of damage. And the worst thing is, for a second I want it. I want to lean into him, let him claim me.

But if I do that, then I'm nothing more than another pawn.

He will own me, the same way my father does.

"It was just one night," I whisper.

"It was more than that." His glare is furious. "*Mine.* You said you were mine."

"Did you ever think that maybe I want to belong to myself?" I snap, shoving at his chest. He doesn't move an inch, and it feels like slamming up against a stone wall. Inexorable. I push against his chest again. Again. Until he captures my wrists and shackles them there, forcing my fingers wide over his pectorals. A shiver runs through me. "I've never had true freedom." I look up, into shockingly bright eyes. "Even now, I can't escape you until you allow me to."

A hand locks around my nape and then he's hauling me toward him. I spin into his arms as his mouth locks over mine.

Claimed.

A gasp escapes me.

It's a kiss forged of desperation and fury. A kiss designed to punish. I can taste his anger and his unspoken demand in the heated lash of his tongue, in the bruising crush of his mouth. *Mine.* The sheer possession inherent in the way he cups my skull speaks its own language, and for a second, just one second, every inch of me yearns to submit to him. All I want is bare skin under my hands, even if it will cost me. Even if this one night of bliss will only chew me up and spit me back out into a world where I'm fighting to find my feet again.

Because it will.

This doesn't exist beyond tomorrow. Soraya's setting everything in place. She and I have been over the plan so many fucking times that it's imprinted into my brain.

There's just this one last fucking obstacle—and that's

the stupid, wretched weakness in my chest. The way my heart skips a beat when his palms skate up my flanks.

Once more, I promise myself. Just one more time. He'll never forgive me, but maybe I can give him this. Maybe I can steal just a moment of happiness for myself. No pros. No cons. Just pleasure.

The moment his tongue strokes against mine, all the defiance melts out of me.

Fuck the gods. Fuck my father. Fuck this entire bloody situation.

I just want *him*.

"*Mira*." It's a breath. A curse. A plea. And I can't help thinking that maybe he's as trapped in this moment as I am. "Mira, what do you want?"

"You." I kiss him hard. "*Everything*." And then I'm laughing against his mouth. A bitter, wretched sound that cleaves my heart in two. "Everything that I can't have."

The silk of my dress tears beneath his hands. A gasp escapes me, but his hot mouth closes over my breast in that instant, and suddenly I don't want this to end.

I capture fistfuls of his wet hair, yanking his face up to mine. Our mouths meet again. Clash. Keir slides both hands over my ass and then hauls me into the air, my thighs closing around his hips. One step. Two. My back hits the column of the folly and I moan as he grinds against me.

He kisses his way down my stomach, fists bunching the wet fabric of my skirts around my thighs. *Gods*. I slide my fingers through his hair, arching my head back against the column as he finds me. Hot breath stirs over my damp skin and then the roughened graze of his stubble marks my thighs.

"You're so fucking stubborn," he growls.

"Why? Because I won't fall at your feet like every other pretty little fae princess in this fucking court? Sorry, Your Highness." I laugh. "I'm never going to be an easy conquest."

"There's just one problem with that little scenario...." He looks up the length of his body, his amber eyes feral with heated desire.

A shiver works its way through me. There's no hiding the dragon tonight. He wants me. He wants to claim me. To own me. "What little problem?"

Keir nuzzles against my thighs. "You keep thinking I'm a fae prince." His fingers dig into the back of my thighs. "I'm not fae, Mira. I was born of fire and fury. I was Named when this world was but a whisper in the ears of your fae ancestors. I owned these lands. I ruled this world. I was the creature that everything else feared. I hunted and I took, and I claimed. And while I'll play your little fae games, my love, you should know.... I took one look at you and I knew want for the first time in thousands of years. You were mine, promised to me by the stars themselves. I've spent millennia waiting for you and I'm not about to let you go now."

The words spill through me, carving themselves on my heart.

I don't know what to do with them. Or him. I never have and—

He captures my ass in his hands and then grinds his face into my wet flesh. His heated tongue spears within me, tearing a shocked cry from my lips. The hard steel of his hands are inescapable, but it's his tongue that wreaks the most damage. Driving into me. Stroking up in slow unhurried swipes, before he pauses to lazily trace little circles around my clit.

The world vanishes. Fractures. Reforms. All I can hear are the soft, breathy gasps that escape me. More. I want more. "Fuck. *Please.*"

"Beg me for release," he growls the words into my wet flesh. "Plead for mercy, Mira."

"*Please.*"

Pinning me against the column, he moves his mouth in lazy swirls, the rasp of his stubble marking my sensitive thighs. It's too much. Not enough. It feels as though he's settled in to feast and I need him to devour me whole.

"How much do you want me?" he demands.

"Fuck, please. Just do it." I curl my fists in his hair, losing all sense of composure. "Make me come."

Two fingers drive inside me. Then the soft pads of his fingertips are curling up, finding that spot deep inside me that will bring so much ruin. The hard suction of his mouth locks around me and then his tongue flickers lightly, teasing at me, driving me wild.

I grind into his face. So close.... So close. Panting. Gasping for breath. For release.

My spine arches, my fingernails digging into his scalp. It's as though he senses my urgency because every movement suddenly gains intensity.

"*Keir.*" Every inch of my spine arches as pleasure drives through me.

It's breathtaking. Endless. And he rides me through it,

fingers and mouth and tongue forcing me over the edge into pure obliteration.

I can't stop a scream from tearing loose.

"You're so fucking perfect," he growls into my wet flesh. "And mine, Mira. *Mine*. You think this ends like this? You think you have any hope of escaping me? *Never*."

It's like riding lightning. And then something he does drives me off the edge of that mountain again.

Pleasure. So much pleasure it feels like my nerves are raw.

"Stop! Stop, please." I collapse against the folly as he presses a soft kiss to the silk covering my abdomen, shockwaves lancing through me. So fucking sensitive. I don't think I'll ever be able to move again. Every inch of me feels raw and contained, as if I were slammed back into my body, only my skin's too tight.

A tongue circles my navel through the gap in the silk, and then he laughs under his breath. "Mine."

Another sharp nip that makes me shiver. I can't even protest. I don't think I would even if I had the breath to do so. The world settles back into being around me. "You don't have to sound so smug about it."

A rough laugh rumbles through his chest as he climbs his way up my body, his heavy weight driving me back into the steel column. "Mmm." Keir licks the taste of me from his fingers, the heated amber of his eyes alight with a self-satisfied humor. "The sounds you make are… delicious."

I want to bury my face in his throat. "You're impossible."

"Relentless," he agrees, kissing my throat. "You nearly vanished in my hands. I had to pin you down."

"I noticed that."

"The pinning you down bit?" A rumbling laugh vibrates through his chest, sending a delicious shiver through me. "You liked it. Do you want me to pin you down, Mira? Do you want me to hold you down and fuck you? Hard?"

His words ignite another shiver within me.

I reach between us, finding the heated length of him. There's too much fucking material between us. I want him. *Now*. I tear at his clothing, ignoring the roughened laugh that rumbles through his chest as I find him.

"So impatient, my love."

Capturing my ass in his hands, he braces me against the pillar.

And then he drives inside me in one single thrust.

I throw my head back and scream as every inch of my body sheathes itself around him.

The golden fire in those eyes fills me. Hot possession stakes its claim on me. Keir's lip curls, and then he's looking around for the daybed in the folly.

Capturing me in his arms, he takes two steps and then we're both falling, my thighs locking around his hips as he grinds against me. I can see the tension in his spine, the self-restraint—

"I'm not going to break," I whisper.

"Good." He slams inside me, piledriving me into the daybed.

Oh gods. Maybe I was a touch too cocky. It's been a

long time since I was this sexually active, and he was right…. He's more than fae in all the ways that count.

There's no mercy. This is more than a punishment. It's a claiming, pure and simple, and I want to steal this moment from him. I want to remember every single second of this encounter.

I kiss him and undulate into every rough stroke. Maybe he senses the unspoken yearning that fills my heart, because he captures my face in his hands and kisses me so deeply and savagely, that a tear leaks from my eye.

Hauling my thigh up in a spill of skirts, he drives into me. "Look at me, Mira."

I can't help myself. I do.

"Look at me and know my truth." There's a tremor in his hands, as he levers himself off me with his elbows. "I have never known feelings such as this. It's you. It's always going to be you. And I've known it since the first time I kissed you."

I grip his wrists, turning my face to press a kiss into his palms. I don't know how we went from fucking to this sweet torture. Another hot tear slides down my cheek as he thrusts within me.

"Nor have I," I whisper, because it's the only truth I can give him.

It's hours later, and I can barely move.

Keir helped me get dressed and then we stole back to our chambers in the lull of the storm before stripping each other down and tumbling into bed again. The ache between my thighs feels deliciously bruised in the best way.

Never a bad thing in this particular case, even if my heart is giving me trouble.

Or maybe it's only giving me trouble because he's kissing his way down my arms, as if he intends to pay homage to every single rune he marked me with. The second his mouth touches them, a shiver lights through me, like localized goose bumps.

It's magic of some sort.

Maybe he wants to remind me of what I owe him.

Stop being so cynical. I close my eyes as his lips skate up my throat. *Just enjoy the moment. Pretend… pretend he feels the same way.*

"You missed one," I whisper as he finally comes up for breath.

"No, I didn't." He breathes the words into my hair. "Three hundred and forty-three."

My breath catches. I thought it was just me, but he must have been able to feel them too. For some reason, I feel vaguely naked and cold.

It's a sense of cold so deep in my bones, it feels as though I've been warming myself by the fire for months, only to be shoved out into the blizzard.

Maybe that's just prescience—a glimpse of tomorrow's future when I play my hand.

"What's wrong?" he whispers.

"Nothing's wrong."

"You're such a liar."

I allow myself a shiver. "I feel cold."

Instantly, his arms are around me. "Then let me warm you."

"Mmm." I bury my face in his throat, my arms wrapped around him. He's so warm it's like snuggling with a bedwarmer. "When you were trying to convince me to be your bride, you should have led with this."

"Would it have convinced you to accept my suit?"

I glance up coyly from beneath my lashes. There's something teasing about his tone, as if we're just playing make believe. But the look in his eyes is anything but.

"No," I whisper. "I was there to do a job and steal the Dragon's Heart. Instead, I failed."

"Did you?" he muses, his voice rough with the dragon. Keir rolls onto his side, his amber eyes locked upon me. I don't know what he's thinking. I never do. He has the kind of eyes that can see straight through you, picking apart all your unspoken secrets, and yet his own are locked away and guarded.

"Can I ask you something?" I whisper, our faces mere inches apart.

A smile curls over his mouth. "Always."

My focus shifts to his mouth. "Why do you want the cauldron so badly?"

I *need* to know.

Instantly, tension skates through him. It strips the past few hours away from us; once again we're on different fields of the game board. "What do you mean?"

"You said you wanted me to find the horn, but you never told me exactly why you want to get *your* hands on the cauldron." I've been distracted. It's the only excuse I let such an important fact slip under my guard.

Keir pushes upright, the sheets falling into his lap. Shadows play over his face, and his hair falls forward, half obscuring his eyes. "You never asked."

Grabbing the sheets, I haul them up around my breasts as I sit up too. Maybe it's the timbre of his voice or the fact he didn't directly answer me, but something tells me this conversation is not one I want to hold naked. Dragging a pillow behind me and propping it against the wall, I face him. "I'm asking now."

Keir hauls a knee up to his chest, resting his arm on it. Ancient eyes examine me. "I don't want to find it. I *need* to find it. Before someone else gets their hands on it."

"It was washed into the sea," I point out. "Maybe no one will find it."

He doesn't look convinced. "It will be found. It has its own part to play in the future."

"Tell me," I whisper.

He leans back against the window, his arms crossed over his massive chest. "I guess the story starts with Calliope."

Calliope. I hug my knees to my chest. I don't know what she has to do with—

His expression hardens. "Calliope told you she could trace her bloodlines all the way back to Queen Mab."

"She said there was a treaty between the king of the dragons and Queen Mab, forged by a marriage between them."

"There was. The fae feared us for our power. There was rumor of war. We could all sense it in the air and see it spun to life in our dreams. It was coming, whether we liked it or not.

"And so King Vorvane gave Mab his word there would be peace between our kinds. There was a child born of their union—"

"Princess Igrainne."

"Half fae," he whispers. "Half dragon. But it was the dragon side that was submerged within her. She held the power of the stars in her blood but she couldn't touch it. And she wanted to."

There's something about the way he says her name. "You knew her."

"I knew her." He looks at me. "I was a dragon prince, and she was the daughter of my king. We were of an age, and it was expected...." He considers how best to use his words. "We were betrothed from the moment she was born. I was three years older, so we grew up together."

There's a sinking feeling in the pit of my stomach. I know what he's going to say, even before he says it. It feels like being a long-ago voyager, charting your map and knowing what lives in the seas ahead. *Here lies dragons….*

"You loved her."

"Of course I loved her. She was beautiful and wild and headstrong. She was promised to me from the cradle, and yet, she yearned for adventure. She hungered for power, and I was not her path to power. When they spoke of her father, you could see the fury in her eyes. Her mother whispered poison in her ear every day of her life, and Igrainne wanted his crown. She played me like a fool."

"We were mated, and there was… a child. Arianna." His eyes grow distant. "She was the most beautiful child that was ever born. She had her mother's pale hair and face, but her eyes, her eyes were like a dragon's."

There's a lump in my throat. He'd had a child. A daughter. And he loved her.

I often think of what that would be like, to have a father who loved me.

A father who would protect me before anything else.

I can see it in Keir.

He'd have moved mountains for a child of his own. He'd have slain armies and set fire to the world if it tried to harm her.

"What happened?"

He jerks out of his reverie. "Igrainne killed her father and ate his heart. It woke his power within her—the power of a dragon queen. But it disturbed the others, for they felt she was her mother's creature, and Mab could not be trusted."

"And you?"

His mouth twists. "I knew Mab could not be trusted. I wasn't even certain if Igrainne could be by this stage. Our mating was beginning to sour. I had suspicions…. And she could be spiteful, willful, and her fury at times was all encompassing. But what was I meant to do? My love for Igrainne grew strained, but Arianna…. She would curl her little finger around mine and I could not walk away.

"In those days there were seven kingdoms of dragonkind ruled over by the High King. I was the ruling prince of Tarronais, mated to the new High Queen. But the other princes wished to treat with me. They were concerned about Igrainne's growing need for power. They urged me to take Arianna and run." His lashes shield the pain in his eyes. "But Igrainne was her mother. And while I wondered if I could trust the woman she was becoming, I knew Arianna loved her. When Igrainne walked into the room, she was the whole and center of Arianna's universe. I could no more steal her away from her mother than I could cut off her hand."

He leans forward, clasping both hands together. "I let myself be blinded to the truth. Arianna became all I could see. By this stage, Igrainne and I had separate chambers. I knew she had other lovers. She'd forged an entire guard of powerful dragon males in their prime, and they catered to her whims. I won't pretend it didn't hurt, but if that was the price I paid to be with Arianna, then I would pay it."

All I can taste is ash in my mouth. If there's one thing I know well, it's blackmail.

What would you do for the safety of your soul?

What would you do for a child you love?

There's a horrible suspicion in my chest. This Igrainne sounds as though she was cunning and manipulative, and I know her kind well. Keir would be a powerful ally, but he's headstrong and willful himself. To bind such a prince to your side, you would need to do it with chains so strong they'd never shatter.

I swallow hard. *Arianna. It's always Arianna.* "You don't call her your daughter."

Tension exists in the hard line of his shoulders, but there's heat in his eyes when he looks up at me. And pain. "I said she had the eyes of a dragon. I did not say she had my eyes."

Confirmation. It's a knife through the heart. I wish I'd been wrong. "I'm so sorry."

He shrugs. "There was a point at which I knew the truth. She'd been born nearly a month early, and our mating had not been consummated until the ceremony. And as I said, Igrainne had her loyal guard, particularly a captain, Theomides." His mouth twists. "I would look at him sometimes, and I would see her. And... for all his faults, he loved Arianna too. I knew. I knew in my heart of hearts. I knew. But I was the one who rocked Arianna to sleep. I was the one who fed her goat's milk when her mother preferred not to nurse. I was the one who sang her songs and laced my power through her, so she would know a dragon's magic. She was my daughter as much as she was his."

I go to my knees on the bed before him, taking his hands in mine.

There's a knot in my throat, and it tastes of treachery.

I've told myself a thousand times that he knows better than to expect anything else from me. But this…. How do I steel my heart against this?

"And the cauldron?" I ask, for it's a safer topic to speak of.

"As I said, I had my suspicions. Igrainne was growing in power. I could no longer blind myself to what was going on when servants came to me, desperate for mercy." He clasps both hands between his thighs. "Some of them were vanishing. At first it was one or two. But soon it was nightly. And Igrainne would lock herself away in her tower with her squadron of guards every night.

"I hid myself within her tower and that night her guards brought one of the servants, kicking and screaming, into her solar. They bound him to a heavy marble slab in the center of the room and Igrainne entered with a knife. She intended to cut his heart out with a knife and eat it. It's what she'd done to all of them."

It's the same thing Calliope intended to do to him.

"A dragon's heart wields its power for only so long. Igrainne's hunger grew, but without the ability to constantly renew her magic source, her power would eventually fade. And then Prince Theramon fell to her in battle, and she consumed his power. This time it was different. A dragon prince—a king in the making—is not a mere servant. She'd finally found a source that could renew her.

"The fae flocked to her banners. The echoes of war filled the skies. I could hear the stars screaming. Hear the prophecy they'd once proclaimed echoing through the air.

War would come. The world would be torn apart. Both peoples would suffer. And the dragons would die.

"Igrainne blazed like a supernova. If one more of us fell, then she would be unstoppable. I asked the goddess how I could end this madness. And she gave her answer." He sighs. "The age of dragons must come to an end. The power of the dragon kings must fade from this world. We were to give up our magic to a cauldron forged from the metal that came from the skies. And I was to kill her and end her line."

Arianna. The heat drains from my face.

I know how this story ends now.

Keir gives me a merciless look. "And so I did. We gave up our magic so that if Igrainne took one of us, she would no longer be able to consume our power. We marched to war and I faced her across the field." Another hint of anguish. "I slew her. I broke her armies. A queen faded on that field and a king arose, as is the way of my people. The prophecy came to pass. One would rule over all of us, and yet he would have nothing. The High King fated to destroy his people. It was me. It was always meant to be me."

"And Arianna? What happened to her?"

"It was what I had promised the other kings. I would end Igrainne's line." His voice roughens. "I swore I would do it myself. I swore…. And I went to Igrainne's keep, and I cut down all who stood before me until finally I was at the door to her chambers. And he was there. Theomides was there, Arianna in his arms and a sword held against me. There were tears in his eyes. And she looked at me, and her little face lit up, and she called me 'Da.'"

And he couldn't do it.

I slide a hand down his face. "You were never going to be able to do it. I know you, Keir. You are honorable and loyal." *And you love so fiercely.* I close my eyes, unable to let him see the truth in my face.

"I told him to flee," he grates out. "I told him to take Arianna and raise her far away from these lands. To never even breathe her name. To never tell her of her mother. To protect her and love her… for me. And that was the last time I saw her. I made a promise to my people, to the goddess—and I broke it."

I ease out a breath. How hard must it have been for him to kill Calliope? Knowing she came of Arianna's line.

"There's something I haven't told you."

Stillness creeps through me. "What?"

Keir's look slays me. "Do you remember when Calliope came into the Court of Dreams and sought to kill me?"

The wall. Narcissa's lifeless hands reaching out of them forever, desperate to be saved…. I close my eyes. "I've been trying to forget it."

"Calliope was dragonborn, Mira. She could manipulate an Other World. She could manipulate my world and conjure monstrosities to life." He rubs his knuckles against the sheet straining over his thigh. "Did you ever think her death came too easily?"

There's a dull, throbbing beat in my chest. My heart, kicking like a mule. "What?"

Our eyes meet.

"She died with a single strike of my sword," he murmurs. "Or did she? After all, the Court of Dreams is a place where one sees what I want them to see…. And

Calliope has the same abilities I do. She could warp the dream."

I shove up onto my knees. "She's still alive?"

"I don't know."

"What do you mean you don't know?" All I can feel is stone around me, my body sinking into it like quicksand. "You killed her."

Thick lashes paint over his eyes. "Sometimes I hear whispers through the court. A mocking laugh. A pair of claws trailing over the stone walls of my palace. I thought at first it was her spirit haunting the court, but there's no sign of anything unnatural. And yet...."

"And yet?"

A dark heated knowledge fills his amber eyes. "There's one line of the prophecy that has always stayed with me: A queen will Awaken, and the dragons will fall. Until the line of Igrainne breathes its last, no peace will be found." He bares his teeth. "Calliope wasn't a queen. She was just... some poor wretch who didn't understand her powers. But if she gets her hands on that cauldron, she could become something even I'm not able to thwart."

Keir eases out a slow breath, lacing his fingers through mine. "I need to find the cauldron." His voice is rough gravel, thick with emotion. "Before Calliope does. I need to take both it and the horn and hide them away from this world. Calliope.... If she's still out there.... If she—or her mother—manages to get her hands on that cauldron.... Or if a fae king somehow discovers how to use its powers...." His face hardens. "This is my burden because I failed the first time. I am the guardian of the cauldron. I have to be. I have to end this."

The power of the cauldron is the only thing remaining in play with the strength to break the curse laid upon my people.

Without it, we'll wither and die.

And if I don't bring it home to my father, then he will....

Let's just say drowning will be the least of my worries.

I clasp a hand to my throat. All that power. My father will never stop with a broken curse. It will be war and no matter what I think of the fae I've never truly wished for war. "What if we could destroy the horn?"

Keir looks at me sharply. "What?"

"We find the horn, and we destroy it." I push to my knees as the idea starts to gain hold within me. "No one can use it to find the cauldron."

Keir shakes his head. "The horn cannot be destroyed. It's protected by the goddess."

"Then maybe we can sink it in the deepest part of the ocean so no one ever finds it," I growl.

Keir brushes his knuckles against my lips, his eyes sleepy-lidded and satisfied.

"Why are you smiling?" He's just told me a story of horrific consequences.

"You said 'we,'" Keir says as he kisses me.

19

I Sift inside Belladonna's rooms the next morning and reform, stalking toward her bed with the intent of whipping the blankets off her. "Wake up, Sleeping Beauty. You want me to kill your groom? Then you have to—"

The blankets burst upwards, and two startled heads appeared.

My hand jerks back.

"What in the Cauldron's name are you doing in here?" Belladonna hisses, as Anissa ducks back beneath the covers with a yelp.

I slam to a halt. A great many things suddenly make sense in hindsight. Letters. *Oh.* Those kinds of letters. "Well. Aren't I a fool?" Mistmark's imminent execution suddenly makes a great deal of sense. I circle the bed. "This is why you want your groom dead, isn't it?"

Belladonna slips from the bed, icily cool even as she draws a silk robe on. The expression on her face would be a threat if her hair didn't look like she'd spent hours with her face between her lover's thighs last night. "What in the

Shadow Lands are you doing in here? How dare you? If you think this gives you any leverage, think again. My cousin is well aware of my proclivities."

She curls her fingers into claws, gathering her magic, and I Sift out of reach, wagging a finger at her. "Relax, my lady. I have no intention of telling anyone what I saw here." I glance toward the bed. Anissa still hasn't made a reappearance. "None of this is my business. I was merely hoping to gain your assistance with a small task."

Her eyes narrow.

We stare at each other like two cats entering each other's territories.

Finally, Belladonna turns toward a bowl of water set out for her morning ablutions. She cups her hands within it and wipes them down her face. "You think I'm fool enough to fall in with your little scheme and name myself conspirator? Think again. I told you what you need to do—"

I pluck an apple from her breakfast tray and toss it in the air. "Killing Mistmark's a little more difficult than originally intended. He's protected far too well. Besides"—the bed appears to be moving; Anissa is clearly curious about this turn of events—"it's not Mistmark you have a problem with. Don't you want to throw this mistake in your cousin's face? Don't you want to see Malechus humbled before his entire court? He's forcing you to marry, isn't he? He took your letters, made some sort of threat against you…. Or no, Anissa, wasn't it? He threatened Anissa."

Belladonna stills. I have to admire both her restraint and her posture. Her shoulders are so square she makes even the effort of drying her face with a linen look arrogant. Tricking her is going to require the kind of play that makes my fingers itch.

But everyone has their weakness.

And Malechus is hers.

"What did you have in mind?" she finally asks.

Perfect. She's on the hook. I snap my fingers, and as if she was waiting for this moment, Soraya shoves both panels of the bedchamber doors open and stalks inside with her shoulders squared. An enormous train of dark green velvet rasps over the floor behind her, and her sleek brown hair has been swept back with waxed hands, so that it falls in a straight line down her back. Her sharpened nails are painted scarlet, and the gown brings out the malicious emerald glint in her eyes.

Belladonna gasps, which draws Anissa out from beneath the blankets.

"What do you think?" I ask Anissa, because she would know best, after all.

Her jaw drops open, and her head jerks between Belladonna and Soraya as if even she can't tell the difference.

"*Who*. Is. This?" Belladonna demands, facing her exact replica.

I sink into a chair and kick my heels up on the small table in front of me, taking a bite out of the apple. "I think we're going to have to work on your delivery," I tell Soraya.

"Get your *filthy* boots off my table," my sister tells me in an almost perfect rendition of Belladonna's tone as she stalks toward me. "How was that?" Then she gives a little twirl before giving Belladonna a nasty grin. "You may remember me…. I had weeks to learn your mannerisms."

The glamor bleeds off her until Anissa is scrambling from the bed, wrapping herself in the sheets as she cowers beside her lover. "*Violet?* What are you doing here?"

I exchange a knowing look with Soraya. "Violet? Really? I meant to take you to task for that. Isn't it getting a little old?"

She shrugs. "I retired Rose, and Iris was getting a little too well-known in the eastern courts."

With every role she plays, she takes on an alias, and for some reason she likes flowers.

"Pretty. Potent. And sometimes deadly," she once told me.

"I presume this has a point." Belladonna's voice drips ice.

I grin at the reluctant bride as her eyebrows hit her hairline. "This is what we call bait and switch."

"You want to exchange me with my *maid?*"

"Technically—" Soraya gives her a little smile. "—I'm an assassin. Not a maid."

Both she and Anissa grow pale, but Soraya saunters toward me, resting on the arm of my chair. "Oh, relax," she says. "I was never here for you. You were just an easy way to get into the court, once I realized your previous maid was bundled away to the country. Not that you'd know anything about that."

I feel like I'm missing a vital piece of information.

"The previous maid was working for Malechus." Soraya reads me well. "So Belladonna removed her. She's currently convalescing in the country."

"Convalescing." It's an interesting word.

"I'm not the only one with a gift for poisons," Soraya murmurs. Her eyes lock with Belladonna's. "Although her ladyship's a little less refined with them. You nearly killed her."

Belladonna's finger twitches as though she'd almost like to curse Soraya.

"Careful with that finger, my lady," Soraya purrs. "You're still recovering from what you did to Zemira. I'm very well aware of the extent of your powers, and you're days away from recovering the strength to commit a second curse. But just in case, my knife will be in your throat before you can even twitch it again."

She definitely hasn't told me everything.

Belladonna's eyes narrow, and she takes a long time before she sinks into the chair opposite me, crossing one smooth leg over the other. "I assume there's more to this lovely little get-together than a chance to exchange threats." She drags Anissa down beside her, somewhat protectively. "You have my interest. Proceed." And then she smiles. "Give me one good reason not to detonate the curse twined around your heart."

"Simple." I toss the half-eaten apple back on the plate and lean forward. "Two words: Malechus. Dead."

"In a way that cannot lead back to you," Soraya adds.

"I'm listening," Belladonna purrs.

The plan is simple.

Belladonna conceded Mistmark isn't her true target—

merely a means to sidestep this marriage, since her cousin insists she must go through with it—but she's not interested in lifting the curse or allowing me to avoid the terms of it unless it's done.

Mistmark must die before she'll remove the curse.

She will *not* marry him.

Someone has trust issues, though I daresay I can't blame her after spending over a week in the Court of Blood. The only hint of softness the lady reveals is when she looks at Anissa, and she absolutely refuses to allow even the slightest chance this marriage will take place.

Which means we're back to the beginning—but then, I never expected otherwise.

With Falion hovering attentively over Mistmark like a mother duck clucking over its ducklings, Mistmark is out of reach. If Soraya can't see a way to do it, then it doesn't exist.

But there's one person who can get close to him.

One person who is *expected* to get close to him.

Besides, sometimes I can be a little theatrical.

Soraya and I sit in the rafters overlooking the grotto where the wedding will take place. The servants are hauling in boughs of mistletoe and bloodstar. Snow dusts the grotto floor, hiding any lingering remnants of lechery.

"Exits." Soraya points. "One to the right, one to the left, and there's the antechamber Malechus likes to use for his more private entertainments."

I rub my hands together. The snow started last night, followed by a light rain. It was enough to wash away the snow in the garden above, but here in the grotto the protective overhang of rock shields certain corners of the room, and the overall effect is a little chilly.

It's pretty though.

Especially against the backdrop of scarlet leaves and berries.

"Think you can go through with this?" I mutter. "If you mistime it, then Mistmark is dead."

"Oh, I know I can." Soraya doesn't move, her hawkish eyes surveying the room. "And if he dies, then I can tell father I succeeded in my task."

She doesn't even flinch. But I learned long ago that my sister can lock away her heart as easily as breathing. It doesn't mean it doesn't occasionally bother her.

"I know you won't kill him."

"What?" She cuts me a look.

I blow into my cupped hands. "He got to you. Somehow. And you got to him."

Color blooms in her cheekbones. "What do you mean by that?"

"You haven't said a word about the fact Malechus used you to blackmail Mistmark into marriage." My voice softens. "If he didn't care, then he would have told Malechus to toss you off a cliff."

Soraya stares across the grotto for such a long time I'm starting to think she's not going to answer. And then her lashes lower over her eyes. "Then he's a fool," she says, but her voice lacks the chilliness I think she's striving for. "You can't fall in love with a weapon. And that's all I am. That's all I can ever be."

"Soraya—"

"And what about Keir?" Her voice hardens. "Since

we're speaking of *complications*. Is Keir going to be a problem? Because I know your heart is softer than mine."

The problem with knowing someone as well as this is that they know all your tells. "He's unaware you're in play. I can keep him distracted."

Her eyebrow arches.

"I can," I repeat. "And don't give me that look."

"You're fucking him."

I uncap the water flask I have at my belt, focusing on keeping all my emotions off my face. "Why wouldn't I be? He's gorgeous." I aim for insouciance. "Good in bed too."

"Good?" She reaches out and taps my throat. "You have bruises everywhere. I'm fairly certain they look like teeth marks."

I slap her finger away. "Fine. *Great* in bed."

She grumbles under her breath.

"What?" I demand. "Why not enjoy the moment? I'm never going to see him again once this is done."

"Really?" The way she drawls the word makes me want to punch her. "You see, there's just a little problem with that...."

"Oh?"

"Teeth marks, Z. Possessive, territorial marks. All over you. And you're blushing like a maiden after her first tumble."

I roll my eyes. "Ridiculously mind-blowing in bed. It's just sex."

She's so still, sitting on the ledge of the grotto like some sort of gargoyle. Her gaze grows distant as she returns her focus to the altar. "I keep thinking about that last quest. About the way we both failed."

"I'm fairly certain *you* succeeded." I can't help it if my voice grows a little rough. Like most of our relationship, it's easier if we don't pretend it's built on a foundation of betrayal.

This is getting dangerously close to topics we really shouldn't be discussing right before we try to pull off the heist of the century.

"Did I?" Soraya turns all of her focus upon me. "The Dragon's Heart. A relic with enough alleged power to tear apart the curse upon our people, and yet, when I placed it in Father's hands it barely had enough magic within it to light a candle. Someone got their information wrong."

My heart skips a beat. "Fine. I fucked up."

"I was locked in a sarcophagus for a long time, Z." Her voice becomes silken. "I had a lot of time to think about where it all went wrong. And I *know* you. You know what my mind keeps tripping over? The fact I was about to drive my knife through Keir's heart when you appeared. You threw me off him and the amulet hit the floor. But you didn't go for it. You stepped between us. You were protecting *him*."

There's a chill in the center of my chest. I can't let her guess the truth. "Maybe I was a little furious. You had your tongue down his throat."

"What can I say? The best way to get a man's mind off his defenses is to give him a taste of what he wants." She eyes me, noticing the way I shift onto my toes. "Jealous, Z?"

"You know what would be fun?" I turn the conversation on its head and smile sweetly at her. "Asking Mistmark what happened between the two of you. I'm fairly certain *that* would be an interesting tale."

A scowl darkens her face. "Nothing happened. And nice attempt to deflect. You're right. You fucked up. But it has nothing to do with getting the location of the relic *wrong*." She laughs under her breath. "Your soul was on the line, Z. You had a chance to get it back and break free of Father's geas. You had a chance for freedom. But you chose *him*. You chose his life over yours. Does he even know that?"

"I'm sure you have a point to make."

"You knew the amulet was a decoy. You knew it wasn't the Dragon's Heart. That's why you didn't even glance at the amulet." She shakes her head. "It was right there in front of me the entire time. He's the key to our freedom, but you were protecting him."

I tense.

"He's a dragon," she says softly. "He has the power to change an entire world—or to break our curse. His heart will power the entire spell by itself."

Fuck. She knows. Indecision makes my hand hesitate, but she catches the way it hovers near my belt.

"Don't," she warns. "We both know who's going to walk away from this if you draw that knife."

"Maybe we did once, but I didn't have anything to lose then." I let my hand settle on the hilt. "You can't say anything. If Father finds out—"

"Father underestimated the play," she says coldly. "*I* underestimated the play. And I learned my lesson. I've also been doing a little bit of research since then." Her expression sobers. "Everyone knows dragons were powerful, but all the books skirt around the fact there was no way to win that war against them. A single dragon king tore apart the combined forces of nearly all the Blessed courts. The only way they were defeated was to destroy them from within." She shudders. "I'm not dipping my toe in that pool again, Z. I know when I'm outclassed. Whoever Keir is—whatever he is—I'm staying well and truly away. He can keep his heart. I can't enjoy my soul if I'm dead."

If there's one thing I know about my sister, it's that she weighs the risks of *everything*. It's why she's the best.

"You won't tell Father?"

"If I tell Father where the real Dragon's Heart is, he's only going to send me after it. You may as well put me back in Malechus's little stone box."

The tension finally eases from my muscles. "Thank you."

"You're a fool, you know?" Her voice softens again. "He's only going to get you dead. There is no escape for either of us. That's another little reckoning I was forced to accept while I was contemplating life."

I'm not going to give up. "What's the point in surviving if you have nothing left to live for?"

The muscle in Soraya's jaw twitches before the faintest of smiles escapes. "Stubborn bitch."

I eye the grotto again. "Someone has to be. I'm going to beat him one day, Sora. Father's not invincible. I just need my soul-trap—"

"And then what?" she demands bluntly. "You think he'll just let you go? Father can't afford to be merciful. He's bred this little army of murderers and thieves. If he shows a weak flank—if he lets one of them get away—then the rest will start eyeing him like a pack of dogs. The only way to escape Father's hold is to slit his throat and burn him to ashes. And you're not a killer. Not at heart, you little fool. It's always been your weakness."

"It's a good thing I know someone who is."

There's a moment of shock in her eyes, as if she's never truly contemplated it before. "He's better than I am."

So, she's weighed those risks too…. That's interesting.

"I've been thinking about it…. What if we could get our souls back?" My breath catches because I've never dared put this into words. "I'm his best thief. You're his best assassin. Together—"

She shoves to her feet and stalks away from the ledge, back into the shadows. "You can't say that. Not out loud," she hisses over her shoulder.

Because Father's eyes and ears are everywhere.

"Think about it," I call as I follow her.

"I *am* thinking about it." She turns on me, her expression livid. "This is all *his* fault. I told you Keir's dangerous. In more ways than one. You're starting to think there's hope for the two of you."

"I'm fairly certain I'm about to betray him. I don't think he'll forgive me a second time." My voice is steady, but I can't help feeling my heart skip a beat.

I haven't decided what I'm going to do.

I didn't tell Keir about Soraya—or what my plans are today—only that I have things to set in place.

But I also can't forget the way his voice caught on Arianna's name.

If I give that horn to my father, then I'm effectively starting a war.

But I'll make a decision once I have the horn in hand.

A good thief doesn't look at her haul until she's well away from danger…. And a good thief doesn't dwell on the future when she's right in the thick of the heist.

"You don't understand, do you?" For once there's almost a hint of sympathy in her dark eyes. "Those marks on your neck? That look in his eyes? You know what they say about the dragons? They were possessive, territorial bastards. If they saw something they wanted, then they'd take it." Her voice softens. "I was there when he chose his bride, Zemira. He wants *you*. He's chosen you. He's not going to let you go now, betrayal or no betrayal. You woke the dragon. You captured his interest. And now you're going to have to pay the consequences."

The words send a little shiver down my spine.

"If that's the worst thing I have to worry about today," I tell her, "then I'll take it. I can handle Keir, but right now, we have a wedding to ruin. You need to get dressed. Maybe you'll thank me once this is all said and done."

Our gazes clash.

Then Soraya snorts. "If we're still alive, I'll thank you. Until then, try not to get us both killed. Now go and get ready for the wedding."

20

The entire amphitheater—where the ceremony is being held—is bedecked with blood lilies.

"Interesting choice," Keir murmurs as he leads me beneath the arch and into the natural stone amphitheater. "Adds a certain… ambiance."

"For a funeral." I don't know if that's tempting fate or not, or whether Belladonna is making a pointed statement to me.

"The groom looks nervous."

"I'd be nervous too if I was marrying Belladonna."

Keir gestures me toward our seats, which are several rows back from the front of the natural grotto. But I can't stop myself from examining the layout of the terrain.

Red leaves rain down softly from the blood oaks that surround the top of the grotto, as if they're weeping. The floor is smooth, polished stone, and enormous limestone columns line the amphitheater, ensuring that those cavernous walls stay in place. The stone sarcophagi line the rooms, bedecked with flowers and candles as if to hide that they are, effectively, tombs for some of the lesser dragonkind that stepped into mortal flesh. This is a place of power, and I can feel it in the hush of the room.

"Relax," Keir tells me, his fingertips resting in the center of my back.

Instantly, I still. My brain is racing at a hundred miles an hour, but I thought I'd managed to keep it off my face. The ability to consume such emotions and choke them down is what saw me through the first nineteen years of my life, until I finally graduated from the training camps.

If it's showing….

Keir cuts me a sidelong look, and his hand slides over my hip and draws me into the curve of his waist. "That's not relaxing."

I force my shoulders to drop and ease out a slow breath as I rest against him. All the better to commune privately. "Forgive me if I'm running to a deadline," I mutter. "You're not the one with a curse entwined around your heart."

"Nothing's going to go wrong," he reminds me, his lashes smothering those wicked, dragon eyes. "We have this entirely in hand. We just need to play our cards. "

About this "we" business….

He still thinks we're going to run with this illusion.

Keir can manipulate reality, and he *is* the Prince of Dreams. If anyone can make it look like Mistmark is dead….

"Glamor's tricky," I whisper into the curve of his neck. "If even a single fae in this room realizes that what is about to happen didn't actually happen…."

"We only need to fool one of them. As long as the bride believes it—"

"The entire room needs to believe," I whisper fiercely. "I can't risk it."

Keir looks into my eyes. I don't know what he sees.

A lover. A liar.

A *fool*.

One who doesn't dare wear her heart on her sleeve.

"We risk nothing," he growls. The room goes silent, and I know he's encased us in one of his little warded bubbles so that no one can hear us. Indeed, everyone around us seems frozen in some sort of tableaux. Even the leaves hover in the air, as if they hang suspended in time. "You know what I am, Mira. I don't just create illusions, I breathe them into reality. I can change the very existence of the world around us. Belladonna will believe what I want her to believe. I can make it look like the Lord of Mistmark dies with but a flicker of my will. The entire gathering will believe it—"

"And you would bet my life upon your skills?"

"Yes." Fury lights within his eyes. "I wish you would trust me."

There it is. The crux of the matter. I don't. I don't entirely trust anyone. "But I—"

Everyone's head turns as the bride appears. The ward evaporates, but silence falls over the guests, the entire room settling with a single hush. A stream of natural light falls over the entrance, highlighting Belladonna.

My breath catches.

She's beautiful. Stunning. The red of her dress is cut to accentuate her waist, and the bodice caresses her full breasts, making more of them. The fae are rarely curvaceous, but Belladonna's curves threaten to spill out of her dress.

A single split up the center of the skirts reveals creamy white legs, and the train of elegant red ruffles is almost ten feet long.

A girl could kill for a dress like that.

Let's hope it doesn't come to that.

The Lord of Mistmark cuts a look toward his bride, the muscle in his jaw tightening imperceptibly. And then his lashes shield his eyes, but I know his attention is shifting to the side.

Toward the shadows that linger between the enormous columns that support the roof of the amphitheater. And the lean figure that stands there.

Falion.

His assassin.

Shit. Maybe Belladonna isn't the only one who's been plotting to stop this wedding in its tracks.

Stalking toward her betrothed, Belladonna's eyes find me in the crowd. Her eyebrow arches challengingly, as if to demand whether I've fulfilled my part of the assignment or not.

I roll my eyes. The second Mistmark left his rooms, I went through them. There was no sign of a map to the horn, but when I placed a piece of paper over his desk blotter and scribbled graphite over it, words showed through.

Mistmark has a letter tucked in his pocket revealing the whereabouts of the horn—presumably to give to Malechus the second the vows are said.

Except, I also know the contents of said letter.

And I'm going to get there first.

I just need a distraction.

The priestess steps forward wearing a gauzy white gown, roses bedecking her hair. "Goddess bless thee."

"And thee," intones the gathering.

"Who stands before Her Holiness today?" she calls.

There's a long drawn-out moment before Mistmark clears his throat. "Alaric of the Summervein, Lord of Mistmark."

She turns to the bride. "And thee?"

A clear voice rings through the grotto. "Belladonna of the Blood Lily, Lady of Mariangettes."

The priestess settles into her usual spiel about the goddess's blessing. Belladonna's voice is quiet as she repeats the words she needs to say to make her pledge— too many people might recognize the slight changes of timbre in her voice.

Mistmark's cool tone is almost a shock after her quiet words.

The priestess summons her page forward, and he presents a dagger on a plush velvet cushion. "By blood I bind thee," she calls, taking the dagger and slicing a nick into the tip of Mistmark's finger.

Holding his hand over a golden goblet, she forces three droplets of blood to mix with the elderberry wine within.

She repeats the gesture with the bride and then presses the cuts together, mingling their blood. A velvet ribbon binds their wrists together—if they remain bound until the following morning, it's said their union will be blessed with bounty. To strike the cord early means drama and strife.

"Drink and Goddess bless," she says, lifting the wine to Mistmark's mouth and then the bride's.

"Ready?" Keir murmurs.

"Wait," I urge, tucking my arm through his elbow.

He's giving me a look, as though he's starting to suspect I've another plan up my sleeve. "Not until after the ceremony," I caution.

Thick lashes shield his eyes from view. "Just what are you up to, Mira?"

"I don't want to bring misfortune down upon this hall," I whisper. It's said the goddess watches each blessing, and to defy her will is to draw her attention. "Just a few moments more. Once it's done, the goddess will turn her face away."

"I didn't know you were superstitious."

"A good thief doesn't invite bad luck."

He nods, thank the goddess.

"By Blood, Ash, and Cord, I name thee bound before the goddess," the priestess calls, dipping her thumb into a pot of ash, before she paints it between each of their eyes. "Goddess bless this union."

Everyone leans forward in anticipation, because this is the moment we've all been waiting for. A single kiss to seal the ceremony.

The Lord of Mistmark steps toward his bride, his lips pressing together thinly as his face lowers toward hers. There's no sign of distaste upon his face—Mistmark's an expert at keeping his horses well in hand. I've met him several times this past week, and I still don't know a cursed thing about him.

It's the bride who hesitates, casting a slightly stricken look toward the crowd as if searching for a particular guest.

Come on. Come on.

Play the game. Do your part....

I squeeze my fingers into a fist even as the bride does the same.

Even as she tilts her painted red mouth toward her new husband's.

Their lips meet.

It's a breathless moment as all the guests shift, some of them leaning forward hungrily as if in search of a hint of discord, and some of them merely curious.

Instead, the bride slides her hand behind Mistmark's neck, hauling his mouth against hers. Her hips tilt toward him, a hint of unexpected longing echoing in the curve of her spine.

Malechus allows a dangerous smile to stretch across his face.

But it's Mistmark I didn't account for.

The groom draws back sharply, touching his hands to his lips and staring at his bride's face. Confusion draws his brows together.

My heart sinks through my chest like lead.

He knows.

And then he staggers to the side, going to one knee as if he's a puppet with cut strings. The color drains from his face, his fingers bleeding red. The same red as the bride's lipstick. The same red as the miroire flower, renowned for its ability to murder a fae within minutes.

Anger flashes over Mistmark's expression as he grabs a fistful of the wedding gown. It's too late. He doesn't have the strength to fight, even as he knows what has happened.

The last thing he whispers is "Sora?"

Before he collapses on the dais at the bride's feet.

21

Time to roll the dice.

Malechus is no longer smiling. The crowd gasps. And the bride looks ready to flee.

She can't escape now. I still need her to play her part.

I move to Sift, even as someone screams, but Keir snatches my wrist, searching my gaze. "What did you do?"

I try and pry him free, but there's no shifting him. "I took care of Belladonna's threat."

"You *killed* him?"

"I just need Belladonna to think I've killed him," I whisper in his ear. "Let me go. I need to finish this. I need to fetch the horn."

"You were supposed to wait for *me*. If they realize you're gone—"

"They won't. Because you're going to summon an illusion of me," I whisper. "Make it look real."

He stares at me.

"Please."

"And the questing beast?" he finally asks.

"I have a plan. *Trust* me."

Keir's lips thin, but he waves his finger.

A cloaked figure bumps into me and an elegant young woman steps between us, whipping back the hood of her cloak.

It's… a little shocking to stare myself in the face. I have to assume no one can see the real me.

"Make sure I'm seen," I tell him. "Make sure *you're* seen."

I can't have him interrupting my plans, after all.

And then I take a step back into the shadows, even as Keir shoots me an absolutely furious look.

He's going to make me pay once this is all said and done, but I have to finish what I started.

Distraction gets you dead. Put Keir out of your mind and focus.

I bury him so deep in my heart that those treacherous longings will never see the light of day again. And then I Sift toward the side of the amphitheater.

There's a hooded figure in one of the side chambers, pacing the floor like a caged wolf. The second I enter, she stills, those malevolent green eyes locking upon me. "Well?"

"It's done," I tell Belladonna.

"He's dead?" she demands.

I gesture over my shoulder to where Malechus and Falion are desperately trying to revive the Lord of Mistmark. "If you wait ten minutes, he will be. But I don't think we have the time."

"Just break the curse," Anissa murmurs from where she's slumped against the wall. "Let's be done with this.

Let's be done with all of this. I just want to go home, Bella. No more murderous games. No more blackmail and curses. I want our life back. You, me, and our sunny pavilion by the lake."

Eagerness leaps in my heart, but this isn't the moment to reveal it.

Belladonna stares at me, before her gaze cuts to the side. She doesn't say a thing, but I know—if she gets her way and Malechus dies—that she and Anissa won't be returning to what sounds like their summer retreat. The Blood Lily is ambitious. I can't forget the hunger in her eyes when I spoke of Malechus's death. Without a crown prince the path to the throne is open, and maybe Belladonna's tired of dancing to someone else's tune.

But that's their problem.

Not mine.

"Fine." Belladonna yanks me toward her, wearing an exact replica of the bridal gown. I don't know whether she's wearing the illusion, or Soraya is. Both dresses look like they required several hundred hours of stitching each, which makes Soraya's gifts of glamor impressive. I knew she was good, but I didn't know she was *this* good.

Belladonna's fingers curl into shadowy claws, and then she strikes at my chest.

I gasp as I feel them sinking within me.

My heart throbs in her grasp, but it's the curse that drives me to my knees as she wraps her hand around it and wrenches it from my chest.

"I told you we didn't have to be enemies," Belladonna purrs as she curls her fingers around the wretched black tangle that writhes in her palm. It sinks into her skin and vanishes, and I can finally breathe again.

Yeah, well.... "That was before you tried to kill me." Somehow I make it back to my feet. The curse is gone. *Gone.* I'm free of her entanglements.

There's a strange look in her eyes. "Sometimes I react hastily when the people I love are threatened."

"That's her way of saying thank you," Anissa murmurs as she captures her lover's hand. There's a relieved smile on her face. "And we do. We both thank you. Without you, there would be no hope for us."

One look at Belladonna reveals the haughty cock of her brow. She's not *that* grateful. Or maybe she just has difficulty conceding it.

"Long live true love," I tell her, bending over and panting as I try to recover. "And you're welcome. Now go. The pair of you need to play your parts."

Drawing her hood over her gorgeous mahogany hair, Belladonna arches a brow. "Your friend's glamor is ridiculously good."

"It almost fooled me," Anissa grumbles.

"Don't tell *her* that."

Belladonna smiles that little smirk I hate so much. "You do realize my dearest cousin is going to try and torture her?"

"He can try. I don't think she'll appreciate that."

"As long as the truth comes out."

"Well, that's where you have to play your role," I point out.

She rolls her eyes and stalks toward the door. "Where

the fuck are my flowers? If I'm going to do this, then I'm going to do it right."

Anissa grabs the bunch of night-blooming lilies and hands them to her.

"You breathe a word of this," Belladonna tells me, "and I'll ruin you. I can curse you again just as easily as breathing."

I roll my eyes, but Anissa pokes her in the ribs. "Bella!"

"Thank you," Belladonna says stiffly.

The last thing I see is the excited flash of Anissa's smile. In her eyes, once Malechus dies, they're finally free to live their lives the way they choose. No more political marriages bound to separate them. Without Malechus trying to drive a wedge between them, they may love each other openly.

The second they're gone, I breathe a sigh of relief and allow myself a moment to lean back against the wall.

The first part of the plan succeeded beyond my wildest expectations.

Now Belladonna needs to make her entrance and make it clear she had nothing to do with the attempted assassination. She'll be shocked. Speechless. Then furious as she demands to know who this imposter is.

The fun begins when she realizes I'm the one using her as a pawn—and not the other way around.

Phase two of the plan needs to be set in place.

I have a horn to find.

A fae lord to revive.

And then a sister's rage to quell.

Soraya is going to kill me once she realizes what I'd failed to mention.

After all, the ceremony wasn't fake. Not even I dare circumvent something while the goddess is watching, and it doesn't matter what names they gave if their blood is bound.

Mistmark just found himself married to the wrong woman.

22

SORAYA

"Let go of me!" My skirts hiss around my legs as the prince of the Court of Blood drags me into a side chamber.

Malechus shoves me through the door and slams it behind him, locking us away from the curious guests. "Are you out of your mind? What have you *done*? You've cost us everything!"

"Cost you," I point out, taking a step away from his towering rage.

"Cost *us*," he hisses, advancing upon me. "Cost this entire fucking court. We cannot afford to go to war with Mistmark. I gave my word to Angmar of the Court of Storms that nothing would go awry. And now the fucking Lord of Mistmark is *dying*! His fae will arm themselves for war, and that frigid fucking wraith he has up his sleeve will come after me!"

I can't help myself. "Ooops."

He freezes. "What did you say?"

I shrug. Sometimes it's best not to say anything at all.

Besides, if I wasted my breath on words, I wouldn't be able to sit back and watch a thousand furious emotions dance across his face.

And then his expression stills, his rage sliding off him like he's locked it away. "You don't care. You knew the risks associated with this—that Anissa would pay the price of your insubordination. But you don't care."

What can I say? That my cold dead wraithen heart would bleed for the two lovers—soon to be torn apart—but it turned to ice so long ago it barely beats anymore.

"But my cousin *would* care," Malechus says, and suddenly he's a hound on the scent of its prey. "Belladonna would die for Anissa. She would prostrate herself at my feet if it meant she could stop me from cutting her lover's heart out of her chest."

He's figured it out.

Now to lure him closer.

"She would," I purr.

"Who are you?" he demands, his dark eyes glittering as he snatches at my upper arm. "For you're not my cousin."

I let the glamor I've been holding dissolve, and it feels like I step out of Belladonna's skin. The discarded glamor settles around my ankles like a shed snake skin, before it wisps into nothingness. "You're right. I'm not. Remember me?"

Oh, this moment feels *good*.

His eyes widen even as I summon my dirk. The goblin-forged metal materializes in my hand, and before Malechus can recover from his shock, I drive it into his side. Right between the fourth and fifth ribs.

It's the best way to a man's heart, after all.

And it takes care of any nasty surprises like blood curses. They're difficult to conjure when you're trying to stop your arteries from gushing like a scarlet fountain.

His fingers dig into my arm, and we both go to our knees in a semblance of an embrace.

"Do you remember when you put me in that sarcophagus?" I whisper, caressing his face. "And I promised I would make you pay?"

"How… did you…?"

"Get free?" I purr. "I had a little help from an old friend."

Malechus's fingers snatch at the gossamer of my skirts. From the wheeze hissing between his ribs, it sounds like I might have hit a lung. Excellent. I slide the dirk free, and trail my bloody fingers over his lips.

"Shhh," I whisper. "This won't take long."

Rage ignites in his eyes. He coughs blood. Definitely a lung.

I kiss him, painting the poison across his mouth—just in case he actually can heal the knife wound—and then I ease to my feet.

"I'd stay to watch, really I would, but I have a certain sleeping beauty to wake." Grabbing a fistful of my skirts, careless of the bloody knife, I step over him as he slumps to the floor. "Do be a good little prince and die."

I stalk out into the amphitheater just as Belladonna appears at the head of the aisle.

Perfect.

Her mouth drops open when she sees me and then her flowers fall at her feet. "Who are you?" she demands. Loudly. Half the guests crane their neck to look. "What is going on here?" Her gaze falls upon the dais, where half a dozen solemn fae stand around waiting. They took Mist-mark elsewhere, sending desperately for a medic.

"Sorry, my lady." I blow her a bloody kiss. "But I had a prior engagement with the groom."

The entire hall falls into shocked silence as heads swing between the two of us.

"What's going on here?" someone demands.

"Imposter!" Belladonna screeches, and I can't help thinking she's enjoying this a little too much.

With a wink, I throw myself into the crowd. Ladies screech as I trample through them, and someone calls out behind me, "Stop her! She's an assassin!"

I don't have my sister's skill at parting shadows, but I have a few little gifts of my own. As I lunge between two ladies, I catch a glimpse of a fae lord's face and then am wearing it myself, even as an illusion of his blue cloak spills from my shoulders. The illusion of the red dress hits the floor behind me like a second skin. My skirts vanish, encasing my legs in tight leather trousers. Perfect. All the better to kick a man's head off his neck.

Fae yell and grab at the dress, and it's only as I finally find the edge of the guests that I glance back to see them fighting over the torn fabric, arguing about what happened to the assassin. It shreds apart in their hands, turning to wisps of insubstantial smoke.

Guests whisper and gasp. Some are crying. It's a crush of braying donkeys begging for the slaughter, and I'm forced to become a little generous with my elbows to make my way out of the crush.

Fools. Ducking into the shadows that line the columns,

I head for the chamber where I saw them taking Mist-mark's body.

Time is ticking out.

I had ten minutes from the moment I kissed him, and right now I have to guess that only three minutes remain. Malechus dragging me into that antechamber cost me precious time I don't have.

Even if I can always make a little time for murder.

A guard steps forward to stop me as I enter the cavern that leads toward the lord who is dying. "Here, you. You can't go back there—"

I grab the wrist of the hand that reaches for me and twirl beneath it, driving my dirk up into his armpit. Axillary artery. My favorite. Close enough to the heart to leak a few decent pints. Nobody ever thinks to protect themselves there and a single slice can make a man bleed out in a few minutes.

As he hits the ground, I flip my dirk and keep walking. It's almost tempting to hum.

Blood spatters lie on the floor, and I track them.

Blood that Mistmark no doubt coughed from his lungs as they carried him away from the amphitheater. I track it toward a set of doors, but even if I hadn't seen the blood, the four fae standing guard would have told me this is where they took him.

Four Blood Court guards. Not particularly great odds, but hardly something that will stop me.

The captain snaps to attention when she sees me. "Here, you. What are you doing—?"

"Do they train you with such language?" I chide, as I stalk toward her. "'Here, you?' That's the best you can offer?" The handle of the dirk flips into my hand as I mock her. "And what am I doing? I'm here to save the day, don't you know?"

She reaches for her sword, but I'm in and under her guard before she can blink. I have a particular respect for females who've reached the pinnacle of their male-dominated careers, so I merely spin beneath the sweep of her sword and slice across her Achilles. She'll thank me later. Maybe.

As she goes down with a scream, I drive my elbow into the back of her head and then lunge up, burying the dirk in the belly of the next guard. Right between the rings in his chain mail.

It's why I like the dirk so much. It's such a thin, delicate weapon, and when you're facing guards armed with swords, they're always terribly smug about the fact they have an extra sixteen or eighteen inches on me.

The problem is, those extra inches are a liability in close quarters.

I grab the guard's collar and yank him closer, making sure I skewer his liver, before I spin him to take the strike of his fellow guardsman. The sword glances off his chainmail—there has to be some use for it, after all—and then I kick him in the chest.

They both go down with a clatter, like turtles on their backs.

And I face the last guard.

This one is no fool.

He held back while the others attacked and he crouches low, his spear held in steady hands. "Thou shalt not pass."

Oh, we have Mr. Determined here.

I spin my dirk between my fingers and grin. Suddenly, there are two of them, one in each hand.

His gaze flickers down, focusing on the spinning knives, but I'm already slipping my skin. I put the dirk through his throat and the image behind me—a grinning young woman with two knives twirling—vanishes in a puff of smoke.

"Never even saw it coming," I whisper in his ear as the light goes out of his eyes.

Glamor. The next best thing to an entire arsenal of goblin-forged blades. Too many of the fae focus on what they can see.

And if there's one thing that growing up with my sister taught me, it's that being able to "vanish" into thin air is a powerful weapon.

I step through the doors, sheathing the knife.

The room is quiet. Still.

There's a marble slab in the center of it and someone's laid the Lord of Mistmark there in quiet repose.

The sight of Alaric lying so still is a shock that makes my feet slow. He's always seemed so energetic to me; a whirlwind of determination that would stop at nothing and no one. I've fought with him, kissed him, tried to kill him…. And every time we've clashed, he's been the one in control.

Now he looks like he's sleeping.

It takes me right back to that first night I crept within his chambers, intent upon murdering him. He was so beautiful that I hesitated for a moment, and that hesitation cost me. Just as I summoned my goblin blade, he suddenly woke, grabbing my wrist.

It even feels like that night again—like fate is going to reach out and kick me in the teeth—though the weight in my chest is different.

I could let him die.

I could let this entire twisted knot that binds us together die.

All I have to do is tell Zemira I was too slow to bring him the antidote.

He'd be gone from my life. I'd never lie awake again, twisted in knots as I fight the urge to go to him. I'll never wake from dreams where his name is on my lips even as I can still feel his tongue between my thighs. The scars on my body—the ones my father graced me with when I returned from my assassination attempt in failure—will fade.

There'll be no more shame.

No more fear.

No more desperate yearning that wakes me at nights.

I'll never see those blazing eyes lock upon me across a room again until everything around us fades.

"Just you and me, little wraith," comes the whispered memory of his voice. *"Forever."*

And any chance I ever had of escaping his hold over me vanishes.

Curse him.

Alaric doesn't move. He's barely even breathing.

The poison must be working through his system even faster than I could have imagined.

It spurs me to action.

"Don't think you're escaping me so easily," I whisper

as I slide to my knees beside the stone bier he's lying on. "You still owe me a reckoning."

Where the fuck are the healers? Surely they didn't just leave him here to die?

It's not as though they would have been able to do anything against the poison he ingested when he licked my lying little lips, but if he dies in Malechus's court, there will be an accounting.

Two minutes left, at best.

I kneel by his side, and for some ridiculous reason my heart hammers in my chest.

I can't help thinking of the way he kissed me that long-ago summer.

Every day I'd promised to kill him, and every day he'd simply laughed and said, "*No, you won't.*"

And I hadn't. I hadn't been *able* to.

It's the one time my knife has hesitated, the one time I've failed. It cost me more than he will ever know.

It cost me my heart.

My cruel, treacherous heart.

"Curse you," I whisper as I run my tongue over my teeth, searching for the capped one. I break the tiny glass vial embedded there, and as the antidote floods my mouth, I lean down and kiss him.

Shoving my tongue into his mouth, I force the antidote within him. Tiny shards of glass cut my lips until I can taste my own blood. Taste his mouth. Taste him.

One single stolen kiss.

It reminds me of so many others. It reminds me of everything I forced myself to forget.

A hand suddenly sinks into my hair, and then I gasp as Mistmark wakes beneath me, sucking in a huge breath.

I jerk back, patting his cheek. He's alive. I wasn't too late.

But as his lashes flutter against his cheeks, I know I have to get out of here. He cannot discover I was here.

I barely escaped him last time.

A hand catches at mine as I turn to flee. "Sora?" His glazed eyes search for me.

He shouldn't be able to sense me.

Once again, that fucking inexplicable bond between us has bound me in place.

"I thought… you tried… to kill me…?" His vision finally seems to focus upon my face.

My heart skips another beat as a thousand emotions wage war within me. "I did," I whisper, and then, unable to help myself, I lower my face to his, stealing another kiss from his cold mouth.

One last desperate taste of him before I vanish.

He's fading as I come up for air, his eyes rolling back in his head. The antidote will take several minutes to work its magic, and he'll be weakened for weeks. It was the best I could come up with when Zemira first worked over this plan with me.

This poison is an inevitable death once ingested.

But the recovery is swift, and the consequences few.

As much as I want to kill him, I don't actually want to hurt him.

He's got you twisted in so many knots, you don't even know yourself.

Cupping my palm over his eyes, I slowly close them.

Maybe he'll remember me. Maybe he won't. But I can't just leave without saying goodbye. "Sleep well, my lord."

And then I steel myself and push to my feet, turning toward the doors.

Except I'm no longer alone.

"I wondered what you would do," Falion says, leaning against them and watching me from beneath his silvery lashes.

Mistmark's assassin.

The one I never knew about until it was too late.

I freeze in my tracks.

Of course. No wonder there were no healers. Only this faithful dog, waiting at his master's heels to see how the game would play out.

I've never quite understood the bond between them.

"What I would do?" I lick away the blood. "Have you been watching me again?" I force a laugh. "The same way you watched me then? Tell me, Falion. Do you ever step out of the shadows? Or do you simply enjoy peeking through windows when nobody knows you're there?"

There's no sign I scored a point. He tugs one glove off as he steps forward into the light. "I enjoyed watching you stab Malechus. I was about to cut your throat myself, except you didn't run for the exit, you made straight for this room. I'd smelled the poison on your breath and knew you had to have the antidote on you somewhere. You had to take it yourself, of course, before you could paint it across your lips…."

"Somewhat presumptuous." I summon a small pouch of powder into my hands, curling my fingers around it even as I wave the point of my knife at him. *Look at the knife, go on.... Just focus on the knife....* "I've been sipping miroire for years in order to acquire a certain immunity. It's my favorite. The kiss of death.... Nobody ever sees it coming, and most males are too fucking stupid to look beyond what I'm offering them."

"Not this one," he whispers, and as our eyes meet, I know he's about to repay everything I did to Mistmark that long ago summer.

I throw the pouch at him and he bats it aside, the spill of crushed bone and grave dust painting across his chest.

"You missed," he says with a dangerous smile, before he vanishes.

"Did I?" I mutter, feeling him pop into being behind me. Dropping into a crouch, I spin and slice my second knife across his thigh—the one dipped in poison.

He sucks in a startled breath, but he's a professional. He Sifts out of reach in order to regather himself, instead of coming at me again.

I straighten, pretending to wince. "That cut looks nasty. You'd better clean it before it gets infected. Or... before the monksflower on the blade starts to work its way through your leg." This time, it's my turn to smile. "I'd estimate that you have a good half minute before your leg feels like it's on fire."

He growls under his breath and plucks at his shirt, where my mixture of bone and grave dust paints the fabric. "You can track me."

"Oh, please." I barely resist the urge to roll my eyes. "My sister is a Shadow Walker. Did you think I wouldn't have somehow accounted for someone of her skills?"

"Sister, huh?" Falion's eyes narrow. "Ah, I thought the

sweet Lady Merisel looked familiar. Well, if I've only got another twenty seconds, then I guess I'd best make them count, eh?"

He vanishes again.

My wards tug at me a second before he reappears to the right of me.

My knife cuts through the air, but he's ready this time. Slamming a hand to my elbow, he blocks the blow, and then he's angling his own knife straight toward my chest. I twist and block, but the tip slashes through my shirt.

I can't move my fucking arm. The block he has on me is excellent, and he's stronger than me, with a greater reach.

It's a good thing I'm ambidextrous.

I drop the knife and catch it with my left hand, slicing a fine line of blood across his chest as he leaps back. Free again. But not for long. Our blades duel even as our bodies slam against each other. I throw everything I have at him, and he counters almost elegantly. My fist meets his cupped palm. His blade retorts with a stinging swipe across my cheek, even as I drive my heel into his instep.

It's a blur of violence, carefully choreographed by long-gone masters who taught us our trade.

And I can't find a fucking weakness.

We break apart for a second, both aware we've met our match as we circle each other like panthers. It's been a long time since I've come across a foe who can keep me on my toes.

I'd almost be enjoying myself if I didn't need to get out of here in a hurry.

I glance toward the bier, and Mistmark is stirring.

Dragon's scurvy.

I cannot let him catch me here.

"Thought you were going to show me the error of my ways?" I taunt, lunging forward. "Looks like you're just an average assassin when your feet are grounded in reality."

"Do you want to know the best thing about your sister?" Falion muses as he flips me over his back and nearly puts a heel through my kneecap when I land.

"What?"

Falion holds out his palm toward me, before making a twisting move with his finger. "She's a baby compared to me. She barely even knows what she's doing. Sifting? That's one of the first things we learn. But when you can make the shadows themselves walk…."

Something snatches my shirt, and I'm hauled back into the gloom along the wall. Ethereal arms wrap around me, and as I grab at them, my hands go right through them.

Shadows.

He's somehow entrapped me with shadows.

One of them hauls my wrist back, slamming my knife against the wall.

I glare at him as he stalks toward me, smirking that smirky smirk.

"Oh, you want to play dirty?" It's never bothered me to pull my punches, but I always like to hold back until the last moment—once you show all your tricks, you've got nothing up your sleeve for later. But now seems to be a good moment…. "Let me show you what I can do."

I lock onto the suit of armor in the far corner and Summon it toward me. It's a trick I learned when I was a little girl. But instead of conjuring it into my hand, I simply yank it through the air.

Falion Sifts a second before it hits him, but he's moving a little slower now.

The shadows dissipate, and I'm free, driving toward the ring of torches that guard the bier. Mistmark stirs, as if he can almost hear us clashing, but the only safety to be found when you're fighting a Shadow Walker is in the light.

Shadows ripple around the ring of light, some of them forming faces.

I dance on my toes, trying to keep them all in sight, but it's the silvery-haired assassin stalking through them that earns my full attention.

I arch my eyebrow and point mockingly at the ring of light.

Falion merely smiles.

And then the torch to my right hisses out.

I spin, just in time to see a shadowy figure pinching the wick.

My protective circle becomes a little smaller.

Cauldron's piss.

"When we Shadow Walkers openly walked this realm, every court in the land learned to fear us." Falion takes a step closer and a second torch sizzles out. "They used to light torches along their walls to guard them from the night, but the greatest of our kind learned not to fear the light."

A third torch hisses, and then there's only one last torch remaining. I back around it, knife in hand and heart in my throat.

If he plunges us into darkness, then he'll have the upper hand—

Or… will he?

My heart skips a beat. Shadows need light to exist.

And I'm a wraith.

I was born in darkness. I hate it, but to let yourself bear such a weakness is like offering your throat to an enemy, so I trained for years with a blindfold. It paid off. When Zemira and I were sent into our final testing, they dropped us in the mines of Wraithenghul for the first leg of the three-part challenge, and only those who managed to escape that darkened tomb were offered a chance at claiming our place among the ranks of the wraithen court.

Falion's smile is a knife edge as he puts one foot on the step that leads to the bier.

But he doesn't extinguish the last torch.

No, he's counting on my fear to force me to make a preemptive strike—one he's ready for.

This time, it's my turn to smile back. "When your kind walked the world," I whisper, "my kind learned not to fear the darkness."

And then I Summon the last torch into my hand, close my eyes in preparation, and extinguish the flame with a single breath.

We're plunged into utter darkness.

I hear his sharp inhale before I throw the torch behind him and move.

I had a moment to prepare for this. I don't know if his head turns to track the sudden clatter the torch makes as it lands, but I'm crouching low, moving like liquid night in the sudden darkness.

I don't have to move far. I just have to wait.

I slow my breath, my heartbeat. I let my body sink into stillness as I listen.

He's good. He's frozen in place too, waiting for me to make my move. I don't know if he can Sift in this moment. Zemira needs some hint of a shadow to do it, but Falion's already proven he's well beyond her capabilities.

Mistmark stirs again, his breath loud in the silence of the tomb.

And I get an idea.

I reach out for his boot, trying to imagine it. I need to lock on to it first, before I can Summon it, and it's ridiculously hard to do when I can't see it.

But then I sense it quiver, and it tugs free of his foot, rattling across the floor toward me. Noisy enough to draw his attention.

Falion makes his move. But it's not the one I imagined.

Instead, his skin suddenly lights up, illuminated from within just as I lunge toward him.

"Clever," he mocks as the boot thumps into his back.

Because he's already turning to counter my strike, the light from his skin searing my vision.

It's over in an instant.

I can't see him—he seems a blur of light—and I miscalculate the blow. Then there's a hand locking around my wrist, spinning me off balance as a strong arm curls around my throat from behind and draws me back into a fatal embrace.

"But not clever enough," he whispers as his knife rises to strike—

"Don't. Kill. Her."

Both of us freeze as Mistmark sits up on the bier, sucking in a sharp gasp of breath.

Falion has me against his chest, his arm around my throat and the tip of his knife resting against my carotid. A tremor runs through him. He wants to finish this. He wants to end me. But to do so means going against what his lord and master has commanded.

The breath bursts out of me, and I see stars.

He's gripping me so tight, but it's relief that nearly sends me to my knees.

Two minutes ago, I never wanted to see Mistmark again. Right now, he's my hope and salvation in one.

I nearly died.

Mistmark snaps his fingers, and suddenly all the torches burst alight. He sags back on one hand as if the poison still has its hold on him, and his lips are shockingly blue. "Don't kill her."

Falion releases a breath. "She's going to ruin you. Let me end this foolishness before she makes a mockery of you again—"

"If you kill her," Mistmark says, "then you'll kill me."

"What?" The word bursts out of me. Suddenly, the knife at my throat is the least of my worries.

"What?" Falion sounds just as surprised.

Mistmark slowly pushes to his feet, his gaze sliding over me. The flickering light from the torch gilds his olive skin, but it's the look in his eyes that incinerates me. "I should have known who you were the second you walked down that aisle. Nobody else has that particular swagger."

"I'm touched that you would remember it." Somehow the words sound cockier than I feel. My heart's still skipping beats, strangely out of rhythm. "Now let's go back to that interesting little statement. If you die, I die? What in the cauldron's name do you mean by that?"

And Mistmark smiles at me, holding up his wrist where the bloodred ribbon is still tied in a neat little bow. "It's a little something I insisted be added to the vows. Let's just say that I didn't trust Belladonna."

"But I'm not your bride," I blurt.

"You pledged your troth to the goddess, as did I." There's a dangerous, predatory look in his eyes. "You bound yourself by the sun and the moon and the stars. It doesn't matter if you weren't who you said you were. Your blood still lingered with mine. You gave your word. The goddess heard it all. Did you not think about what would happen if you mixed your blood with mine and gave me your oath?"

Right now, my blood is draining out of all my extremities. No. *No.* I did not. "That scheming little bitch." I know exactly who has to pay for this. Who trapped me. She knew. Zemira *knew.*

Maybe you'll thank me some day....

I am going to wring her bloody neck.

"Like it or not, Soraya, you are now my wife. It doesn't matter what name you used, or what face you wore. Your blood. Your pledge. Your oath. And now you're mine." Mistmark's smile holds a thousand dangerous edges. "But the funniest thing about this entire situation is that you *can't* kill me. You don't dare let me die. 'Til we meet the endless night, my love… you are bound to me, body and soul." His gaze lifts to a point over my shoulder. "Now let her go."

"*Fuck*," Falion grates out as he shoves me forward.

I don't think we've ever agreed on anything before. "Fuck."

But then his face tightens. "Hang on a minute.... If you're here... then where in the blighted lands is your sister?"

Ooops.

23

ZEMIRA

There's one thing the best thieves have in common: Patience.

Pulling off a heist like this requires exquisite planning. You have to get the lay of the land.

And you need to locate the thing you're trying to steal.

You need information about what you're going to encounter. Guards. Opposition. Vaults and magical deterrents. The wards you're likely to breach…. Everything.

Then the magic happens: You create a distraction, something that's going to pull everyone's attention like an explosion. Something like… a wedding where the groom seemingly dies. Throw in a fake bride. An assassination of the prince of the court. Mix it with hundreds of wedding guests all trying to play their own power games, and you have one potent moment in time where nobody's going to be thinking about the horn.

But the secret ingredient that binds everything together?

Timing.

You have to know *when* to make the grab.

I Sift along the hallway, alighting in each shadow only long enough to get my bearings before I vanish again. I can't afford to have anyone see me, but what I really needed was to take Falion out of the equation.

Good thing I have his secret weakness up my sleeve.

He's been itching to get the upper hand on my sister ever since the summer she tried to kill Mistmark, Soraya said.

She's going to kill me when she discovers the truth about those wedding vows. But I'm starting to learn my lessons. I can't trust anybody. Not truly. She'll betray me the second she gets a chance, and so this time, I took the leap first.

Now how are you going to work your way around Keir?

Later, conscience. We'll have this discussion later.

The whiny little bitch sighs, but she gives up. Maybe she knows this is not the right moment to be trying to get me to be a better woman.

Two seconds later, I'm standing at the entrance to the maze.

The questing beast lurks in there somewhere. I just know it.

There's a reason the fae have been vanishing. It's got nothing to do with the antics of the Court of Blood, and everything to do with an enormous chimera of nightmarish form who might not be getting fed as frequently as she'd like.

I think about everything I know about Mistmark and Falion.

The first time I saw them conspiring, they were in the checkerboard garden. And according to Mistmark's letter, the horn is "right where the queen should be."

Checkerboard.

Or chess board?

I Sift through the maze, bouncing between each dapple of shadow until I reach the magnificent checkerboard of lawn. Nothing moves but the whisper of wind through the trees, but I can smell something gamey.

Perfect. The beast must be close by.

Wrapping the shadows around me, I creep along the wall of the hedge as I scan the area.

There's something hidden there in the shadows of the enormous bloodstar tree. I don't think I'd have even noticed it myself if there wasn't something about the way the shadows twist that catches my eye as *wrong*. And I certainly wouldn't have noticed it if I wasn't looking for it.

Taking a slow breath, I ease toward it, hoping the beast can't scent me.

It's a casket woven of shadows themselves. They're bound together so tightly I can barely see through them, and if not for my gifts, the golden chest beneath them would be almost invisible.

The Horn of Shadows.

Falion.

It's incredible work, somewhat like that cloak of his. I've never even thought it was possible.

But how to pierce the shadows?

I can hear the questing beast's breath writhing through its lungs like the sound of three dozen distant hounds wheezing. The echoing timbre of that sound makes it difficult to pinpoint, but I know it's here somewhere. Each breath is slow and steady.

Asleep.

Sifting closer, I try and shield myself in the shadows.

Nothing moves.

But every instinct is on alert as I kneel before the casket.

I tentatively touch the casket before me. It's chill and cool and somehow impenetrable. And yet, it stirs beneath my touch, like a cat arching into a pat.

Somehow, the shadows meld around my fingers. It's not unlike the way I can slip *through* them, but this time, I'm using them to coat my skin. Allowing them to part around me like a glove.

Is this how he does it?

I coax them to part, feeling the cool slip and slide of them. The chest appears, gold lock dulled by years of wear. It's a simple thing to pick for a master thief.

I glance around as I slowly open the chest. The hinges squeal, and I freeze.

Only the wind stirs through the trees of bloodstar, but there's a different timbre to that wheeze now. If the beast was asleep, then it's only dozing now.

I ease the chest open, and my breath catches as I find the horn, nestled in a bed of red velvet.

The Horn of Shadows is cast of ancient brass, and you can almost see the marks where someone has lovingly polished it in the past.

I stroke the smooth curve of the horn. It was created by the same dwarf who crafted the cauldron. They say a single blow of the horn will bring the ghostly hunt to life, the hounds who guard the cauldron riding at the bidding of the horn blower.

But the horn can only be blown by one.

Your life will be tied to it forever—or at least, until death.

"Well," says a voice behind me. "It's all starting to make sense now. You've grown a little more ruthless, dearest sister. You lied right to my face. We were supposed to retrieve the horn *together,* but imagine my surprise when I came across that brainless little apparition that's perched on Keir's lap, eating sweetmeats."

Leaves rustle as if something enormous is moving behind them. I slash a hand through the air in desperation as Soraya stalks into the clearing, trying to urge her to shut up.

It's too late.

I finally realize where the bloody beast is.

It's not hiding behind the bloodstar trees.

It's been there all along, right in plain sight, the scales on its body rippling into a patterned background that matches the maze as it moves. Dapples of its hide appear. It has the body of a leopard, the head and neck of a serpent, and the legs and feet of a hart—though I didn't know it could camouflage itself like that.

It's also three times as tall as me and can spit poison that can sear the skin from your bones.

"Run!" I scream as the questing beast suddenly appears against the trees, a reptilian eye blinking open and locking upon me. Snatching the horn, I tuck it under my arm. "Run!"

~

"WHAT IN THE BLIGHTED LANDS ARE YOU DOING HERE?" I demand as we sprint through the maze. "You were supposed to be taking care of Mistmark!"

"I did take care of Mistmark! I married the bastard, after all! And then I managed to slip him and his nurse-maid," Soraya yells. "I didn't realize the ceremony was real and binding!"

I shoot her a glance.

She slams me into the hedge just as an enormous green spitball hisses past us. It cuts right through the bloodstar, eating its way into the hedge as though it doesn't exist.

"You knew." Soraya can obviously see it on my face, and she's furious. "You said 'you'll thank me later.' That's what you meant, isn't it?"

I push off from her and drag her through the newly opened hole in the maze. It's too small for the questing beast. It might hold it for a moment. "This way! And yes, I knew." I haul her to the right. "You've only been pining after him for three years."

"Pining?"

"Don't think I don't know you," I snap at her as the entire hedge to our right shudders. I throw a glance over my shoulder as the beast simply forces its way through the tightly bound trees. *Curse it. Guess that wasn't going to slow it down at all.* "'I'm fine,' you used to say. 'He'll get his comeuppance one day soon.' 'His heart has my name on it, and I'm going to shove my fucking blade so deep inside it that you'll hear his scream from here.'"

"What part of *that* has anything to do with pining?"

"He's the one who got away, Soraya." We reach a T-intersection and I take two seconds to decide which way to go before hurling her toward the left. "You don't miss when Father sends you after a target. But for some reason, you couldn't kill Mistmark, and I don't think it's got anything to do with Falion, and everything to do with those pretty blue eyes."

"Goddess, I hate you!"

I grin at her. "I knew it!"

Soraya makes a frustrated screaming sound. "Well, don't get too excited. He's sent Falion after you. I managed to escape and led that fucking prick on a merry chase before I came here, but I think he'll realize where we are the second he hears that huge furry bastard rampaging behind us." She looks over her shoulder. "Down!"

I dive, and another enormous, sizzling spitball burns a hole through the hedge in front of us.

"How do we kill it?" she snaps as we both scramble to our feet.

Teeth clash as I leap halfway up the hedge and snatch a hold of one of the branches. The questing beast misses me by an inch, and I'm dangerously close to where its spitball is eating its way outward in the hedge.

"We don't!" I Sift out of the way, rendezvousing with Soraya on the other side of the beast. "It's impervious to mortal weapons."

"Falion's idea, no doubt. I swear, I'm going to drown that smug prick in the blood lily pool. He's going to be picking weed out of his crushed velvet for weeks."

"You're starting to sound a little fond of him," I muse. "I thought you'd simply try to kill him."

"I did try," Soraya growls. "Let's just say, I think he's got my measure. Although, apparently he can't kill me because my life is bound to Mistmark's."

I ignore her glare. "I did actually think of that. Hand-fasted couples are bound to each other for a year and a day."

It's an ancient custom between warring fae courts that's probably saved many a life. By the time a year and a day has ended, often cooler heads have prevailed, and in some cases both bride and groom no longer want to kill each other.

We skid around a corner and slide to a halt.

"Dead end. Curse it." Soraya looks this way and that. "And no way out."

"Here." I cup my hands and kneel. "The way out is *up*."

"With this bloody hedge trying to take a swipe at me at every step," she grumbles, but she steps into my hands, and I throw her into the air.

Grabbing the horn, I Sift after her just as the beast crashes right through the hedge beneath us.

The shock as it hits the trees takes my feet out from under me. I catch a glimpse of Soraya's startled expression and then she's falling too. A branch stabs into my shoulder, and the horn is torn from my grip.

No!

The ground comes at me too fast to Sift, but the second I land I vanish into the shadows, punching back into reality several feet away. Lucky. The questing beast's slavering jaw closes right where I should have been, its teeth clashing over nothing more than empty air.

"Z!" Soraya launches beneath it, her knife slicing through the tendon in its heel.

I launch into a dive, grabbing the horn and rolling beneath the creature's hooves. The flash of its dappled belly glides over my head, before I'm rolling to my feet on the other side of it. "This way!"

We sprint for the exit of the maze as the questing beast gives another furious roar behind us. A glance over my shoulder reveals its crimson eyes locking on us furiously. Soraya injured it, but the creature heals too fast to remain crippled for too long.

A door appears in the maze walls. I slam against it, and the polished timber bursts open. The cave beyond is dark, leading into the mountain court. We slam the doors shut behind us, but two seconds later an enormous jarring impact throws me off my feet.

Desperation fills me as I scramble across the gravel floor just as the creature appears. It's enormous nostrils flare as it turns its lizard-like head this way and that, a long thin tongue flickering out to taste the air.

"Blow the horn!" Soraya snaps, blood dropping from her temples as she presses her back against the rock wall.

She's trapped there.

Our eyes meet.

"It can only be used once!"

"Then use it! Blow the cursed horn!"

I set the horn to my lips and blow.

Nothing happens. I'd been expecting the bellow of something like the trollhorns they have in the north, but this is silent. All I can hear is my breath, whispering through the brass curve.

"It didn't work." I jerk the blasted thing down.

But Soraya's face pales, as if she sees something I don't. "Stay still," she whispers, sinking back against the rock. "Don't move."

Mist pours into the cavern, lit from above with eerie blue. Little gleaming lights sparkle within it, and it's not until it draws closer that I realize they're eyes.

The grymhounds of the Wild Hunt.

Creatures you can barely see until they're upon you.

The questing beast roars its rage to the pack, and then it lunges toward them, teeth snapping. A hound vanishes into a curl of mist as its ruthless teeth close over it, but another darts beneath its belly, angling for the back of its front hoof.

"Move." Soraya shoves me further into the blackened cave.

A low, echoing growl rumbles from within. I skid to a halt as she slams into me.

And then a creature appears, huge and wolf-like and carved of glowing light. Its eyes shine with blue light—empty and emotionless, but the growl tells me everything I need to know.

"What's it looking at?" Soraya whispers. "Isn't it supposed to respond to the horn blower?"

"Define 'respond,'" I reply grimly, "because Keir said something about how they guard the horn. Maybe it *is* guarding it."

"Guard? *Guard*? It's looking at you like you just murdered its firstborn." Soraya draws her knife and the pair of us glance at its glowing blade.

"What's it doing?" I whisper. "Is it supposed to be doing that?"

"Not that I know of." She whips the knife through the air in a threatening arc. "Stay behind me."

It's been years since we've worked together like this. My back meets hers, and while I draw my own blade, I doubt it's going to do much.

"They're impervious to steel," I tell her. "The only thing that effects them is silver."

"Good old goblin-forged weapons," she says with a smirk. "Come on, you mangy cur. I dare you."

The enormous grymhound stalks toward us. It has to be the alpha of the pack. Others turn away from the questing beast at its growl, falling into place around us.

Then they're upon us. Glowing teeth snapping for my face. The heavy weight of rancid wolf slamming into me, the impact numbing my arm to the wrist.

I Sift out of the way, but something catches on my sleeve as I go, and the ice-cold burn of teeth grazes my wrist. The second I reform, the pain drives me to my knees.

"Z!" Soraya lunges toward me, driving her glowing knife through the heart of the alpha. It vanishes in a swirl of mist, but those glowing eyes reform barely ten feet away.

Teeth chattering with the pain of its bite, I stagger to my feet. "It doesn't like your blade."

"Recall them!" Soraya yells.

Two sharp blows of the horn will draw them back to the Other World from which they came. I blow sharply. Once. Twice.

Instantly the hounds evaporate, curls of light eddying into nothing.

The questing beast looks toward us before it hesitates. Its gaze shifts over my shoulder—into the black interior of the cave—before it makes a desperate sound and limps away, vanishing into one of the smaller caverns that branch out from this one. Blood drips from the bite marks slashed into its hide and the braying sound it makes reminds me of mournful beasts heading for the slaughterhouse.

It's not the poor bastard's fault it was brought into this game.

Both of us sink to the floor.

I can't get over the sensation of how close we came to death. I can feel the beast's breath on the back of my neck still. I can hear its wheezing roar.

"Why didn't you Sift out of here?" Soraya demands, pushing to her feet and offering me a hand.

A tingling sensation burns through the bite marks in my wrist as I let her draw me to my feet. "It all happened too fast."

Soraya makes a growling sound. "You lying wretch. We spent years testing your reflexes. You had more than enough time. You stayed because of me, didn't you?"

The words lie trapped behind my teeth.

Yes, I stayed. I always will, because I can no sooner leave her behind than I ever could.

And she senses it.

"Didn't you?" she snarls, shoving me back with a hard slam to the chest.

Instinct kicks in. I sweep low, taking her feet out from

under her, and the second she moves to retaliate, I'm gone, punching back into being several feet away.

"What was I supposed to do?" I demand, my fists curled at my sides. "Leave you behind? The only thing keeping it off our backs was the fact there were two of us. It couldn't work out which one of us to focus on."

"I don't need you to watch my back—"

"Because you were doing such a good job of it before I found you in Malechus's sarcophagus!"

"I didn't ask you to rescue me," she says coldly, examining the cavern. "When Malechus came back—"

"*If* he came back," I point out. "You could have suffocated in there. And you're welcome. You're always bloody welcome."

Bristling with fury, she stalks past me. "Where are we?"

It's Soraya's way whenever there's conflict. If she knows she's in the wrong, then she simply won't argue any further. I want to scream. I've been bottling this all inside me for years.

"I don't know." Bending to pick up the horn, I wrap it in a piece of my shirt and concentrate, plucking shadows from the air to weave around it. It's nowhere near as good as the protective veil Falion had created, but it will do to guard it from anyone's eyes. "I had a monstrous gnashing beast trying to take a bite out of me. I wasn't mapping where I was running. Why?"

"Because I'm fairly certain something drove that creature off, and it wasn't your grymhounds. Nor was it us."

There's something about the way she stares into the darkness of the cave that sends a shiver down my spine. I take the chance to Sift to the side, hiding the horn in a rocky crevice before I reappear at her side.

Soraya looks at me sharply, as if she sensed the movement, but she's still distracted by the current threat.

The questing beast could be lurking outside.

And she's right. It was injured by the grymhounds, but the second a wound is cut into its hide it starts repairing itself.

Something about the cave unnerved it.

"Guess we're going to find out," I mutter as I turn toward her. "Are we taking bets on what sort of vicious beast lurks in—"

A hiss of air whips past my face, a sting alighting on my cheek. I clap a hand there in surprise, but it's the brief scream Soraya gives that stalls my own shocked cry.

An arrow embeds itself in her chest, and she staggers back, her feet scrambling to keep her upright.

The last thing I see before she hits the ground is the ebony shaft of the arrow.

One glimpse of those short, clipped raven's feathers on the shaft and I know who hunts us.

I *know*.

Ruhle. And his seven.

I spring forward, slamming Soraya back to the floor as she struggles to rise, just as another arrow screams past.

And then they're singing toward us like a flight of ravens. Rolling her, I manage to find cover under an overhang of rock for both of us.

"Get out of here!" Soraya screams, coughing blood.

Leaving her here is leaving her to our bastard brother's mercy. "Not without you!"

Grabbing the arrow, she grits her teeth together as she snaps the shaft. "You stupid fool, you'll only slow me down. The way you always do. The way you did the night of our final test. You're not ruthless enough, Zemira. And you're going to get us both killed."

It's an arrow to the chest.

Suddenly I'm back there, staring into her eyes as I see

recognition slowly dawn there. She was reaching for my hand to haul me up the cliff until a sheet of glacial indifference came over her.

"You're only slowing me down," she'd whispered, her voice cutting through my chest like a rusty hacksaw. *"You're going to get us both killed."*

"Don't leave me! We'll do this together—"

But Soraya only shook her head, her eyes locking down tight and hard as if she was nailing the coffin shut on the love we'd once shared. *"He was right. Father was right. You're weak. And I have to be strong enough for both of us. Goodbye, Z."*

And then she turned and walked out of my life.

Forever.

"Maybe I am weaker than you are," I snarl. "But that doesn't mean I'm going to just walk away right now. I'm better than that."

"Curse you, let me go—"

Grabbing two fistfuls of Soraya's coat, I steel myself. I've done this before.

I can do it again.

"No! Don't you dare!" she yells.

An arrow ricochets off the ledge.

"Come out, come out, little rats," Ruhle whispers, his voice dipping into a laugh that echoes through the cavern.

One day soon, I am going to drown that skulking rodent, and I'm going to enjoy it.

But right now….

"Don't move!" I hiss at Soraya, and then I plunge us both into the shadows.

We punch into darkness, but this time it feels like a

weight keeps dragging me down. Flickering in and out of being, I move as fast as I can. Alighting on a ledge. Slamming into the tree outside the cavern. Toward the lake....

Every time we slam back into the world, Soraya's scream rings out until I'm forced to clamp a hand over her mouth to stop her from giving away our position. Speckles of shadow stream off me until the hem of my cloak is ragged and torn. Somehow I'm losing particles of myself. Maybe I'm not strong enough to hold us both incorporeal for this long, but I knot my fists in Soraya's shirt as though I can somehow hold her together physically. It's like falling through an endless chasm of darkness, screaming, screaming, until you finally hit rock bottom.

We slam into the waters of the lake.

I'm inside out. Blind. Breathless.

And it's so cold here.

The darkness closes over me, and the last thing I think is how heavy my bones feel....

Slap.

Pain ricochets through me.

Water rushes past.

I cough out a lungful of water and try to get my bearings as someone drags me from the lake. The world is spinning, or maybe that's just my eyes rolling back in my head.

Slap.

"You stupid bitch." Someone's rubbing heat into my hands. "Z, wake up." A hand slaps my face, gripping my chin. "Wake up! Or I swear I'll leave you here. I swear I will. *Wake up!*"

She breathes into my mouth, and heated air fills my

lungs. It's like swallowing light. Heat. My eyes pop wide, and then it feels like every ragged edge of my body suddenly melts into liquid.

Coughing again, I roll onto my side and spew out a cloud of darkness. It's like I'm vomiting pure shadow, and Soraya thumps me between the shoulder blades even as that merciless heat eats its way through me.

What the fuck…?

"What'd… you do?" I rasp, finding myself on the banks of the lake.

Soraya wilts over me, barely holding herself up.

Her skin's the color of ash, her lips blue and her skin shivering. Somehow she's aged a year in a single moment.

"What did you do?" I whisper, because I feel like I could leap a small mountain right now.

And she looks like she can barely lift her head.

Soraya staggers to her feet, hauling me with her. "You don't know everything about me, Z. And it's going to stay that way." She trips against me, her body shaking. Weak. "You should have left me there."

"*Never.*" Why can't she see it? Why doesn't she understand? "Do you remember when you had night-mares and I used to crawl into bed with you and hug them away? Do you remember what I promised you then?"

"We were seven," she snaps. "We were children. We knew *nothing* of the world."

I slide a hand through her hair, forcing her to meet my eyes. "I will guard your back," I whisper. "I will shield you from the shadows. Always. Forever. Together. And I will *never* let you go."

Soraya gives me a helpless look. "You're going to get me killed."

Tears prick at my eyes. I don't cry. I never cry. And yet, there they are. "Are we even really living?"

It's a confronting truth.

"Not for long." Soraya claps a hand to her chest as she looks away. "Not if that prick finds us. Here. Where's my knife? I need to cut this out."

I dash away the tears. It's not worth getting my hopes up. She doesn't want to see it, and without her, I'm only half of what I once was. "Give me a look at it."

"Don't—" She tries to shy away, but I get a fistful of her shirt and tear it open. The arrow shaft is embedded just below her clavicle, but—

That's when I see it.

The dark mottling that covers her chest.

Soraya grabs the shirt and whips it back over the wound, but it's too late.

I sit back on my heels in shock. The blight. She's one of the unlucky few afflicted by the blight. It feels like the world drops out from under me. No. *No.* "Why didn't you *say* something?"

Soraya stiffly tears her shirt sleeve to pieces and uses it to blot the blood weeping from her wound. "What was I supposed to say?"

"How long have you known?" Shock makes my voice ring in my ears. "When did you first see it?"

Her jaw works. "A year ago."

So she knew she was afflicted by the curse when we stole into the Court of Dreams to steal the relic. It wasn't just her soul she was trying to save. She was staring her death in the eye—a brutal, violent, painful death.

This changes everything.

There's only one way to fix this. The blight is a cancerous twist on the curse that afflicts wraithenkind. Hundreds die from it each year, and we have no way of knowing who it's going to strike next.

But if we break the curse….

Maybe she'll have a chance.

My heart feels like a leaden weight in my chest.

Keir wants to keep the cauldron safe from those who'd use it for their own misdeeds, but I can't simply let him have it now. And I wanted to. I wanted to… prove myself true for once.

I have my answer.

And I *hate* it.

"Don't," Soraya's voice cuts through me. "Whatever you're thinking, don't. This is why I didn't tell you. Because you'll do something rash—something stupid—in order to save me."

"I'm not going to do something rash." My ears are ringing. "I'm going to do exactly what Father wants me to do. I'm going to bring him the horn. And then I'm going to bring him the cauldron."

And afterward?

I promised myself there would be no war. I promised myself I'd do right by Keir, just this once.

I can steal the cauldron back.

After all, I'm the best thief in the north.

I can fix this. I can fix all of this.

Soraya's eyes go shiny, and she turns her face away.

"It's almost painful to see how stupid you are. You're going to get yourself killed. And for what? For me? *Why*?"

"Because you're my sister." My voice roughens. "You're my only sister. You're all I have. And maybe I'm stupid to trust you again...." My throat fills thick with unshed tears. "But you're the one warning me away time and again. I have to believe that means something. I have to believe there's even a single hint of love left in your heart."

Her gaze jerks to mine again.

Her jaw works.

But she can't say it.

All I can see is the impossible pain in her eyes.

"Love will ruin you," she finally says. "And leave nothing but ashes in its wake."

"That's what you always say." I push to my feet, offering her a hand. "And I don't care. Now are you going to give me the knife? We need to cut that out of you and get out of here. I have a cauldron to find."

THE FIRST SIGN WE HAVE COMPANY COMES WHEN WE'RE half a mile from the lake.

Gravel rains down over us as we cut through a narrow ravine.

Soraya pales as she looks up. There's no sign of anyone on the ridgeline above us, but there doesn't have to be.

When our brother and his seven are hunting someone, they're rarely seen.

"Why is he here?" she gasps, sweat tracking rivulets through her hair. "What does Father want now?"

I think of the questing beast. "They've been there for a few days. The creature knew danger lurked within those caves. They must have scared it off at some stage."

"What in the Shadow Lands can scare a creature like that away?"

"Ruhle's face," I say with a grimace. "Maybe it knew he was the bigger monster."

Our eyes meet. I managed to cut the arrow out of her chest, and her right arm is strapped to her body, but she's still losing a lot of blood. Whatever she did to me cost her. And while my feet feel as light as air, I don't dare try and Sift us both again.

"Run," she says, shoving me in the back.

She's right on my heels as we slip and slide down the shale-covered hillside. The forest is crawling with shadows, some of them keeping pace with us.

An arrow hisses through the air, and I shove Soraya ahead of me as it sinks into a nearby tree with a thunk.

Ripping it from the wood, I stash it behind my belt, and then follow her.

On and on, with arrows hissing out of the weak afternoon light, as if Ruhle wants to taunt us with how easily he could kill us.

He's playing with us.

Or no, herding us somewhere.

And the worst thing is, we're not going to make it.

Enormous beech trees climb the rocky mountain slope beside us. There's no help for it. I dart within their lingering gloom. Two steps in, and there's an eerie silence that falls like a curtain. I swallow as I lead Soraya further.

The trees provide the cover we need, but we're not the only ones who can hide in here.

"Give me your knife," I tell her grimly.

The look she gives me tells me exactly what she's thinking. A goblin-forged blade? *When the sun rises in the Shadow Lands*....

"I'll bring it back to you," I promise.

A certain bleak acceptance darkens her eyes as she passes it over. "Kill," she says. "Don't hesitate. Not today. This isn't the Court of Shadows. Father isn't here to whip Ruhle and his filthy brethren into line. If he gets his hands on either of us—"

"He won't," I promise. "Hide."

She's right.

She's only slowing me down.

And there's only one way to end this.

I have to become her.

I Sift away, slinking from shadow to shadow. I don't know whether it's the fact we're being hunted, but I can't help feeling as though there's something dangerous about this place.

A figure appears, creeping through the forest on silent feet. Nocking an arrow to his bow, he eases over fallen trees, ghosting over dry leaves that ought to betray him.

Semirhyn. My brother's tracker.

I meld back into being, my spine pressed against a beech trunk and my hand curving around the hilt of the knife.

Of all the wraiths in my brother's hand-picked seven, he's the most dangerous.

You never see him coming. I've been ambushed in hallways within the Court of Shadows and nearly knifed in my own bedroom. One night, when I was asleep, a knee drove into my back and someone looped a garrote around my throat. I thrashed and fought just long enough to drive my attacker into the wall, and then I Sifted to safety.

The next day, Semirhyn stared across the dining hall as I took my seat, his black eyes cold and emotionless.

There'd been a bruise on his cheekbone.

I'd learned how to lay nasty traps over my door after that. Sleep is difficult to find at the best of times, but since that night, I tend to wake at the slightest provocation.

It all boils within my chest.

All the sleepless nights. The nervous way I can't walk through the castle without my hand twitching over my blade. The tripping beat of my heart….

I've never fought back. You don't dare fight back against my brother's seven, but this time I'm not alone.

And that prick put an arrow in my sister.

I can fight as good as Soraya can, but I've always lacked the ruthless edge she owns.

But this time…. This time there will be no mercy.

I punch into the shadows, alighting just long enough to kick a branch behind him. Semirhyn spins, his arrow driving into the tree root I was just on, but I'm already gone.

I slide into being on my knees, driving the knife across the back of his heel to cut the tendon.

With a scream he goes down, and I lunge to bury the knife in his throat, punching in and out of black smoke.

"She's here!" someone yells, and then sunlight bursts over the clearing as though someone's jerked a curtain from the window.

Rhyvaen. My brother's little sun mage. It's his one gift: the ability to conjure a shocking amount of light, although he can only hold it for seven seconds at best.

It's long enough.

I scream as the light hits me and then vanish.

Through the trees. Rippling through shadows. Trying to smother the burns on my skin. When I'm shadow melding, I'm incredibly vulnerable to searing light.

The sound of a cantering horse suddenly captures my attention.

Shades of white and black glint between the trees. A rider clad in elegant finery, completely alone—

And then I see his face.

Keir.

Curse it. *No*. What is he *doing* here?

And he looks like he's alone.

I flash to his side, startling the horse. It dances to the side, threatening to bolt, and Keir brings it back into line with the squeeze of his powerful thighs.

"Goddess's mercy," he hisses, as he wheels it around me. "Where have you—?"

I press a finger to my lips. "We're not alone."

That amber gaze locks on the blood dripping from my knife. "Mira?"

An arrow hisses out of the trees. The gelding rears,

taking the shaft right in the chest. Its frightened whinny turns into a scream as it starts to fall.

Keir throws himself free of the stirrups at the last second, rolling to his feet beside me.

"What's going on?" he snaps, scrambling to the side of his horse.

It screams in pain, its legs thrashing.

"It's complicated!"

"It always is when it comes to you!"

"What are you doing here?" I demand. "You're supposed to be at the court!"

"And you were supposed to be back by now!" He snaps the arrow, teeth gritting in fury as he strokes the beast's frothed flanks. A certain kind of chilly rage settles over his face as the horse grunts and falls still. "I came to help you."

There's something about the way he soothes it that sends calm through it as it dies. It's a particular kind of kindness, and the grief on his face is real. He couldn't heal it. Not in time. So instead, he took its pain away.

And I know what he's not saying.

I was supposed to be back—and so he came to find me. All the way out here, as if he somehow knew where I was.

"Are you *tracking* me?"

Keir gives me a withering look. "You have a habit of disappearing, my love."

The breath bursts from me. I have a habit of betraying him too, but he's kind enough not to say it.

And I don't have time to argue.

"We have to move," I warn him.

"I'm not going anywhere." There's a rough timbre to his voice as he pushes to his feet. The heat in his amber eyes flickers as the dragon rises. Wind whips through his air. It rips through the trees around us all of a sudden, tearing the leaves from branches and earning a startled cry from a distant figure. Keir turns in that direction as if he's finally found a target for his fury. "Don't you know where we are? Can't you feel it?"

"Feel what?" I yell as my hair whips past my face. What is he doing?

There's a particular quiver in the air, as if detonations of silent force vibrate out from him.

Keir's lip curls as he smiles. "This is a dragon's barrow. They're in my playground now."

And then he flings up a hand.

Trees fall violently, as if they were simply clipped at the roots. Branches simply shatter. A scream rings out, and I see a blur of black crushed by one of the toppling trees. Semirhyn.

He just... crushed him.

"Wait!" I scream, grabbing hold of his leather-clad arm. "Soraya's out there!"

The wind cuts off as if it didn't exist.

The devastation remains.

We're surrounded by fallen trees, all of them radiating out from us in a circle. And right in the center lurks a dragon's bleached skull, its knobby vertebrae covered in moss as they blend into the forest floor.

He simply... cut the trees down as if they weren't towering giants with roots that wove through the forest floor. The power required to do such a thing.... It's just... beyond comprehension.

"This way," I yell, dragging him toward where I left Soraya.

The forest lies silent.

Maybe my brother caught a glimpse of my companion. Or maybe he found Semirhyn. Ruhle's a coward at heart. He likes odds his enemies can't match.

"Soraya!" I hiss as I slip down the slope toward where I left her.

She appears out of the hollowed-out center of a tree, her face strained and a knife in her hand. "What are you doing? Did you kill the archer?"

"Not I." I jerk a thumb over my shoulder toward Keir. "Keir crushed Semirhyn with a tree."

The two of them stare at each other, and all of a sudden I realize he wasn't aware she was even here.

Indeed, the last time he saw her, she was trying to kill him.

I spin toward him, stepping between them. "Don't."

Keir rips his leather gloves off, one finger at a time. "Don't what? Don't ask what's going on here?" Tension hardens his jaw. "Then I won't. I have a fairly good idea already, considering you don't look surprised to see your sister alive." His gaze cuts over Soraya. "I assume this was planned. I assume you intended to double-cross me."

I hold my hands in a pleading gesture. "Originally, yes. But…. I heard what you said about Calliope. About the cauldron. I was going to…. I just needed to get my hands on the horn. I was going to give it to you."

"Was?" There's acid in his voice.

It's complicated.

He sees it in my eyes.

"The King Beyond the Shadowfangs wants to break the curse upon our people." It bursts from my lips. "He sent me here to bring him the horn. If he finds the cauldron, then he'll use it to set us free."

"And you think he's going to stop there?" Keir growls, his shadow falling across me as he steps closer. "I know what manner of creature your king is, Zemira. It doesn't end there. It never does. It will end in war. Your king doesn't want to set you free. He wants vengeance against the fae."

"I know!"

"And you'll what?" Anger darkens his brow as he stares at me in disbelief. "You'll just give it to him?"

I rake my hands through my hair. "If he uses it to break the curse, then I can steal it back from him. I can get it back for you."

Keir looks as though I just slapped him. "You've been planning this from the start."

"Not from the start, no! He was the one who tore me from that dream. I couldn't believe it when he gave me the same assignment. I didn't intend to.... I never wanted to...."

"Betray me?" There's a sense of bleakness in his eyes. "I kept telling myself it was different this time. I thought I knew the truth." He scrapes a hand over his mouth. "But every time you open your mouth, lies fall out."

There's a piercing ache in my chest.

It's better this way.

It has to be better.

"Why?" His voice breaks. "*Why?* I've offered you everything—"

"Because I can't give you *anything!*" My chest heaves as we stand there staring at each other. "I can't."

"Can't? Or won't?"

Looking him in the eye is beyond me right now. "It's not just me. We're not all monsters. There are those among the wraithenkind who deserve a chance to live their lives free of this curse. There's a blight afflicting our kind, a twist of the curse that is killing us. And... Soraya...." I gesture toward her, still seeing that dark mottling on her skin. "I was going to get it back for you."

But even as I say the words, I can't help sensing how pathetic they sound.

His expression closes over, and he gives a bitter laugh. "I was a fool once. And I knew when you walked into my dreams again I was taking the risk that I would be a fool again, but I didn't truly believe...." He shakes his head. "Thank you. For making it very clear to me what your intentions are."

I've lost him.

Forever.

And it hurts, even though a part of me knew it was never going to be.

That's the cost of hope—you know it's a lie and yet you still want it. You still want to believe its gentle whispers. You see a single reason to believe in it, and your heart throws itself wholeheartedly into the cause.

"I'm sorry." The whisper steals over my dry lips. I don't know whether it's the look in his eyes or the steel in his voice that hurts the most. "I've warned you dozens of times. I tried to tell you—"

"Tried what?" he snaps. "Tried to tell me the truth?

Was that before or after you kissed me? Before or after you fucked me?" He breathes out an incredulous laugh. "Did you even want me, or were you just trying to lure me where you wanted me?"

"You make me sound like some sort of conniving witch." It's just one blow after the other. "I kissed you because…."

His gaze sharpens with savage intensity, and he leans closer. "Because… *why*?"

It's all there in his face. The want. The need. The… hope.

"Because I wanted you," I breathe. "Because for once in my fucking life I wanted to pretend it could be this way. You want to know the *truth*?" My voice lifts, right there at the end. "I know what my future holds, and it's *not you*. But I just wanted to believe in it for a moment. Every time you kissed me… I couldn't stop you. I couldn't stop you because I wanted you too much. And I hate it. I hate that you make me feel this way." The words come thick and choking. "I'm a wraith-born bastard of a murderous king. I don't belong in this world, Keir. I don't belong in *your* world."

I press the heels of my hands to my eyes, turning away from him. It's better this way. It has to be better.

"Mira—"

"No." I hold out a hand, cutting him a sharp look. "I have a job to do. That's all that remains between us now. And my half brother is still out there with his murderous little sycophants." I can't stop the tide of anger rising within me. "I'm done running. I'm so fucking done. You want to help? Then get her out of here!" I shove Soraya into his arms.

Keir flashes me a heated look. "Mira—"

"Don't." There's no time to talk about what could have been or what we both want. It was a dream. It was always a dream. And girls like me don't get to live those kind of dreams. "Just get her out." And then I say the one word I've never allowed myself to let past my lips. "*Please.*"

"You're leaving me with him?" Soraya demands, as if she's well aware he still hasn't forgiven her for trying to kill him.

"I trust him." I stare into his eyes. "He won't hurt you. I know he won't hurt you."

It's a breathtaking moment.

Because it's the truth.

I trust *him.*

Even if he can't trust me.

Keir glances toward the rocks behind me. The look he gives me is absolutely furious. "And what are you going to do?"

I gesture with Soraya's goblin-forged blade. "I'm going to kill Ruhle."

Soraya grabs my wrist, hauling me toward her with a strength I didn't expect. "You *can't*. He's the heir apparent. Father will *destroy* you."

These are dangerous games.

I rub my thumb over the hilt of her dagger. Ruhle is my father's favored child. What Soraya's saying has merit. Father won't care if Ruhle attacked us.

But I care.

I am done playing these games. "Maybe it's time for a new heir then?"

I've never been ruthless enough to kill easily. Not the way Ruhle and Soraya are.

I've never wanted to before.

But as my hand closes over the hilt of the blade, it's surprising how easily it fits there. I have nothing left but this.

"Zemira!"

"*Complicated*," I grind out, taking a step back into the forest. "I'll tell you everything. I promise I'll tell you everything when I return. Keep her safe for me," I beg Keir. "I'll take care of them and then come back to you. I promise. I *promise*."

And then I Sift out of existence, before either of them can grab me.

The caves. They returned to the caves.

Of course. Ruhle knows I secreted the horn within them, and he won't give up until he's got his hands on it.

When we were in the training camps, we played a game. An ambush, really.

It was called Shadows and Assassins.

Soraya and I were the best at it.

But I'm alone now as I hunt my brothers. I have to draw them away from the horn. Soraya is counting on me. I don't know how long she has left until the blight eats away at her—the healers within Castle Blackrock will be able to give me a better idea.

The main cavern is full of a lingering sense of silence.

I know that silence as I slip from shadow to shadow.

One little raven, perching on a rock…. I mark him and move on. Patience isn't only a virtue for thieves. It's also the best weapon in an assassin's arsenal.

Another raven, his spine pressed against the tunnel wall as he watches the cavern.

Two of Ruhle's seven.

Semirhyn is dead; Rhyvaen is injured, which leaves five. But where are the other three?

And most importantly, where is Ruhle?

I flit across the cavern, knife held low as I stalk the wraith sitting on the rock. Nothing moves. His attention is focused purely on the cave mouth….

I step out of the Sift, grabbing a fistful of his hair and jerking his head back even as my knife finds his throat—

Light sears the cavern. A thousand bats overhead rustle and scream, their voices too high-pitched for fae ears, but perfectly attuned for mine.

I try to Sift, but the light is everywhere.

And then I'm surrounded by a cloud of bats as they flee for the opening of the cave. Tiny bodies whipping past me. Little claws catching in my hair. And through it all, the light burning, burning, burning….

And then it's all gone.

Seven seconds of misery, all in all, but my knees hit the floor as I try to blink away the afterimage. I can barely even see the shadows…. All I can hear is the soft crunch of footsteps stalking over the gravel floor of the cave toward me.

Ruhle.

He materializes in front of me, just as my eyes finally recover.

Ruhle stares down at me, his teeth bared. "You little slut. You think we weren't prepared for you?"

A web of finely spun spider silk from the demorari on

the Gilded Isles is flung into the air above me. I recognize it from the gilded gleam of that silk; the enormous, bloated spiders weave pure light into a net so tight that nothing can break the strands or escape.

Not even a shadow.

I punch into nothing, but I'm too late.

Thin razor-fine wires of light sink over me—through me—and then I'm gasping on the ground like a beached fish, landing back in my corporeal body with a heavy thud.

It hurts. I can feel those little burning lines all over my skin, but it's the dull ache in my bones that warns me that the jarring thud hurt me more than I immediately suspect.

A boot drives into my stomach.

The shock of such pain wrenches a gasp from me, but I barely have time to absorb it, because another one replaces it.

"I've spent years waiting for this moment," Ruhle whispers, advancing on me menacingly. He grabs a fistful of my shirt and the net, his knee sinking into my stomach even as he presses the tip of his knife against my throat. "Beg me for mercy."

Sharp iron trails down my throat, leaving behind the wet slide of blood.

I grab his wrist, but it's like straining against steel. He's always been stronger than me.

I can't escape. I can't even feel the shadows here. All I can feel is those thin strands of light seeking to sink right through my skin.

The burn of the light. And the kiss of the knife.

"Beg," he insists, and the knife cuts a little deeper.

"No!" I slam a palm into his arm. Desperately.

Uselessly. "You think… I don't know that nothing will come of it?" I kick and strain, but his weight's too heavy to move. "You like them to beg," I gasp. "You like to have us… on our knees before you. You want us to have a moment of hope…. Before you take it away from us!"

He laughs. "Maybe. Now where's the fucking horn? I know you hid it here somewhere."

"I'll never tell you! I'll never beg!" I scream, even as the knife drives through my chest with slow, inexorable pressure. It hurts. It hurts so much. I kick and scream, but there's no stopping him.

Until the wraith right next to us suddenly slumps to his knees with a gasp, clasping at his throat before he slams face-first into the stone beside us.

Ruhle pauses.

"What the fuck?" he demands, pushing to his feet.

I grab the knife, gasping against the feel of it embedded just below my collarbone. *Hurts…. Fuck.* I don't want to die, but even as I drag the knife out of my flesh, my vision wavers.

What happened?

I blink and find Karseem's wide eyes staring blankly at me as Ruhle rolls his friend over.

His throat bleeds red. Someone cut it open to the spine.

I scramble upright, holding onto Ruhle's bloody knife.

"Karseem?" This from Gwyvaen.

Ruhle draws another knife, his gaze cutting around the cavern. "Who did this? Show yourself."

"A pity I don't obey the whims of wraith born bastards," a voice mocks.

Ruhle freezes, his knife hovering in his hand.

The breath I inhaled leaves me in a rush as I slowly lower my hands. My heart pounds fit to tear through my ribs. I recognize that mocking drawl. And while I don't dare call the emotion I feel hope, I can't help feeling as though… there may be a way out of this.

"Serruen?" Ruhle hisses. "I thought these caverns were secured?"

Serruen straightens, drawing the vicious scimitar he prefers. "They were."

He takes one step toward where the voice came from and then he jerks back, as if something grabs him by the hair. A hiss of movement glints, and then blood spatters through the air as his throat is cut.

Serruen goes down like a bag of wheat. He slams to the floor, grabbing at his throat and choking. Blood wells and spurts through his fingers. His heels kick the floor. A death rattle echoes in his throat.

Cauldron's piss. I kick my way free of the net of demorari silk, still bleeding like a stuck pig. A shadow grabbed him. A fucking shadow.

Falion.

I try to shove to my feet, but the world sways around me. *Curse it.* I have to get out of here. Ruhle wants my head. And who knows what Falion wants of me.

He surely didn't just save my life because he likes me.

It happens so slowly, I almost think my eyes are playing tricks. A shadow forms, one tapping a knife against the stone wall.

"Blast it," Ruhle snaps to the side, toward Rhyvaen.

"I can't," the light bringer returns. "I need time to recover."

Grabbing a torch from the wall, Ruhle shoves it toward Rhyvaen. "Then fucking light this. Lights! Everyone get a torch!"

"All the better to see you with," says the shadow, as three torches flare into flame. The light only paints it larger across the walls.

"Who are you?" Ruhle demands.

"I'm your nightmare, little wraith princeling," Falion mocks. Suddenly there are a dozen shadows circling us. One of them actually holds a knife, which I thought was impossible.

Is he half-Sifting?

How is he holding that knife?

"Two down," says the disembodied voice, as the knife draws sparks as it trails down the granite. "Four to go. Interesting to find a horde of wraiths daring to walk among the fae lands…. I wonder what brought them here?"

"Kill it," Ruhle says.

One of his wraiths lunges forward, driving for the floating knife.

The shadow simply vanishes, and then the wraith is screaming—a brutal, tortured sound as if something drove a hand through his chest and grabbed his windpipe.

He dies with a gurgle, blood spilling from his lips as he falls but no other apparent injury.

The glimpse I catch of Ruhle's face will warm my heart for centuries. He is actually shitting himself right now.

Falion steps out of the shadows, wiping at his hand with a linen handkerchief. His shock of silvery blond hair gleams in the light, and he's still wearing the elegant silvery-blue doublet he wore for the wedding ceremony.

"No matter," says Ruhle, cutting me a sharp look I have no trouble interpreting, considering it lingers on my face and hair. Clearly, he sees the resemblance as he steps back toward the mouth of the cavern. "We'll deal with this development later. Retreat."

"But we were just getting acquainted," Falion mocks, spreading his hands.

Ruhle and his remaining companions flee, and while I've always thought I'd enjoy the sight, I can't turn my back on the real monster in the room.

The smile falls off Falion's face. "Get up."

"What do you want with me?" I demand, shoving to my feet.

His eyebrow quirks and then he rakes me over with a disdainful look. "Where's the horn?"

"Somewhere you'll never find it. Stay back," I warn, waving my knife at him.

He stills, but there's a dangerous look in his merciless blue eyes. "I'm not here to kill you."

"No?"

"If I wanted you dead, all I had to do was wait. You were about to have your throat slit by that two-bit wraith," he sneers.

I stare at him, but there's no hint he's lying. He wants something from me. It's not the horn, or he wouldn't be here. It's not to see me dead, or he could have merely waited.

"Fine," I say, flipping the knife and sheathing it at my

hip. "I'll play. Why did you save my life? What do you want?"

"Want?" His gaze hardens. "Haven't you figured it out yet? I want answers. I want to know who you are and where you came from. And I want to know how you can walk in my shadows...."

"Who I am?" Of all the things I expected, it wasn't this. I spread my hands wide. "I'm Merisel of Greenslieves, the beloved betrothed of Prince K—"

"You're wraithenborn," Falion says, his lip curling. "With fae magic in your veins. You're an impossibility. You should never have been bred. But you...." He takes a dangerous step toward me, making me regret the impulse to sheathe the knife. "You are an abomination."

The words strike me where they hadn't been able to hit earlier. "Like I had any choice in the matter. I was born into this body. I didn't choose it."

"Who is your father?"

"That's none of your business."

"It's Raesh, isn't it?" Every step he takes is tight with menace, but it's the unsettling intensity in his eyes that unnerves me.

I don't know what he wants.

I don't know why he's looking at me like that—like

he's one step short of violence—but this is personal for him, somehow.

He's a Shadow Walker.

A gift granted to me by my mother.

And she was…. She was…. The heat bleeds out of my face. It's impossible, but then fae magic tends to run through family bloodlines.

"Answer me," he snaps. "Your father is Raesh Ghul, the King Beyond the Shadowfangs, isn't he?"

"What do I get if I say yes?" I drown my sudden terror in a smirk. "A sweetmeat?"

His thumb rasps over the hilt sheathed at his hip. "Maybe I don't kill you."

"Maybe you can't," I taunt. "You seem to be having some difficulty killing wraithenborn today, considering my sister is walking free."

Oh, yes, he's definitely still feeling the weight of losing to Soraya.

We circle each other, and he chokes down the emotion lighting bonfires in his eyes. "Who was your mother?"

It's an old hurt, but it lances through me like an arrow to the chest. "I don't know."

"I overheard Keir call you Zemira," he says, sauntering toward me nonchalantly despite the wraith blood dripping from his knife. "What's your real name?"

"You want my *name*?" I blurt. He's got to be joking. My father's the only one who knows my three names, and the giving of such a gift is merely another manacle to shackle myself with.

"Did your mother name you?" Falion demands.

"That's none of your business."

"No?" He gives me an evil smile as he spreads his hands. "You walk the shadows. There's only one fae bloodline that can do that."

"Two," I point out. "The Court of Shadows and the Court of the Moon and Stars."

"One," he says coldly. "The Court of Shadows took one of our Shadow Walker's as queen long ago, but her bloodline has long-since died out. I would know. My people kept immaculate records. You *shouldn't* exist."

And then he disappears.

I'm so used to being the only one who can do that, that I hesitate a fraction of a moment too long. *Idiot*. I spin, driving my knife toward where I expect him to appear, but it merely cuts through the air harmlessly.

Instead, something swipes across the back of my calf.

I scream as I fall, my shadow bleeding across the floor in some amorphous shape. He didn't cut *me*. He cut through my shadow, and now it's untethered and leaves me feeling dizzy.

"You wraithblighted asshole," I growl.

Falion suddenly reappears, flipping his dagger from hilt to blade and back again as he circles me. "You're a Shadow Walker," he confirms, "but you barely know the basics. You're barely a baby."

I hiss and lunge toward him, ungainly and heavy in my flesh.

He vanishes again, but this time so do I, even if it's like clawing my way through quicksand.

The world turns to shadows.

I try to Sift, but something grabs me by the hair and then I'm staggering back into cold, merciless arms.

"You know nothing," Falion says in disgust, his voice an odd echo in my ear.

I'm little more than a mass of black smoke, a shadow rippling and straining to escape his arms. He wrestles with me, but he's far more skilled than I am. My inky form keeps breaking away. Instinct wants me to Sift again, but he's holding me here, like two shadows tangled in each other.

I slam back into reality and hit my knees.

For the first time in my life I have no idea where my knife has gone.

A thin line of light appears in the air in front of me, and Falion steps through it. This time he has two knives, which he juggles with apparent ease. One of them is mine.

Light. He's… manipulating light as *well?*

"A baby Shadow Walker who's never been trained," he muses. "One born to a wraith king. But the question remains: Who was the mother?"

I can't help feeling Keir's words lancing through my heart. Zyra. Zyra Starsworn. It's a truth I haven't even allowed myself to consider.

Hope, once again taunting me.

"Why do you care?" I spit the words. "You want a name to add to your list of kills? You want to gloat about how you killed the Wraith King's bastard daughter? Fine." I push to my feet. "I don't know my mother's name but whoever she was, she named me thrice. She *loved* me. She loved me enough to give me three names. Gravekissed, the Black Hawk, Winterborn. And that's all I know."

Falion freezes.

I lunge forward, kicking my knife out of his hand. It whirls through the air, and I spin, driving the same heel high into his chest. He staggers back as the knife lands in my hand and then we're facing each other again, and though I caught him by surprise I know it won't happen again.

But then he surprises me, because he bows his head and sheathes his knife. "I know who you are. I know who your mother was. And I'm not here to kill you."

"No?" My fists clenches around the blade. It would be nice to believe him, but I've seen this trick played a thousand times before. "Then who was she?"

There's a wealth of sadness in his blue eyes. "She was Zyra Starsworn. Lost to the world when I was but a baby. Stolen from her bed in the middle of the night and never returned." A hint of anger clouds his expression. "Zyra Starsworn. Starblessed. Lightkissed. The Queen Who Was Promised. The queen who never had a chance to live up to the promise in her name. And now I know. Now I know what became of her." His face locks down tight and hard. "How did she die?"

I lower the knife. The weight in my chest feels like it's going to drown me. I don't dare hope. I don't. But this is the second fae male who's confirmed that name. "If she was truly my mother then she died in childbirth. My…. My father cut me from her womb. Her magic was killing me." I taste the truth on my tongue like bitter acid. "And mine was killing her."

We stare at each other.

It's a little akin to looking in a mirror. My face holds more feminine softness, but there are… hints….

"You knew her?" I ask, barely daring to breathe through the hope.

I may as well be speaking to a frost-glazed lake. "I knew her but briefly." His voice drops. "She was *everything* to me. Everything. And yet, I have only one true memory of her—the one my father gave me. A memory trapped in a crystal ball. A beautiful woman who smiles down at me as I lie bloodied and bruised on her chest." His gaze seems far away in that moment. "She kissed my head and she drew me to her breast, and then she named me thrice."

The heat drains from my face.

Only a fae mother gives such a gift.

Falion smiles as if he knows exactly what just went through my mind. It's a bitter, twisted smile, one that holds the edge of a knife. "I was four when she was stolen from us. And now I am the sole remaining heir to the throne of the Court of Stars and Moon. I am Falion Starforged. The Prince Who Shall Never Rule." He takes a deep breath. "And you are my sister."

No. *No.*

"How do you *know*?"

"Because you are Gravekissed," he whispers, "for your father. Winterborn for the time of your birth. But the Black Hawk was all for you. It was the mark she wore, inked into her skin. The mark of her warband, her own personal coat of arms. The mark she would have embossed on her banners had she ever come to her throne. The promise of her name and future glory." His voice falls away. "A glory that never came. A throne that was never claimed. And now a court that is nothing more than rubble and ashes."

Because of me.

"Well, it's a lovely family reunion," I snap, "but you'll forgive me if I doubt your intentions. As you can see, those I call brothers tend to have a tendency to try and drown me in wells or put arrows through me."

"My intentions are this: You're pathetic. You're weak. You're half-trained and know nothing—"

"It wasn't as though I had someone to instruct me!"

"As such, you're an embarrassment to my family line." He eases out a breath. "But you are also my sister. She named you, and in so doing, she has forced my hand. I cannot walk away and allow her sacrifice to be without meaning." He closes his eyes. "I will train you."

Train me?

I can't stop myself from thinking of how easily he walks through shadows. He trapped me with but a single move.

If I knew how to do that, then maybe…. Maybe I could steal back the soul-trap with my soul in it. Maybe I could… kill my father and set myself free. Set us all free.

For the first time in my life, I see a way out of the trap I've found myself in.

"Now come," he says, turning on his heel and glancing toward where I'd hidden the horn as if he can see right through the shadows I wove around it. "Fetch your horn."

"*My* horn?"

"You blew it," he points out. "And as such, you are bound to it until you die."

"I thought it was Mistmark's?"

Falion gives me a sidelong look. "Alaric no longer needs it."

And then he's gone, leaving me to wonder what in the Shadow Lands that meant....

KEIR

"Zemira!" I snatch for her wrist, but she's gone, evaporating into black smoke. My fingers plunge through it, and then even that is gone.

Damn it. Damn *it.*

She's out there.

All alone.

"She can do this," Soraya rasps as she sinks to her knees in the heather at my feet.

I cut her a look. None of this makes any sense. Soraya tried to kill me and allowed Zemira to take the fall for her actions. Every time I've seen them, one of them has been trying to murder the other, and yet there's a connection between them I can't deny.

Keep her safe for me….

Goddess' breath, the things I do for this woman.

I cut my wrist with a swift jerk of my knife and then bring her lips to my skin. "Drink."

Soraya jerks her mouth away. "Thanks, but—"

I shove her face against my wrist. "I wasn't asking.

Drink. I need you on your feet so I can go after your sister."

Soraya gasps as my blood hits her system. Warmth and color spreads through her skin as if my magic heals her inch by inch. Tugging my hand free, I swiftly seal the cut with a hint of magic.

"You stupid fool." She laughs under her breath as her head sinks back on the heather. A single tear glints in her eye before she blinks it away. "You love her, don't you? You still love her, even after everything...."

I haul her to her feet, where she trembles against me.

She's healed, but that doesn't mean she's going to be putting a knife through anyone anytime soon. Even my blood has its limits.

"You can't have her," she whispers.

The dragon within me bares its teeth. "Watch me."

I swing her up into my arms. She's pathetically weak, but she grabs a fistful of my shirt and if she had a knife, it would be at my throat. It stills the rage. There's a wariness in her actions that reminds me of Mira.

Tough armored shells.

Careless attitudes.

A yearning neither of them can quite hide.

In that they could be twins.

"*No.*" Soraya bites her lip. "Father will kill her the second he realizes you want her. He'll snuff her light, her soul, all so that he can deny you. He'll do it to hurt you. He won't even spare *her* a thought. You *can't* love her. You can't have her. Because you will cost her *everything*. I know what you are, but you can't have her."

Stillness radiates through me. I know Zemira is

bound to her father's will. It's my one eternal frustration: that she can never simply cast off the yoke of his demands.

But….

"What do you mean, he will snuff her soul?"

Soraya's shoulders sink. "He cuts our souls from us the second we're born and wears them in a soul-trap around his neck. He has hundreds of them. Thousands. If he thinks she's betrayed him, then he'll crush her soul-trap and kill her instantly." Those hard black eyes meet mine. "He promised her that if she brought him the Dragon's Heart, then he would return her soul. She'd be free of him, free from our court."

The words expand within me, leaving me breathless. When Soraya stole the amulet, I thought little of it—just another fae king or prince making a power play.

But Zemira knew the truth.

She knew it was never the amulet.

And all she had to do to save herself was betray my secret.

But she clearly kept it instead.

It changes everything. It all finally makes sense. And even though there's a heavy weight inside my chest, I can't help feeling a little breathless.

Zemira never wanted to betray me. She's warned me a hundred times. *Don't fall in love with me. I will betray you. I will always betray you.*

I always wondered what sort of hold he had on her.

And now I know.

Now I know what the transaction will be.

"I didn't think you would care," I tell Soraya quietly.

"She told me about the final test. She said you betrayed her. You left her behind to die."

Soraya looks away. "You don't know my sister. I was the one holding her back. I knew she'd stay with me physically. I knew I was slowing her down. And when she slipped and was hanging off that cliff…. She can punch into shadows. All she had to do was let me go and she would make it to the finish line. But she had to let me go first. She had to let me go."

"So you let her believe you left her to die?"

Soraya's lashes lift, revealing eyes as bleak and hard as obsidian. "Love is a weakness. Love will get you killed. I finally understood that."

And now I understand it too. "We would do anything for love. Despite the cost."

I slowly set her down. Soraya grabs my arm. "What are you planning to do?"

"What makes you think I'm planning anything?"

"You have that look in your eye," she retorts. "Don't do it. Whatever you're planning, don't do it. You'll kill her."

"You've got it wrong." Maybe it's reckless, but I can't help smiling at her. "I'm a dragon. We don't let go once we've found something we want. Now I just have to find something *he* wants."

I set a finger to her nose, drawing on the enormous well of power that binds me to these lands.

Soraya opens her mouth to argue, leaves swirling around her and lacing in her dark hair—

Freeze. I breathe power into the world.

Everything comes to a standpoint.

The leaves hover in the air.

The wind stops.

Soraya stands mute, frozen in motion.

Time is a held breath, pressure building and building, like a set of lungs forced to endure. I have minutes at best before the structure of the world starts to strain at its bindings. Once I walked through time with the ease of a master, but now, all I have left is this…. Stolen minutes.

I sense half a dozen others turning toward me from wherever they stand, curious to know who has wrought such a working of power. Even the fae will sense it when I restart time. They will sense it, and they will wonder.

"I am done hiding," I whisper into the world, and my power carries those words across courts and kingdoms. *"I have found my true mate. Don't interfere."*

Their minds brush against me, curious and distant, and then, one by one, all six of them turn away.

They will not interfere.

But Asmeroth leaves me one last parting note. *"You risk us all with this decision. They will sense the truth."*

I risk nothing I'm not willing to pay.

I am Enkeirammon.

King of kings.

Heir to a throne that no longer exists.

And I have finally found the treasure I've spent my entire lifetime searching for.

Nothing is going to stop me from having it.

Tearing apart time and space, I step Between, and then I'm standing in front of a brass horn wrapped in shadows. I can sense it whispering to the world here in the Between, the song of the cauldron hissing through it.

Zemira thinks she's secured the horn.

And maybe she did, because I can still hear it singing her sweet tune.

But now I'm going to take it.

I'm going to take it all.

But first, I have to let her go.

ZEMIRA

The court is in uproar.

We barely managed to slip our way inside, for Belladonna—the new ruler of the court—has guards stationed at every door.

Particularly mine and Keir's.

"This could be a problem," I whisper, as Falion and I watch from the shadows. "I made a deal with Belladonna. Right now, I'm the only one who knows she wanted your lord and master dead."

And if Belladonna is cleaning up the court, then she'll most likely be interested in tidying up any other sort of loose ends she can find.

Falion sighs. "This way then. I need to check on Alaric anyway. And you need me to look at that knife wound."

"It's fine." No one has ever offered to look at my wounds, beyond Soraya. I don't know how I feel about that. "You don't think Belladonna will be trying to ensure Mistmark doesn't breathe another day? There might be some confusion about whether she's married to him or not…."

"There's no confusion. The court is aware he survived and has since found himself hand fasted to an assassin. He thinks it's amusing," Falion grumbles. "One thing you will learn is that Alaric thinks a dozen paces ahead. He's already accounted for Belladonna. And there's a reason she didn't dare try and kill him herself."

I thought that had something to do with not daring to thwart Malechus, but maybe I was wrong.

I shoot one last look at Keir's door. The horn is hidden. I didn't dare risk bringing it into the court until we knew the state of affairs, so I put it in the one place I know nobody will find it. And Belladonna won't dare confront *him*. But I still haven't seen him. I know he'll be watching over Soraya. I know they'll both be safe, but I can't help wondering what's going through Keir's head.

I didn't have a chance to talk it through with him.

The last time he saw me, he'd just realized the depths of my betrayal….

"Are you going to stand there like a lovesick puppy forever?" Falion growls. "It's a little embarrassing."

So much for brotherly love. I glare at him. "It's a good thing you're so powerful, otherwise I'm fairly certain there'd be no reason for Mistmark to keep you around."

"Oh, there's a reason." He stalks into the shadows and vanishes. "Now are you coming or not?"

I SINK INTO AN ENORMOUS ARMCHAIR ACROSS FROM THE Lord of Mistmark, nursing a cup of warmed tea that Falion brewed. My shoulder is bandaged, and Falion cleansed a half-dozen other minor wounds he found on me. The tea is filled with herbs, but there's nothing that strikes me as poisonous or drugging.

Falion sees me inhaling the fumes and raises a brow. "If I wanted to kill you, I would have used my knife. I could have buried you in the forest and then I wouldn't have to drag your body out of the heart of the court, where hundreds of assholes are simply looking for a reason to tear my lord down. It would have been considerably easier."

"What he means," the Lord of Mistmark says, examining me with the most amused expression I've ever seen him wear, "is that we don't intend to harm you."

The two males share a look.

Mistmark seems to have recovered from his poisoning well, though he doesn't bother to shift off the sofa, and I can smell something restorative in his drink. Dark shadows haunt the circles beneath his eyes, however, and he's not as well put-together as he usually is.

I'm fairly certain his mouth is stained a vicious pink, as if he couldn't quite manage to remove all the lip paint Soraya was wearing.

So much has happened in the space of an afternoon.

"So," Mistmark muses. "You're Falion's little sister."

"So…." I draw my knees up under the blanket Falion gave me. "You're my sister's husband."

If anything, the tension in the room grows thick. Falion

turns to put his teapot away, and Mistmark rests his hand over his mouth and leans on it. Rings glitter on his fingers.

"It seems that way," he finally says.

"You don't appear to be as unhappy about that fact as either Falion or Soraya," I point out.

Mistmark runs his tongue over his upper teeth. "Let us just say that... I have long believed my path was going to cross your sister's again one day. Indeed, while it was a shock to realize it was actually *while* I was kissing my new bride, I've been expecting her."

He has? My fingers itch. "Just what did happen between you all those years ago, Mistmark?"

"Alaric," he says in a warm voice. "And nothing happened. She tried to kill me. She failed, much to her disapproval."

I stare at him. Alaric has the best card playing face I've ever seen. "Strange…. That's not what she says."

And there it is.

A slight narrowing of his merciless blue eyes. He lasts twenty seconds. "What did she say about the situation?"

"Oh, it's a 'situation' now, is it?" I set my cup down with a smile. "My sister doesn't say much at all. Which is more telling than anything she might actually mention. But I'll trade you an answer for an answer."

"What sort of answer?" His curiosity is definitely winning now.

"An answer to whatever sort of question you would like to ask. And likewise."

"Don't," Falion warns him.

But Mistmark smiles. "Fine. I'll play. But I'm going first…. And I will have the truth from you, little wraith."

"I will answer as truthfully as I may."

He sinks back onto the sofa, considering his cup. "Your sister has tried to kill me thrice now. The first two times she failed. Badly. But today, she would have succeeded. I was poisoned, and there was nothing Falion could do to try and save me." He leans forward. "But she saved me. She poisoned me and then she gave me the antidote. Why?"

Because I'm fairly certain she's half in love with you.... "Belladonna had cursed me. She wanted the marriage to fail, and unless I killed you before today was done, I was going to die." I tell him about our little heist. "You were the perfect distraction, but if there's one thing we are ever taught, it's not to let the situation get too messy. If you'd died, it was quite clear Falion would be intent upon exacting his revenge, and we already had Malechus and Belladonna to worry about."

"Not to mention the Crown Prince of the Forbidden Court," Falion mutters.

"I wasn't entirely certain Ruhle was in play," I say with a shrug. "I also had no particular desire to see you dead. I just needed Belladonna to think you were."

He seems slightly disappointed with the response.

"But that is me," I add gently. "If my sister wanted you dead, then you would *be* dead." And then, because I've always been a romantic at heart, I add, "Three years ago, my sister was sent to kill you. I have to presume it's because my father knew you had the horn and wanted it. I don't know why she didn't kill you. I don't know how she failed, or what occurred between you, but I do know this." My voice hardens. "My father doesn't tolerate failure. You get one chance, and your punishment is severe. When my sister returned home from your court, she knelt before him and told him she'd failed. Just that. She gave no explanation. She gave no excuses. She did not beg for mercy. And so he locked her away in a windowless, lightless, frigid cell for four months. She was given just enough food and water to survive at irregular intervals. No one spoke to her. No one touched her. She had not a single blanket with her, and she's terrified of the dark.

"But she accepted that punishment without a single complaint." I sip from my tea, cooling now. "It always surprised me, because Soraya is selfish and argumentative. I've never seen her deal before Father like that before. But then... sometimes I'd wonder if she did it because she was trying to protect someone else—someone she needed to convince Father not to kill."

There's trouble in his eyes, and I don't think he knows what to believe. But there's also something thoughtful there too. "She's afraid of the dark?"

It's not the concept I would have thought him to focus upon. I shrug. "I was born within my father's court, but Soraya was not. Her mother managed to escape him when she was heavily pregnant, and she spent five years in hiding, before his wraithen scouts finally tracked them down. They killed Sora's mother right in front of her and locked her in a chest for weeks on end until they'd smuggled her back into our lands." It's not my story to tell, but.... "She suffers from nightmares sometimes. Her entire life changed in a single day, and while she forged armor around her heart and grew calluses on her soul, she still prefers to have a light burning in the night."

Mistmark considers my words. And then he nods.

"More than what I asked, and I'm grateful for it. I will try to reply in kind."

"There have been a few questions plaguing me about this entire situation. At first I wondered why you agreed to marry Belladonna, but it soon became clear Malechus was blackmailing you. He wanted the horn, and he forced you into a corner in which you would marry his cousin and yield it to him as a bridal tithe." It's the one question that's always bothered me. "Why? What was he holding over your head?"

Mistmark sighs. "Your sister."

So far my theory is correct. Ruhle must have approached the prince in order to set this entire thing up—but I don't know what Malechus thought he'd gain from the arrangement. The horn, clearly, but what did he intend to do with my brother when Ruhle came for it?

"You know what Soraya is."

"I do."

"And it doesn't bother you?"

Mistmark strokes his thumb over his cup. "I'm the guardian of Mistmark, and the castle is a repository of information. While I wasn't yet born when the Court of Shadows was cursed, I've read everything about it that I could get my hands on."

Was that before or after you met my sister? "My father believes the curse can be broken."

Falion pauses at that, his mouth thinning.

But Mistmark stays him with a hand. "It's possible, yes. You would need an enormous amount of power to do so."

"How much power?" It's something I've given

thought to several times of late. "My father believes it would require something like the cauldron. Or a dragon's heart."

Mistmark chews on his nail. "Both would definitely break the spell." He looks a little pained. "Both could tear apart the world while you're at it. You speak of taking a war hammer and using it to shell peas." His eyes narrow upon me. "But the cauldron is lost, and there are no more dragons."

I sink back a little. "Of course not. Hence my question. I wanted to know if there was anything else that could do it."

"Of course. You'll forgive me if I cannot answer such a question from memory. I would be willing to open the library at Mistmark to you, if you sought an answer."

"Thank you." I can't help fighting a yawn.

"Tired?" Mistmark asks.

Falion tops up my cup. "Do you need somewhere to stay for the night?"

Mistmark shoots him a quizzical look.

"What?" Falion asks blandly.

"I'm just trying to work out what you're plotting," he tells his friend. "That was... generous."

Falion scowls. "She's my sister."

"And I'm your friend." Mistmark leans back in his chair, his arms crossing. "Do you remember when you threw me out into the mud and told me to find my own fucking bed?"

"You were drunk." Heat climbs up Falion's throat. "And you snore like a wounded bear."

"Precisely my point. I was in a precarious state of mind

and you made me sleep in a barn. Anyone could have slit my throat."

"I set a shadow to watch over you."

Mistmark shoots me an amused look. "There is one thing you should know about your brother, my lady. Don't ever trust him when he's trying to be polite. He's up to something."

Falion throws his hands in the air.

I don't know what to make of this good-natured play. "I'd begun to realize that. He looks slightly constipated whenever he tries to smile."

Mistmark coughs a laugh into his hand, his blue eyes twinkling as he glances to see his friend's reaction.

"Cauldron's icy kiss," Falion says. "You two are as bad as each other. Fine." He glares at me. "I tried to be kind. Sleep in the hallway. Crawl back to Keir's bed. I don't care. Just don't come sniveling to me when he casts you out."

Yanking his cloak over his shoulder, he slams the door as he stalks through it.

"He's out of sorts," Mistmark explains, stretching his arm along the back of his sofa and watching the door with an affectionate look. "Your appearance in his life is very confusing for him." His gaze softens. "He's spent years hoping his mother was still alive. And now he knows what happened to her. He won't ever say it, but he doesn't like surprises. He doesn't know what to do with you."

"He offered to train me."

It startles a laugh out of him. "Did he?"

I sink back into the sofa. I'm so fucking tired. Every inch of me feels like I'm covered in bruises, but it's the one painted across my heart that hurts the most. I've been avoiding Keir ever since I returned to the court, but I can still hear our last argument.

"What now?"

Now? It's an explosive question. The last time I saw Keir, he'd just discovered the depths of my betrayal. I drain the rest of my tea in a single gulp. "Now I have to go beard the dragon in its den."

"You're going back?" His smile is kind, even as his eyes remain watchful. It's a reminder. Mistmark is still sounding me out.

Falion isn't the only one I cannot quite trust.

I push out of the chair. "Someone has to go see if your bride is still alive."

"Oh, she's alive." He swirls the rest of his drink, staring into it. "At least until I get my hands on her."

I slip over the edge of the balcony and come face to face with a furious dragon.

There's no surprise in Keir's eyes as he wrenches the curtains aside. Only frustration.

"Where have you been?" he growls. "It's been hours."

"Making friends." I stagger over the doorstep. "Where's Soraya?"

"Sleeping." He jerks his head toward my bedroom. "I healed her with my blood and put her to bed." His eyes narrow. "Where have you been?"

There it is.

The first thrust of the knife in this game of parry.

"Somewhere safe," I tell him, because I haven't entirely decided what I'm going to share with him. Somewhere in my head, I'm still trying to sort out what this revelation about Falion means.

He prowls back into his bedchambers as my dry tongue cleaves to the roof of my mouth. I follow him slowly, uncertain whether I'm truly welcome here. If he put

Soraya in my bed then does he mean for me to stay here with him?

My heart skips a beat. I never meant to be here once my deception was discovered. Until Keir told me that story and made me question where the horn truly belongs, I was planning to slip away before he could confront me.

I've never had to face the consequences for my actions before. Not like this. I've never had to stare a prince in the eye and beg for forgiveness. I've never... wanted forgiveness before.

And I can't read him.

What is going on in his head? I want to be ill.

"What?" he finally asks.

"You're... not as angry as I expected you to be."

His expression is cold. Stark. Unforgiving. "Oh, I'm angry."

"I told you the truth of what happened. I changed my mind. I was going to give you the horn. I was going to let you throw it in the deepest trench in the ocean, if you wanted to keep it secret—"

"But?"

"Then I saw Soraya's chest. I saw the blight spreading through her." My voice drops to a whisper. "It's a wasting sickness that afflicts my kind—the backlash of the curse that transformed us. It's brutal and unforgiving, and I've seen what those who suffer it go through. It will eat away at her, inch by inch, until there's nothing left. There *is* no cure. Do you know what they do to those afflicted with the blight? They kill them, Keir. A quick knife across the throat is the cleanest death we can offer them, but there's another truth my father wants to keep hidden.... Every year the blight affects more and more of my kind. It's not contagious—not the way an illness is—but there are some factions at the Court of Shadows who think my father's stranglehold over the court is what is causing the increase in cases. He'll have her killed if he sees the rash." I swallow. Hard. "The only way to stop the blight from spreading is to break the curse that ties us to this flesh. I have to give my father the horn." It's the only way I can save her. "I have to find the cauldron for him. *Please*. Please understand. It was never about betraying you." I give a bitter laugh. "For the first time in my life, I was actually tempted to give you everything you wanted, even if it cost me. But she's the one price I won't pay."

The harsh line of his shoulders doesn't soften. "I never asked you to pay such a price."

"You want the horn—"

"I don't *care* about the fucking horn. Do I want to keep it out of the hands of those who will abuse its power? *Yes*. But if it takes its place in the world, then I will deal with it." Hot anger flashes over his face. "I understand why you made the choices you made. You love her. She's your sister. I understand that. Do you know why I'm angry, Zemira?"

I'm a mess of confusion. "Not really, no."

"I'm tired of the lies," he says, advancing upon me. "I'm tired of being right here, only you won't look to me for help. I told you everything; about my past, about Igrainne, about Arianna. Do you know how many times I've breathed those words in the past three thousand years? *Never*. I told you because I wanted you to understand. I wasn't telling you that you *had* to give me the horn. I was asking you to trust me. I was asking you to share your side of the story, so we could work through a solution together. You want to save your sister? Then why the fuck didn't you tell me about her? About this blight? You think I wouldn't care? You think I wouldn't help you?"

The words take me like a fist to the throat. "I…."

The harsh line between his brows deepens as he hears my hesitation. Somehow, he's backed me against the door. "Don't you dare insult me like that."

"I'm not insulting you! Have you ever thought that maybe the problem is me?" I shove at his chest. "I don't know what you want of me. I don't understand *any of this*."

His eyes blaze. "You know what I want of you. I told you once"—he presses his fingertips on the wall on either side of my hips—"that I was searching for my truemate."

There it is again, the panic clawing its way up my throat. "I can't be your truemate."

"Why?" His breath whispers over my lips, his expression savage. "Because your father has your soul?"

I rear back in shock.

"Soraya warned me away from you. She told me everything. She thinks I'm going to get you killed."

"I…."

"No more lies," he tells me, pressing his finger to my lips.

No more secrets. No more lies.

And so I kiss him.

This is my truth, right here. It's the only one I can give him. The only one I can give myself.

Keir captures my face in his hands, and the second our lips touch, the control within him shatters.

His hands are on my skin…. His tongue in my mouth. The sheer force of his body hammers me back against the wall as if whatever dam he had in place to shield the torrent of his emotions has failed. Need pours out of him. Fury. I'm drowning in it and I want it, and maybe this would be the sweetest death of all.

Destroy me. Please.

A tremor runs through him as if he heard me. A hand slides into my hair, pinning me there as his kiss turns hot and punishing.

It's a desperate clash, all my emotions riding me like a whip. I don't know what today has brought, but I do know it's changed my future forever.

I can't pretend anymore. The cracks around my heart were hammered by the finest of chisels, and though my shield was strong, it was never meant to guard me against this. Against my own wants and desires.

"Keir," I gasp.

Capturing me behind the thighs, he hauls me into his arms and then strides for the bed. We hit the mattress together, the shock of his weight driving me into the soft blankets. Another savage kiss obliterates my senses. There are hands on my skin, shoving my shirt out of the way. Teeth grazing their way down my throat.

"You're so cold," he whispers, crawling up my body.

"Then kiss away the shadows," I whisper back.

A glint of something I can't quite name darts through those wicked eyes. He pauses, and somehow, he sees right through me. "As you wish," he finally breathes.

Those wicked lips find my skin.

Roughened hands glide beneath my half-ruined shirt. He parts it with a sharp jerk, tearing the fabric I used to bind my breasts free and then his mouth follows, closing over my nipple.

A spear of delicious agony jolts through me. There's a hollow inside me, desperate to be filled.

All those empty nights, dreaming of a lover I knew waited for me....

I never knew until this moment that it was him I dreamed of.

He's the one I've been waiting for all these years.

I kiss him. Hard. Seeking to drive out the doubts plaguing me. Keir tugs my leathers down my legs and flings them aside.

Fingers find me through the sheer silk of my drawers. He tugs the silk aside and drives them into me, a curse leaving his mouth.

"Fuck, you're so wet." A kiss obliterates every thought in my head as he pumps those fingers slowly within me, scissoring them.

I can barely retain a moan. Whatever this male is, he knows what he's doing in the bedchamber. A spear of jealousy lights through me at the thought, and I shouldn't be jealous.

I can't stop thinking of the cauldron.

Of Calliope.

Of the oath he pledged to his people.

And of Soraya, trying to fight against the curse's blight.

He said he'd help me save her, but what am I dragging him into?

My father will kill him. My father will—

"Stop thinking," he whispers in my ear as he curls his fingers up, just so. They rasp over something so sensitive I moan and arch into him. "There is nothing outside this room. Not tonight. Just you. Just me. Us."

He's right. I kiss him again, forcing my sister and her deadly illness out of my mind. Maybe, just maybe, if I give him this moment, he'll understand.

Then he's shoving my knees apart, diving between them.

His hands grip my thighs and pin them down as he plunges his tongue inside me. Dragging his tongue out of me slowly, he lets it flicker against that sensitive bundle of nerves there. *Oh, fuck.* Again and again. A brutal, furious fucking of his tongue, leaving me writhing and wretched on the sheets. And then his fingers join him, thrusting inside me the second his tongue darts around my clit, before he replaces it with his tongue again. A scream tears loose. He's taking no prisoners tonight. There's none of his usual control, his curiosity. Instead, he's a marauding barbarian, driving me hard toward the edge, as if he intends to stake his claim.

I tumble over it with another jagged cry, my fingers sinking into his hair. Too hard. Too fast.

The entire room is whirling.

"Gods, Mira." He kisses his way up my thigh, his mouth wet with my juices. "I could spend forever worshipping you like this."

"Maybe it's not worship I want."

"Then what is it?"

Punishment.

He sees it in my eyes, and his own darken. His thumb drags over my mouth, his gaze following the teasing trace of it. "No. Not that either. Though I can make you beg for mercy. Is that what you want?" He thrusts his thumb inside my mouth, where I suck on it. Hard. "Do you want to beg me, Mira? Do you want pain? Will it make it easier for you to submit to me?" Those two fingers slide over my lips until I can taste the musk of my own body. "Because let me assure you, by the time the sun rises, you will submit. I'm done with this fucking game. Mine, Mira. *Mine.* I'm going to claim you so hard you'll feel the bruises for weeks."

My heart erupts like a flock of birds taking flight. *Panic.* I haul him toward me with a fistful of hair, our mouths clashing even as I lick the taste of myself off him. I want him inside me. *Now.*

I want him to still all the doubts.

Getting a hand around his cock, I urge him toward me, but he smiles against my mouth. The brutish head of his erection dips into me, then it's gone again, like a tease.

"Are you ready for me?" he whispers.

"I've been ready forever," I gasp.

There's something savage and possessive about the look he gives me. "So be it."

Flipping me onto my hands and knees, he drives inside me with one smooth thrust.

If I'd thought him a barbarian before, then I knew nothing. The savage way he takes me is wild and desperate. Teeth sink into my shoulder, even as he knots my hair around his fist. Harsh, sharp thrusts hammer into me. It's an assault on all my senses, but it's not until he pushes my face down into the pillow and slides those fingers over my clit that I realize I knew nothing of fucking until I met this prince.

Am you ready? he asked, and I didn't understand what he meant until I was moaning into the pillow.

"Come, Mira," he commands, his fingers doing their damage.

I cry out, fingers curling in the sheets as I shatter.

Body clenching around his, I ride him through each and every mind shattering thrust. "*Mine*." His teeth sink into my neck. I'll be painted with bruises on the morrow. "Forever, mine. Say it. *Say it*."

"Yours. Oh, Gods," I gasp. "Yours."

And then his thrusts slow, his fingers digging into my hips as he grinds within me.

A roar escapes him, and then we're both spilling onto the mattress, his body still sheathed in mine. I gasp and pant, every inch of me trembling with aftershock. I want to keep him inside me forever. He's relentless, both in and out of bed, and I wouldn't have it any other way.

Breathing hard, I try to seek some sort of equilibrium. It was just sex—just pleasure—and yet, in some ways, it was so much more than that.

Keir rolls to the side, drawing me into his arms as his cock slips from my body. His seed paints my thighs, leaving me milky-wet and aching. Every inch of me is tender and trembling. Maybe I'll be able to walk on the morrow. Maybe not.

I can't resist a laugh.

Good luck getting the horn out of here. I can barely move.

He's ruined all my plans simply by fucking me into oblivion.

"What is it?" His brusque whisper stirs the sweat-formed curls at the base of my neck.

Oh gods. Instantly, the laughter dies, choked off and brittle. I grind the heels of my palms against my eyes. I have the stupid urge to cry again, and I never cry.

"What's wrong?" he whispers.

Relentless.

I tear my face away and bury it against his throat. "Nothing."

Keir arches back, forcing me to meet his eyes. "I will have all of you or I will have none of you."

It bursts from me in a whisper. "Then you will have none of me."

Frustration darkens his brow. He kisses my mouth, chasing after my lips as he draws me into another caress. He's inside me with another smooth glide, hard already. I whimper and arch, still shattered by the throes of our last orgasm.

Keir laces his fingers through mine, pressing them to the bed as he rocks against me. There's something heated about this long, slow kiss. His lips chase their way down my throat, but it's the sensation of his palms against mine that undoes me.

There's an entirely different tone to this moment.

It's no longer fucking.

I can see the possession in his eyes. I can taste it on his tongue. And I can feel it as he fucks me with slow, gentle, torturous thrusts that would threaten to steal my soul if I still had it.

"All of you, Mira. I'm taking it all," he promises, as I cry out again and surrender to the pleasure. "And this time, I'm not asking."

I slip from the bed hours later, leaving Keir lying on his side, the breath easing in and out of his massive lungs. For a second, I pause beside the bed and simply drink in the sight of him. The faint lamplight gilds his olive skin, and the sheet barely covers the muscular globes of his ass. I'd like to say I could spend forever staring at that ass, but it's his lips that draw my attention. His lips and his hands.

Soft lips.

Gentle hands.

Unless he's using them to unleash ruin upon me.

But even then, there's a certain sort of devastation they wreak.

Because I yearn for the taste of his mouth and the touch of his hands.

Not merely for sex, but in those quiet moments where he draws me into his arms.

It's the single most brutal realization of my life.

I could love him. I could love him.

Suddenly, there's a gaping chasm beneath my feet. My heart plunges into freefall, but this time there are no shadows to catch me. Digging my nails into my palm to ground myself, I turn and grab the glass of water on the nightstand, gulping it down.

By the time I lower my hand, it's easier to breathe. Easier to think.

I'm only going to get him killed. If Father knew the truth about him… he wouldn't stop until he was cutting Keir's heart from his chest. He'd let the truth get out to the fae courts. He'd try and back Keir into a corner and come at him from the shadows. He'd use me against him, if he had any idea of what Keir feels for me. Of what I feel for him.

This fucking curse…. I half wish it would end us all.

But I promised him.

No more lies.

Together.

Trust.

I know what I have to do now.

Brushing a kiss against his temples, I turn and head for the horn.

I have to give him the horn.

Drawing my robe over my naked body, I clean up as best I can in the wash chambers, dress in my leathers, and then Sift out into the night to where I've hidden it.

The grotto is silent and dark now the wedding is over and I doubt any of the revelers will linger here. Not while Malechus is dead. Not while Mistmark's prognosis is so uncertain. *I* know he's going to survive, but no one else knows that.

I light the torch that guards the heavy stone sarcophagus that Soraya was trapped in, staring at the carvings on the tomb. It was the safest place to leave it. The stone lid's too heavy to shift by mortal hands, and Falion—the only other fae who might be able to Sift through the stone and retrieve the box—told me the horn is mine now.

"The weight of its being rests on your shoulders now," he'd said. *"Mistmark and I are done with it."*

I don't know what that means, but I'm fairly certain he never wants to see it again.

I Sift through the stone, releasing a sigh of relief when I find the box untouched. The second I reform. I dart a glance around the room, but there's no one here. The hairs down the back of my spine lift, but that's not unusual, nor is the pounding of my heart.

Time to get out of here....

Except that whispering sensation that filled my chest is gone. No disciplined thief would ever take the time to check the loot right in the middle of a heist, but doubt pools through me like fermented wine.

Just one little look.... When the fate of the world lies in your hands it pays to be—

The chest is empty.

Empty.

"What the fuck?" I blurt, scrubbing my hand over the insides of the box I found. No horn.

The breath explodes out of me. *No.* How did this happen? Who took it?

I jerk the lid down sharply, but a sound behind me steals my attention.

There's a shadow rippling across the walls.

Kicking the box out of the way, I turn to face the intruder, both knives slipping into my hands. "Show yourself."

Blue skirts slip into the pool of light, and then a woman steps forward, her cheeks gaunt and her arms wrapped around her. I have several inches on her, and there's no sign of a weapon, but that doesn't still my suddenly racing heart.

"Ismena?" What is she doing down here? How did she even get in? As far as I know, the grotto is locked and guarded.

There's something broken about her eyes. Something fractured. "I wish I'd never met you," she hisses. "I wish she'd killed *you* and not Narcissa."

Calliope.

"Look," I start, lowering my knives. "Everyone wants to forget what happened at the Court of Dreams. You think I enjoyed it—?"

"I think you're a lying bitch," she spits, "who ruined my life."

"I was inclined to be tolerant, because you don't seem at all yourself right now, but I've had enough. It's been a tremendously shitty day. I didn't *ruin your life*. You think you had a chance with Keir? He didn't even *notice* you. Even now the extent of his feelings toward you seem to be guilt. I never stole him from you. I didn't ruin anything. Because it didn't exist, except for whatever ridiculous notion is playing through your—"

"You think this has anything to do with Keir?" she half screams.

A glint of gold echoes in the torchlight. I get a glimpse of a tiny crossbow, and then she pulls the trigger.

I go to Sift, but the tiny bolt slams into my hip just

before I make the leap. It jolts me through the shadows, spitting me out on the floor by her feet.

I yank the bolt out of my upper thigh, hissing at her through my teeth. "You think that little prick is going to bring me down?"

"No." She launches herself at me, the silk of her dress flying. "But this will."

She throws a handful of powder in my face, and my body reacts before I can think it through. I inhale sharply, even as I try to roll out of the cloud of drug.

Because that's what it is.

The first acrid taste of the drug coats my tongue. Metallic. Metallic, *shit*. Snake root. I need to get out of here, get to Keir—

I try to Sift, but the shadows bleed away from me even as my knees hit the marble floor. The entire room is spinning. I knew it worked within seconds, but I didn't realize it was *this* potent.

"Ismena." Her face comes into focus as I sway. "*Don't. I saved… your life.*"

"And then you threw me to the wolves," she says, tears streaming down her face as she withdraws something bright and shiny from her pocket.

Light erupts within the room, searing my eyes.

I try to shield them, but it only throws me off-balance, and I slam to the cold tiles. Ismena grabs my hand, locking that burning, searing band of light around my wrist.

"A little gift from the Court of Dawn," she says. "No more shadows for you."

Pure light.

Rhea.

I try to scream as she snaps both ends into place. Burning, burning, right through to my bones…. A hand clamps over my mouth, and then my eyes roll back in my head as I taste one last mouthful of snake root.

The last thing I hear is a dragon bellowing before Ismena jerks a turnkey portal from her pocket.

I swear I imagine it—did he somehow sense I was gone?—but then she throws her arms around me and activates the portal.

The world sucks me into a pinprick point.

And then it vanishes.

3 0

Don't *show a single hint of weakness.*

I stalk through the hallways of the Court of Shadows, every nerve in my body screaming at me as dozens of wraiths flock to see me make the long, silent walk toward the throne room. My whole body hurts after I came to in the dungeons nearly two days ago, but it's the burning brand biting into the skin around my wrist that sets my teeth on edge.

And the presence of my captor.

I underestimated Ismena.

Or maybe I underestimated just how far Ruhle would go.

He prowls just behind me, his leather cloak flaring like bat like wings. "Not quite as mouthy now, little wraith," he taunts.

Swallowing down the lump in my throat, I try to ignore the burning manacles around my wrists. I tried to Sift out of the dungeon, but the light merely burned right through me, leaving me shaking and gasping on the floor. I can't

Sift right now, but I'll get free. Somehow. Falion manipulated the light. That has to mean I might be able to do it too. And I'm too valuable to my father for him to break me and toss me to the scrap heap....

It doesn't still the nervous twisting in my stomach.

He doesn't need me whole, after all, and there are many tortures I can survive.

Ruhle reaches for my arm as we reach the throne room doors, and I yank free with a hiss. "Keep your hands off me."

He gives a menacing laugh. "I'm enjoying every second of this." His eyes flash with dark fire. "I'll make you beg for mercy before this is done, Zemira. You killed my brothers. I'm going to cut their deaths out of your hide."

I lean close enough to see the glint of rage in his eyes. "I don't think he'll let you. You might play at being the wolf here at court, but the truth remains: You're just one of Father's hounds like the rest of us."

There's no point struggling or trying to run. Facing Father is inevitable—it's merely a matter of whether I do it on my own two feet or not.

So I don't give him the satisfaction of having the last word. Instead, I turn and stride toward the doors as if they'll part before me. The guards jerk them open just in time, and my breath catches as I catch a glimpse of the enormous throne in front of me.

An eerie figure waits in silence.

Torchlight flickers behind the king—a ploy I know is intended to make him appear more foreboding—but despite that knowledge, I can't help feeling the weight of his gaze upon me.

"Father." I go to one knee before the dais, my fingers curled into fists and my heart thundering in my chest.

I failed.

The horn is gone. I don't even know who took it.

And there is only one answer for failure.

Boots crunch across the cold slate tiles. I steel myself, teeth clenched against the blow—

Instead, a hand slides through my hair. "You have done well, child."

What? My head jerks up, but I'm not imagining the smirk on the king's lips.

"You succeeded beyond my wildest imaginings," he purrs, capturing my chin in a brutal grip. "And played your part to perfection."

I don't know why, but my stomach drops through my heels. *Never trust his smile.* "What do you mean? I failed," I whisper. "I had the horn in my hands, and I lost it."

"We no longer need the horn." He reaches within his cloak and produces a letter. "I found this on my throne this morning."

And with that, he tosses it at my feet, looking strangely ecstatic over the fact someone clearly slipped past his personal security.

I flip the envelope open with my thumbnail. The envelope was sealed with red wax, and my heart starts to flutter when I see the impression of the broken seal. A dragon rampant.

Keir's mark.

And his words, direct and to the point.

. . .

YOU HAVE SOMETHING I WANT.

I have something you want.

Meet me at the Easternwick ruins to make the trade by sundown and bring your daughter.

KEIR

THE HEAT DRAINS OUT OF MY FACE AS I LOWER THE letter. "I… don't understand."

"Simple," my father replies, sinking back onto his throne. He snaps his fingers and Ruhle appears from the shadows behind the throne, dragging a young fae woman.

Ruhle throws her at my feet, and Ismena scrambles upright, panting with fright. Her skirts are torn and tattered. "I did everything you asked," she blurted. "You promised you would let me go if I told you everything."

I surge to my feet. Ismena. *Here?* It makes no sense….

Or does it?

Blood slides from my extremities with a clammy touch. My father's spies are excellent, but not even they can penetrate the Court of Dreams.

If Father wanted to truly know what happened within the court three months ago, then he would have needed an eyewitness.

Ruhle offers me the faintest of smiles—and the edge of his teeth. "I did tell you I wasn't in exile among the border forts. I was setting up the play." He drags his gloves off, then captures Ismena's chin. "*My* play. This pretty little princess hates you, did you know? She hates you for having what she wants... a prince's heart—"

"I *don't* have his heart."

"That's not what she says." He shoves her aside as if she's merely collateral damage, and it's only then that I see the bruises she's been hiding beneath the silk of her gown.

I wish I'd never met you....

My heart goes still.

I understand what she meant now. If Ruhle got to her....

It doesn't matter if she hated me. I know how he works. I know who he idolizes. Even if she wanted to tell him everything she knew about me, it wouldn't have mattered. He'd have hurt her. Violated her. Perhaps even worse.

Sorrow fills me as we stare at each other. I don't blame her.

I don't blame her for any of this.

No. I know who I have to kill.

Slowly, my gaze lifts to my half brother.

"Is that fury I see in your eyes, Zemira?" Ruhle grabs a fistful of her hair, pressing her face against his thigh as if she's a dog. Ismena flinches, looking down. "You thought you were in control, didn't you? But all I was doing was testing a little theory, and it seems I was right."

"*No.*" I can see where this is going now. I wasn't the fucking card in play when I was sent to the Court of Blood; I was the bait. If I managed to capture the horn, then my father would have used it. But now he's going to make another play, and I can't let that happen. I lunge forward, but one of the guards yanks me back. Another kicks my feet out from under me, slamming me back to my knees.

And the fucking manacle of light stops me from Sifting.

"Tsk, tsk, tsk." Ruhle prowls in a small circle around me, his eyes glittering maliciously. "I knew something had occurred when you came back from the Court of Dreams long after your sister returned. I know Keir's reputation. Regardless of your skills, he wouldn't have just let you go like that. I wanted to know more…. And so I found this pretty little bird and made it sing." He wrenches Ismena's head back with a fistful of her hair, squatting down and setting his face close to hers. Grazing his fingertips against her cheek he smiles when she flinches. "And what a story she told. About a prince who couldn't take his eyes off our little wraith. About stolen kisses. Dinners alone. About the fury in his expression when you betrayed him. It made me start to wonder…. Did our little thief steal something more precious than a relic when she entered the Court of Dreams?"

"He's a prince," I scoff. "He doesn't like to lose. And if you think he'll trade me for the horn then you're quite mistaken." He wouldn't dare. Not with the suspicion that Calliope survived the massacre within the Court of Dreams. Not with the cauldron still out there.

"The horn…." His smile is sinister. "You're always so many steps behind, Zemira. Keir's in love with you. And he's going to give us everything we need if he ever wants to see you alive again."

"You son of a bitch!" I lunge for him again, but one of the guards drives a boot into my ribs.

"How's your sister?" Ruhle mocks as he paces around me where I lie gasping on the floor.

I try to suck in a breath, try to stop the pain. Something's broken, I think, but it doesn't matter. I can't fight my way out of here. I need to be *smart*. They'll know Soraya's alive—Father will be able to see her soul writhing within its trap—but I'm not about to volunteer any information on Soraya's whereabouts.

What I do know is that she isn't *here*.

She's with Keir. With Mistmark and Falion. Maybe I'm not entirely reliant upon the mercy of wolves.

"Soraya's probably imagining a target right in the center of your back right now," I whisper to him. "Don't start sleeping easily, Crown Prince. Especially now you only have two or three of your seven left to watch your back."

His eyes narrow, but his smile is nasty. "I'm going to enjoy cutting the heart from your lover's chest. In fact, I might make you eat it once we've used it to power the spell."

Ice floods through my veins.

A dragon's heart.

They *know*.

Ruhle grabs my upper arm as I lunge forward, his fingers digging in cruelly as he leans toward me. "Did you think Father was going to make the trade? Your precious soul in exchange for the horn? Did you think you were going to be finally free?" He laughs. "We know the truth now. We don't need the horn. We don't need the cauldron.

What we need is waiting for us at the Easternwick ruins. The dragon's heart was right there in front of us the entire time." He lets me go, brushing imaginary dust from my shoulders. "I do thank you, dearest sister. If you hadn't spoken such a thing so loudly, my little sparrow here would never have overheard you, and we'd still be none the wiser."

Ismena flinches, scrambling away from me with her head bowed.

And despite myself, I can't quite summon complete hatred for her.

If Ruhle speaks the truth, then she's only trying to save her own skin.

He's our father's favorite child for a reason, after all.

She's just another victim of these vicious creatures.

Just like my mother. Just like me. Like Soraya. I curse and yank at the sunlit bracelet around my wrist, but all it does is burn my fingers.

I turn all my rage, all my focus upon Ruhle. "I will kill you," I whisper. "You won't hurt him. You *won't*." Maybe it's a declaration of my feelings, but they've already got me bent over the altar with the knife to my ribs. There's no point in keeping my silence now. "I swear I will stop you. Somehow. I'm going to burn your entire kingdom down."

He throws his head back and laughs. "Where you're going, you won't have a chance. Prepare her for the trap."

Hands grab me, dragging me away from the throne.

"Stop!" I scream, kicking at the floor. "Stop! Don't do this!" I turn my attention to Father. "I'll bring you the cauldron. I'll break the curse. I swear!"

But there's no hint of mercy in his expression.

There never is.

"I don't need the cauldron," Father says, waving a hand dismissively, "when I have the dragon's heart right in front of me. Throw her in the cage and ready the horses. But don't harm her. Keir will want to see her before we spring the trap."

"No!" I scream as they drag me across the throne room floors.

I can't Sift. I can't warn him.

I don't have a single ally in this place.

But I swear I will stop them.

Somehow.

To find out what happens next, Zemira and Keir's story will reach its epic conclusion in *Thief of Hearts*.

Dear Reader,

Thank you so much for reading **Thief of Souls**. I hope you enjoyed it.

To find out what happens next, Zemira and Keir's story will reach its epic conclusion in *Thief of Hearts*.

Books in series:

Thief of Dreams
Thief of Souls
Thief of Hearts

Want to know more about future release dates?

Make sure you sign up to my newsletter to be the first to know when they're available.

Here are some other ways to stay updated:

* Follow me on Bookbub
* Visit my website at becmcmaster.com

*Or join my Facebook group,
The Company Of Rogues

I hope we meet again between the pages of another book!

Cheers,
Bec McMaster

P.S While waiting for **THIEF OF HEARTS**, why not try
PROMISE BY DARKNESS? Turn the page to find out
more….

Princess. Tribute. Sacrifice. Is she the one prophesied to unite two warring Fae courts? Or the one bound to destroy them?

In a realm ruled by magic, the ruthless Queen of Thorns is determined to destroy her nemesis, the cursed Prince of Evernight.

With war brewing between the bitter enemies, the prince forces Queen Adaia to uphold an ancient treaty: she will send one of her daughters to his court as a political hostage for three months.

The queen insists it's the perfect opportunity for Princess Iskvien to end the war before it begins. But one look into Thiago's smouldering eyes and Vi knows she's no assassin.

The more secrets she uncovers about the prince and his

court, the more she begins to question her mother's motives.

Who is the true enemy? The dark prince who threatens her heart? Or the ruthless queen who will stop at nothing to destroy him?

And when the curse threatens to shatter both courts, is she strong enough to break it?

A fairytale twist inspired by the Hades and Persephone myth.

Keep reading for an excerpt from Promise of Darkness....

CHAPTER 1

Kill the beast.

And don't disappoint me this time….

My mother's words play in my head in time to the drumming hoofbeats of my gelding. It's a song that's been repeating itself for years, though the verses often change depending on her latest critique. Disappointing my mother seems to be my greatest ability these days.

Golden leaves drip from the trees in a steady tumble as autumn starts its slow, seductive slide into winter. I ease Jaeger to a halt, and he snorts, no doubt catching scent of the rank musk I too can smell.

"I know, boy." I pat his neck as I slip from the saddle, landing lightly on the leaf mulch. Smells like a troll's breath the morning after a feast of decayed corpse.

Late afternoon sunlight ripples over the ground, the wind whispering through silent trees. The forest itself seems to be holding its breath.

Watching.

Waiting.

Drawing my sword, I tie Jaeger to a tree and then creep toward the ruins.

There are eyes upon me.

I can feel them.

"That's right, you ugly bastard. I'm here."

The trail of blood leads directly toward the ruins ahead. Where it fell, the leaves have shriveled into brittle shreds, as if the blood itself is tainted.

The news came from the borders three days ago. An empty hamlet discovered on the edges of Vervain Forest, the woodcutters within vanished. Instead, there'd been claw marks in the door and a bloodied fingernail on the floor inside, as if someone had been dragged out by the ankles.

Other empty cabins were slowly discovered. Tales of a beast stalking the edges of Vervain and whispers of hunters not returning from relatively easy hunts began to grow in strength. Chickens slaughtered in their coops over the summer months, though nobody had mentioned it until it was too late.

It always starts with the chickens.

Banes are violent, magic-twisted beasts, cursed to live in a half-animal, half-human shape. It takes a powerful witch or spell to create them; and to break the curse is both dangerous and difficult. True love's kiss. Eating the heart of the witch. Sometimes another spell will gift them with the ability to remain a man during the day and a beast at night, but magic often sloughs off them.

Which leaves me with one option.

The cold kiss of iron, straight through the heart.

It's my first bane hunt.

Preferably not my last.

"Let's make this nice and easy," I mutter as I slip through the forest with murder—or mercy—on my mind.

Thorns encircle the ruins, some of them bearing spikes as long as my forearm. Poison drips from their tips; they call this particular bramble Sorrow's Tears. It sprang from the ground the night the King of the Sorrows was slaughtered by his new Unseelie queen. Where his people wept, the brambles grew. It's deadly to the Unseelie and excruciating to my kind, though it won't kill us.

How, in Maia's name, am I going to get inside the ruins?

The snuffling of the bane echoes in the distance. No doubt it made its lair deep inside where it will be safe from predators.

Skirting the brambles, I hold my sword low. Demi-fey peer at me from the shadows, their golden eyes vicious and unblinking. Sweat drips down my spine. I'm practically jumping at shadows, my skin prickling at the faint whisper of claws on stone.

"You can do this," I tell myself quietly.

I have to do this. I have to slay the beast at my mother's behest or suffer her consequences.

After all, if it tears my head from my shoulders, then at least I won't have to hear about it for the next ten years.

Or worse.

Girding myself, I follow the bane's blood trail to an overgrown arch. Shadows loom beneath it.

This was once the ancient stronghold of my kingdom, many years before my mother took power. The king who ruled wore a gauntlet coated with pure iron. A literal iron fist. Though the main tower's half-shattered, with stones strewn about it like rumpled skirts, it wouldn't surprise me if the tower once bore a certain phallic resemblance.

My mother overthrew him nearly a thousand years ago.

Nobody even remembers his name—she had it wiped from public record, and no one dared speak it upon pain of death. The years passed, and he faded from memory, crushed to dust just like this keep. Now only the forest remembers him, slowly swallowing what remains of his grandeur.

I wonder what he did to her to earn such a fate, such enmity. My mother is petty and vicious, but to ensure even history forgot him speaks of an enemy she saved her most vengeful acts for.

"This way, Princess!" a voice cries through the ruins. "I can see its tracks!"

I freeze.

Hooves echo on half-buried cobblestones, and then a glint of gold shines through the brambles as a young woman canters into view. Her blonde hair knots into tight braids that circle her head like a coronet. A trio of Seelie hunters clad in hard leathers are at her heels.

Curse it.

The Crown Princess Andraste. Strong. Dangerous. Powerful.

She looks like the epitome of a warrior princess, with a battle-hardened leather corset protecting her slim waist and boots that cling to her calves. A lush dark green cloak wraps around her shoulders, but it's the bow at her back and the knives tucked into her boots that make her dangerous.

Andraste doesn't miss. She doesn't fail.

I might have once called her sister, though it's been so long since we've been close enough for such a word. It's not encouraged anymore.

After all, in my mother's kingdom, there is only one ruler, only one heir.

And I'm not the favored child.

I have to kill the bane first.

Darting up the spiral staircase of the tower, I slip my knife from its sheath so I'm well armed. I can't afford to rush this and make a mistake, but I cannot afford to lose the chance.

Thighs burning, I make it to the highest level, my steps slowing.

Wounded grunts echo from within the chamber at the top. I slip toward the door, pressing my back to the stone wall beside it and softening my breath. A glance shows the turret room inside, dust and dead leaves covering the floor. In the middle of the room is an enormous, twisted mass of fur and sinew.

It looks like a wolf and a lion had a baby.

Or no, not quite.

There are enormous teeth that don't belong to either animal, and claws over two inches long. It moves like a man, though its spine is curved like a cat's, and it loped along on all fours when we were hunting it.

Blood drips from the wound on its flank where my arrow sank between its ribs, and it licks the ravaged wound, wincing a little.

The movement's so familiar my fingers curl around the knife. The sound it made when my arrow sank into soft gray fur lingers in my memory. A cry. It sounded like a man's pained cry.

No mercy for the monsters, sneers my mother's voice.

But is it a monster?

It was fae once, whispers my conscience.

Aye, and now it's terrorizing local villages.

Year by year, it will lose itself to the curse, until all it craves is blood. All it will hunger for is flesh. There's no turning back. If the curse hasn't been broken yet, then I doubt it ever will be.

This is mercy.

Or at least, that's what I tell myself.

My fingers flex around the knife as I creep closer, picking my way between dead leaves.

The creature freezes.

So do I.

"Schmell you," it whispers. "Coming to finish job." The word comes from an inhuman mouth, but it freezes me right to the core.

There's no reasoning with a bane. All you can do is put them out of their misery and stop them before they slaughter entire villages.

But this one is fae enough still to speak.

The slight hesitation almost costs me.

The bane lunges toward me, muscle rippling beneath its fur. I drive to the side, blade swinging up. Its claws lash out, smashing my sword to the side. The weight of it slams into me, and then I'm going down. Only pure luck—or years and years of practice with my mother's swordmaster —mean that my knife drives into its side.

Stupid. So stupid.

As my back slams into the stone floor, I kick my heels up, driving it over the top of me. Lines of heat sear my thigh as its claws glance off me, but if I hadn't reacted so quickly, they'd be buried in my gut.

Rolling ungracefully to my knees, I scramble for my sword. I have no idea where the knife went. Probably still in its flank.

The bane lashes out, claws swiping my boots from under me. I hit the floor, my hand closing over the hilt as I flip over. Like a turtle on its back, I shove the sword between us, scrambling back across the floor until my back hits the wall.

The beast stretches its spine, eyes glowing an amber gold in the dying afternoon light that pours through the open arch window.

It laughs, a faint, wheezing sound, as it prowls back and forth. "In trouvle now, little fae."

It's between the door and me, and even though it's bleeding heavily, it's still twice my size. And I'm down a weapon.

Curse it.

I clamber to my feet, forcing my voice full of a false bravado I don't feel. If in doubt... bluff. "I don't know. It seems I swapped the knife for a star-forged sword. I'd say I just traded up."

It snarls and swipes the air threateningly in a mine-is-bigger-than-yours kind of way.

Okay, fine. "Yes, I know. My, what big claws you have...."

"Come closer and see dem," it hisses.

I lunge forward, sword whining as it cuts through the

air. Right into the sunlight that streams through the arched window, which blinds me for half a second. The bane avoids the blow, but instead of lashing out and taking advantage of my blunder, it hesitates.

"Prinshess...."

What? My sword hovers in the air. "Do you know who I am?"

Its lip curls as it backs away. "Ish-vien."

Close enough. I stare at it in horror. There's only one way it could recognize me by sight. "Who are you?"

"I am loyal, my princhess. I am Evernight," it whispers, holding up one paw, claws curled inward. "Pleashe. Pleashe don't hurt me."

Evernight?

The Kingdom of Evernight is the enemy. Evernight and Asturia have been at war for centuries. How would it know me?

When I was a little girl, I played games of Strategy across from my mother. Each game was a lesson, and if I played well, I would not be punished. It made me wary, thoughtful, hesitant.... And Mother noticed. *Trust your instincts*, Mother would say, eyes alight upon me. *Instinct is the cold kiss of warning that something is wrong, but hesitation is a death knell.*

And right now, mine are blaring.

It knows my face. My name. And I swear I've never come across an envoy from the Kingdom of Evernight. Mother will barely let us speak its name, let alone encourage mingling.

I lower the sword. "How do you know who I am?"

Movement shifts behind it.

"Don't move," says Andraste, stepping inside the room with her bow drawn.

The bane hisses, rising onto two feet, its hackles lifting. Amber fury rolls across its eyes, driving away any last vestiges of its humanity. All that's left is rage.

"Don't kill it!"

"Did you hit your head? That's what we're here to do."

"Something's wrong." I don't take my eyes off the beast. "How does it know who I am?"

Andraste steps to the side, her bow nocked, the string tight with tension. "Step back, Iskvien."

Before I can even move, the bane roars and rams me. My sword lands with a clatter as I slam onto the stone floor, the beast leaping over me.

An arrow flashes, and it screams.

Then it's upon my sister, driving her into the wall. Andraste whirls beneath its lashing claws, swirling her cloak in a flourish that traps them. She ducks free of the fabric, draws the knife from her right boot, and lunges forward.

It should have been an easy kill, but the beast shoves away from the wall and throws her off-balance.

She staggers back, boots clipping against my side and sending her sprawling. We're both down, scrambling to get out of the way as the enraged monster launches itself toward us.

A hand shoves me in the back as I stagger to my feet, knocking me clear. Claws rake down my arm, spilling blood, but it's my sister who grunts as she barely deflects a killing blow. My sister who pushed me aside.

Curse her. She wants to steal the glory of this kill, but I need to know how the beast knows who I am.

If it doesn't kill us first.

There's no hint of those fae eyes in its monstrous face. Not anymore. Only rage and fury and pain.

I grab Andraste's fallen cloak and throw it over the bane's head. Andraste drives her knife between its ribs just as I kick the back of its knee. For one shining, precious moment, we're moving in unison. A deadly, unstoppable force to be reckoned with.

"Don't kill it!"

Andraste's eyes flicker to mine as she slashes through its hamstring. The bane screams. Her knife flashes, catching the last dying rays of sunlight that glint through the arch, and then it's burying itself in the bane's throat.

"No!"

Blood gurgles from the stab wound. The bane's roar chokes off.

She stabs it again, right in the kidneys.

Those amber eyes lock upon me, breath wheezing from its lungs as it slumps forward. "Prinshess...."

And then the light in those eyes fades, and the beast hits the floor.

My sister turns to me, alight with fury as she wipes the blade on her thigh. "What in Maia's name were you thinking? Were you *trying* to get yourself killed?"

"I was *trying* to discover how he knew me."

Light shimmers around the bane, as though the curse isn't quite done with him. Its fur shrinks, claws sinking back into flesh and becoming fingers right before my eyes.

When the light fades, there's a fae male on the floor,

naked and bloody. Scratches mar his back and buttocks, and his blond hair is long and ragged. I can't stop myself from squatting beside him, trying to avoid the growing pool of blood.

I don't know his face.

I would swear I've never seen him before.

But he's seen me, which sends a shiver down my spine. Catching the attention of the vicious prince who rules Evernight is never a wise idea.

There's a chain around his throat, and I slide my hand along its length, revealing a golden amulet shaped in a wolf's snarling head.

"Leave it," Andraste says.

"It knew me," I insist, slipping the amulet free. I don't know why, but I feel the urge to keep it.

"It was Evernight."

"Precisely the problem," I snap, fetching my sword and pocketing the amulet. Won't Mother be thrilled with her now. "A pity you're not going to get a nice fur throw for your floor."

"Haven't you learned anything, Iskvien? We do not treat with the enemy. And we show the beasts no mercy. Both are only likely to get you killed."

"And we wouldn't want that." I slide my sword home with a steely rasp. "Or do we?"

Andraste startles. "I don't want you dead."

Only bowing at her feet.

"There can be only one." One queen. One heir. It's how the Kingdom of Asturia operates. "Let's not pretend I wouldn't be a threat to you if you left me alive." Every scheming courtier in the castle would see me as an opportunity to climb the ladder at court. "Let's not pretend I'm stupid enough to think you wouldn't. You should have waited. You should have let the bane have me."

"Vi." She snags my wrist as I turn to go.

I arch a brow, waiting for her to protest that it's not like that at all. That we're sisters, not a threat to each other. But Mother has done her job far too well.

"I am either Mother's heir or I am dead," I say quietly. "I don't even want the throne. I just want to stay alive. And so do you."

"There are other options."

"Oh, really? I would love to hear your proposition."

Her lips press thinly together.

"Marriage into another kingdom? You know we'd both be merely pawns. And Mother's done too good a job in alienating every other royal court. Besides, I'd prefer to choose my own husband rather than become some petty prince's little plaything."

None of the royal options are anything short of skin-crawling. The fae can be merciless and malicious. Royals never sit on an easy throne, and the truth is, no innocent ever holds a position of power in this world.

Not for long anyway.

Those who rule kingdoms are rarely kind.

"Maybe marriage doesn't have to be a death sentence," she says.

"And maybe that bane didn't intend to kill either of us. Maybe it was trying to give me a hug."

Andraste lets me go. "We're not enemies, Vi. I would protect you."

She doesn't understand. She never will. She's always

been Mother's favorite. The one who sits in on council meetings. The one who receives gifts from visiting nobles, as if they already consider her to be Mother's heir.

The one who can wield her own magic, when mine dies on my fingertips in a shower of sparks.

"I wish that was the truth." I miss my sister. But neither of us are children anymore, and I can't afford to forget that. "And I'd stay to help you lug your trophy home, but I think I'd best get a head start before night falls. Got to watch my back out there. The forests are dark and full of monsters."

But nowhere near as dangerous as court.

CHAPTER 2

Two dresses hang in the closet in front of me, both gauzy and overflowing with far too much fabric. Neither are my preferred style, but that's not the point.

Tonight is Lammastide and appearances have to be met.

Tonight I'm not Iskvien, second daughter of a merciless queen. Tonight I'm an Asturian princess, ruthless in her own right, invulnerable to those who might seek to bring down my mother's court. It might only be silk, but it's armor of a kind, though I'd far prefer a chain mail vest.

"Wear the red," says a clipped voice from the doorway. "It will accentuate your dark hair and olive skin."

My fingers still on the fabric. "Mother. What a pleasant surprise."

It is neither.

She wasn't here when we returned from the hunt. It's been three days. And I know Andraste made her report.

I've been waiting for the queen to make an appearance, and point out all the ways in which I fail her. Queen Adaia is not the type to strike immediately. She likes to let her opponents wait. And each day she hesitates is one more hint of her displeasure, one more sign it's going to be fatal.

Three days…. Not quite a storm of rage that could threaten to tear the palace apart, but a quiet, deadly chill, I suspect. Like the breath of winter down your spine.

I turn as the queen sweeps inside the room, her heavy silver gown dragging over the marble tiles with a rasp. We're as different as night and day, and I see Andraste in the queen's features, which is simply another reminder of whom the favorite daughter is. They share the same stubborn chin and full mouth, high-swept cheekbones highlighting the vaguely feline shape of their blue eyes.

But Mother's hair is wheaten gold, drawn up into a coronet of braids upon which rests her sharp-pointed crown. And she's taller, slightly thinner. More dangerous.

Anyone looking at the two of us might wonder if we shared any blood at all.

"To what do I owe this pleasure, Mother?" It's the edge of impertinence, which is all she will allow. "Won't we be late to the Queensmoot?"

"They'll wait."

"You expect an attack?" Lammastide is the one night of the year when all five surviving kingdoms of the Seelie Alliance come together to bring in the new year. Drinking, dancing, bloodshed, and assassinations are all to be expected.

Because allied we may be, but it's only against a common enemy. If my mother could destroy the other rulers of the alliance, she wouldn't hesitate.

In some part of her mind, she sees herself sitting on a

throne that rules over the entire southern half of the continent.

"Sit," she says.

The only option is to obey.

"No attack." She slinks behind me as I take a seat at the vanity. "Or nothing beyond the usual. The Prince of Evernight will be there, after all. He craves my downfall."

Someone's projecting.

"I thought the Unseelie delegation would be the greater danger?"

Five hundred years ago we defeated them in the Wars of Light and Shadow, but the peace has always been tenuous. This recent treaty between Seelie and Unseelie courts is a relatively new development, and if I were my mother's daughter, I wouldn't trust it.

The three witch queens of the Unseelie court are bloodthirsty, vicious, and powerful. If my mother has delusions of grandeur, then they're nothing compared to the Unseelie, who want to cast us all into chains.

The queen lifts the heavy strands of my hair from my shoulders and runs her jeweled claws through it. "Queen Angharad is still bleeding from that last skirmish, and some say she doesn't have the full support of her sister queens any more. She's trying to fight a war on two fronts, so she won't have the courage to cause trouble for us. Focus on the real danger, Iskvien. Those at your back. Those with a knife to your throat." Her claws caress my collarbone. "Those who were never meant to rule the earth beneath their feet."

She's speaking of the two Seelie princes who forced their way onto the thrones of their own kingdoms. The

Seelie kingdoms have been matrilineal for centuries—queens are tied to the lands, and the earth beneath them flourishes from the bond. Any kings that sought to elevate themselves were slowly and mercilessly destroyed. My mother considers Prince Thiago and Prince Kyrian's claims to be unnatural, and she's been working on ruining them ever since they proclaimed themselves.

Prince Kyrian never attends the Lammastide rites in person. Mother once mocked him for the loss of the woman he loved, and he swore an oath that if he ever set eyes upon her again, he'd have her head. To uphold the peace, he sends an envoy to the rites in his stead.

So she's talking of Evernight.

Always Evernight.

My thoughts stray to the forest and the bane. The creature who knew me.

And the Prince of Evernight, who rules the dark kingdom.

"What should I expect?" I've never met the prince. These are the first Lammastide rites my mother's allowed me to attend. "Will the Prince of Evernight avoid us?"

"Unfortunately, not. He considers me responsible for the loss of his wife, and I daresay he's still determined to have his revenge upon me. In fact, he's the reason I'm here."

Here it is. I still, like prey catching scent of a dangerous predator as she moves to the side, considering the array of scents and powders on my vanity.

"What does he have to do with me?"

"You're not coming home with us tonight, Iskvien,"

my mother says, lifting the stopper of my perfume vial and sniffing delicately at the scent within. Her nose wrinkles.

I blink.

"*What?*"

"The Prince of Evernight agreed to a truce over the territories of Mistmere after that unfortunate clash near the border, but it has come at a price."

I feel the edges of the world sucking at me. "What price?"

"There are to be hostages, to prove our good faith. His cousin is to be exchanged tonight, for you."

The jaws of the trap spring shut. I shouldn't have trusted her sweet smile, her gentle touch.

"You bartered me away? Like a fucking trinket?"

The queen's eyes narrow. "Watch your tone, daughter."

Rage fills me, but it's tempered with the quicksilver flash of fear. All these years I've been wary of her temper, but this is…. How do I…?

"It's only for three months," she continues, as if I've accepted it.

The prince could do anything to me in the space of three months. If he thinks my mother killed his wife, then I daresay I'm to be a proxy for his vengeance.

"Is this punishment?" The words erupt from my mouth. "For failing to kill that bane? It was just a hesitation, Mother. Andraste stole the kill. It won't happen again."

"*What* hesitation?"

Andraste didn't tell her?

The queen's face tightens imperceptibly, and her hands come to rest upon my shoulders. The tip of each of her fingers is covered in a silver claw, the points pressing into my collarbone. Thin chains connect them to the gauntlets around her wrist. It's nothing more than a focus for her powers—not that many know that—but the effect is also eerily threatening.

She doesn't say a word.

She doesn't have to.

"Andraste was faster than I," I say swiftly, to cover my misstep. "I thought she'd told you."

"The bane is of little consequence."

I square my shoulders. "Why worry about a ferocious beast when you're throwing me to the wolves?"

"You are not to be harmed."

"Of course not. Am I to be his whore instead?"

She arches a brow at my tone. "You are to be his political hostage, Iskvien. Make whatever bargains you need to, to keep yourself safe. But remember…, his cousin will be in my hands."

And any harm that befalls me will be returned in kind.

"Forgive me, Mother, if such a concept brings me little peace. They say the prince betrayed his queen and murdered her sons. I daresay he'll not hesitate to consider his cousin to be an acceptable loss if he can strike a blow upon you."

"You disappoint me, daughter. I offer you an opportunity, and you throw it in my face."

This is another one of her challenges. *Prove yourself,* she's telling me. *Show me you have the strength and wit to survive.*

"What opportunity?"

"There is a way you could serve your queen while you

are there." My mother unsheathes the dagger at her belt and places it on the vanity in front of me.

Star-forged steel. No trueborn fae can wield the iron that lies on this world, but this knife was forged from the heart of a fallen comet, and its iron came from beyond the stars.

As long as I don't touch the blade itself, I can use it.

For a second, I see his blood splashed across the marble tiles of his palace, the knife planted between his shoulder blades. An end to the monstrous lord of the Evernight court, and freedom for those Asturians who've been imprisoned in the war camps. No more fighting. No more endless wars. No more scheming and politicking.

But murder, just the same.

"No," I say abruptly. "I'm no assassin."

Adaia leans down, her face resting on my shoulder and her gaze meeting mine in the mirror. "Perhaps not. But he'd never expect it. Not from you, with your soft heart and those pretty eyes. And perhaps you should consider your people. The Kingdom of Asturia has been at war with Evernight for centuries. Whilst this treaty sparks a fragile truce, it doesn't mean anything. We could end this war with a single strike. We would own Mistmere, perhaps more...."

I push away from her, the hem of my silk wrap brushing against my calves. "Murder, Mother. I'm the first person they'll point the finger at. Who do you think they'll blame? If I kill the prince, then his people will execute me immediately, and their armies will rise against you."

"Not if it's self-defense," she points out.

So now I'm to frame an assassination as an assault by the prince.

"Thiago has no heir," she continues. "Without him, his generals will fight for control of his armies. It will be chaos, and I will crush them."

I notice she doesn't address the part where I lose my head.

"Take the dagger."

It's not a suggestion.

I pick it up, feeling the weight of it. Accepting it doesn't mean I have to go through with anything.

"I'll consider it." I catch a glimpse of my mother's dangerous smile in the reflection as the queen backs away. It wouldn't surprise me if she made this bargain with this end in mind.

"You have an hour. Get dressed and meet us in the courtyard. We ride for the Hallow. Wear the red."

Then she's gone.

Leaving me trembling.

I can't believe she gave me no warning. Or maybe that was deliberate: With a hint of what was to come, I might have been able to flee or outmaneuver this treaty. Now, I don't have a choice. The stamp of the guard's feet as they settle outside my door is jarringly loud, and my mother expects me in the courtyard within an hour.

This isn't merely hesitating to strike a killing blow against a monster.

This is politics, and she will brook no refusal.

But who would I rather face? My mother or a volatile, dangerous prince who might think me a plaything?

My resolve firms. If he thinks he's getting a trinket to toy with, then he had best think again.

The prince of the Kingdom of Evernight is Unseelie to his bones, despite the fact he claims to be Seelie. I can't afford to show him even a hint of my weak underbelly.

And curse my mother, but I'll be damned to the Underworld if I'll let her think me her puppet.

I fling the wardrobe open, both the red and the white gowns tumbling in a frothy mess to the floor. Inside the wardrobe, right at the back, is *the* dress.

It's like a piece of pure midnight was carved from the sky, diamond stars glittering down its silken length. I don't know what urged me to have it made. Mother's right: vibrant colors suit me best. And yet, I'd been unable to think of anything else the moment I saw the material.

Red would be a sign of groveling.

The white is probably what she intended me to wear all along.

But this…. Time to show her I refuse to bow to her whims. This princess has claws. And she's not afraid to use them.

CHAPTER 3

The guards are on edge as we take the portal from Hawthorne Castle to the Hallow that lies by the grassy plains of the Queensmoot, where the Seelie Alliance will meet for the Lammastide rites.

It's the only Hallow in the area, which means every queen—and prince—will be using it. Despite their vigilance, there's no sign of danger as we step through the circle of standing stones that guards the portal. Power hums through the ley line it's set upon, setting my teeth on edge, but the night is quiet and dark.

And probably full of surprises.

In the distance, enormous bonfires glow like a necklet of starfire gems draped around the throat of the nearby mountains. The moment takes my breath away. I've heard the court bard speak of the unbroken chain of Lammastide fires that ward against the thinning of the Veil. It's said the fires protect the realm from the Others who occasionally slip through the portals from the Underworld on nights like these, when both worlds pass each other so closely they almost touch.

"If I was an assassin, you'd be dead right now." My sister materializes out of the shadows, tearing my gaze from the mountains.

"The only thing you've killed of late, appears to be a flock of ravens," I point out. "Does mother approve? Where's your pretty gown?"

She wears black leather from head to toe, with a ruff of raven's feathers around her throat. That moonlight hair is braided back fiercely, and silver moons drip from her ears. No dress for her. She's a warrior princess, prepared to hold a sword at someone's throat if needed.

"I'm not here to play nice with the other nobles."

No, I'm the one dressed up like a gift, though the black silk cape I wear hides my starlight dress. I'm not quite prepared to reveal it just yet.

Curse it. I feel like a peacock, displayed on a platter on the dining table.

"You didn't tell her about the bane."

My sister doesn't flinch.

And a thought occurs. "You knew."

Andraste didn't need to tell mother about my failure. She's already won. I'm to be sent as tribute to another kingdom, a sacrifice to peace. The path to being named heir is clear for her without so much as a hint of bloodshed.

It's so well done, I'd almost clap, if I wasn't about to be sacrificed.

"It's not like that," she finally says. "I—"

"It sounds exactly like that. You've won. You barely even had to lift a finger. All that talk about finding another court…."

"Vi—"

"Don't." We both know anything that comes from her mouth next is insincere. She can afford to be gracious. "You're Mother's heir. That's all that matters."

My mouth tastes like ash. What am I going to do? When I return in three months' time—if I return—what am I coming back to?

It's unwise for a princess of the blood to remain in another's court. It creates too many opportunities for politicking nobles. Too many pathways to dissent. I'll always be a knife held to my sister's throat unless….

Unless I disappear.

"Vi, there are things you don't know." She finally looks at me.

More cursed secrets. I'm starting to realize how peripheral I am to Mother's court.

"All these little secrets," I murmur, twitching at my cloak. "It's starting to make the skin between my shoulder blades tickle."

"You'll understand, one day."

"Oh, I think I understand now."

Andraste's gaze drops to the hem of my skirt, and her eyebrows hit her hairline. "You're not wearing the dress Mother had made for you."

My fingers brush against the midnight-dark silk that caresses my legs. Tiny pinprick diamonds are woven throughout the fabric, so it seems as though a cloak of pure night clings to my body. "I thought the white lace seemed a touch too virgin sacrifice. This suits me better."

"Where did you find it?"

"Find it?" Andraste spends most of her time in hunting leathers. I'd have thought fashion would have been the last thing my sister would ever willingly discuss. "I had it made on a whim several weeks ago. It seemed a little more fitting for the night."

The faintest of smiles plays about Andraste's lips. "Has Mother seen it?"

"Not yet."

I can't explain why I withheld the dress. Only a gnawing sense the queen will not approve.

Andraste laughs. "Oh, I can't wait to see her face when she does. Wait until the last moment to reveal it, or she'll strip you to your skin."

The precise thought I'd had. For a second, some of the old camaraderie we'd once shared whispers in the night.

Of course, she's happy. You won't be around to block her path to being named princess-heir.

My smile dies on my lips.

Only three minutes separate the pair of us, and from the moment we were birthed into the world, we were inseparable. I remember rolling in the grass as children, chasing demi-fey through the trees, stealing into Mother's chambers and trying on her jewelry and her crowns....

I don't know where it all went wrong.

I can't remember a single fight or betrayal that tore us apart. It was a slow creep of realization, I suppose. Leaving childhood behind and realizing my sister was now my competitor.

It was one of my tutors who pointed out the future to me. I'd never wanted the crown. Andraste could have it for all I cared, but my hob tutor had slapped his cane on the desk in front of me one day when I wasn't paying attention and snapped that if I didn't focus on my lessons, then my future was bound to be short and inconsequential.

She'd never hurt me, I protested.

But every ball, I'd see the pair of us on display. Nobles would circle around us, and I realized Andraste was making her own little court.

It soon became clear she was the favorite. The one who began to be seated at Mother's right hand on the dais. The one who was asked for advice in Mother's Round Chamber. The doors would close in my face, and I'd see my sister through them, shooting me a sad, apologetic look.

It's been years since I've seen that expression.

The sister I knew is gone, replaced by this hard, implacable woman. Though she wears no crown, the circlet of braids reminds me of a coronet every time I see it.

"You should make the most of it," she finally says.

"My three months in Evernight?"

"Yes."

I give an incredulous laugh. "I think you've been drinking too much elderberry wine, sister."

"Perhaps it won't be so bad."

Won't be so bad? "Which part?" My voice roughens. "The part where I'm handed over to a monster? The part where I have to bargain for my safety?"

For a moment, Andraste looks like she wants to tell me something.

Then the queen stalks toward us, surrounded by her advisors and guard. The moment's lost.

"Are you ready?" she demands of both of us, though I know she's looking at me.

I can't help myself.

Some part of me always has to challenge her.

So I step forward and brush the cloak from my shoulders, where it falls in a spill around my skirts.

The queen's face hardens when she sees the dress. For a second, rage ignites her magic, and glints of pure gold streak through her irises.

Defiance is her least favorite attribute.

But it's too late now.

I arch a brow in her direction. "I don't want him thinking how nice the red dress looks against my skin, and the white gives the impression I'm some pure little dove ripe for the plucking. Considering I don't have any chain mail in my wardrobe, I settled on the least offensive option."

"Oh, Iskvien." Her jeweled claws capture my chin, the heat of her magic banking in her eyes. "Why must you always defy me?"

"Because I want to make my own destiny, Mother."

"You've already made it," she whispers, the claws biting into my skin. "And now, you can lie in your bed and bear the consequences."

"Mother," Andraste murmurs.

They share a look, and I hate the fact they're clearly communicating something I don't understand.

"Let Vi wear what she likes," Andraste says. "There are too many witnesses."

There's no time for the queen to punish me for the transgression. Trumpets blare, and a malicious whispering wind suddenly springs through the trees, announcing the arrival of another court.

The queen lets me go, her spine straightening. It's one thing to punish defiance, quite another to have it witnessed by the enemy.

I breathe a sigh of relief and glance at my sister. It irks to have to say it but… *"Thank you,"* I mouth.

Andraste gives me a sad little smile.

Time to throw the dice and play the game of my life.

I don't join the dancing.

There's nothing to celebrate.

And I can't stand to remain with my mother's delegation, watching as she introduces Andraste to envoys and foreign nobles from other courts.

Instead, I grab two glasses of elderberry wine, drain one, and then sip the other as I weave through the gathering.

There has to be some way to escape this trap, though I'm aware that two of my mother's guards stalk me circumspectively. Running is clearly not an option.

Perhaps the Queen of Aska will take mercy on me and welcome me into her court in exchange for every little secret I know about my mother? Unlikely, though, and my mother would make it her life's duty to have me assassinated.

Painfully.

I'm running out of options when a shiver trickles down my spine; a sense of trepidation hovering in the air, like the lingering portent of a lightning strike about to detonate.

I turn.

For a second, there's nothing there but myriad dancing fae.

Then shadows melt together, forming into a tall, masked figure that stalks through the crowd as if it doesn't exist. It's as if Kato, the god of death, walks among us. But this is no god, slumbering now in the memories of the fae. This male is carved out of hard, heated flesh and practically poured into black leather. Despite my anxiety, I can't help noticing the breadth of those shoulders and the powerful flex of his thighs.

The fae of mother's court flee before him like deer scattering before an approaching predator.

Because that's exactly what he is.

Even I feel it.

Piercing eyes meet mine through the eyeholes of the mask he wears; a feathered raven's beak cascading over his brow. Though no crown graces his temples, power drips from him, leaving me with no doubt of whom I face.

Thiago, Prince of Evernight.

Lord of Whispers and Lies. Master of Darkness.

I hadn't expected the sheer boiling power contained within him, or the shock of anticipation—the feeling I'd somehow spent my entire life drifting toward this single moment. The sensation punches the breath out of my lungs and sets my heart racing.

I've never been afraid of man or immortal, but I suffer

a moment of trepidation as I realize the black cloak eddying behind him isn't fabric, but a pair of black wings that hint at his impure heritage. He calls himself Seelie, but my mother claims he has impure blood. And the wings betray him, for no Seelie bears the features of a beast.

I blink, and the wings vanish. There's only a man before me, draped in a black cloak.

But I swear I saw them.

"Princess," he says. The way he looks at me makes me feel as though nothing else exists. "I've been waiting for you."

All night, I'm sure.

I force my spine to straighten. To become steel. *You are an Asturian princess, and you will not yield to the Prince of Evernight.* "Prince Thiago, you honor us with your presence."

His gaze drops, the faintest flicker of—is it disappointment?—marring those dangerous eyes. "The pleasure is mine."

Why, then, do I feel as if I've somehow failed some test?

Perhaps he thought I'd be more welcoming.

If so, then he's a fool.

"I don't believe pleasure has anything to do with it."

His eyes sparkle as he lifts my hand to his mouth, his lips ghosting over the back of it. "Yet."

Oh, so that's the way he means to play.

I tear my hand free, though I can't deny a shiver runs down my spine, and the sensation of his caress lingers. "Ever."

"Did your mother not warn you? I've never met a challenge I've failed to surmount."

"But you've never met me before."

"Haven't I?" Another mysterious smile. "We're to spend the next three months together. Be careful with your challenges. I always play to win."

"Ah, but what precisely are we playing for?"

"Hearts, perhaps."

It steals a laugh from me. Oh, he's so polished, he's practically gleaming. "You think to steal my heart?"

"I don't think that at all. I think you'll give it to me."

"Never in a thousand years."

The prince leans closer. "There you go again, Princess. Opposing me. Daring me. I think I'm going to enjoy the next three months. Very much so."

Of course, he will. He's the one with the power. "Perhaps. You might regret them instead."

"Regret meeting *you*? Never. Dance with me," he says.

I press my hand to his chest. "But you didn't say please."

The faintest of smiles graces his hard mouth. "I never say please."

I've heard that about him too—I can see it in the flex of his jaw, as if a part of him yearns to reach out and take my arm. He's not the sort of male you deny. A warlord, a conqueror, a prince who stole his kingdom from its rightful heirs.

Time to prove I'm no mere pushover. "Sorry. You don't own me just yet."

And then I whirl away into the watching crowd, leaving him staring after me.

Want to know more about the Prince of Evernight?

Click here to keep reading.

Kiss Of Steel

Heart Of Iron

My Lady Quicksilver

Forged By Desire

Of Silk And Steam

Novellas in same series:

Tarnished Knight

The Clockwork Menace

LONDON STEAMPUNK: THE BLUE BLOOD CONSPIRACY

Mission: Improper

The Mech Who Loved Me

You Only Love Twice

To Catch A Rogue

Dukes Are Forever

From London, With Love

London Steampunk: The Blue Blood Conspiracy Boxset 1-3

London Steampunk: The Blue Blood Conspiracy Boxset 4-6

London Steampunk: The Blue Blood Conspiracy Complete Series Boxset

DARK ARTS SERIES

Shadowbound

Hexbound

Soulbound

Dark Arts Box set 1-3

BURNED LANDS SERIES

Nobody's Hero

The Last True Hero

The Hero Within

The Burned Lands Complete Trilogy Boxset

SHORT STORIES

The Many Lives Of Hadley Monroe

Burn Bright